Michael Malik

Ghost Thief

Oak Moon Press

Oak Moon Press, Raleigh NC 27606 U.S.A.

ISBN 978-0-9913360-0-5
LCCN 201392365

Dedication

Thanks:

To my wife, for her love and support during the creation of this book.

To my family. They are my first and most generous fans.

To my friends, who acted as useful and trusted sources of constructive criticism.

To my editor, who helped fix the stuff that needed fixing.

"The most beautiful and deepest experience a man can have is the sense of the mysterious. It is the underlying principle of religion as well as of all serious endeavor in art and science."

Albert Einstein

Prologue

The Condemned Man

**London
The Year of our Lord, 1606**

The prisoner had been locked in his new cell for almost two days. At one time it was a predicament he would have found unremarkable, almost preferable. This time it was pure agony. The reason for the difference was simple. His new cell was so small and misshapen he had nowhere to rest.

Struggling against the constant pain of his confinement and dangling at the edge of madness, he began to mumble softly to himself. After several uninterrupted minutes of incoherent rambling a faint sound made him falter. He went silent and, cringing in fear, strained to hear what caused it.

The noise started out soft and indistinct but quickly turned into a padding rhythm. It then grew progressively louder until, after a brief halt, the prisoner's cell door burst open and two oafish-looking guards shuffled into his sight.

"Hello precious," the shorter of the two said, peering down at him, "missed us?"

Without waiting for an answer, the guards pulled the prisoner out from between the cell's thick stone walls and dragged him across the outer chamber's cobbled floor. They came to a stop next to a tall table and, grabbing his wrists and ankles, heaved his battered body on top of it like he was a sack of potatoes.

Through the pain, the prisoner noticed a flicker of warmth wash over him from a fireplace across the room.

Compared to the cold slab he now occupied, it was a small but welcome bit of consolation.

"Lash him down," the shorter guard ordered.

"Why? He stays put."

"Because I said so!"

"Alright, alright."

"And besides that, a guest is coming to see him." The guard accompanied his pronouncement with a short snigger. When he turned his attention back to the prisoner, however, all of the mirth wilted out of his voice. "And no going on today about saving me from myself or this will take longer."

The prisoner nodded mutely. He then attempted to slow his sharp, panting breaths as he watched his legs being bound to the table. The guard's words, however, inflamed his thoughts.

When he was first caught, he thought that eventually he would be released from the desperate hellhole he was trapped in. Even after his torture started, he held religiously to this hope. But as the days wore on, as the guards knives and whips cut deeper into his flesh, he realized the truth. The men who sponsored his mission, the reason he was captured and imprisoned in the first place, possessed more than enough money to buy a hundred prisoners their freedom. Instead of exercising their power, they lied and abandoned him. They were just as corrupt as the house of rot and decay that he tried to destroy.

The knowledge of his betrayal hardened his will, and he vowed that someday they would all pay for their sins. But now a guest wanted entry to his sphere of misery. Was it possible? Had they finally come to save him?

"We still have some time before he gets here," the shorter guard said once the prisoner's arms were bound.

A slack expression crossed his partner's face. He nodded and, with sickening eagerness, went over to the fireplace and prodded the blazing logs. The ones near the bottom fractured, releasing a shower of glowing hot embers. The man grabbed a particularly large one with a crude set of iron tongs and pulled it free.

"Feeling bold, eh. Just remember, no killing, else-wise we end up where he is."

2

Ten minutes later, whatever reserve the prisoner once held onto was gone. The pain of this latest assault, combined with the force of his screams, stole it from him.

"Not dead, is he?" The man with the tongs asked without much concern as he flicked the spent coal back on the fire.

"He damned well better not be."

The sound of voices echoed in the corridor behind them.

"Quick," the shorter man said.

His partner dropped the tongs, grabbed a bucket of filthy water and passed it over. The freezing cold liquid was emptied in one toss over the prisoner's torso. This aroused him back to semi-consciousness. He was then covered with an equally filthy blanket.

When the door to the outer chamber opened the guards stood stiffly on either side of their charge and waited, filled with curiosity. They seemed eager to see who was interested enough in the prisoner to breach their foul world.

"I shall go on alone," the man at the door said to another, unseen person. He entered the chamber and closed the door behind him. The sight of the two guards made him pause. He inspected them for a moment with a jaundiced eye then said, "Leave."

"But—but—he is a danger," the shorter guard said with surprise.

The visitor shifted his gaze to the prisoner, who started to shiver uncontrollably beneath his threadbare covering. "I doubt it."

"Please, milord, consider the risk."

"I said leave."

The guard kicked at a pile of straw near his feet and, without looking up, said, "Aye, milord." He nodded at his partner and the two of them shuffled toward the deep bowels of the prison. When their footsteps were faint the visitor walked over to the table.

The prisoner sensed the man's closeness and opened his eyes. His blurry vision prevented him from seeing the man's face. He did, however, manage to make out the man's clothes; a scarlet doublet beneath a light brown jerkin, covered by a matching ankle-length, fur-lined gown.

3

Michael Malik

The familiar combination allowed him to identify who was there to see him. Before he could stop himself, a single word escaped his dry, cracked lips. "No—"

The visitor lifted the blanket and inspected the prisoner's wounds. "Brutes," he whispered as he reached into his pocket and pulled out a small jar. He raised it to the man's mouth and gave him a small sip of the liquid it held. "Believe me, I did not wish this," he said after administering his tonic.

Despite his pain and raw throat, the prisoner found the strength to respond. "Too late."

"Yes, unfortunately, it is too late. The decision cannot be changed. I tried. They would have none of it."

"I meant too late for them."

The visitor looked at the prisoner quizzically for a moment then said, "I cannot change the verdict but I can end the torment." He reached into his other pocket and pulled out a document.

"What is that?"

"A confession. Sign it and all of this will be over."

To the prisoner's surprise his pain, unbearable a moment earlier, was now almost gone. One of the burn scars on his arm also faded away. He even managed to lift his head and shake it at the visitor, something that a moment earlier would have been impossible. What manner of magic was in the small jar that it could do such a thing?

"There is no escape," the visitor said in reply. "Fail to sign and the torture will resume. It will carry on for days, perhaps weeks. Sign now and it ends tomorrow. I will not be allowed back here after today so decide—before it is too late."

"I shall be victorious."

"How? By being tortured into madness?"

"I shall be victorious," the prisoner repeated then added with a faltering whisper, "Mankind shall someday know that I was right."

"What shall he know? That bombs and explosions are the path to truth? I think not."

"My old friend, ever so simple."

"We are wasting time. Sign the confession before the guards return."

4

The prisoner shook his head again, but weakly as his brief burst of energy was already fading away.

The visitor looked down at him with exasperation. Finally he said, "Stubborn fool," then turned to leave.

At that moment, the prisoner's brief respite from the pain began to recede. Agony washed through him again and it diluted his will to nothingness. His defiance leeched away with it and he began to panic at the sight of the retreating visitor. A faint "wait," barely escaped his lips, but it was enough.

The visitor returned to the table and untied the prisoner's right arm. He then put the document by his hand and watched him scrawl his signature on it. Once the prisoner was finished, he took the page and put it back into his pocket. The small jar was once again brought out. He fumbled it in his fingers for a few seconds before laying it in the prisoner's hand. "For tomorrow," he said as he closed the man's fingers around it.

The prisoner looked down at his hand then up at the visitor. His eyes were filled with hate.

The prisoner's gaze startled the visitor. He broke off eye contact and hastily made his way to the exit. As he stood next to the half-open door he uttered, "I am truly sorry." He then turned and strode away, shutting the door firmly behind him.

* * *

When the guards came for the prisoner early the next morning, he knew his time was out. Unsure what to expect, he retrieved the jar the visitor had given him and drank the last of the liquid it held.

Once again, he was pulled roughly from his cell. The guards, aware it was their last chance, used the time left to give him a severe beating. When they were done, they dragged him out of the prison and tossed him into a horse-drawn cart.

The prisoner was wheeled slowly out to the great yard. A bloodthirsty mass had already gathered in the acre of open ground. They had all come to witness what was sure to be a gruesome spectacle. Despite the mixture of fear and disgust he felt, he did not blame them. They were what their masters made them.

"Filth!" a woman screamed at him.

"Traitor!" he heard a man yell.

The ride to the scaffolding came to a quick end. The guards kicked the prisoner off the cart, into the cold mud below, and the crowd burst into laughter. He somehow managed to regain his footing and, to his semi-amazement, stand up. This saved him from being trampled, which upset his guards. They immediately grabbed him again and dragged him up the stairs. He glanced upwards for a last look at the sky but his head was quickly pushed back down, and he was forced to gaze upon the rough-hewn and grimly stained floor. Just as he feared, the men caught with him had already received the ultimate punishment. They had been drawn and quartered. And now his captors meant to do the same to him.

"Keep moving," the shorter guard ordered.

Suddenly, the prisoner's sight plunged into darkness as a coarse cloth hood was placed over his head. The time finally arrived. Escape or pardon was now impossible.

A thick rope was placed around his neck and tightened. As the pressure settled across his windpipe, a furious flash of panic coursed through his body.

"I shall be victorious!" he said with a final, guttural shout.

Filled with a strength that surprised even him, he managed to break free from the guards. Forgetting the noose around his neck, he ran blindly forward. At the edge of the scaffolding, he suddenly became aware again of where he was. He tried to stop, teetered for a moment then pitched forward. There was a sudden intense pain around his neck, a flash, and then—nothing.

A thin, scar-pocked man with flaxen-colored hair and his disheveled companion stood among the rowdy and jostling crowd at the base of the scaffolding. The sight of the prisoner swinging above him seemed to break the flaxen-haired man from a trance. An expression of fear combined with disbelief filled his previously blank face. His pinched features and scrawny shoulders then sagged as if a great weight suddenly attached itself to them. A rucksack was strapped around the man's midsection. He glanced down nervously at the bulge it made in his waistline then looked back at the figure above him. The rope that held the battered and lifeless body of the prisoner continued to sway for several minutes. Once it finally stopped moving the small man turned his bloodshot eyes away from the dismaying sight.

"Fret not, Mister Taylor," the disheveled man said. "He was past saving long ago." He shuffled his feet in the dirt. "Can we go now?"

Taylor nodded and, pushing himself through the crowd of cheering men and women, wandered back into the heart of the dark and dangerous city that surrounded him.

1
The Mysterious Delivery

Detective Constable Benjamin Crisp cracked open his eyes, glanced at his alarm clock and groaned. Only five hours had passed since he had fallen asleep. Despite still being exhausted, he automatically started to swing his athletic, six foot frame out of bed. His feet were almost on the floor when he remembered there was no need to rush. He flopped back on his pillow and began to stare up at the ceiling.

Ten minutes later he was still in the same position, his mind tumbling aimlessly. Normally, he was buried in a number of challenging cases. This meant, more often than not, he was up before his alarm went off and didn't return to his flat before late night. Deciding how to spend his day was never a problem. But now, suddenly, he had nothing to do.

His predicament was all the more vexing because it had been forced upon him. He could still hear Detective Chief Inspector Fuller's words from their meeting at New Scotland Yard the day before. *Everyone has a breaking point, Crisp. You've obviously reached yours. I think the best thing for you to do is spend some time away from here. Two weeks should about do it.*

At the time, Crisp didn't offer much resistance. He didn't feel he could after the way his last case ended. The smuggling activity he'd been tracking had mysteriously vanished. Whoever was responsible for it must have become suspicious and shut his operation down. Months of hard work was wasted.

Now he wished he had spoken up. He hated unfinished business.

As he returned to staring at the ceiling a short, loud buzzing sound filled his flat. It was the call button for the front door. Since he had no close friends and rarely any visitors, it was a noise he hardly ever heard. His curiosity was aroused a bit but not enough to get him up. He settled deeper into the covers of his bed determined to ignore what he assumed was a mistake.

Another, longer, buzzing sound filled the flat again. Annoyed, he rolled out of his bed and walked back through the length of his flat. Halfway through the reception room his call buzzer went off a third time. He reached the control panel and pushed the button for the intercom.

"I hope this is vitally important."

"Post delivery," a cheerful voice came back through the speaker.

Crisp was surprised. What was a postman doing at his front door at 7:00 in the morning? And an especially jolly postman at that?

"Come up then," he said into the speaker as he pushed the button unlocking the entranceway.

He listened for the sounds of footsteps up the stairway. A dull scuffle rapidly approached the second floor landing then paused briefly just outside his door. Crisp opened it just as the postman was reaching forward to knock.

The door startled the postman when it opened. He reacted with a nervous step back but then quickly recovered and stepped forward again. Instead of just standing in place, however, he bounced on his heels, like a dog eager to go for a walk.

He was average height but appeared taller due to the blue cap set upon his head. His thinning hair tufted out from beneath its edges. Gold rimmed wire spectacles rested over his thin straight nose. His mouth displayed the typical polite smile of someone used to dealing with impatient people. He wore a standard blue uniform and seemed to be full of remarkable energy for the time of day.

"Detective Constable Crisp." The postman said this more as a statement than a question.

"Yes, I'm Benjamin Crisp."

"Good morning sir. I was already quite sure it was you."

The postman seemed to wait for a response from Crisp. When none came he cleared his throat and continued.

"I'm Deputy Postmaster Harold Tuttle of the Royal Mail. Sorry to disturb you at this early hour. I hope I didn't wake you."

"No, I was already up."

"Excellent. There was a bit of a mix up down at the post station. I wanted to personally clear it up and express our apologies. We don't like for this sort of thing to happen, not at all. Especially something related to the business of a distinguished knight of the British Empire such as this."

"I'm sorry but I'm having a bit of trouble following you. What sort of mix up? What does this have to do with me?"

Tuttle looked around the stairwell. No one was there but he lowered his voice anyway. "May I step inside, sir?"

Crisp suddenly realized that he was standing in his doorstep like a bouncer at a pub. "Of course, my apologies, I didn't mean to be rude." He swung his door wide and stepped out of the way.

Tuttle gave Crisp an understanding look and entered the flat. As the postman walked past him, Crisp caught sight of the package he was holding behind his back. Tuttle walked the same way as he stood, with an energetic bounce. The package bounced slightly up and down with him. He stopped in the center of the reception room. Crisp closed the front door and followed him in.

"I appreciate your discretion," Tuttle said. "I don't want anyone else to overhear what I am about to tell you. We would prefer that this matter stay out of the public eye. It wouldn't do to have certain people questioning the efficiency and safety of their mail delivery."

Tuttle took the package out from behind his back and extended it out to Crisp. It was medium sized and wrapped in plain brown packing paper. His name was written on the front but oddly his address was listed only as London. He looked at the upper left corner. The return address was listed as Sir Albert Price-Mills, Cambridge. Crisp gave Tuttle a quizzical look.

"Sir Price-Mills, as per his privilege, occasionally requests that the Royal Mail handle important deliveries for him. This is done with the absolute understanding that the parcel in question will reach its intended recipient within a certain time period. In addition, the parcel must never be misplaced or delivered to the wrong hands. This is a duty that we have been honored to provide to certain select subjects of the Crown for centuries. I regret to inform you that the period Sir Price-Mills specified lapsed at midnight

10

just passed."

"What happened?" Crisp was more curious than concerned. He wasn't used to the intensely serious tone that Tuttle displayed over a seven hour delay in post-delivery.

"Somehow, the parcel that you are holding was temporarily re-routed. Incorrect information was inserted into the process. Where the information came from is what we cannot seem to figure out. More importantly, the information led to the parcel almost," Tuttle put particular emphasis on the word almost, "being given to someone other than its intended recipient, that being you of course."

Tuttle seemed to cringe a bit, as if expecting a thorough tongue lashing. When Crisp simply said, "Please go on," Tuttle visibly relaxed.

"First, let me assure you that this is the first time the Royal Mail has failed in this particular duty. It's restricted to our most senior and experienced workers."

"How did you discover something was wrong?"

"As the postman was getting the certification document signed he noticed some hesitation and nervousness that was out of place. Because of this the postman quite correctly passed a dummy."

"What do you mean he passed a dummy?"

"There's always a second parcel that's a reproduction of the proper one carried during the delivery. This is in case the postman is forced against his will to give up a parcel or he notices anything out of the ordinary during the delivery. If the postman decides to not pass the original then passing a dummy helps avoid a confrontation."

Crisp held up the package to look at it again. "So is this a dummy or the real thing?"

Tuttle let out a low chuckle. "It's the real thing, all right. We weren't about to make another error. I'll be surprised if we make another in my lifetime. But, just to be sure, before coming here I personally verified that you are Detective Constable Benjamin Crisp, great nephew of Sir Albert Price-Mills, the brother of your late father's mother and the proper recipient of the package in your hand." Tuttle finished with a satisfied look on his face and an extra bounce in his already active stance. "Now, would you please sign here?" Tuttle held out a form with several carbon paper layers and a pen. Crisp scanned the paper then signed the bottom of the page.

"Just one more question," he spoke as Tuttle started back to the front door. "How did the package end up in the wrong place?"

"As I said, improper information was inserted into the process. We interviewed the local postmaster where the mistake originated. He maintains it was a freak accident. He has no prior record to make us doubt him."

"What do you think?"

"I don't believe in freak accidents," replied Tuttle in a matter of fact way. "Good day to you." He then bounced out of Crisp's front door without looking back.

Crisp turned the package over and pulled the taped portion apart. The brown paper fell away leaving only an antique-looking soft-covered book. He opened to the middle of the book and saw a beautifully rendered map. It depicted a segment of northern England and was obviously from a much earlier time in history. He turned the atlas to examine the map in better light. As he did so, a note slipped from its pages and fluttered to the floor. He picked it up and read:

> Benjamin,
> I need you to safeguard this for me. Please keep it well hidden and tell no one else that you have it. I will retrieve it when the time is right.
> With Gratitude,
> Uncle Albert

He looked at the note for a moment. The last time he saw his great-uncle Albert was years ago. Now, unexpectedly and in quite an unusual way, here he was sending stuff with a cordial note. It was like their last meeting was playing bridge at the club a fortnight past.

Suddenly he was thirsty. He headed for the kitchen and placed the atlas on the table. The kettle was half full on the stove top. He reached over and turned the burner on and set a mug up to make tea. When he was done he sat down in front of the atlas and began to inspect its pages.

The contents of the book his uncle sent him were impressive. There were a dozen pages of beautifully rendered cartographs of England. He tried to make out the writing in the corner of the maps but it was cramped and slightly faded and the light coming from the kitchen window was still minimal. The date 1598 finally showed itself on the second map.

The kettle began to whistle. Getting up, he poured boiling water into his mug. With his tea in one hand, he leaned against the counter and stared down at the atlas. Why on earth did Albert send it to him? There had to be a good reason for it.

When he was done, he placed his mug in the sink with a slight clatter. Then, reaching down, he gingerly lifted the atlas off of the table. He carried it back to his bedroom and set it on the bed.

His curiosity was still running high but his questions would have to wait. His first job was to make sure the atlas remained safe. Luckily, he knew the perfect hiding place for it.

Besides, how much harm could come from doing a small favor for his last living relative?

* * *

Crisp spent the next several days alternately sleeping, eating and looking at the atlas. Its age and his desire to keep it hidden stopped him from handling it much at first. Instead, he tried several times to ring Albert and ask some questions about it. His uncle never picked up the phone. Next, he tried searching the internet for information. This also turned up nothing. Eventually, he decided the only way he was going to learn more about it was to examine it himself.

A full body portrait of two men standing side by side filled the frontispiece. He didn't know who they were and was unlikely to find out. Water damage marred the facial features of both of the men. The damage struck other places as well. One of the men held some sort of device in his hand. It looked a bit like a telescope but its blurred lines made it hard to tell. No names or caption were listed under the portrait, adding to the mystery.

The maps themselves were wonderful. They were brilliantly inked with varying colors. The rivers were a light sky blue. Little green trees were depicted individually in the wooded areas. The larger cities and their surrounding areas were shaded with muted hues. Each also contained a half-dozen or so isolated spots that were marked and labeled with a series of numbers. They looked like they denoted the spot's latitude and longitude but there was no pattern to them. They seemed to be placed randomly.

He was particularly drawn to two of the maps. One was primarily of East London and parts of Essex. The other covered West London and continued out to Maidenhead. Both seemed to have received special attention, and they proved that whoever created them was clearly a master at his craft. The trees seemed to jut off their pages and the Thames seemed to flow. It was a remarkable optical illusion. He passed his fingertips over the pages each time he viewed them. It seemed like he should be able to feel the contours that he was seeing but the only difference in their texture that he could make out was a slight roughness, like fine sandpaper. They were also different because they didn't have any of the numbered marks. Instead there were unusual symbols he didn't recognize in each corner.

Despite the hours of fascination the atlas provided him, he realized he couldn't spend an entire fortnight indoors. His self-induced seclusion was slowly turning his flat into something more like a prison cell than a home. It was time to go outside, even if just for a little while. After mulling his options, he decided to go on a light jog in the park. A bit of exercise seemed like the ideal way to blunt his mounting boredom.

He returned to his flat just as it was turning dark. The first thing he did as he opened his door was reach for the light switch. As his arm extended outward, he sensed something was wrong. He was a split second too late. A shadowy figure pounced from behind the door and grabbed his arms. Crisp was expertly tripped and then guided down to the floor. Even with both arms held his fall was quick and a bit awkward. He landed with a muffled thud. His chest absorbed most of the impact but his right cheekbone also hit hard against the wood floor. He let out a gasp of pain. He then felt a knee grinding into the middle of his back, pinning him down. He struggled for a moment then felt the knee dig deeper into his spine.

"Hold still bobby," a raspy voice whispered down at him. "I can break your back from this position." Crisp stopped moving. "That's better." The voice then spoke to someone else. "Call Taylor. Tell him it's done and he can come up now."

Crisp was unable to see either the speaker or his accomplice. He did manage to hear a two-way radio being engaged followed by mumbled words that he couldn't decipher.

His assailant addressed him again. "You're going to stay mum for a few minutes. Don't move a muscle neither. If you behave yourself I might let you get up when he gets here. Don't matter much to me either way. If you don't behave," he paused for effect, "the next chair you buy will need wheels." There was no trace of humor in his voice.

While keeping his body motionless, Crisp's mind started to race. The first thing he realized was he was helpless in his current position. If there was some chance to alter it he would be perfectly willing to cooperate. More than anything he needed to remain calm.

He began to gather as much information as he could. The pressure holding him down and the power being used to pull back his arms told him that the man restraining him weighed at least sixteen stone and possessed brute strength. He was able to barely see the rubber soled shoes of the radio operator over by the window. The shoes kept shifting around, which made him think the man was feeling a bit nervous. Bluster and confidence were likely to be his only weapons. The man by the window might be someone he could put a scare into. Unfortunately, he doubted the man on his back could be intimidated at all.

His eyes roved around and examined the mess the intruders had made. His furniture was overturned. His books were piled up on the floor next to the bottom of their shelf. His reception room had been thoroughly searched. He assumed that the rest of his flat had received the same treatment.

The sound of the front door swinging open caused him to instinctively turn his head. The knee pressed down again. "Stay still I told ya," came another low rasp. Then another voice, calm and soft, carried over from the door.

"Has he given you any trouble?" The voice moved closer to him. "No of course he hasn't. Your usual methods of persuasion are as effective as ever."

The sound of a chair leg scraping across the floor was immediately followed by a dull thud. The man spoke once again to the big guy kneeling on Crisp's back. "I think the detective realizes your capabilities, my friend. I need to have a short conversation with him."

Crisp felt the pressure on his back easing up. His arms were pulled upwards, drawing him into a standing position. He was pushed forward then roughly turned and forced into a sitting position on the chair.

His reaction the moment he was released came from a mixture of instinct and training. Every muscle in his body tensed like a coiled spring. It was an almost imperceptible shift but it didn't go unnoticed.

"I wouldn't if I were you, Detective. While I am sure the Special Air Service instructed you in hand-to-hand combat, my friend," he pointed at his companion, "is as close to invincible as anyone I have ever met. Even if he wasn't, you are still outnumbered three to one."

Crisp reluctantly agreed with the man, whose name evidently was Taylor, about one thing. His chance of fighting his way free was pretty low. He settled back into the chair and began to warily appraise the three intruders. One was short, but squat and built like a gorilla. His hair was barely stubble and his nose was pushed flat against his face like clay squished by a board. The one next to the window looked almost like a smaller, thinner version of the first man. He was stoop shouldered and looking down at the floor. He glanced out the window every few seconds, like he was waiting for late company. Taylor was tall and well-built. His head was covered with a mop of grayish-blond hair, his mouth frozen in a patronizing smile. He stood straight and looked directly into Crisp's eyes.

"I will further warn you Detective, if you do not

cooperate I will need to ask my friend to utilize his preferred methods of interrogation. You would do well to avoid this."

Taylor's words made him realize something important about his adversaries. They counted on threats and the considerable strength and ability of his attacker to cause intimidation and submission in their victims. He was sure the technique was effective for them whenever they had used it before. They hadn't even bothered to tie him to the chair.

"Where to begin?" Taylor asked rhetorically. "The plan was to complete our search while you were out of the way. It would've been much simpler. The first snag occurred when you seemed determined to spend almost all of your time for the past few days here." He swept his right arm around, indicating Crisp's flat. "That problem was finally solved when you were observed leaving today. The second snag has occurred because you seem to have hidden what we want too well. We are in the process of resolving this second problem this moment. Tell me Detective," Taylor moved closer to Crisp in order to inspect him with his intense eyes, "where did you hide the package Sir Albert Price-Mills sent you? Do be careful. The wrong answer may cost you your life."

Crisp let the man's words sink in for a moment. He figured the reason his uncle wanted to hide the atlas was to keep it from being stolen but he never expected someone would threaten to kill him for it.

"The package, Detective Crisp."

He decided there was no point in playing dumb. Taylor was too well informed for it to work. But he wasn't going to give in either.

"I'm afraid you're too late." He stared directly back into Taylor's eyes. "The theater tickets he sent me were good for last night's show. If you want I can check if there are three seats still available for tonight."

Taylor frowned slightly. "You joke. Let me assure you, now is not the time for jokes. I am quite willing to be patient but you must learn that we are serious."

He nodded almost imperceptibly at the gorilla-like man, who acted with lightning swiftness. His hairy left arm came down in a crashing blow against Crisp's already bruised cheekbone. The pain was sharp and exquisite. His head started to throb and he wondered if he had a concussion.

"Several more similar blows are enough to kill a man. I have seen it happen. I think we are done with jokes. Once again, where is the package?" The thin smile was back on Taylor's face.

"I am an officer in the Metropolitan police service," Crisp gasped out as he shook off the grogginess he was feeling. "If I die you are going to be tracked down. There's nothing my mates love more than a fox hunt, especially when they're after slimy gits like you."

"I don't want no part of killing a bobby. It's not like our other jobs. It's suicide, that's what it is!" came a sudden outburst from over by the window.

Taylor's face flashed with anger. "Silence!"

Crisp stopped a satisfied grin from appearing across his face. Impatience was another thing he needed from his captors. That coupled with a desire to get away from his flat as soon as possible. He already clearly saw this combination in the radio-man.

"Let me assure you Detective Crisp, I am in charge here."

He nodded to the gorilla-like man again and another fierce blow landed on Crisp's cheek. His head snapped back violently this time. He held it there for a moment, then let it slump slowly forward. A trickle of blood traveled down to his chin. The cobwebs began to clear but slower this time.

"Enough. Hurts—"

"I will tell my friend to stop when you cooperate, Detective."

"Yes—please stop." Crisp turned his head a bit toward the radio-man. "False wall. Kitchen cupboard—next to sink." Once the words were out, his head flopped back into a defeated position.

Taylor waved at the man by the window. He eagerly left for the kitchen. After a bit of grunting and scraping, they heard a muffled shout of "got it" come from the kitchen door. The radio-man came back in to the reception room holding a brown paper package.

"It says it's from that Albert bloke up here in the

corner." He walked straight to the front door as he reported the information. The door remained closed but he stood eagerly next to it, waiting for an order to leave.

Taylor peered down at Crisp. "Your willingness to cooperate has saved your life tonight." He gave one last slight nod at the gorilla-like man and the two of them followed their companion out the door.

Crisp sat still until he was sure his attackers were gone. Then, rising unsteadily from his chair, he headed straight toward the bathroom. The first thing he checked once he got there was his reflection in the mirror. It wasn't a pretty sight. His dark wavy hair was disheveled and his light brown eyes were red-rimmed and watering. Worst of all, his right cheek looked like an over-ripe tomato. The skin at the center of the ugly bruise was split open a few centimeters. Blood oozed from the spot and was trickling down to his chin. He found some antibiotic ointment and put a dab on the open wound.

Despite the painful swelling a smile spread across his face. He decided he would have to drop Deputy Postmaster Tuttle a thank you note. It was from Tuttle, after all, that he learned the trick about dummy packages.

After un-wrapping the atlas he had found an old history book and used the same brown paper on it. He then put it in the cupboard hiding place. He figured it would satisfy any snoops that came around. His only bad luck was his attackers' inability to properly search a room. If they found the dummy in the first place he would be short a few cuts and bruises. The atlas was safe. He decided to leave it where it was in case he was still being watched.

There was now only one thing left that he needed to do. He walked to his bedroom and picked up the phone. The number he dialed was to his uncle's home in Cambridge. If Albert didn't answer this time he was going to contact the local constable and have him check things out. The phone rang the sixth time and he was about to hang up when the receiver finally picked up.

"Hello, who is this?" His uncle's voice was as recognizable as ever. It was clear and sonorous, having been honed over his many years teaching at Cambridge University.

"Uncle Albert, its Benjamin. I've been trying to catch up with you for days. Where have you been?"

"Benjamin?" there was a slight pause. "Thank God it's you. I need you to come to Cambridge right away. Something quite terrible has happened. I have tried and tried but I can't find it. Come right away. You must say yes!"

"Hold up a second," Crisp said. His uncle seemed to be rambling. "I need to ask you about the package you sent me. Why are there people willing to kill me to get it?"

"Is it safe?" His uncle did not seem to be paying close attention to him. He didn't react to his comment about the threat on his life at all.

"Yes."

"Good, thank you for helping me with it. But something much more troubling has taken place. It's vital that you come to Cambridge. I have no one else to turn to. Time is of the essence. You must come as soon as possible."

"But—"

Uncle Albert interrupted him again, "You must come. I'll explain what I can once you get here." There was a loud click then silence.

Crisp hung up the phone. His uncle was right. He had no choice. If he wanted any answers to his questions, he was going to Cambridge.

2

Uncle Albert's Secret

Crisp decided to take the train to Cambridge. When he arrived at the station he walked out front and began to look for a taxi. One black cab was available. A short, thin and balding man stood next to it. His gaze looked past the other passengers milling about and settled on Crisp. After a rapid but thorough appraisal, the man seemed to make up his mind. He unglued his feet and shuffled over.

"Lieutenant Crisp, sir?" The man straightened himself as much as he was able to. "I'm Wilkins, sir, Mortimer Wilkins, Sergeant Major of the 1st parachute regiment, retired."

"I'm pleased to meet you Sergeant Major," Crisp smiled down on the diminutive man as he spoke, "but my army days are over now. I would be happy if you just addressed me as Benjamin."

"As you wish, Lieutenant. Sir Price-Mills sent me. I'm to take you to his house."

"I thought as much when you knew my name."

"May I have your bag, sir?"

"I can manage."

"If all's the same with you, sir, I'd rather you let me take it." Crisp shrugged and held out his leather weekend valise. Wilkins took it, shuffled to the back of the car and put it in the boot of the well-worn vehicle. He then held the back door open for him.

Crisp shook his head. "I prefer riding in the front. Do you mind?"

"Of course not, sir." Before Wilkins could move to open the front passenger side door, Crisp helped himself into the auto. Wilkins got into the driver's seat. He quickly turned the car over. After a few grinding gear shifts the cab pulled away from the station.

"How did you know who I was?" Crisp asked Wilkins once they were passing through the town.

"I didn't expect you to remember but I used to drive you and your parents to see Sir Price-Mills. That was many years ago of course. You were nothing more than a wee sprite then."

"You recognized me from when I was a boy?"

"It wasn't all of it. You're a fair likeness of your uncle. He was a handsome bloke like you when he was younger."

The regular visits to his father's kindly, if a bit eccentric, uncle were some of the happiest of his childhood. Albert's large Manor was full of artifacts from centuries of English history and perfect for exploring. He always managed to find some medieval shield or weapon to play King Arthur with. His mother never enjoyed the visits for this reason. He was invariably caught with his purloined object. His mother would scold him and spend the rest the time apologizing to Albert, who always seemed more amused than anything. Once the treasure was safely returned, Albert would sneak him a brand new pound note with a wink.

After his father died he saw his uncle just once. He was in the SAS and participating in a training exercise near Cambridge. Somehow Albert knew he was in the vicinity. Crisp received a message that asked him to stop by if he had time.

During his visit, Albert was enthusiastic to see him and full of questions about his life in the SAS. Crisp stayed over one night and then returned to duty. Since then, he had neither seen nor spoken to him until the phone call last night.

"Almost there, sir." Wilkins voice broke through Crisp's reminiscence. He looked out of his window at a large green field they were passing to their left. It was all part of Albert's estate. In the distance he could make out the chimneys and the roof of the manor house.

"May I ask you another question, Mr. Wilkins?"

"Certainly, sir."

"How has my uncle been?"

"Begging your pardon, sir?"

"Is he getting along well? I haven't seen him for several years. When I spoke with him last night he seemed different. He has one of the most organized minds I've ever encountered. I spoke with him on the phone and couldn't get him to focus on a few simple questions. It wasn't like him at all."

"I'm not sure how to answer that, sir."

Wilkins looked slightly uncomfortable. Crisp assumed he didn't like talking about a prominent local citizen to an outsider. Even if he was Albert's nephew, he was not from this part of the country. That made him someone subject to mistrust until proven otherwise.

"I didn't mean to put you on the spot. I was just hoping to get an idea of what to expect when I see him."

"It's not that, sir." Wilkins continued to fidget a bit as he spoke. "Sir Price-Mills hasn't traveled to town much lately. I'd say it's been at least six months since he last asked me to pick him up. It was a right shock when he rang me this morning. The lot of us figured he'd moved back north somewhere, if not something worse. We've always seen him as a friendly and social part of the community. I never figured he would turn into a shut-in like he has. Begging your pardon if I've overstepped, sir."

"No I don't think you have, Mr. Wilkins. If my uncle needs help then I want to know about it. Thank you."

They pulled into the circular drive that led to the house. Once the tree line was behind them, Crisp caught a clear view of the house and, even though he was no longer a young boy, it still looked massive to him. Its two-and-a-half stories of solid red brick Georgian design sat on one hundred acres of lush Cambridgeshire farmland. The house itself dated back to the 18th century. Seven large windows lined the rectangular front face on each of the first and second stories. Seven smaller windows lined the front of the top story. The middle third of the building buttressed forward a few feet. The roof was made of gray slate. Four chimneys grew from it, one in each corner, looking like the truncated legs of an upside-down parlor table. A triangular section stuck out from the roof on top of the middle buttress. A shield and crossed axe design sat in the center of the triangle. On the right of the house was an acre of formal gardens. Off to the left was a solid-looking brick carriage house with a matching gray slate roof.

The circular drive came around to within a few yards of an ornate white front door. The cab rolled to a slow stop a few feet in front of it. Wilkins immediately hopped out of the auto and shuffled to its rear. Crisp climbed out of his door and turned to help him.

"I've got it, sir." Wilkins said as he opened the boot. "Sir Price-Mills told me he'd leave the door open for you. Go on in. I'll be right behind you."

Despite Wilkins's prodding, Crisp hesitated. Many of his best memories were made in this place. To him it was a refuge, a symbol of fun and innocence. Was this about to change forever? Taking a deep breath, he walked up to the door and tested the knob. It turned easily, as Wilkins said it would. He took a tentative step into the entrance hall and looked around.

For a moment he felt like an eight year old boy again. Everything was exactly the same as he remembered it. The large portrait of Sir Harold Mills was hanging directly across the room. Sir Harold had been a Captain with Wellington's army at Waterloo. The tables were decorated with delicate oriental porcelain vases. There was a grandfather clock that once belonged to Winston Churchill's father. Several smaller portraits mixed in with watercolors of the English coast dotted the remaining wall space. The banister curved up to the second floor landing. Looking down at him from the top of the stairs was his great-uncle Albert.

Sir Albert Price-Mills looked exactly like the retired Professor of Physics that he was. His mostly bald head was neatly trimmed. His jaw line was clean shaven with the typical extra fold of an older man. He wore a striped bow tie. A cardigan sweater showed beneath his tweed jacket. A smile was on his face but it was out of place somehow. It was less wide, more melancholy, than Crisp remembered.

"Benjamin, it's a great pleasure to see you again. Other than that rather ghastly bruise on your face, you seem to be fit and prosperous." The older man's deep voice easily reached the entranceway from his high perch.

Crisp reached up to his right cheek. "This bruise is one of the major reasons I'm here, uncle. I have a few important questions for you."

"All in good time, Benjamin, all in good time." Albert worked his way down the stairs. Once he reached the first floor he grabbed Crisp's right hand and eagerly shook it with both of his. He then looked over Crisp's shoulder.

"Sergeant Major," Crisp turned around as Albert spoke, "I wish to apologize for neglecting your services. I do thank you for being kind enough to forgive me and for assisting my fine young nephew."

Wilkins dropped Crisp's bag and bowed slightly to Albert. "It was my pleasure, Sir Price-Mills."

"Will you be available tomorrow morning? I planned to call you once Benjamin is ready to depart. I anticipate our business will last at least until then."

"As you wish, Sir." Wilkins took Albert's words as the polite dismissal they were. He gave a smart salute to Crisp. "Pleasure to meet you, Lieutenant."

"And you Mr. Wilkins."

Wilkins turned and shuffled out the door, leaving Crisp alone with his uncle.

Albert addressed him again. "Your usual room has been prepared for you. I realize it has been four years since you were last here. In case you don't remember, it's on the second floor, third room on the left. Once you're settled in would you be so kind as to join me in my study?"

Crisp took his bag upstairs. After placing it in his room and freshening up, he wandered back downstairs. The study was in the front right corner of the house. A full-length set of closed double doors blocked the way in. He tested them. They swung open with a gentle push.

The study was oak paneled with bookshelves and a fireplace. The furniture was covered with sturdy cordovan leather. In the rear of the room, Albert sat behind his desk with his eyes closed. He looked like he was concentrating on something.

Crisp walked toward the desk, surveying the room as he went. At first glance, everything was neat and properly arranged. As he looked closer, however, the books were placed out of their usual precise order. He saw classic literature mixed in with theological texts and history mixed with poetry. It was as if someone jumbled them and then put them back on the shelves randomly. He reached the desk and sat down in a chair. A few silent moments passed before he leaned forward and said softly, "Uncle Albert."

Albert opened his eyes. Close up they looked tired. They were still inquisitive, however. Crisp felt them searching deeply into his own eyes. They seemed to be looking for the answer to an unaskable question.

"I'm sorry to drag you up here, Benjamin. I wish it hadn't been necessary. I tried to manage things myself at first. I'm afraid I'm just not as capable as I used to be."

"Does this problem have anything to do with the atlas you sent me?"

"Why do you ask?"

"Some rough types broke into my flat last night and made quite a bit of fuss over it."

"I assume, then, that they were the source of your injury."

"Yeah, they were the source all right."

"Are you going to be okay?"

"Never mind about me; I've dealt with their kind before. You, however, are a different matter. I need to know whether or not you're mixed up in something dodgy. If you are, tell me now. That way I can do something to get us out of trouble before it's too late."

Albert shifted in his chair then replied "I appreciate what you're saying, believe me I do. You said the atlas was safe, though, did you not?"

"Yes, it's safe."

"Then there is no further reason to discuss it, at least for now."

"That's tough to do, uncle. I get reminded of it every time I look in the mirror."

"Yes, that bruise is quite difficult to miss. Once again, I'm terribly sorry it's there. But let me reassure you, I didn't know I was putting you in any danger when I sent you the atlas."

"At least tell me why someone wanted to steal it from you."

"I don't know. Honestly, Benjamin, the atlas is not the reason I asked you to come here. I need to talk to you about something else, something much more urgent."

"Are you sure? They seem to be awful important to someone."

26

"I'm quite positive. Let me reassure you, all you've done is perform a favor for me—nothing dodgy, as you say. The atlas is my property. It's also, I imagine, quite valuable. I'm distressed that passing it to you led to the events you describe. It also bothers me to think that someone was able to trace the atlas to you so easily. As for the reason you were attacked—I suppose, as with anything of worth, there will always be men eager to take what they have not earned."

Albert paused a moment to sip from a tall glass of water then continued. "Now that we have dispensed with your questions about the atlas, we must move on. There's a much bigger problem that I need you to help me with. It will require your full attention since it needs a solution fairly quickly. I'm not ashamed to admit, you may be my only hope."

"Go on," Crisp said as he continued to watch Albert closely.

"Two nights ago my home was vandalized. My study was turned into quite a mess. Thankfully, no other room was disturbed. In the process, however, a treasured heirloom went missing."

"What heirloom? Which one?"

Albert stood up and walked over to the bookshelf. The spot he pointed to was bare.

"This is the usual position for an over four hundred year old bust of Doctor John Dee. It is the missing item."

"Excuse me uncle, doctor who?"

"John Dee—a brilliant scientist who was once a close advisor to the first Queen Elizabeth."

"And you're sure it's gone? It hasn't been tucked away another shelf somewhere?"

Albert shook his head. "I've searched the house and the grounds. There's no doubt it's been taken. I've even made some inquiries with some of my old sources in an attempt to locate it and met nothing but failure. Now, sadly, I am unable to venture forward any further. Age and time has made difficult that which once would have been simple for me. Nevertheless, I must retrieve it within the next five days." Albert shuddered slightly. "The price of

27

failure is too high. That's why I need you. You must find it for me. I'm certain you can if you try."

Crisp stared, speechless, at his uncle. He was talking about the statue of someone's head as if it was the Crown Jewels. He remembered the bust dimly. It was a plain metal cast of a rather homely man with a full pointed beard. It was never the source of any special interest during his past visits. What could have changed in his uncle's mind?

"Did you contact the local constable?" Crisp asked.

"I cannot allow the police to get involved in this matter."

"I don't know if you're aware of it uncle, but I'm a Detective Constable in London."

"I'm fully aware of your status with the Arts and Antiques division of the Metropolitan Police Service. I gave the Chief Inspector an unsolicited but fairly persuasive recommendation when you applied for the post. And the fact that you are in London is actually of great benefit. After my inquiries, I have reason to believe that's where the bust has been taken. But I'm not asking for your help as a police officer. What I'm asking for is another favor. You're someone I trust and this must be managed confidentially. Of course, I didn't anticipate having to test your good will so soon again. I do hope I didn't use it all up with my last favor."

"Uncle, I want to help you, honestly I do. I wouldn't have come all this way if I didn't."

Crisp got up from his chair and went to Albert's side, grabbed his elbow and gave it a gentle squeeze. "Have you been to see Doctor Foster recently? He was the local GP you spoke about during my last visit, wasn't he? I think I should call him and make an appointment for you."

Albert fixed his penetrating gaze on him again. "I assure you that I am in full control of my faculties. Doctor Foster is not required here. It is Doctor Dee who I need to retrieve to my study." There was no hint of mental weakness in his eyes as he spoke.

Crisp shook his head as he let go of Albert's elbow. "It just doesn't make any sense."

"I thought I was being quite clear."

28

"But how can a statue, no matter how old, be as important as you say it is?"

"Trust me; it's everything I've said and more."

"I'm afraid that's not good enough. How am I supposed to find something that you claim is so vital without having any idea why it's so vital? I'm afraid that without more information it'll be impossible for me to find the bust. You've asked me to manage this confidentially. It's your turn. Take me into your confidence. Unless you do I'll be unable to help you, not because I don't want to but because I won't have a clue where to start."

Albert returned to his desk chair and sat down again. He seemed lost in thought for a moment. "There's truth in what you say but what you ask is no small matter. I have to think it over. There's food in the kitchen. You must be hungry. Please help yourself. I'll have an answer for you within the hour."

* * *

The refrigerator in the kitchen held some roast beef and cold potatoes. Crisp cut several slices of meat and dished some potatoes on a plate. His uncle was right about one thing; he was hungry.

As he stood at the counter and chewed his food, he noticed how quiet the rest of the house was. The usual attendants were absent. There wasn't a cook or butler to be found. He wondered how Albert kept the house in order without any help.

When an hour passed, he returned to the study. Albert was not there. He sat down in the same chair as before and waited. After about five minutes he heard a muffled clunking noise that seemed to emanate from behind a bookshelf. He turned his head toward its direction. The bookshelf swung outward and his great-uncle entered the study from behind it. As the bookshelf closed the muffled clunking sounded again.

"I apologize for making you wait," Albert said to a stunned Crisp. "I needed to double check the rules regarding this particular situation. I thought I found a narrow loophole. Upon further review, I now am certain it will satisfy at least the majority of my colleagues. It will not matter, of course, unless they find out about it," he added with a hopeful afterthought.

"I thought you were going to clear things up. So far you've managed to confuse me even further. By the way, where are Geoffrey and Matilda? You didn't sack them I hope?" They were the married couple Crisp remembered once worked for Albert.

"No, I didn't sack them. They returned to Australia about a year ago. Geoffrey said something about inheriting a sheep ranch. They seemed quite happy about it."

"And you didn't hire replacements?"

"I haven't bothered. A woman down the way comes to cook and clean once a week. It has been a satisfactory arrangement so far. But enough about that. Time is, as I said, precious. Before we can move forward there is one essential thing I must ask of you. You must promise me on your life, on your very soul even, that what I am about to divulge to you remains an absolute secret. This restriction includes all of your personal and professional acquaintances, even your superiors in the police service. I know that it's a lot to ask. I know that I'm the one in need and in a poor position to demand anything. Without your solemn vow of silence, however, I'll be in violation of an oath that I have upheld my entire adult life. I need to find Doctor Dee quite urgently, but I will not forfeit my pledge of secrecy no matter how desperate I am to retrieve him."

Crisp considered his uncle's words carefully before answering. "I have also taken an oath. It says I must enforce the law and protect others from harm. I won't violate it, even if I give you my promise."

"Your condition seems reasonable. Do we have an agreement then?" Albert asked as he peered over his glasses.

Crisp hesitated for a moment then said, "Yes."

Albert fished a sheet of paper from the breast pocket of his jacket. He took a pen from his desk and wrote something along the bottom. He then signed it and put it back in his pocket. "It's my personal affidavit. I'm required to keep a record of your promise and any conditions in the archives. I'll have Miss Pimsby file it in the morning. You don't need to sign as only a member's signature is valid in this situation."

"Member? Of what?"

Albert reflexively dropped the volume of his deep voice. "Now that you are sworn to secrecy I can answer that question. For the past fifty years I've been affiliated with the Academy of Natural Philosophers. The Academy has never been open about its existence, a condition I am obligated to protect. That's why your silence is so imperative."

"And what exactly is this Academy of Natural Philosophers? Something you joined while at Cambridge?"

"No, no, the Academy is made up of scientists and university men and women from around the world. They've been gathering for centuries to discuss natural and paranormal phenomena and to conduct experiments with the elements."

"You make it sound as though you belong to a group of medieval alchemists."

"While that term is technically correct, we Academy members frown upon it. Being an alchemist is associated with turning lumps of metal into gold and elixirs of immortality."

Crisp twisted in his chair. Albert's answer wasn't the one he expected. "You mean like the Philosopher's Stone?" he asked, hoping his uncle would back down from his ridiculous assertion.

"Absolute rubbish. Unfortunately, legends can be difficult to separate from facts, which means when someone is thought to be an alchemist he is in considerable danger. In the past, the local dignitary would imprison people caught practicing it until they produced a room full of gold. Many good men and women languished under these cruel circumstances. Nowadays we much prefer to speak of ourselves as experimentalists or philosophists, not alchemists."

Crisp stared at his uncle, incredulous. However, instead of arguing with his elderly relative, he decided it was best to play along. "Call yourselves what you like, I still don't understand why it is so important for the Academy to stay a secret. I can't imagine anyone nowadays objecting to a bunch of scientists getting together to chat once in a while."

Albert sighed. "The Academy is much more than that. I don't expect you to understand all of the important ways the Academy has contributed to the betterment of mankind. Suffice it to say the knowledge it has accumulated has helped change the course of civilization. Unfortunately, some of the 'unique' ways we use to protect and maintain this knowledge and wisdom would be rendered useless if they became common knowledge—which brings me back to the reason you are here; my bust of John Dee."

"Was Dee a member of the Academy when he was alive?" Crisp asked.

"Oh yes, he is one of our most influential and active members. It will interest you to know it was his idea to send the atlas to you. I'm not sure what prompted his sudden insistence to be rid of it. It seemed a minor matter so I was happy to comply with his wishes."

Crisp wasn't sure he heard right. "Wait a second, didn't you tell me earlier that he lived four hundred years ago?"

"Yes, of course I did. As I was saying, the Academy has preserved certain discoveries for the exclusive use of its members. The manipulation of certain elements and the existence of other rare ones are examples of the discoveries I'm talking about. One of the rarest and most precious of these elements was discovered during Academy investigations into paranormal activity. It's called ambrosium. It's most easily found in areas where such activity is consistently reported. Unfortunately, deposits exist only in minute quantities. These small amounts of ambrosium, however, are capable of capturing intensely emotional brain wave patterns, such as anger and fear, which are typically released at the point just before death. Once captured, the ambrosium will intermittently project the electrical potential from the brain waves into the surrounding atmosphere. The result is a crude spectral vision that is capable only of mimicking the emotions captured at the time of death. The perceived haunting is actually an explainable scientific process based on the existence and properties of ambrosium."

"So ghosts aren't souls that are trapped on earth like most people think?"

"I'm afraid not. The soul is, as far as anyone knows, not detectable or trappable. The afterlife is as much a mystery to the Academy as everyone else."

"I admit your story is intriguing. The one thing I haven't figured out is what any of it has to do with the missing bust?" Crisp asked.

"It has everything to do with it. The Academy discovered long ago how to find and collect deposits of ambrosium. When enough of the element is collected we refine it with a special process. Concentrated amounts of refined ambrosium can store much more extensive and more complex brain wave energy than the crude form found in nature.

"For centuries, when a prominent member of the Academy has died, refined ambrosium has been used to capture his or her knowledge. It is the most important method we use to preserve and build upon their accumulated wisdom."

"I think I'm beginning to understand. The bust of Dee is made from ambrosium and you don't want to risk that whoever finds it will learn about your secret element."

"That is part of it," Albert replied. "But you're missing the crucial point. As I said earlier, crude ambrosium creates a rudimentary and fleeting spectral vision. As you alluded to earlier, these visions are commonly known as ghosts. Refined ambrosium has the power to create a sophisticated spectral vision that can be reproduced at will. We Academy members, however, tend to still use the common term for the image that is created."

"So the bust of Dee is vitally important because it actually holds his wisdom and knowledge, which can be spectrally projected in the form of a ghost."

"You have summed the situation up admirably," Albert said with a satisfied smile.

"There's one thing I'm still not clear about." Actually he wasn't clear about any of his uncle's wild claims. He just didn't see the point in challenging Albert right now. Instead, he was storing everything in his memory so that he could make sense of it later. "Why do you need to find the bust so quickly? The ambrosium isn't radioactive or unstable, is it?"

Albert shook his head. "No, there's nothing dangerous about formed ambrosium. I need to have Dee back before the Academy holds its International Meeting next week. Unfortunately, there's no way I can go without him and it's imperative that I attend. There are two reasons for this. First, I cannot bear the shame. Losing a precious Ghost of the Academy is an unprecedented error. Going without Dee will expose my carelessness to a major assembly of my colleagues."

"I'm sure you can get past that somehow."

"Yes, you are correct. Eventually I would. But the second problem is the meeting itself. The news cannot get out that a ghost thief may be at large. If it does, the other members will not risk exposing their own ambrosium busts. They will leave them at home or not come at all. As a result, the meeting will fail to achieve anything or may even be cancelled."

"Maybe it should get cancelled. It would be safer."

"Actually, the exact opposite is true. There are several vitally important matters that I need to bring before the Academy. I am not exaggerating when I say that all of our past achievements are in danger of being wiped away. So as you can see, I must go to the meeting, which means I urgently need to find the bust of Dee."

Crisp massaged his swollen cheekbone. Doing a favor for his uncle had already yielded some unexpected risks. He was tempted to say no. But then he saw the desperation in Albert's eyes.

"I'm usually not someone who fancies a fantastic tale like yours, uncle. But, luckily, I happen to have a bit free time on my hands. I'll do what I can to help you find the bust."

"I'm quite willing to accept that you have doubts, Benjamin. On the rare occasion the Academy has needed outside assistance before, it has always come with a healthy dose of disbelief. It doesn't matter right now. I'm simply relieved that you're willing to help."

"So what do we do next?"

"You're now a Special Investigator for the Academy. You have volunteered to render expert services that no other member has the ability to provide. As such, I am authorized to provide the limited but normally confidential information that I just divulged to assist you in the performance of your duties. I'm also allowed to provide certain 'secret weapons' to aid you in your quest. It's the loophole I spoke of. Some members would undoubtedly frown on detective work counting as expert services. I say if it was acceptable to appoint Arthur Conan Doyle a special investigator in 1898 you pass muster as well!"

Albert coughed lightly as he finished. He reached for his water and carefully and slowly downed the rest of it. The grandfather clock in the hall chimed midnight as he put his glass down.

"My goodness, time has simply flown by tonight." Albert suddenly looked every bit of his eighty years. "Perhaps we should retire for the night. Rest is essential for the proper functioning of the body and mind and you will need to get an early start in the morning."

Albert walked over to Crisp and gave him a soft pat on the back. "Putting business aside, it has been good to chat with you again, Benjamin. It has been far too long since we last had the chance."

"I'm sorry, uncle. I should've visited sooner. I don't know why I haven't."

Albert looked at him again with his penetrating gaze. It seemed to carry a measure of pity this time around. "Never mind that now, it doesn't matter."

They walked up the stairs to the second floor together. Crisp watched his uncle until he made it to his bedroom door at the end of the hall. He waved goodnight as Albert disappeared then opened his door and entered his room.

Crisp sat down on his four-poster canopy bed. He wasn't sure what he just got himself into. Nevertheless, finding the bust seemed like the best course for now. Returning it to his uncle would hopefully break him out of whatever delusion he seemed to be trapped in.

As he picked up his overnight bag to get his toiletries he realized it was vibrating. He reached to the bottom and found the source. It was his mobile phone. He flipped it open and saw there were several missed calls. They were from his immediate superior, Detective Inspector Smythe. For a moment he considered throwing the phone back in his bag but his better nature took control. He pushed the call button and put the phone to his ear.

"Crisp, where in blazes have you been?" the DI's voice boomed through the phone.

"Good evening, Detective Inspector. Or should I say good morning? To what do I owe the pleasure?"

"Where are you? I sent a car to your apartment to get you but they said you didn't answer. Never mind. Wherever you are, get back to the Yard as soon as possible."

"I'm in Cambridge. I took the train so I can't get back until the morning. What's going on? Did someone raid the Bank of England?"

"Cambridge?" This seemed to confuse the DI for a moment. "Listen up Crisp. It's a bloody mess around here. The British Museum got hit and it was a bang-bang job. They managed to get away with some stuff from an exhibit."

"What does that have to do with me? I'm not allowed to play. Fuller said so."

"All leaves and holidays have been temporarily rescinded. Report back here tomorrow afternoon at the latest. That's an order."

3
Help Arrives

Crisp took his time getting packed and dressed to leave. Then, when he was done, he spent an extra twenty minutes studying a dust covered archer's helmet that he found in his room. It was one of the 'borrowed' items he played with as a boy. For some reason he couldn't put it down. Even though he needed to get going he just sat on the edge of his bed and spun it on the palm of his hand, over and over.

Albert was up and waiting for him when he finally made his way downstairs. Crisp gave him the news about the break-in at the museum and, even though it wasn't his fault, made sure to apologize for his sudden loss of free time. He assured him he would still do what he could to help, but he had to follow orders first.

Albert tried but couldn't hide his disappointment. Fortunately, he didn't argue or try to plead his case like Crisp expected he would. He simply went to his study and called Wilkins back to the manor.

On the ride back to Cambridge, Crisp decided he had done the right thing. Promise or no promise, how was he supposed to ignore a direct in order to go chasing windmills?

Once he was back in London, Crisp took the Undergound to New Scotland Yard. Detective Sergeant Reginald Little waiting for him when he arrived. His awkward stance and stooped shoulders made him easy to recognize from across the room.

Little was perhaps the person he knew best in the Department. He always found him to be a bit of a strange bird. Crisp doubted Little had it in him to hurt another living creature. It was a curious trait for a police detective and he often wondered what had driven him to join the service. The only answer he could ever come up with was Little's well documented obsession about following proper rules and regulations.

"Hello, Reggie." Crisp said once he reached his desk.

"Hello, Benjamin."

Michael Malik

"I'm not used to the VIP greeting. A bee's obviously in someone's bonnet over the museum robbery."

"Sorry to be a pest but Detective Chief Inspector Fuller told me to get you over to the museum as soon as you got here. You're supposed to go over the scene thoroughly. I think he's hoping you'll see something the rest of us have missed."

"And we certainly wouldn't want to upset Fuller," Crisp said. "Let's get cracking."

Little gave him a curious look. "How are you, mate? Everything alright?"

"Sure, why wouldn't it be?"

"It's just that you seem kind of—I mean, after what happened anyone would be—" Little seemed to be searching for a description as Crisp stared impatiently back at him. "Oh, never mind," he finally said, giving up with a shrug.

They arrived at the British Museum thirty minutes later. The area around Great Russell Street was cordoned off and there were police vehicles lining the street. After showing identification, they drove toward the east wing. As the side of the building came into view, Crisp let out a gasp. A mild breeze was causing the large tarpaulin that had been hastily hung from the roof to billow. The glimpse he caught of the wall beneath it revealed a giant hole over a large a pile of rubble.

"They took a big hunk of explosive and blew the side of the building off," Little explained. He must have caught the look of shock and horror on Crisp's face. "They must have been desperate to get in there."

"It doesn't make sense," Crisp said. "An explosion of this size would generate a rapid and overwhelming response. They would hardly have any time to take anything."

"Funny you should say that. The museum has done a quick inventory. The only thing missing is a herald trumpet. It was part of a special display of artifacts from the court of Queen Elizabeth I. Granted, it's practically priceless, but they could have gotten away with a few other pieces that would have been even more valuable, either as collectors' items or as jewels to fence. And the weirdest thing is there were four trumpets in the set, but only one

38

was taken. It seems like a remarkably thorough undertaking for it to be botched by taking a single item, and a second rate piece at that."

"Is there anything else I should be aware of?"

"I saved the best for last." Little's expression turned sour. "The herald trumpet is part of the Queen's private collection. As soon as the crown's representatives found out what was gone they started raising the roof. Any wiggle room we might have hoped for is officially gone."

Little found an open space to park. They got out of the car and filtered through the temporary barricades that were now in place. As they approached the crumbling wall, a uniformed man wearing the protective equipment of the bomb squad came over to meet them.

"Hello, Trevor," Crisp said to the large man. "Staying busy, I see." He pointed at the padding Trevor was wearing. "What's with the suit of armor? Is there another bomb left behind?"

"I just finished clearing the site," replied Sergeant Trevor Dunston. He was a thick set man with a midsection that looked like fat but was mostly muscle, short but powerful-looking legs and a large bristled mustache that dominated his round, friendly face. The rumor was that Dunston once competed in the Olympics as a power-lifter. He was even supposed to have just missed winning a medal. As he watched the man's massive body move closer, Crisp found the story easy to believe.

Reaching his right arm out, he grabbed Crisp's hand and gave it a crushing shake.

"Thanks."

"How are you? Everything alright?"

"Why does everyone keep asking me that?"

Dunston released his grip. "Take it easy, mate. No offense meant."

Crisp felt a twinge of guilt for snapping at Dunston so sharply. "Sorry," he said. "I'm fine, honestly, ready to get back to work."

An easy smile spread below the massive man's mustache. "Never mind, mate, it happens. Every detective I know has gotten a bit twitchy when a bomb's involved in the job."

"Have you found anything useful yet?" Little asked.

Dunston shook his head. "Afraid not. Just a major headache for the most part. They used plastic explosives, more than I've seen in one place before, remotely detonated. I've gone over that last bit. There weren't any of the usual fingerprints. It was a totally unique set up, wires and radio both, so I won't be able to lean on any of the coaches for information."

"Coaches?" Crisp asked.

"Bomb makers who've been caught and are still in prison. If they've trained other bombers then getting one to talk usually gives us a short list of suspects."

Dunston wasn't painting a very pretty picture. Crisp eyed the museum again. There wouldn't be many clues left in the pile of crumbling brick and mortar. "Is it safe enough for us to look things over?"

"Sure, just don't go out too close to the outer wall on the second level blast area. The floor is unstable in places."

"Okay, thanks for the warning."

Crisp and Little walked over to the main entrance. Inside the front hall, another member of the bomb squad directed them to use the south stairway. They followed the signs and soon found themselves in the east wing European exhibit.

Despite the large tarpaulin flapping loudly against the museum's crumbling wall, Crisp's attention focused squarely on the scene before him. Several of the displays holding Elizabethan artifacts were blown askew. Most of the pieces they once held were still scattered on the floor. Some, however, appeared to have been picked up and lined along a wall. A few, including an oddly familiar looking telescope-like instrument, were even dusted clean. The museum staff must have been tampering with the crime scene before someone stopped them. He imagined the incensed curators arguing with the police as they were told to leave the valuable artifacts spread out and dusty on the floor. Hopefully their understandable desire to restore things back to normal hadn't destroyed any evidence.

The main display case was in the center of the room. Its Plexiglass top was neatly cut away and lying on the floor. He saw some suction cup handles affixed to it. They must have been used to lift the top away once it was free. They'd need to be removed and tested for fingerprints even though he knew they wouldn't have any.

He moved closer to get a better view of the case. The line where the top once sat looked bubbled, like it had been melted. All that remained inside of it were four short stands. Three still held gleaming brass trumpets. The fourth was empty.

"What's so special about the things," he asked Little as he leaned over and inspected the remaining trumpets.

"I don't know."

"We should probably find out. It might help us figure out why someone would blow up a good bit of the museum to steal one."

"Perhaps we should talk to the manager of this special exhibit. He would know more about them."

"Just a few more minutes." Crisp looked around in a circle, sweeping the floor, the walls, and the ceiling with his eyes. "What about the surveillance cameras?"

"Destroyed by the blast, I'm afraid."

"I mean before tonight. Look at the segment of wall and the blast area. It could've caught this display case if the explosives were placed a few feet over. But the case is untouched. The robbers knew exactly where to place their charges. At least one of them was in here checking things over. The recordings from when the display opened need to be checked thoroughly. Maybe there's a video of someone who's acting strange, maybe pacing the distance out between the case and the wall."

Little looked back and forth from the case to the wall. "I believe you're on to something. You find the manager and ask about the trumpets. I'll go to security and get the tapes. After we're done we'll meet back at the car."

They left the east wing of the museum and returned to the main floor. After another inquiry for directions, Little parted ways for the security office. He gave Crisp a slight wave as he ambled away. After a short walk, Crisp found the exhibit managers office. He knocked on the door. A voice said, "Enter". Crisp opened the door and walked into a small room. An older, flustered looking woman who could've passed for Margaret Thatcher's sister was on the phone. She motioned Crisp to a chair but he remained standing in his spot.

"Yes, it was at my request that they were loaned to the exhibit. I quite understand and I accept full responsibility for the loss." The look on her face showed that she meant what she said. It was a mix of shock and embarrassment. "I don't know what else I can say." She glanced up at Crisp. "I believe a police officer has entered my office. Perhaps he has some new information. Let me speak to him and I'll ring you back." She hung up the phone with obvious relief.

"The Queen's representatives," she explained. "Was I correct in assuming you're from the police?" Her look turned hopeful.

"I'm Detective Constable Crisp. I was hoping you could answer a few questions Miss—"

"Melanie Fairfield. This means you haven't found it yet, I take it. The missing trumpet, I mean."

"Not yet ma'am, we've just started our investigation. Can you tell me what makes it worth blowing up a building to steal? It's not encrusted with rubies or cast from solid gold, is it?"

"No, it's a rare historical artifact and priceless for that reason. Jewels or gold wouldn't add much to it's worth."

Crisp doubted that. Most criminals weren't exactly history enthusiasts. "Do you have any idea what special interest the missing trumpet could have held for the robbers."

Fairfield stared at him blankly for a moment. "I suppose there's no reason for you to know the interesting story behind it."

"Feel free to enlighten me, then."

"Robert Cecil presented Elizabeth I the trumpet, along with the three others, upon the fortieth anniversary of her coronation. The people met her ascension to the throne with a great musical celebration. The trumpets were meant to symbolize the elation that existed in her subjects that day and how it would be an undying presence for her entire rule.

"After Elizabeth died the trumpets were bequeathed to the estates of the ruling monarch of England. They have

42

retained a sense of majesty through time that has kept them protected and cherished through upheaval and changes in the line of succession. They have survived all this, only to have one unceremoniously pilfered last night on my watch."

She began to get teary eyed. "I'm sorry detective. Please, please find it. As a complete set, the trumpets are an irreplaceable national treasure. To have only three is as good as having none."

"We'll do our best, ma'am," Crisp said with as much conviction as he could muster.

Fairfield wiped her eyes and then reached for a piece of museum stationary. She wrote something on it and handed it to him. "If you learn anything, anything at all, please, ring me at this number."

* * *

When Crisp arrived at the front door of his flat later that night he was surprised to find a woman waiting for him. She had somehow found a chair and was sitting patiently on the landing. As soon as she saw him she stood up, revealing a large handbag slung under her left arm. After the crazy events of the past several days, he couldn't help feeling suspicious of an unexpected visitor.

"Detective Constable Crisp?" the woman inquired after he stopped at the top step.

"Yes, and who might you be?'

"I'm Miss Sophia Pimsby, Sir Albert's personal secretary."

Miss Pimsby appeared to be in her mid to late twenties. She was of average height but had a petite build. Her reddish-brown hair was worn up and pulled tightly behind her head. She wore glasses with thick, black rims. This did nothing to detract from the obvious beauty of her face. Her tight lipped serious look along with the standard white blouse and pleated below-the-knee skirt she was wearing gave him the impression of a pretty librarian informing him about an overdue book.

She reached forward and handed Crisp a sealed envelope. He opened it and pulled out the small card it

43

Michael Malik

held. The unmistakable scrawl of his uncle traced across it.

> Benjamin
> Miss Pimsby is my personal representative. She has something that will help locate the item we discussed. Please give her a moment of your time.
> Uncle Albert

He put the card back in the envelope and returned it to Miss Pimsby. "How long have you been waiting here?"

"I arrived approximately four hours ago. I'm afraid I didn't have another way to contact you and I couldn't afford to miss you once you came home, so I decided it was most expedient to wait for your return."

"That's a bit of a slog. You must be tired."

"It hasn't been too bad. The woman in the next flat was kind enough to lend me this chair."

"You best come inside. I'll give Mrs. Cratch her chair back later."

Miss Pimsby followed him into his flat. Once inside, she looked about with undisguised bewilderment. "Is this some new trend in home decorating that I'm unaware of?"

"Don't mind the mess. It's a leftover from some unexpected guests."

"Were your 'guests' also the reason you have that awful bruise on your face?"

"Yes."

"What on earth did they do that for?"

"I suppose they didn't think I was much of a host." He righted an overturned chair and brushed it off. "Have a seat. You must be hungry and thirsty after your long wait. Can I get you something?"

"Tea would be lovely, thank you."

Crisp went to the kitchen and put a teapot on the stove. After finding two clean mugs he sat at the kitchen table and tried to figure out what to do with his newest problem.

The arrival of Miss Pimsby was inconvenient at best. He told his uncle he would do what he could to locate the bust. Her sudden presence felt like undue pressure to make it a priority. As he waited for the kettle to boil, he tried to work out a polite method to send her on her way.

When the tea was ready, Crisp carried it out to the reception room. He almost spilled all of it on the floor when he turned the corner. Everything was perfectly clean and tidy. Miss Pimsby sat straight up in her chair, her large purse at her feet.

"Much better, don't you think?"

"Yes, much." He handed her the tea and sat on the couch. "You're a ruddy miracle worker. Don't tell me you're the secret weapon my uncle mentioned last night?"

"Oh, no," replied Miss Pimsby with a stifled giggle. Crisp found it curiously at odds with the somewhat severe personality she otherwise projected. She seemed to notice the look on his face and quickly recovered her terse mannerism. "I have the 'secret weapon', as you call it, in my handbag. You'd be surprised at the things that can be carried about in a woman's purse."

"Secret weapon or not, I'm afraid you've wasted your time coming here. The assignment I'm dealing with is a top priority problem. In case you don't watch the news, the British Museum was bombed last night. A herald trumpet dating to Queen Elizabeth I was stolen. That happens to be confidential information, by the way."

Miss Pimsby put up her hands and said, "Not a word."

"The point is, there's pressure from very high places to solve the museum robbery sooner rather than later. If I devote too much time to other things I'll be in dereliction of duty and would be letting my mates on the service down. I'm sure you can understand my predicament."

"I do understand. Your explanation was quite thorough. I just don't believe you."

"And why is that, exactly?"

"Well, for starters, you invited me inside to chat. That implies you are open to a change of heart."

"No, all it means is I didn't want to be rude."

She leaned back in her chair, took a furtive peek at him over her glasses as she sipped her tea, and then said, "That's true. You seem like a considerate person. That's another reason I don't believe you."

Michael Malik

Crisp tried to figure out the logic of her statement. He quickly gave up. "I don't see how my manners matter much in this situation. In fact, I would say they're pretty irrelevant."

"It's just that I've heard so much about you from Albert and you're the same as he described. It makes me think that you want to help him. Badly."

"Of course I want to help him." He set his mug awkwardly on the table, causing the tea inside to splash over the rim and trickle down its side. "But it's not a matter of wanting to do anything, is it? I can't do two things at once and hope to do either well. All that ends up happening is I make a bloody mess of both."

"Then you're in luck," she said as she picked her purse off the floor and put it in her lap. "I'm here to help you do exactly what you said you can't do—complete both tasks at once."

"I don't know how I can be much clearer," Crisp said with a sigh. "Do I want to find Dee's bust for Albert? Of course I do. I just don't have time to go looking for it right now. I'll help him, but he needs to be patient."

"That's what I'm trying to tell you. Looking for the bust will not waste any of your time. In fact, it may actually assist you in solving the museum robbery."

Crisp stared at Miss Pimsby in disbelief. Linking the two crimes seemed like a desperate reach, even for her. Be that as it may, she held an important advantage over him. Despite his earlier assertions, he hated leaving Albert in the lurch. If there really was a chance he could kill two birds with one stone, he was willing to listen to what she had to say.

"I should explain one thing before I go on. I am not just Albert's secretary. Technically, my position is an archivist for the Academy."

"I think I remember your name now. Albert mentioned you when I visited him. He was going to have you file something."

"You're referring to your confidentiality pledge. It's an official document in the Academy archives as of this morning. That's one of my many duties. I also catalogue important discoveries. Much of what I see, I freely admit, is

46

beyond my comprehension. Some things, however, are quite simple to understand. Which brings me to my point. Do you know anything about Doctor Dee, Detective?"

"Just that he's some bloke who lived four hundred years ago," he said.

"That means he was alive during the reign of Elizabeth I."

"Yes, but there must be hundreds of Elizabethan artifacts out there. What make you so sure that, just because a few go missing, the thefts are related?"

"When Dee was alive he was a well-known mathematician and astronomer. He was also an influential member of the court of Elizabeth. Don't you find it a bit curious that artifacts directly related to her court here in London have gone missing within days of each other?"

Crisp paused. He saw what she meant. It was unlikely that two different thieves were suddenly interested in Elizabethan artifacts. He was impressed. She was making a good case. He wasn't going to give in to her quite yet, however.

"Maybe, but it doesn't add up as neatly as you're trying to make it," he countered. "The bust has been in the possession of the Academy for generations. The trumpet has been a part of the royal family's private collection for hundreds of years. There's no one alive who can make a connection between the two."

"Then perhaps there is someone already dead who can shed some light on the subject."

"I'm not inclined to believe in ghosts Miss Pimsby."

"That's understandable, but I think there's a way I can convince you." She opened the top of her purse and began groping into its depths. Crisp wondered if she was going to pull out a crystal ball. What else did someone use to talk to ghosts? When her hand resurfaced it held a battered looking copper disk about the size of a saucer with two clear crystals embedded in its center.

"What's that?" he asked, his curiosity piqued.

"It's an ambrosium detector. It's an antique model but Albert says it still works well enough. It took him a while to find it this morning. He only had a few moments to explain how it works before I left for my train. These sapphire crystals cover two separate gauges. The bottom gauge shows whether or not there is any ambrosium present. The more ambrosium that's detected the higher this pointer goes." She was pointing at the bottom crystal. She then moved her finger up to point at the top gage. "This one is a directional indicator. Once the ambrosium shows on the bottom gauge, this one will point out the direction to follow to get to it. According to Albert, it's not easy to pick up ambrosium in nature, even with the detector. Experienced Academy members have difficulty harvesting it, even at sites where it tends to replenish itself. Luckily, the refined ambrosium in the bust sends off a much stronger signal. The detector might be able to pick it up from as far as a half mile away."

Crisp took the disk from her and examined it closely. Although it was unlike anything he'd ever seen, it appeared genuine enough.

"When we find the bust with the detector, I'm sure Albert will introduce you to Doctor Dee. It would be the decent thing to do after rescuing him," Miss Pimsby said.

"Have you seen the ghost that Albert is referring to?" he asked as he put the detector down on the table.

"Of course. Doctor Dee is charming and quite brilliant. I hate to think that something bad might happen to him. That's why I'm hanging around to help until you find him."

Crisp was expecting a different answer. He thought his uncle had simply drifted into a delusional state brought on by old age. But Miss Pimsby was a young, no-nonsense type of person. The fact that she confirmed his uncle's story left him suddenly feeling uncertain about things he had been sure of a moment earlier. What if his uncle truly was in big trouble?

"I'll concede, you've made a few good points," he said to her.

"Does that mean you'll help?"

"And I suppose a promise is a promise."

"It does mean you'll help." Miss Pimsby said, jumping excitedly from her seat and knocking her purse to the ground with a loud jangle.

"Hold on now. Finding the stolen museum piece will still have to be my number one priority. But while I'm doing my job, having you around to monitor the ambrosium detector couldn't hurt. One way or another, we'll find out if your theory is right."

"You're a good person, Detective, just like Albert said you were." She picked his mug up from the table and took it to the kitchen. When she returned a few moments later she didn't sit back down. Instead, she lifted the ambrosium detector from the table and put it back in her purse. "It's time for me to go. I'll return first thing in the morning. In the meanwhile, please be careful." She lightly touched the bruise on his cheek. "I'd hate for any more harm to come to you."

4

Long Shots

Miss Pimsby arrived at his flat the next morning carrying tea, fried eggs and sausage from the shop across the street. She seemed determined to start the day in Crisp's good graces. He understood and appreciated her effort. There was a good chance that they would be spending a fair amount of time together. All the same, he was determined that finding the stolen museum trumpet would come first. Bribes, even tasty ones, wouldn't change this.

After finishing breakfast he and Miss Pimsby remained at the kitchen table. Their conversation to this point had been polite banter. As he sipped the remnants of his tea, she turned the talk back to business.

"Well, Detective, where should we start?" She tried to assume a serious look, but wasn't very successful. There was an irrepressible eagerness that lay beneath her stern veneer. Crisp couldn't help thinking it was, in its own odd way, charming.

"That's an excellent question. The answer is I don't know exactly." He took another sip of his tea and tried to concentrate. "The museum crime scene didn't provide any clues. It was mostly a pile of rubble. Plus, the chaos after the explosion gave the burglars a chance to get away cleanly. No one even knew which direction they went off in."

"Someone must have seen them."

"Not yet. The customs people are on alert of course. There are road checks that are searching vehicles coming in and out of London. But I don't think they'll turn up much."

"Why do you think that?"

"It just makes more sense for the trumpet to still be in London. If the merchandise needed to be moved there were other things they could have stolen—stuff that would have been much easier to smuggle, smaller objects or artifacts that would have retained value after being broken down.

The trumpet is bulky and worthless if melted and recast. So why try to smuggle it out now? It's too risky."

"I think I see what you mean."

"The burglars also created a storm by blowing up the place. Every policeman in London will be on the look-out for them now."

"If they're not smuggling the trumpet out of here what are they doing?"

"I'm not sure, but they may plan to lay low for a considerable time. It's also possible that the trumpet is meant for delivery somewhere here in the city. Either way, it should still be within our reach. If your theory that the stolen trumpet and bust of Dee are related is correct then if we find the trumpet we find Dee."

"Or vice versa," she said quickly in response to his last statement. "If we find the bust then we find your trumpet."

"Only if you're right," he replied. "Like I said last night, I'll do what I can to help you while I'm looking for the trumpet. We'll both have to hope that's enough."

"For some reason I'm certain it will be Detective."

"I'm afraid it's not as easy as that. Artifacts get stolen or go missing from museums on a regular basis. Despite my department's best efforts, some of them are never seen again."

"I guess I just don't see you as someone willing to give up easily."

"Don't get me wrong. I'm not saying it's a lost cause. In fact we may have a minor advantage. The museum job was a frontal assault. Most frontal assaults are the result of desperation. So even if the smart play is to lay low for a while, the robbers might be pressed for time. And if they're desperate and pressing their luck, it may lead to a mistake. We have to be in a position to take advantage of that mistake if and when it comes. That, of course, is the hard part. I'm not sure how we get there yet."

"There must be something that can point us in the right direction," said Miss Pimsby. "The way they went about breaking into the museum sounds unique. Doesn't anything that differentiates them from the crowd make them easier to spot?"

"Not necessarily. It may even be a liability here. Known bomb makers can be linked to a job by their tendencies to use certain materials. I was told that there isn't a signature pattern in the detonator or wiring this time."

"If you're stuck and don't know what to do next then there shouldn't be any harm in taking a ride with the ambrosium detector. If Albert is right, it will be very sensitive to a large collection of refined ambrosium. We may get lucky and catch a hint of it. After that the detector will do the job and lead us right to the bust. As I said, find it and you'll find what you're after as well."

"That may well end up being the plan. Until then, there are a few people I need to visit and I can't see the harm in having you tag along." Crisp saw excitement welling up in Miss Pimsby's eyes. "Don't get your hopes too high. Even if that detector works like you say it does, London is an awful big target zone. It would be nice if we could narrow things down a bit."

"How do we do that?"

"I have one or two ideas. Of course there's always a chance that they'll come to nothing. That means I'm willing to put up with anything at the moment that might generate a lead." He frowned at the copper disk Miss Pimsby was putting back in her purse. "No matter how crazy it sounds."

Crisp and Miss Pimsby left his flat and went out to the road. They stopped in front of a small canvas covered car. He lifted the tarpaulin to reveal a racing green Triumph Spitfire MK3. It was slightly battered but clean, with tan leather seats. Miss Pimsby opened the door and sat down in the passenger seat. He went around to the driver side and got behind the wheel. The engine started with a low growl and he pulled them into the city traffic. As soon as they were moving Miss Pimsby took the ambrosium detector out of her purse and laid it on her lap. After it was safely in place, she looked over at him.

"So, where are we off to?"

"To visit someone I was hoping to avoid, at least for a while."

"Why's that?"

"He's an obnoxious prat."

"Lovely."

"Don't worry, Rat's harmless enough now. Just hold on tight to your handbag until we leave."

"And why exactly do you want to see this Rat person?"

"He provides me information, albeit reluctantly, from time to time. Most recently it was when I was looking for some smugglers. If anyone bought or stole a cache of plastic explosive, he's someone who might have an idea where it went."

"Did you catch the smugglers?"

"Unfortunately not," he replied with a grimace.

Miss Pimsby noticed the look he made and must have decided against asking any more questions. They drove along without talking for a few miles before Crisp felt it was time to break the silence. "Tell me more about yourself Miss Pimsby. The only thing I know about you is you work with Albert."

"I actually come from a long line of family members who worked for the Academy," she answered, the eager smile returning instantly to her face. "It's a tradition. The oldest male heir inherits the job from his father."

"How did you get it then?"

"I have seven sisters but no brothers. Thankfully, I was still offered the position. So far it has been a marvelous experience."

"How long has your family worked for the Academy?"

"Two hundred and twenty six years," she replied proudly.

"How long have you been on the job?'

"A little less than a year now. Daddy simply couldn't do the work anymore. His eyesight is quite poor. Mother kept insisting he retire until he gave in. I think he was worried that the Academy wouldn't accept me for the job or he would've quit earlier. He couldn't bear the thought that he would be responsible for losing the family's traditional position. It turned out the Academy was happy to take me on; Daddy had worried for nothing. Most of the members I've met are older like Albert, and a bit eccentric too. But they're sweet and not as old fashioned as you would think."

"So there are more of them around here. How many?" He asked as the car passed over Waterloo Bridge.

Michael Malik

"Actually, the few I've met have been visiting from abroad. I haven't met another British member since I started."

The car was traveling along Belvedere road now. They drove alongside the Royal Festival Hall and Crisp parked the car in Hayward parking deck.

"What are we doing here?" Miss Pimsby asked.

"I told you, I want to talk to Rat."

"Who exactly is this Rat person again?"

"His full name is Rupert Archibald Tattingbone."

"You can't mean the head conductor for the Philharmonic Orchestra," Miss Pimsby said, her eyes wide.

"The same," he said while exiting the car. "It's a lot easier to say Rat. It fits him too."

"How did you meet?

"In school. Back then he was a bully with money. He tried his act on me once. For some odd reason he took a liking to me when I wouldn't let him push me around."

"How does he know about this sort of stuff?"

"You mean stolen explosives?"

"It is why we're going to see him, isn't it?" Miss Pimsby said as she hurried beside him toward the Hall.

"The organization his father built knows what's coming off every ship at the docks, legal or not. He makes sure to take a cut of whatever cargo goes 'unclaimed'."

"By unclaimed do you mean stolen?"

Crisp nodded. "That's where his money came from."

"So a criminal boyhood friend of yours now runs the Philharmonic. Smashing. What does he do, stash narcotics in the violin cases?"

Crisp shook his head. "Rat isn't interested in the family business that way. He's only interested in spending the fortune his father stole."

"But how did he end up working here then?" Miss Pimsby asked while indicating the large glass facade of the Royal Festival Hall.

"His father wanted to add some respectability to the family name so Rat was encouraged to get an education. It turned out he's a musical genius. When the head conductor job opened they came looking for him. But Rat's not about to let his father's money get too far from him. He

54

still keeps his eyes and ears open when it comes to that side of things. The main problem I have with him these days is he doesn't like the police. It's a hereditary aversion he's never cared to shake."

Instead of going through the front entrance they walked toward a side door. When the hulking giant guarding it noticed them approaching a menacing scowl appeared on his face. Miss Pimsby stopped to stow the ambrosium detector back in her purse. When she looked up and saw the man's unpleasant expression she quickly tucked herself behind Crisp. She stayed there all the way to the door.

"Hello Dexter, is Rat here? I want to have a chat with him."

The large man leaned his body against the door, using his bulk as an impressive barricade. "You know he doesn't like being called that anymore. Besides, I'm not supposed to let you in again." His voice was remarkably high pitched and polished for such a large man. It sounded like it belonged to an usher at the opera, not an imposing doorman.

Crisp pulled an envelope out of his jacket pocket and waved it in the air. "If Rat won't speak to me, maybe this will change his mind." He handed it to Dexter. "Give that to him. I promise we'll wait here. If he still doesn't want to talk to me after he's read it, I'll go away peacefully."

Dexter eyed Crisp suspiciously for a moment. Then, certain that nothing foolish was about to be attempted, he turned and lumbered through the side door. When he shuffled back out a few minutes later, his menacing scowl had transformed into a sulk.

"He said to let you up."

Crisp and Miss Pimsby walked through the door into a poorly lit backstage area. "Follow me. Rat's office is this way."

They squeezed through a narrow hallway, the sound of distant music becoming louder as they pressed forward. They finally arrived at a closed door. The music they heard was clearly coming from behind it. Without bothering to knock, Crisp swung the door open and motioned for Miss Pimsby to follow him.

The music blared as they entered the room, which was large and furnished with expensive looking furniture. There were several framed posters of past London Philharmonic Orchestra performances hanging on the walls. These were scattered amongst numerous pictures of a man in various poses with different celebrities.

The man in all the pictures was sitting on a chaise lounge in the corner, his feet propped up on a footstool. A remote control dangled in his left hand. His right hand was waving a conductor's wand in time with the music. When he saw them enter he pushed a button on the remote and the music cut off. The man then stood up. He was dressed in a tuxedo shirt and pants but no jacket or tie. He would have been handsome if not for the effects of alcohol and fatigue on his puffy and worn face.

"Schubert's Trout Quartet," said Rupert Archibald Tattingbone. "I'm considering it for next season's repertoire. The recording you just heard has several major flaws that I can improve on. What do you think Benjamin?"

"It's been a long time since I analyzed a composition, Rat. I'm sure you don't want my advice."

A pained expression crossed Tattingbone's face. "Why do you insist on using my old moniker? I discarded it long ago."

"Some old habits are hard to break. I'm sure you know what I mean."

He bowed slightly. "Touché." He then turned his attention to Miss Pimsby. "And who is this lovely creature? You've been holding out on me, Benjamin."

"This is Miss Pimsby. She's helping me with my little problem, the one in the envelope Dexter brought you."

"Ah, yes the envelope." Tattingbone recovered from his momentary distraction. "Is the information it holds true?"

"It is."

"The remuneration wouldn't hurt, of course, but it's the other teaser that intrigues me most. That would be quite a feather in my cap. Father would like that." He seemed lost in thought. Crisp was sure he was recalling the bottom line of his father's bank account. "I can only do so much, of course. Nothing that could get back to the wrong people."

"Fair enough."

"What do you need to know?"

"Where a big delivery of plastic explosive went. The more you can find out the better. And I need to know relatively quickly." He tried to sound indifferent. Allowing Rat to realize he might actually end up helping someone other than himself was the surest way to lose his interest.

"Plastic explosive is a common package, Benjamin. That stuff is being passed about like cucumber sandwiches at a tea party, both legally and otherwise. You'll have to give me more to go on."

"It was sold to the chaps who did the British Museum job. They were probably also in the market for security plans. Maybe you can tie the two together."

Tattingbone gave him a look that said 'not bloody likely'.

"It's all I have right now. If I can get more I'll let you know."

"You're asking for a miracle."

"You've performed them for me before."

Tattingbone sighed and said, "One of these days I'm going to tell you to bugger off."

"But not today. Not this time. You'll regret it forever if you do."

"You bloody bastard—why did I agree to let you in here?"

Crisp fought off a satisfied grin. "Does this mean you'll answer my phone calls now?"

"Yes it does. But could you try to remember that I spend most of my time with my music, which means I usually don't hear the phone ring."

"What do you want me to do, then?"

"If you leave a message I promise to return it—if I have anything worthwhile to share."

"Thanks Rat. And by the way, the tempo was off in that last bit."

"What's that you say?"

"You asked about the Trout Quartet. Slow it down a bit and the strings will sound more distinct."

"Hmm—yes—I believe you're right."

Tattingbone gave Miss Pimsby a lingering glance then flopped back into his chair. "Now, if you will both excuse me, duty calls." With a click of the remote Schubert's Trout Quartet once again filled the room.

* * *

"Anything on the device yet?" Crisp asked Miss Pimsby as they drove away from the Royal Festival Hall.

"I'm afraid not," she replied as she set the ambrosium detector in her lap. "I get the impression you were hoping for more than what came out of that conference."

"Yeah, but like I said earlier, I'm working long shots."

He glanced at his watch. "It's almost time to test long shot number two. We're going to meet a Sergeant in the bomb squad. His name is Trevor Dunston. I think you'll like him. I called this morning to see if he had some early test results to share with me. He said he should have something by tonight. He wanted me to stop by the bomb lab after he was through to talk it over."

"And I get to come with you?" Miss Pimsby asked suspiciously. "It sounds like official police business. Am I even allowed in there?"

"I told him I would have a guest with me, so we're meeting at a pub on the way back to my place. By the way, I told him you were my cousin. I want him to think you're family. Trevor has one thing in common with Rat. Both are a sap for a pretty girl, so practice being charming on the drive over."

Miss Pimsby shot him a slight scowl but he noticed it was meant as camouflage. The compliment clearly pleased her.

"I want him to show off." Crisp continued. "I want to be sure he isn't holding anything back on me."

"Why would he hold back? You're on the same side aren't you?"

"Professional pride, mostly. Don't get me wrong. Trevor's good at his job. He just won't want to go out on a limb, especially if he found anything that doesn't add up quite right. He'd be the one blamed if it doesn't work out."

Miss Pimsby was now giving Crisp the same look as when she saw his wrecked flat the first time.

"Don't make that face. He's an honest chap. It's just human nature to play the safe hand."

They pulled up to a pub with 'The Ginger Grenadier' written on its front window. The picture of a Napoleonic era red-headed soldier was painted beneath the name. Crisp parked the car in front of it. He opened the door for Miss Pimsby as she once again stowed the ambrosium detector.

A scattering of patrons were inside the building. Most sat along a long wooden bar and had pints of the same dark amber liquid in front of them. A rotund red-headed man was serving them their drinks. When he saw Crisp he lifted a thick arm, pointed and said, "back right." Crisp waved to him in thanks and then followed his directions to the rear of the pub. Trevor Dunston was already sitting in the booth waiting for them. When he saw that Miss Pimsby was with Crisp a broad grin spread across his face. He stood up and motioned them into the seat across from him.

"You never told me you had such a pretty cousin, Benjamin" Dunston said.

Crisp was pleased to see his instincts were correct.

Dunston turned to Miss Pimsby. "Can I get you something to drink?" He gestured at the glass in front of him. "The specialty of the house is the ginger beer. By the way, Benjamin didn't give me your name on the phone this morning."

"I'm Sophia Pimsby. Benjamin's told me so much about you, Sergeant Dunston."

Miss Pimsby smiled at Dunston. Crisp thought it was a weak effort but it didn't seem to matter.

"Please call me Trevor." Dunston hailed a passing server. "Two more ginger beers." He then turned his attention back to Miss Pimsby. Crisp cleared his throat. When that didn't get any results he decided to be blunt.

"Oi, Dunston. While we're waiting why don't you fill us in on what you found today? Police work fascinates my cousin. She's been bugging me all day about my job. It's wearing me down. Maybe you can fill in for a bit."

"Sure," replied Dunston, the return to business blunting his attention to Miss Pimsby in only a minor way. He turned back to her and said. "The bomb squad has the most dangerous and interesting job in the police service.

We have to be the smartest, too. Take the case we're working on now. The British Museum was opened like a can of tuna. I'm sure you saw it on the telly."

"Yes, it was hard to miss," Miss Pimsby said. Her hands were folded under her chin and she kept her eyes squarely on Dunston as he continued.

"The job was done with plastic explosives. After evaluating the components we know that the stuff used was PE4."

Crisp looked intently at Dunston. "It was high grade military stuff, then? It wasn't commercial grade?"

Dunston shifted his focus to Crisp for a moment. "And I haven't even told you the weirdest bit. There were traces of gunpowder in the debris." Dunston lowered his voice to a whisper, even though there was no one within earshot. "Gunpowder with a high sulfur content. It was like it had been sprinkled over the PE4. It's just plain odd."

"Contamination?"

"Must be. What caused it is still a head scratcher, though." The ginger beers arrived and Dunston turned back to Miss Pimsby for some more small talk.

Crisp drank in silence as he mulled over Dunston's information. It was an odd bit of evidence. It was also disturbing. How could such a large amount of military explosive be on the market? The only possibilities were security had been inadequate and the stuff had been stolen or someone had disregarded an oath and sold the PE4 for personal gain. Both cases were unacceptable. It made him even more determined to find the people responsible for the explosion and burglary. He drained the last of his pint and turned his attention back to his companions.

"So you can see it's quite safe when the proper precautions are taken." Dunston was finishing an explanation of something to Miss Pimsby. She was doing her best to follow along, obviously taking his instructions to be charming at face value.

"Sorry to interrupt, mate, but we have to be off now," he said while dropping a ten pound note on the table. "I need to finish up a bit of work."

Dunston was about to protest. He was clearly enjoying Miss Pimsby's company. Crisp politely cut him off.

60

"I'm sure you understand, Trevor. It's already getting late. The information you've passed on is brilliant. Now I need to see if it turns into something more. The sooner I get cracking the more likely your hard work will pay off."

"Sure, I know this is important to you, Benjamin. That's why I agreed to rush things a bit and meet you here tonight. Still, you can't blame me for wanting your company a bit longer," Dunston said.

"Goodbye, Sergeant." Miss Pimsby said as she stood up.

"It's been a pleasure, Sophia."

"I rather liked Sergeant Dunston. I'm also fond of that establishment," she said once they were traveling again.

But Crisp wasn't paying much attention to her at the moment. He was retrieving his mobile phone from his jacket pocket. When they stopped at a red light he quickly dialed a number.

"Rat, its Benjamin. It was PE4. There was gunpowder mixed in with it. Maybe that'll be something you can work with."

"What did he say?" Miss Pimsby asked after he put his phone away.

"It was his voicemail."

"Oh. So what do we do now?"

"We wait."

5

Blow of the Trumpet

Crisp spent most of the following day driving with Miss Pimsby and the ambrosium detector while waiting for his mobile phone to ring. The route he took allowed him to stop and chat with a few more people who had provided useful information before. Unfortunately, his sources were not very helpful. The detector and his phone also remained stubbornly quiet.

The next day, their third together, Crisp couldn't meet Miss Pimsby for their usual early morning start. He needed to spend some time at New Scotland Yard in meetings. One of them was with Little. They spent a few hours reviewing the museum's closed circuit TV records together but turned up nothing. In fact, the entire investigation was going nowhere.

When he got home it was almost night time. Miss Pimsby was waiting for him outside his building. She wore a pea coat to guard against the chilly evening air and carried her usual oversized hand bag.

"Anything new to report?" she asked as soon as they were close enough to speak confidentially.

"Afraid not," Crisp said. "Unless something else comes up we'll drive around again and hope for a break."

They got back in the car. Once they were moving, Miss Pimsby, as usual, pulled out the ambrosium detector and set it on her lap. They then began to banter about the small things like the weather and what they had for lunch. After a few minutes of this, Miss Pimsby became silent. Crisp glanced over at her. She appeared to be building her courage for something.

"May I ask you a question?" she finally said.

"I suppose so."

"I was thinking that the other night I told you quite a bit about myself. It seems only fair that you have a turn."

Crisp hesitated a bit before answering. He wasn't comfortable talking about himself but she was right. It was only fair. "What would you like to know?" he replied.

"I've been curious; why did Rupert Tattingbone ask you about the music he was reviewing? He seemed to value your opinion. I don't mean to sound judgmental but you don't seem the artistic type to me."

"That was my mother's doing. She thought music would help me, probably because it was always such a big comfort to her."

"So she was a music teacher, or a musician maybe?"

"Both."

"That's not so unusual, is it? Plenty of parents want their children to follow in their footsteps. I'm following in my father's."

"True."

"So why did you give it up?"

"Music?"

"Of course music, silly. Isn't that what we've been talking about?"

"I gave it up because, despite her good intentions, I needed something more—something music couldn't give me."

This seemed to confuse Miss Pimsby. "What do you mean? What was music supposed to give you?"

He hesitated. Normally he wouldn't have answered the kind of questions she was asking. But there was something innocent and caring about her inquiries that made him want to continue.

"My dad died when I was twelve. I didn't take it well. I blamed everyone for his death, anyone close to me, especially my mother."

"Oh—I'm sorry. That must have been hard. But I'm sure everyone understood what you were going through."

"Maybe they did, I don't know. It still didn't stop me from turning into the world's biggest prat. My mother decided I needed something interesting to fill the void that'd been left. Since she loved music, she hoped it might do the trick. That's how I ended up in classes with Rat. We went to the Royal Academy of Music together.

"To my mother's great disappointment, it turned out that playing an instrument wasn't enough to straighten me out. I needed a much bigger kick in the pants. It took the army to supply it."

"So you were in the army as well?"

"Two years in the infantry, two years in the SAS."

"Why did you leave?"

"When my mother got sick, I felt I'd been away from home long enough."

There was an awkward silence that followed when he didn't elaborate. Miss Pimsby twiddled with the ambrosium detector, staring at it for a few minutes, finally out of questions. They were saved any further discomfort when his mobile phone rang. He retrieved it from his coat pocket and flipped it open.

"Hello."

"Camden Town," Tattingbone's voice said over the receiver.

"What?"

"The merchandise you were interested in was shipped to customers in Camden Town. I can't confirm any relationship with the second ingredient you inquired about. That's the most I'm going to be able to give you. Happy hunting." He hung up the phone.

Miss Pimsby gave Crisp a questioning look.

"It was Rat," he said. "He gave us a lead. Let's go see if it's worth anything."

The car was traveling in New Cross. He turned it around and headed north. They crossed the Thames and continued at high speed toward Camden Town.

The wind was whistling through Miss Pimsby's hair as they sped along. She was using one hand to hold onto her glasses while the other gripped the ambrosium detector. All of a sudden she let out a squeal of excitement.

"The detector," she lifted it to show him as she spoke. "It's showing activity." She put it down on her lap again and studied it intently. "Albert wasn't kidding when he said refined ambrosium would create a strong response. The needle is reacting quite impressively."

"Brilliant. Which way is the direction finder telling us to go?"

He could hardly believe what he was saying but, after being persistently dormant everywhere else, the detector was now clearly reacting to something. He might as well follow where it was telling them to go.

Miss Pimsby shouted out directions. He drove as fast as he could while minding what she said. He became concerned, however, when they sped through Camden Town. They were now traveling north on Kentish Town road.

"Are you sure you're reading that thing right?" he shouted over the wind noise from the speeding car. "Rat said they were in Camden Town and we're past it now."

"The detector's pinned on maximum," she shouted back. "I'm sure we're heading the right way. Perhaps they're moving. I did notice a brief period when the signal weakened, like the bust was getting farther away." She gasped with sudden concern. "You don't think someone tipped them off we were coming?"

"If they have been there's nothing we can do about it, other than try to catch up." He pushed the accelerator down a bit more.

"Turn right! Turn right!" yelled Miss Pimsby as they came upon another intersection.

He slowed a bit, turned onto Swains Lane, and then pressed down on the accelerator again. They were moving nicely down the one-way street when Miss Pimsby suddenly yelled "Stop, the direction finder has reversed. We must've passed it."

Luckily, there was no traffic on the road. He slammed on the brakes then put the car in reverse.

"Stop," she said, putting a hand on his arm and then pointing at something. "They're in there."

* * *

Crisp turned to look where she was pointing. There was a tall ornate gate overgrown with weeds marking an entrance to the western part of Highgate Cemetery. In the deepening darkness it looked foreboding. He shut the car off and listened but heard nothing unusual.

"The bust is in there?"

"The detector is pointing right at the opening in the gate," she replied, handing over the copper disc for him to examine. A quick glance confirmed what she said.

65

"I'm taking this." He held up the detector. "You stay here."

"You're not leaving me behind; I'm going with you. And I'm not afraid, in case you're worried."

"If," he put extra emphasis on the word 'if', "the museum robbers are in there it could get rough. It's my job to take the risk, not yours."

"Albert gave me the job of finding the bust, too. I'm going with you."

She punctuated her statement with a look of fierce determination. Her eyes were glowing in the moonlight and her usually pulled-back hair was now windswept and hanging around her face. It added a wild edge to her normally reserved appearance.

Crisp tried to think of a way to blunt her eagerness but couldn't come up with one. "Fine, but you have to do exactly what I tell you to do. Is it a deal?" She nodded, which made her glasses slip to the end of her nose. Crisp pushed them back for her and said, "Let's get going then."

They got out of the car and headed for the gate. Miss Pimsby stopped and grabbed his arm. "Wait, I need something to carry the bust in."

"What about your hand bag."

"It's not big enough."

He returned to the car and opened the trunk. After rifling around for a moment he pulled out a worn backpack. "Will this do?"

"What is it?"

"My old army bergen."

"Yes, that should be fine."

He moved toward the stone gate side by side with Miss Pimsby. His eyes were glued to the ambrosium detector. Its indicators gave off a faint incandescent glow which allowed him to make out the needles despite the darkness.

The direction finder led them through the gate and along a path a short way before veering directly toward some dense vegetation. He picked his way through it as quietly as possible while Miss Pimsby followed closely behind him. Finally, after a few minutes of work and several scratches, he broke into a clearing.

The scene that greeted Crisp was eerie. Angelic patterns shimmered on the ground all around him. Several statues scattered about the open space were the source of the shadows. Their presence, however, did little to alleviate his sense of unease. They seemed to be watching him and waiting for something. He stared briefly into the face of the closest one. The cold stone eyes etched into its delicate face somehow managed to convey a mingled sense of pity and remorse. He hastily turned from its frozen gaze. These were the last emotions he wanted or needed to feel at the moment.

He turned his attention back to the detector. It showed him that they needed to move toward the largest angel statue on the other side of the field. He checked on Miss Pimsby, who was lagging slightly to his left.

"How are you holding up?" he whispered under his breath.

"Fine," she replied even though she didn't look it. Crisp gave her credit, though. She wasn't backing out despite the obvious fear she was feeling. He pointed to the large angel statue that was their next point of reference. She understood and followed along behind him.

They were about half-way across the field when the dark sky behind the large statue erupted with a crescent shaped glow. The sight of it made Crisp stop in his tracks. Grabbing Miss Pimsby's arm, he whispered, "get down". As they fell to the ground a lone trumpet began to play. Its music, which came from the same place as the light, suffused the night air in a hauntingly beautiful way. While in school, Crisp had listened to many pieces that had moved him. This was different. It was like the music was flowing inside of him, warming him, making him 'better' in some strange way. When the music stopped, the clouds above them parted and a beam of moonlight pierced the heavens. The clouds then began to swirl, causing the moonlight to disappear like a saber being withdrawn from a deep stab wound. The sky then swept closed again and the darkness of the night was restored to its original state.

When it was over, Crisp warily signaled Miss Pimsby to continue moving. As they got closer to the statue, he went into a crouching position. He turned and pulled Miss

Pimsby down to a crouch as well. They shuffled awkwardly forward until they were behind the statue's large cement base. He motioned for Miss Pimsby to stay put. Just as he started to work his way around to get a better look, he heard a soft thump followed by the sound of something sticky impacting the angel statue. He immediately turned back to Miss Pimsby, grabbed the back of her jacket and tossed her away from the statue.

"Stay down," his shout was like a pistol shot in the cold night air. He saw a brief sparkling fizzle in the corner of his eye. Before he could jump clear, the explosive ignited, throwing him violently to the ground. The ambrosium detector he was holding went spinning through the air and landed out of sight.

Crisp covered his head as bits of dust and cement rained down on him. Once everything stopped falling he turned back to the statue. The angel's body was nearly destroyed. After quickly checking that Miss Pimsby was safe, he got back up and ran to the pedestal. Through the cloud of dust and the murk he caught glimpses of men wearing black suits. Hoods covered their heads and their faces were partially covered with triangular shaped masks. They were evacuating a small circular clearing and melting into the darkness.

One man was still visible. He was in the center of the clearing and seemed stunned by the explosion. His mask was off and the herald trumpet was in his right hand. A large duffel bag sat at his feet. As Crisp watched, the man gathered himself together and moved to pick up the bag.

Crisp recognized him once he leaned over and the moonlight hit his face. It was the man with the radio, the one from his flat. He was sure of it. He charged out of the gloom from behind the pedestal, intent on a bit of payback.

The radio-man must have heard Crisp coming. He abandoned his attempt to bring the bag with him. He also dropped the trumpet when he saw the look on Crisp's face. Without any further hesitation, he turned and fled into the darkness.

When Crisp reached the trumpet he stopped to catch his breath for a few seconds. He was about to lift the bag when he heard a shout. The radio-man was circling back to the clearing with reinforcements. Taylor and his burly enforcer, also clad in black gear, were with him. The short gorilla-like man raised a blunt-shaped weapon to his shoulder and aimed it at Crisp, but Taylor knocked it down.

"Bollocks." They might not want to shoot at him while he had the trumpet but it didn't matter much. There was no way he could outrun all of them while carrying the instrument.

"Detective, is that you?"

He turned and saw Miss Pimsby standing behind him. She was covered head to toe with bits of dust, including her glasses. They rested crookedly on her nose and must have been almost impossible to see through.

"Get out of here," he shouted at her.

"What's the matter?"

"I have no time to explain—just do as I say or else we'll both be trapped."

"Will this help?" She lifted her right arm. One of the blunt looking weapons was in her hand.

"Where on earth did you get that?" Before she could explain he said, "Never mind," and took it from her. He spun around and pumped the firing mechanism at the same time. There was a large headstone a few yards in front of the approaching men. He took careful aim and fired. The blob that was ejected from the gun sailed straight at its target and splattered against its base.

He dropped the gun and yelled, "Run!" Miss Pimsby wiped some of the dust from her glasses and saw the blob start to fizzle. She turned and ran toward a headstone on the opposite side of the clearing. Crisp stuffed the trumpet into the duffel bag, slung it over his shoulder, and hurried after her.

He slowed down before reaching the headstone that Miss Pimsby was hiding behind. Something that looked like a booby trap sat on top of the gravesite next to it. "Wait, not there—"

A loud WHAM sounded behind him. It was closely followed by a second, louder WHAM directly in front of him.

The force of the two blasts buffeted Crisp's body. The duffel bag went flying off his shoulder and he hit the ground hard.

"This is a bad habit to pick up," he said as he pushed himself off the ground for the second time that night. Once he was on one knee he spun around and checked the clearing. It was filled with clouds of statue dust and, at least for the moment, deserted.

"Detective, over here."

It was Miss Pimsby. He picked up the duffel bag and scrabbled over to the sound of her voice. She was tucked behind the large headstone, unharmed by the last explosion. A bust of a man with a full pointed beard, a ruffled collar, and a tight skull cap was in her hands.

"Doctor Dee, I presume." Crisp said.

"He must have been set on top of this headstone. When the explosion went off he fell right into my lap."

"Miracles never cease."

"What happened back there? Are we safe?"

Crisp shook his head. "Something tells me our troubles have just begun. Put that thing in my bergen and follow me. It's time we got out of this cemetery."

6
Dee's Disclosure

The next morning, the satisfaction Crisp felt from retrieving the stolen herald trumpet was rapidly fading. The fact that it was now safely locked in the New Scotland Yard's evidence room and his initial debriefing was complete did nothing to lessen the multiple new problems he needed to deal with. The biggest of these was how to get Miss Pimsby and Doctor Dee's bust back to Cambridge.

He initially hoped Albert would come to London after the bust was found. Unfortunately, his uncle was not answering his phone again. And it wasn't like he could just send Miss Pimsby on her way. He didn't feel comfortable leaving her or the bust unprotected for even a few minutes, much less a long train trip.

His predicament caused some amusing moments as other detectives passed Miss Pimsby sitting next to him at his desk, holding his old army bergen. Crisp used the excuse that she was a witness and he was questioning her. But her continued presence left him an easy target for some good natured ribbing from them. The most common joke involved Miss Pimsby being the first member of the now famous Detective Constable Crisp's fan club. He shrugged it off but was still stuck trying to arrange a way to get free from the Yard as soon as possible.

A break finally came in the early afternoon, not long after his preliminary report was complete and in the hands of Detective Chief Inspector Fuller. By this point, Miss Pimsby had succumbed to exhaustion and was sleeping on a nearby hall bench. He, however, was on his fifth cup of tea and still glued to his desk reviewing crime scene photos. Fortunately, Detective Inspector Smythe passed his station.

"Good God Crisp, you're a sight. Haven't you been home at all? You look like you were brought in on a vagrancy charge. Get out of my department and don't come back until you're decent."

Crisp decided to take his superior's orders literally. He woke Miss Pimsby and the two of them headed straight for

St. James Park station. Since his car was still part of the Highgate Cemetery crime scene, it was necessary to take the train to Cambridge again. On the way he called Wilkins and arranged to be picked up on arrival.

The trip went by like a blur. In what seemed like no time at all, he and Miss Pimsby were standing in front of his uncle's manor home as Wilkins waited in the car. The sun was setting on the horizon and the sky behind the house was awash in dazzling pink and indigo highlights. The front of the house was dimmed with shadow. No lights appeared to be on in any of the rooms.

"Albert didn't answer any of your phone calls?" Miss Pimsby asked as she moved to get a closer look at the house. She was still faithfully carrying his bergen. It was lying over her right shoulder as she stood slightly hunched trying to peer through a window.

"I'm not shocked. He hasn't been answering the phone lately. Still, I'd hoped he would be more attentive since we've been traipsing about after his property."

"It just doesn't seem right."

"Has he been answering when you call, then?"

"Almost all of our appointments are prearranged. If he needs me for something special he calls me and sets it up. I don't recall the last time I needed to ring him. Actually, I don't think I ever have."

Crisp banged on the door loudly then listened carefully for the sound of any movement within the house. There was nothing.

"You don't think something has happened to him do you?" Miss Pimsby said as she stepped back from the window.

"It's becoming a distinct possibility." He walked back toward the black cab. Wilkins rolled down the window as he approached. "Tap on the horn a few times please, Mr. Wilkins."

Wilkins looked scandalized. "I can't disrespect Sir Price-Mills in such a fashion, sir."

"If we don't get him to answer the door soon I'm going to have to kick it in. That will upset him quite a bit more than some noise will." When Wilkins still hesitated Crisp reached through the car window and leaned on the horn. A sharp blast split the quiet country air. He waited a few moments and then, when nothing happened, he leaned on the horn again, this time for a bit longer.

His second blast was rewarded with the sight of the front hall lights going on. After another minute or so the door opened. Albert stood framed by the doorway wearing a red silk robe over blue striped flannel pajamas. A mortified look was on his face. Once he recognized Crisp and Miss Pimsby, however, his expression changed. He smiled and spoke in his resonant voice.

"Benjamin—Sophia—what a welcome surprise. I was, of course, confident you would complete your task successfully. It's just especially heartwarming to have you back safe and sound already."

Albert suddenly noticed Wilkins and his car. Instead of continuing the conversation any further, he motioned at Crisp and Miss Pimsby, "Come in, come in." He was having a hard time containing his excitement.

Crisp thanked Wilkins and watched briefly as he drove away. He then followed Miss Pimsby into the house.

"Albert went to get something from his room. He didn't say what it was but he said he would meet us in the study." She tilted her head at the study doors, which were already open.

He cast his eyes up the stairwell and grimaced. "I suppose we don't have much of a choice."

When they were inside the study Miss Pimsby sat down on the couch. She laid the bergen on the floor next to her but didn't take the bust out. Crisp didn't join her. He preferred to pace in front of the fireplace.

After a ten minute wait Albert finally appeared in the study. A button down shirt, a bow tie, and a vest with matching pants had replaced his robe and pajamas. Instead of heading for his desk chair he stood at the door with his hands clasped together.

"Where is Doctor Dee? He hasn't been harmed, I trust?"

Miss Pimsby opened the bergen and removed the bust of Dee. Albert reached down and took it from her. Crisp watched him carry it across the room with slow, measured steps. Once he was at the bookshelf he gently laid it down in the same spot it had always kept and stared at it with satisfaction.

"Uncle—"

"Hmm, oh—yes, Benjamin, what is it?"

"It's time for you to explain what's going on. What does that bust have to do with a dangerous gang of art thieves— the kind who stockpile explosives and blow up buildings in London?"

Albert frowned. "What's this you say? Art thieves? They're the ones who took Doctor Dee?" He looked at Miss Pimsby.

"It's true," she said.

"Are these the same men who robbed the British Museum? The ones I read about in the Times this morning."

"Yes, and they're the same people that attacked me to get your maps. I recognized them at the cemetery. They would've been more than happy to kill me. These aren't men that can be played with. I need to know what the Academy is mixed up in otherwise you and your friends might get seriously hurt."

"I assure you that the Academy has no affiliation with these thieves you speak of. I don't know why they took Doctor Dee. It's as much a mystery to me as it is to you."

"Excuse me." Miss Pimsby interrupted. Both men turned to her. "Why don't you ask Doctor Dee what's going on? He probably knows."

Albert sat down at his desk. He pulled a rectangular stone from his vest pocket and he fidgeted with it for a moment. "What you suggest is highly irregular, highly irregular indeed. Besides, I should be making my final travel arrangements for the meeting now that the bust has been returned."

"You owe your nephew an explanation for the help he's provided," Miss Pimsby said. Her voice was soothing. The scolding librarian look Crisp was used to was also gone. "It's the least you can do. He deserves to understand what's going on, what he risked his life for. I know I want to learn what this is all about. And I'm sure you do too, Albert."

"Yes, I suppose you're right," Albert said with a heavy sigh. "There's only one proper way to go about this."

He reached for a switch and the lights in the room dimmed. He then turned to the bust and spoke in his deep, clear voice, "Sir Albert Price-Mills, member of the Academy of Natural Philosophers, bids thee to reveal thy wisdom."

Crisp watched as the bust took on a shimmering glow. The air around it thickened and then began to pulsate brightly. A smoky orb of light rose from its surface, grew larger, and moved away from the book shelf. A thin trail of light that looked like a wispy extension cord continued to connect it to the bust. As the ball of light got closer to them, it began to take shape. The light shifted and molded and within a second it turned into the form of a man, a translucent figure that was now standing or, more correctly, floating, in the room with them.

His features were colorless other than a pale sheen but were still recognizable. The same full pointed beard, ruffled collar and tight cap were present. The frozen metallic mask from the bust was softened and humanized in its present form. To Crisp, the vision before him was exactly what he expected a ghost to look like.

"Be gone foul conniving wolves, denizens of the dark." Doctor Dee's deep voice was oddly tinny and seemed to echo slightly, like an amateur tape recording. He was backing away from them, his hands trying to shield his face.

"My dear Doctor Dee, you're back among friends," Albert said in a soothing voice. "It's me, Albert; your guardian. I want to talk to you. Please."

With these words, Dee lowered his hands. His expression of dislike quickly turned to one of relief. "Albert, thy visage is a blessing. I did not think I would see thee again." He looked around and sighed contentedly. "'Tis true then, I am back in Cambridge?"

"Yes, thanks to the efforts of my two young associates."

Dee now took notice of Miss Pimsby and Crisp. "Ah, the fair maiden, I am greatly in your debt." He looked suspiciously at Crisp then turned to Albert. "Who is the stranger? I know him not."

"You haven't formally met him but you know him nonetheless. He's my nephew, Benjamin. I've appointed him a Special Investigator for the Academy. We couldn't have found you without him."

Dee smiled and turned to Crisp. "Then I am in thy debt as well, new friend."

An astonished "my pleasure" trickled out of Crisp's mouth.

"Young man, 'tis not polite to stare."

"Ahh—sorry about that. Umm—"

"Please, excuse my nephew. He never accepted my assertion that you did indeed exist."

"Tis no matter. I have seen as much from neophytes before."

Crisp took a deep breath and gathered his wits. He didn't have time to waste; there was still work to do. "Doctor Dee, who were those men in the cemetery tonight?"

"Thy nephew is also impertinent, Albert. He has no need for proper introductions."

"I cannot fault him for his blunt nature this time, my dear friend. It's a question we would all like answered."

"Then I shall endeavor to make haste to thy liking but, alas, I cannot rejoin thee with satisfaction." Dee paused for a moment to stroke his long beard before continuing. "I know not their names or allegiance," he said. "I confess my interest in the same question. Many times did I bring forth inquiries meant to elucidate the issue. Each attempt met with failure. The brigands did seem quite determined to hide this vital point from mine ears."

"You didn't recognize any of the men who were your captors? Not one?" Crisp asked.

"There once came a voice that was familiar, but I failed to place it. When it sounded no more, I dismissed the episode as a fool's dream."

Crisp sensed hesitation in Dee's voice and the ghost's glowing eyes were downcast. He turned to Albert.

"I need answers, uncle. Before I go wasting my time, how much can he tell us?"

"That which he knew before he died is imprinted the strongest, of course. But refined ambrosium will modify with time." Albert answered. "It doesn't allow learning, per se. But new memories do imprint."

"Does he have to speak up?"

"Not necessarily. Doctor Dee is a distinguished Ghost of the Academy of Natural Philosophers. As such he's honor bound to reveal what he knows only to a full-fledged member like me."

"If you don't mind, I need him to answer my questions as well."

"That's easily arranged." Albert swiveled his chair to face Dee. "I need you to answer my nephew's questions as fully as you are capable, John Dee. Do you understand?"

"Verily, I do Albert and thou dost know I despise conversing in my presence as before an infant."

"My apologies. There you have it, Benjamin. Ask what you like."

"If you don't know who they are, do you know at least why they stole you? And the trumpet for that matter?"

"Indeed I do, Master Benjamin," Dee answered mysteriously. "My heart lies heavy with the certainty that I doth know exactly why the thieves stole me and the trumpet."

He paused and began to stroke his beard again. Crisp recognized the expression that formed on the ghost's face. It belonged to a hesitant witness, someone who was unsure how the information he was about to give would be received. For a moment he thought Dee refuse to continue but his uncle must have sensed the same thing.

"Go on," prompted Albert.

"In order for thee to attain a true understanding of what hath transpired thou must permit me to explain from the beginning. I must go back over four-hundred years. The telling of my tale shall illicit from thee both pride and, I fear, shame. But I hath been given little choice. What lies at stake is greater than an oath I took, no matter the purpose. It is more terrible than any guilt I might feel having to relive the affair."

"My old friend, what's this great sin you allude to? Surely there's some way we can make it right?"

"I fear not. Thou must understand the reign of Elizabeth was a time of great uncertainty. Many good

English folk were afraid.   For this reason I sought a way to soothe the hearts and minds of my countrymen. I shall admit my quest became an obsession. Eventually, I was led to the discovery of Celestial language."

"What the dickens does it have to do with all of this?" Albert asked with obvious surprise.

"Hold up," Crisp said. "What's Celestial language?"

"The language of a class of elemental beings; air elementals to be exact. Some natural philosophers refer to them as sylphs."

"Hold up again. What exactly is a sylph?"

"They're ephemeral beings that protect the earth and help guide and inspire mankind to great deeds," Albert answered again.

"Like some sort of angel?"

"That's the common name for them. It's the one I prefer to use as well."

"You can't be serious."

"Actually. I'm quite serious." Albert turned back to Dee with a frown. "The language is a well-known aspect of your public persona. But no one has been able to reproduce the success you claimed to have with it. It has long been considered among most circles, as well as amongst the Academy, a well-intentioned hoax. You've never dispelled the notion."

"Tis true, that which I shared never did and never shall communicate with the elementals. This is so because that which was shared lacked the essential component."

"What was this essential component you speak of?" Albert asked as he leaned forward and put his hand to his chin. "Please, Doctor Dee, we don't have time for riddles."

"Music. Angels cannot understand Celestial language in spoken form. It must be translated into music. Only then can they comprehend it. 'Twas a discovery I thought would seal my legacy and pacify my restless brethren. Alas, 'twas not to be."

"Why, what happened?" Miss Pimsby asked.

"I enlisted a fellow Academy member, William Byrd, to create the musical elements of the language."

This time it was Crisp's turn to interrupt. "I've heard of him. He was a famous composer when you were alive. He wrote some chorals that are still pretty well known—if you like that kind of stuff."

"Aye, he was a gifted composer and a favorite in Elizabeth's court. This despite being a Romanist. I welcomed his poorly hidden Papal sympathies as an opportunity. All Englishmen would embrace what we learned, no matter their religious allegiance. Following the instructions I explicitly laid out, he worked diligently and in complete secrecy. He did not complain, though it was clear the task that lay before him was the most difficult of his distinguished career."

"Did you complete the translation?" Albert asked. His eyes were locked on Doctor Dee and hadn't wavered for several minutes.

"Forsooth, though there was one key task still required to make a success of our effort."

"Let me guess," Crisp said. "You needed the right instrument to play Byrd's compositions. I'm sensing this is where the herald trumpet comes into play."

"Thou art correct, Master Benjamin. As Byrd worked, so did I. Finding the proper mix of metals was perhaps the most difficult part. Once this was determined, I retired to the experimental chamber. Using methods the Academy established during the time of the Roman emperors, I was able to fashion a single trumpet of magnificent purity. 'Twas the only instrument that was adequate to create the music Byrd composed. Without it, the angels would still not appreciate...our attempt...to communicate..."

Dee's appearance began to change. He was flickering like an old black and white movie and his voice was fading. Crisp gave his uncle a puzzled look.

"Doctor Dee is one of the most brilliant ghosts of the Academy and has been a valuable confidant of mine but for some reason his bust has always been somewhat defective. His ambrosium is limited to releasing energy in short bursts and after a certain period his ghostly projection dissipates. I suspect that his bust was prepared hastily and the ambrosium was inadequately refined. It's of no great consequence. He can be recalled once the ambrosium has rebuilt its electrical charge."

Michael Malik

As Albert spoke, Dee's ghost was contracting and withdrawing back into the bust. "It should take an hour or two, and then I can summon him again. I suggest we use the time wisely. I, for one, am going to finish packing."

* * *

After stretching and refreshing himself, Crisp met Miss Pimsby back in the study. Albert returned from his room a few minutes later and declared his travel arrangements complete. He would be leaving with Dee in the morning. They returned to the same positions they occupied earlier, Crisp in the armchair, Miss Pimsby on the couch and Albert at his desk.

"Quite remarkable," said a clearly stunned Albert. "Dee and Byrd translating the language of angels. The discovery of the musical aspect was ingenious."

"Yes, but we still don't know the bit I'm most interested in, do we?" Crisp said. "What exactly did the thieves want the stolen trumpet for? And why did they take Dee as well?"

"But he needed to tell us all that or we wouldn't understand any of it." Miss Pimsby said.

"I don't think you have a full grasp of the importance of their discovery" added Albert. "The translation of Celestial language, a true one that is, is something some of my old colleagues at the University would have given anything to accomplish. It is, in and of itself, a priceless thing."

"But I'm talking about a bunch of violent criminals, not a bunch of university professors. I doubt they wanted to impress the world with academic laurels."

"Perhaps there's something special about the alloys he used to make the trumpet. Maybe it contains a precious rare element that makes it worth even more than it already is." Miss Pimsby said.

"I think the ambrosium should have charged by now. Let's ask Doctor Dee, shall we?"

Once again Albert addressed the bust. Once again the bright glowing form of Dee materialized. "Welcome back from your rest."

Dee bowed slightly in response to Albert's greeting.

"We're still unsure about several important points. The music was written and the trumpet was complete, but did you get to test your theory? Did the Celestial language work?"

"Once, briefly, but just as our triumph was at its zenith, all was dashed and broken. My apprentice came to me in great distress. He was a man of many means and often associated with those of dubious character."

Crisp caught Miss Pimsby glancing at him. She was no doubt recalling their meeting with Rat. He couldn't fault her. If there was anyone more dubious than Rat, he hadn't met him yet.

"His report was astounding. Despite our precautions, word of our work somehow reached the wrong ears. 'Twas only at this point did Byrd and I realize the danger in what we created. The ability to communicate with such a powerful force carries with it a great responsibility. It can easily be corrupted in terrible ways. In our hands we felt all was safe. But now others were suspicious of our activities. If the language and the horn fell into the hands of black-hearted men the result could be disastrous."

"So what did you do?" Miss Pimsby asked.

"The safest action would have been to destroy all of what we made. This is when foolish pride interfered. We could not bear the thought of our glorious accomplishment being so rudely treated. I took charge and decided to hide the trumpet. The safest place I could think of was in the Court of the Queen. It would become her property and to take it would risk imprisonment and death. There it safely remained these four hundred years."

"What about Byrd's compositions? Do you know what happened to them? Is that why the thieves stole you? So that they could get Byrd's work?" pressed Albert.

Dee shook his head. "'Twas decided that for one to know the hiding spot of each was the same as not hiding them at all. I was forbidden to reveal my chosen destination for the trumpet. All Byrd would tell me of the compositions was they were safe. The deed was properly done. I was secure with this truth until last night."

"What do you mean," Albert asked.

81

"I was taken for one simple purpose. The thieves desired to obtain the one true herald trumpet. They spoke of a great fortune that was to be theirs for obtaining it. But they needed to know which was mine.

"They entreated me to identify which was the proper one to pilfer. Ask me not how they knew I was a ghostly inhabitant within yon bust or that it was I who made the trumpet. I know not. I ignored their pleas and endeavored to hide within my refuge. 'Twas not to be."

"You gave them what they wanted?" Albert said, incredulous.

"I was given but little choice," replied Dee with obvious remorse. "They threatened harm to you if I did not cooperate."

"My life is of no consequence in a matter such as this."

"I was certain thou would feel thusly. Therefore I remained hidden. To my great horror, they next threatened to ignite their incendiaries in another part of London, someplace that would result in the loss of untold innocent lives. I was obligated to relent." He looked at each of them in turn. "The trumpet without the proper music is but a trumpet. Taking all this into account, I decided the danger of the rapscallions knowing which of the four was the one they sought outweighed the risks. I fear I chose poorly."

"How can you say such a thing?" Crisp said.

"You were there. You saw the place that they brought me to."

"What's this?" Albert asked. "What place do you speak of?"

"I got a tip where the thieves were but by the time we tracked them down they were in Highgate Cemetery. It's where we retrieved Doctor Dee and the trumpet."

"You cannot imagine my dismay when I was brought to that place. It is the hallowed warren of the angels. The thieves knew more than they had revealed. All of our precautions, after four hundred years, had come to naught. It was at this moment of my deepest despair that I closed my mind to the outside. I could not face the damage our work has now brought to bear. It has been so until thou summoned me earlier, Albert."

"What's happened?" Miss Pimsby asked. "I'm not sure I understand what Doctor Dee is getting at." She turned to Albert hoping he would clarify things for her.

"I'm afraid I can only guess. You must explain what has shaken you so thoroughly, my friend. Perhaps all is not as dire as you suggest."

"I recognized the music that the bandit played," responded Dee, his head hung with shame. "It was one of the pieces Byrd composed that I paid particular attention to. I was unsure whether it was prudent to have translated it. But once the deed was done, pride was a tonic that once again prevented wisdom.

"It should have been hidden with the other composition. How it was misplaced and allowed to reach the hands of the foul men who were my captives is a mystery. I would give all to know the answer to how it happened."

"How what happened?" Albert asked.

"The piece of music thou did heard in the cemetery last night was called the *Repeto Domus*. 'Tis the Celestial language that, once played, banishes all angels from this plane of existence. It is a catastrophe beyond measure. It is the realization of all of our fears, all that we worked to prevent four hundred years ago. And there is nothing that can be done to stop it."

7

A Ray of Hope

Stunned silence greeted Doctor Dee's last pronouncement.

"Are you certain? Can there be some mistake?" Albert asked when he regained his composure.

Dee lifted his head. His eyes were like large luminescent moons and were rimmed with sadness. "I fear that civilization now faces mortal peril, the likes of which has never existed before. An invaluable force that has allowed man to reach his present state of enlightenment has been lost forever. Nothing but misery can result."

"You said you saw the man with the *Repeto Domus*. I mean the one who actually held the sheet music in his hands. Did he have any of the other compositions? Did they find all of Byrd's works?" Albert was leaning forward in his chair, his brow furrowed and his eyes gazing intently at Dee. He was acting much more like the Albert that Crisp remembered.

"I saw but one sheet. There were no others."

Albert settled into his chair. His brow descended and relief flooded his face. Then, in a self-absorbed daze, he got up and walked toward one of the bookshelves. He pulled an ancient tome off the shelf and flipped lazily through its pages, finally stopping in the middle of the book. His expression was inscrutable as he stared down at the spot he had chosen.

Crisp didn't have time to worry about his uncle's unusual behavior. Something else lurking in the back of his mind bothered him. He knew he better remember quickly as Dee was beginning to waver. Suddenly it came to him.

"I have one last question. Albert said he sent the atlas to me because you asked him to. Why?"

"Truly, 'twas Byrd's last words that induced the delivery. Upon his deathbed he instructed if the trumpet was ever discovered to keep safe the atlas at all costs. Though I was already a spirit, I endeavored to honor his request. All was well until Albert read me the daily news, and the plan for the Elizabeth exhibit was brought to light. I was wary. Though I could not be sure of any danger, I felt I must respect Byrd's last wish. Nor did I wish to act with haste. The prudent course was to place the map in safe hands until the exhibit was over."

"But why me?"

Dee became paler as he spoke. "I overheard thee talking with Albert during thy visit several years ago. Thou did sound...capable and...trustworthy." Dee's words faded as he once again retreated back into his bust.

Crisp watched the bust's glow fade out then turned to his uncle and asked, "Is this some sort of practical joke? Do ghosts have a sense of humor?"

Albert didn't answer. Instead he continued to stare down at the book in his hands. Crisp was about to ask his question again when his uncle finally turned and spoke.

"I'm afraid not, Benjamin. In my opinion, everything that Doctor Dee has told us is, in fact, quite possible. But I believe he was mistaken about one thing. We may have one small ray of hope. The terrible deed that you witnessed and that we've been discussing may yet be undone."

"What's on your mind, uncle?"

Crisp noticed a gleam in Albert's eyes. He didn't know if he was encouraged by it, especially since he was sure it spelt trouble. It was like the fly talking to the spider. He instinctively knew that whatever his uncle was planning would pull him even deeper into the web he was weaving.

"I must take a brief rest and refill my water pitcher." The gleam in Albert's eyes remained intense but the rest of him looked worn out. "When I come back I will tell you what I think must be done."

* * *

Albert returned in ten minutes looking refreshed.

"First let me tell you that I believe that Dee and Byrd acted unwisely," he said once he was seated again. The gaze he leveled at Crisp and Miss Pimsby discouraged disagreement. "Their actions may have jeopardized the balance between good and evil that exists on our world."

85

Michael Malik

"How's that?" Crisp asked.

"One of Doctor Dee's last comments implied that the presence of angels here on Earth was related to a special force. If they have been driven away then the force they wielded will also be forfeit."

"Honestly uncle, do you really believe a bunch of invisible winged creatures are floating around in the sky, acting as our guardians?"

"They may not be there at the moment, considering what happened last night," Albert said with a wry smile. "But yes, I admit I am open to the possibility of their existence."

"Based on what? Dee?"

"We don't have to take his word for it. Legends about winged spirits have existed since antiquity. In fact, Paracelcus, one of my predecessor's in the Academy, decided to study the phenomenon. He concluded that spirit guardians exist for each of the four elements. It was he who named the ones found within the atmosphere sylphs."

"You're talking about myths."

"Yes, I suppose I am and I admit I can't prove they exist. But I do know that something influences society in a positive way and that whatever it is must continue."

"But you don't know for sure whether these sylphs, or angels or whatever you want to call them, influence anything at all, do you?"

"Your objection is well taken, Benjamin. In fact, many of my colleagues would agree with you. Some believe that Type A forces, what you would call goodness, is intrinsic to all humans. If they are correct then there is no need for alarm. However there are others, like Doctor Dee apparently, who feel that the bond is not quite so strong. If it's broken and, as a result, the power of a Type A force is weakened or lost, the ability of man to combat his baser instincts will fly away as surely as a bird from a cage."

"So you think he's right about what happened in the cemetery then."

"I have no way of proving what he's claimed. Let's just say at this point I'm willing to give him the benefit of the doubt."

"Why?"

"Because the Academy has seen a threat like this before. If the situation is indeed similar, the influence angels once provided is now lost and the balance of nature will be seriously disturbed."

"Could you be a bit more specific? What do you mean by disturbed?" Crisp asked.

"Think of the opposing forces in our world, good and evil, pushing on a pendulum. Sometimes the pendulum is over on one side, but inevitably it swings back. This is how history has always played out—periods of destruction tempered by periods of enlightenment. If the angels are truly gone, the pendulum of fate will swing farther toward catastrophe than at any point ever before in history. The usually inevitable swing back will be seriously delayed, perhaps indefinitely," came Albert's answer.

"And then what?" Crisp asked.

"A worldwide cycle of endless war and misery will result."

"We can't let that happen!" Miss Pimsby's said once Albert's point sank in.

"So what we need to do is get these angelic beings to come back. I'm guessing it's much harder to do than say," Crisp said

Albert settled back in his chair, looking somber. "It'll be difficult, yes, but not impossible. Doctor Dee was certain the thieves succeeded in their goal. But he wasn't aware of the seven night period that must pass before the expulsion is irreversible. Many years ago, I read about it in Paracelsus' original sixteenth century manuscript. The book I was just looking at has a copy in it."

"That gives us a bit less than a week," Crisp said. "That's not exactly a lot of time to work with. I hope you have an idea where we can start."

"You said that the men in the cemetery were the same as the ones who were after the maps, didn't you?"

"Yes, I recognized them."

"Then the key lies in the maps contained within the atlas. They must somehow conceal the hiding place of Byrd's compositions. It's the only logical explanation of why you were attacked for them."

Crisp frowned. "I've studied those maps pretty thoroughly. They didn't have any markings that point toward a secret hiding place."

"There must be something you missed. I suspect, now that you are aware of the true purpose for the maps, you will see something that you were blind to before."

"But even if we find the hiding spot, haven't the thieves already been there?" Miss Pimsby asked. "Doctor Dee saw them with a composition. They played it. We actually heard it when we were in the cemetery looking for them."

"She has a good point. If the thieves have one shouldn't they have the rest of them?"

"I can't be sure that what you say isn't true. However, I think logic argues against it. The fact that the thieves tried to take the maps bolsters my belief that they have only one composition in their possession. How they obtained it is, as Doctor Dee said, a mystery. But it's a mystery that holds little importance at the moment. There appears to be something about the still hidden translations that greatly worries them. Otherwise the maps would be insignificant to them. They were ready to kill you for the atlas, isn't that what you told me, Benjamin?"

"Yes."

"That shows the maps are extremely valuable to them, worth at least one person's life. Therefore, the way events have unfolded supports my original assertion. The atlas is the key to finding the rest of the translations. Once found they should contain a work that will reverse the *Repeto Domus*. You still have the atlas safely hidden, I assume?"

"Of course."

"Excellent. You and Miss Pimsby will have to unravel the secrets contained within its pages. Once the maps have shown you the way to Byrd's music, take the trumpet to Highgate Cemetery and play the counter-command there. As I said, you have but one week's time to complete your task. I must proceed with my plans to attend the Academy meeting. Now, the hour is late. You both need to rest for the task that's coming."

Crisp remained where he was. There was a question he still wanted to ask. "I'm a fairly good detective, uncle—"

"Don't be modest Benjamin. From what I've heard you're an excellent one."

"Even so, I don't know anything about alchemy or very much about science for that matter. That's your game. Are you sure you can't come with us?"

"I'm sorry, Benjamin, but I simply can't. Like I said earlier, I must continue on to the meeting. The Academy needs to know the true extent of this new threat. Mobilizing my fellow members' full assistance will be an invaluable asset in the coming fight. But enough talk for now, you two need to rest."

Albert's answer wasn't the one Crisp was hoping for, but he saw the wisdom in his plan. He was leaving the battlefield in order to get reinforcements. Crisp's job, meanwhile, was to spearhead the attack. This, at least, was something he knew he could to do.

Satisfied, he started to exit the study. Miss Pimsby followed him. Albert also got up but, instead of joining them, walked over to the secret bookshelf door. As he opened it, Crisp called over to him.

"What are you up to? You need rest too."

"As I cannot stay here to help you, I want to at least provide you some elemental assistance. I don't have much time and I've much work to do. Now, if you will excuse me."

Crisp watched Albert disappear behind the bookshelf. It then swung shut with a solid and convincing click.

8

Parting Gifts

Despite his uncle's advice, Crisp couldn't rest. After saying goodnight to Miss Pimsby, he retired to his usual room and then proceeded to toss and turn in bed. His mind was racing from the evening's amazing revelations. There was so much new information to figure out and not enough time to do it.

He stared at the canopy that draped the top of his bed and considered the benefits of a warm cup of milk. It was what his mother used to make when he couldn't sleep. He drank loads of the tepid concoction after his father died. Although it never worked, the care she put into preparing it had always been comforting.

"Detective Crisp, are you awake?" Miss Pimsby's whispered voice traveled through his door. "There's something that's bothering me. I don't think I'll be able to sleep until it's out of my mind."

"Yeah, I'm awake. Hang on a moment," he said as he swung out of the bed.

Before letting Miss Pimsby in, he searched the closet for something to wear. The only robe he could find was made from deep purple velour lined with dark green trim. Despite the fact that it made him look like a giant eggplant, he put it on and walked over to answer the door.

By the looks of it, Miss Pimsby had also pilfered the closet in her room for sleepwear. She wore a full length flannel nightgown with a matching night cap. This didn't stop her from arching an eyebrow at the sight of him.

"Don't worry; it's a loaner from there." He pointed at the open closet door.

The eyebrow descended. "May I come in for a moment?"

"You might as well. I can't sleep either."

She followed him in to the room and sat on a well-padded armchair. Once she was settled in she said gave him a tentative look and said, "I hope you're not too upset."

"About what?"

"I'm sure he meant to say it. I just know it was on his mind. But there was so much information being tossed about. I found it hard to keep up with it all. I'm sure he did too. His attention was focused on Doctor Dee so he wouldn't miss anything being said. It could happen to anyone under the circumstances."

"What could happen?" he asked, thoroughly confused.

"Forgetting to thank you properly. Your uncle didn't tell you how grateful he was. It was generous of you to help us the way you did. I was so frightened, for Albert and for you. Albert's heart would have broken if you hadn't found Doctor Dee."

"You mean if we hadn't found him."

"I was there, but it was you who made it all happen. Anyway, he's dedicated so much of his life to the Academy, and now everything it stands for is in danger. I think he feels responsible in some way—that if he'd been stronger none of this would've happened."

"That's rubbish."

"Of course it is. And you placed yourself in harm's way for something you didn't even believe existed," she paused to tighten her nightgown around her legs, "and I'm as bad as your uncle. I haven't thanked you for saving my life in the cemetery. You could've been badly injured when that statue exploded. You could have easily moved away from the blast if you hadn't taken the time to move me first. So here it is—thank you."

Crisp realized Miss Pimsby was trying to be gracious and he appreciated it. At the same time, she was pointing out the considerable danger they'd already faced.

"We may be in over our heads with this one. Although I don't expect you to admit it, I think you know it as well as I do. Part of me can't help wondering if I should go back to New Scotland Yard and tell Detective Chief Inspector Fuller the whole story. He might be able to help us."

"Oh no, you mustn't do that!"

"Why not? Albert said I could break my secrecy oath if the situation warranted it. I'd say the threat of—"

"Bartleby Chichester," she blurted out, interrupting him.

Michael Malik

Her unexpected answer caused a sorely needed laugh to escape him. "I'm sorry, what did you say?"

"Bartleby Chichester," she repeated.

"Perhaps you could explain what you mean by that?"

"He was the person who worked for the Academy before my great, great grandfather, Milton Pimsby, took the job."

"What does any of this have to do with me?"

"It turns out he did exactly what you propose doing now."

"You're still not being very clear."

"One of the first things I looked up when I became Archivist was how my family starting working for the Academy. It was all because of Chichester. He thought he could help his employer, Henry Cavendish, with a difficult problem by going to the authorities. Instead of getting assistance, he was committed as an unfortunate to Bethlem Hospital."

"The mental asylum?"

Miss Pimsby shuddered ever so slightly. "Can't you see? If you go to that Fuller person with a story about angels and ghosts and the end of the world, he'll think you've gone mental. You'll end up locked away somewhere, like poor Bartleby Chichester. Any chance we have of finding the thieves and stopping their plan will get locked up with you."

"I see your point," he conceded.

"So you promise—you won't go to your superiors?"

He couldn't deny the sense in what Miss Pimsby said. Still, it wasn't his safety that concerned him. He was willing to face danger. It was part of his job. He needed to be sure she knew what she was getting herself into.

"This means we're on our own. The two of us may not be enough, especially if we run into the same blokes again. They'll be more than happy to kill us if they get the chance. And Albert himself said he thought Dee was right, but he couldn't be sure. We may be putting our lives at risk for nothing."

"It is a bit scary, isn't it? But what else can we do?"

The look on her face left no doubt in his mind. She was going with him, no matter the cost. This meant it was up to him to protect her. He was growing fond of Miss Pimsby. The last he wanted was her getting hurt.

The downstairs grandfather clock chimed faintly three times. "You should be back in bed." Crisp said. "We need to get up early enough to meet with Albert before he leaves. Do you think you'll be able to sleep now?"

She got up from the chair. "Yes, thank you. And you?"

"I don't know," he answered truthfully as he watched her walk toward the door.

"That won't do." She paused right before exiting the room and looked back at him over her shoulder. "I think I know just what you need."

Crisp waited patiently until a few minutes later when Miss Pimsby reappeared carrying a mug. She strode back into the bedroom and placed it on his night table.

"What's that?"

"Warm milk," she said. "It should get you to sleep in no time." She closed the door behind her as she left.

He eyed the mug with suspicion before picking it up and slowly drinking half of it. As he did, a final question he needed to ask Albert popped into his head. Deciding it could wait until the morning, he finished the milk and lay back down in the bed. Within five minutes he was asleep.

* * *

Crisp awoke as soon as the morning sunlight began to filter through his bedroom window. He dressed quickly and went to his uncle's bedroom. Its door was open and a brief look confirmed that the bed wasn't slept in. Albert's traveling gear, consisting of a large trunk and two smaller leather valises, was neatly arranged in the center of the room. It was proof, at least, that he hadn't left on his trip yet.

He went to the study next, but Albert wasn't there either. A quick inspection of the bookshelf door failed to reveal the latch that opened it. He realized he would have to wait for his uncle to show himself before he could talk with him. He wandered back to the front hall. Miss Pimsby was standing at the bottom of the stairs with a look of anticipation on her face.

"Is Albert up?"

93

"He never went to sleep. I think he's still behind his bookshelf. What's back there, anyway?"

"His laboratory. He told me he doesn't spend as much time in there as he used to. I wonder what he could be doing that would take all night?"

Just as she finished speaking, a clicking noise emanated from the study. The bookshelf door was opening. Crisp swiveled and retraced his footsteps with Miss Pimsby following closely on his heels.

Once Crisp passed through the large double-doors he saw Albert walking slowly across the room carrying a wooden crate. When he reached his desk he laid it down and turned wearily to greet them.

"Good morning. I wasn't sure you'd be up yet. It's helpful, however, that you're early risers. I have a few things left to show you and I must leave soon. Mr. Wilkins should already be on his way."

"And I've something important to ask you before you leave," Crisp said.

"I'll be happy to answer your question, Benjamin. I promise not to forget. I must insist, though, that I finish what I need to say first. As I said, you'll be meeting many difficult challenges in the days ahead. While I cannot stay with you there's still a way I can help. I've created a set of elemental tools for you. They should be of some assistance."

"Weapons?"

"Protection," Albert replied, "designed using special experimentalist methods based on the four elements."

"You mean earth, fire, water and air?" said Miss Pimsby, who was again sitting on the couch.

"Exactly. It was once thought that all things were composed of the four elements. As time went by, this concept became outmoded. Numerous more elements were identified. While many of these are known to the scientific community at large, others are known only to the Academy. The important thing is all of them are subject to certain enhancements. The Academy has taken advantage of this and developed several formulations, known as tools, to help us in various ways."

"Is that what's in the box?" Crisp asked.

"Yes," said Albert as he leaned forward in his chair and pulled the box slightly closer to him. "I'll explain how they work quickly. After all, there's urgent business we must attend to."

He flipped open the box and reached into it. He pulled out a phial the size of a salt shaker. It contained a tan-colored granular material. "This is Sleep Sand. It's useful for subduing adversaries without harming them." He flipped the jar's lid off. Several small perforations became visible in the container's top. "A shake or two of the sand will place a person in a deep sleep for several hours. Be aware, the sand must contact bare skin. And be careful not to spill any on yourself. It's impossible to wake someone until it wears off."

Albert replaced the cap and put the phial on the desk. He then reached into the box with both hands. When he pulled them out they were holding two stones. "Fire is the essential element used to create these."

The stones were rectangular blocks that were smooth on the back and ribbed in the front. Each was the size of a cigarette pack. They were solid looking but seemed to have a faint flickering glow that emanated from their cores.

"What are they?" Crisp asked.

"Pitch Stones. They were originally one stone that was forged in my blast furnace at over one thousand degrees. I split it into the two halves you now see. As twins they share a bond that allows one to transmit sound waves exclusively to the other over a distance of hundreds of miles."

"My mobile phone does as much."

"The difference is, my dear boy, a Pitch Stone's signal cannot be blocked or intercepted, it creates an energy field that keeps listening devices from functioning, and it's a pulse code emitter. It's a quite a useful assistant—especially when one's attempting to guard secrets."

Albert put the Pitch Stones next to the Sleep Sand. He then delved back into the box a third time. When his hand came back up, it held a small metal container that looked like a flask. "This is Aquae Vitae. It has the power to sustain a poorly injured person. It'll revive him and give him strength. Be careful with it; it's not a permanent cure.

It merely provides enough time for the user to get appropriate medical attention. Still, used wisely, it can be a life-saving elixir."

"Now that sounds useful. What's it made of?"

Albert gave Crisp a stern look. "I can't divulge the components or details of the methods that went into creating my parting gifts. That's information a Special Investigator is not privy to. Technically, it's a bit of a stretch for me to share these with you at all. There are things, however, that are more important than rules. Now where were we?"

"The fourth element," Miss Pimsby reminded him.

"Ah yes," said Albert as he rubbed his hands, "my favorite. I had a deuce of a time putting it together, a deuce of a time indeed."

He reached into the box for a final time. The object he pulled out was a long slender tube. "This, my friends, is called the Magic Flute. It has several separate chambers, each filled with a different gas. When the tube is blown into here," he pointed at a hole in one end, "the gases are released into the surrounding atmosphere in a specific sequence. This allows for a vapor deposition reaction that creates a powerful but fleeting shield. It should provide remarkably resilient protection against even the most destructive attack. Remember, the shield lasts at most ten seconds."

He went to place the flute next to the other tools, but stopped midway and lifted it up again. "You should also know that it'll only work one time," he said as he waved it at them with his right hand, "so don't be wasteful. Use it only when you truly have to. You won't have a second chance with it."

Albert finally put the flute down. "Well, I think that was everything I wanted to show you. Now, Benjamin, you said you have a question for me."

Crisp was surprised. The elemental tools had attracted his attention so completely he forgot about the question he mentioned earlier. Albert, true to his word, reminded him when he was finished.

"You said we have a week to reverse things in case the recall was sounded in error. Why can't the angels that were sent away decide that this is just a big bloody mistake made by a band of criminals and ignore them?"

Albert affixed a tolerant smile on him. It was the same look he must have used with his students countless times during his teaching career.

"You have a keen mind, Benjamin. In a few short sentences you've exposed the heart a concept that the Academy has struggled for centuries to explain."

"It wasn't on purpose. I just thought there might be an easier way to get them back."

"I'm afraid there isn't."

"But why not?"

"Because, the thieves in the cemetery invoked what amounts to man's basic right of dominion. You see, whether we like it or not, humans are the stewards of this world, even the parts we can't readily see."

"That sounds a bit dangerous. What's to keep us from buggering it all up?"

"That's another excellent question. Unfortunately, the answer is very little."

"That's not very comforting."

"Perhaps not, but my explanation should have left one thing clear. If man broke the bond that held an elemental force like the angels to us then the actions of another man will be required to repair it. I'm sorry Benjamin but there's no one else I can turn to. You're stuck with the job."

A loud knock sounded at the front door just as Albert finished. "That should be Mr. Wilkins," he said as he got up from his desk chair. "I've believe we're through here. Would you let him in please, Miss Pimsby. Let him know that my luggage is still in my bedroom." After she left to follow his instructions, Albert reached for the now empty crate.

"Let me get that for you, uncle." Crisp walked over and picked the crate off the desk. "What do you want me to do with it?"

Albert went over to where Doctor Dee was resting on the bookshelf. Crisp followed him and then helped him lift the bust into the crate. After the cover was closed, Albert took it back from him.

"Thank you, but I'll have to carry him until I get to the meeting. I might as well start now."

They heard a thumping noise that indicated Mr. Wilkins was moving Albert's large trunk down the stairs.

"I almost forgot," Albert said as they walked toward the study doors. He went over to a coat rack that towered next to the left door. He took down a well-worn mid-length canvas slicker and handed it to Crisp. "This is my old jacket. It has several special pockets within the inner lining. They're useful hiding places for the tools. Keep them there and wear the jacket at all times. You never know when a tool may be useful, perhaps even essential."

Crisp took the jacket, draped it over his left arm then walked out into the front hall with Albert. Wilkins was using a lorry to push Albert's large trunk through the front door as Miss Pimsby held it open for him.

"This is where we part ways," Albert told them. "I'll be traveling on alone. Another car has been ordered for you. It should be here within the hour. I'll leave a key to the house with Mrs. Twilliger. She's the woman who's been helping me for the past several months. Her instructions are to let you in if you've any need to return before I do."

Mr. Wilkins was done packing Albert's things. He now stood by the rear door, holding it open. Albert walked over and climbed into the back of the cab while continuing to gently handle the crate that contained Doctor Dee. Mr. Wilkins closed the door and got into his usual position in the front of the car. Albert rolled down his window as the car started. "I leave you with the words of Lord Byron. 'Good luck to you and take heart, for adversity is the first path to truth'. It seems an appropriate sentiment, does it not?"

The car pulled away as Albert's words reached them. The last they saw of him was his arm extended in a wave through the window as the car drove out of sight.

Crisp and Miss Pimsby returned to the study. The first thing he did was put his uncle's old coat on. It fit him well. He then gathered up the elemental tools and began to place them in its hidden pockets.

The seams were difficult to find at first. If he hadn't known they were supposed to be there he might not have found them at all. He placed the flute in a long thin pocket that extended along the inner portion of his distal right sleeve. There was a small flap under the flared outer left pocket that held the jar of Sleep Sand snugly. The right inseam had a small insulated pocket that held the Pitch Stone while preventing any of its telltale glow from showing. He handed the second Pitch Stone to Miss Pimsby. He decided to carry the Aquae Vitae in the easily accessible inner left breast pocket. It wouldn't be as tucked away as the others but he considered it the most useful thing his uncle had given him. He wanted it somewhere he could easily reach.

"What do we do now?" Miss Pimsby asked as she watched him finish stowing the tools. She was back in her business-like mode. Crisp knew her calm demeanor was only a cover. The departure of Albert had clearly shaken her up. He knew it because he felt the same way. But there was no point talking about it. They had a job to do.

"I'm going back to London to retrieve the atlas." He could already see the argument that was forming behind her eyes. "I'm not ditching you," he said before she could disagree with him. "I need to do what I do best. I'm a detective after all. I have to ask around a bit. I need to learn more about those maps. Perhaps I can find the right person to inquire about them."

He had to stifle another protest before he could continue.

"You have to do what you do best. Go to the archives. Try and find out anything you can about the atlas. Look into Dee and most of all Byrd. See if any clues have been left behind about a key, something that shows how to use the maps to find the compositions."

Now that Miss Pimsby understood what her job was and that she wasn't being left out, her resistance disappeared. Without further interruption, she him finish outlining his plan.

"Once either of us has learned something useful we'll use the Pitch Stones to contact each other."

"The archives are in Greenwich," she said. "If I find anything I should be able to join you fairly quickly. There's quite a bit of material dating from the Elizabethan period.

It might take a day or two to sort through it all.   But if there's something there, I'll find it. I promise."

"It's settled then."

Unfortunately, their plans were not the only thing settled. The clock was ticking. They had less than a week to stop a catastrophe and millions of lives were at stake if they failed.

9
Moonstone Maps

The plan of attack Crisp settled on required the services of an antique map expert. Even though he didn't have the foggiest idea where to find this type of creature, he was confidant locating one wouldn't be too hard. There were bound to be a few such specialists within a city the size of London. Still, discovering their identities would require some research.

He worked out most of the details while on the train ride from Cambridge. As he drove his car home from New Scotland Yard, he went over them again. First he would do a computer search. Once he'd turned up a few names, his next step would be to retrieve the atlas and show it to one of them. If the first one he chose couldn't help him, he'd pick out another one. He'd ask as many experts as it took. Someone had to know something more about the maps than Albert or Doctor Dee did. In his experience, there was always someone who would provide a useful tip.

As with most mysteries, whether it was a serious crime, like homicide, or something like the riddle of the maps, there was only one way to approach things—one step at a time. Any clue might be enough to carry him through to that first step. The next step would follow the first. Once he'd taken enough steps he'd be walking on a path. Then he had to trust his instincts that the path was the right one. He wouldn't have much time to retrace his steps and start anew.

When he arrived at his flat, he went directly to his spare room. It was mostly bare. The only things in it were his old school tuba, which was propped up in one corner, and a small writing desk with his laptop on it.

As soon he was settled in at his desk, he turned his computer on and began to browse through its database. There was no point trying to find information about the map itself. He tried that when it first arrived on his doorstep and turned up nothing. So, just as he planned, his first search was for information on rare book and map shops in London. He compiled some possibilities, which he listed from nearest to farthest using New Scotland Yard as the center of the radius. One of the most promising was a place called Hornbeck's. The biography of the owner indicated he was an expert in maps of England and mainland Europe going back to early medieval times. Crisp put this name at the top of his list.

He was about to move on to the next site when his mobile phone rang.

"Benjamin?" the voice on the other line asked when he answered.

"Reggie, is that you?"

"Yeah, it's me. Thank goodness you're safe."

"What do you mean? Has something happened? Has there been another attack?"

"No, nothing like that. Where on earth have you been?"

Crisp hesitated. "I've been taking care of some personal business. Why do you ask?"

"After reviewing your report, Fuller sent a team up to Camden Town. They found the flat the perpetrators used. Other than lots of bomb residue lying around, the place was cleaned out."

"What about the man I told you about? Can't you trace him?"

"It's weird. No one matching Taylor's description is in the criminal database or any other database we've tried. I'm afraid our pigeons have flown the coup."

"Bollocks. They could be anywhere by now."

"I was thinking the same thing. And then you didn't show up to work this morning, so I got a bit worried."

"Was Smythe looking for me?"

"No. He mumbled something about you being on leave. That didn't sound right to me so I decided to check in."

Crisp quickly realized what had happened. When he hadn't shown up at his desk, Smythe assumed he'd been placed off duty again. He couldn't blame him. The last time they had seen each other Crisp looked like someone sorely in need of rest. Either way, this was a handy development.

"Smythe was right. I'm going to be gone for a few days. Fuller's orders."

"Oh, alright then," Little said, sounding surprised and a bit disappointed. "Well, at least I was able to give you the latest news. Be extra careful out there. I'll catch the bloody gits as soon as possible but, the way I see it, as long as they're mucking about who knows what they'll do. They might even come after you."

"Thanks, Reggie. I will. And I'll keep in touch when I can."

Crisp hung up the phone and tried to get back to work but it was hard for him to concentrate after talking with Little. He realized that giving the false impression he was on holiday couldn't be helped. How was he supposed to explain the predicament he was in? Nevertheless, it bothered him that Reggie thought he was abandoning an unfinished case. Their conversation also left him feeling like an easy target sitting in his flat. He had already been attacked once in his home and was not in the mood for a rematch yet. It was time to gather his research and get moving.

He got up from his desk and went over to his old school tuba. He'd thought of it as soon as he'd decided to hide the atlas. While growing up, he'd used it many times to hide things from his mother. She'd never been able to figure it out.

He reached down for a slender wire hook lying inconspicuously on the floor and then used it to gently probe into the tuba's wide mouth. First, he pulled out a soft black cloth that acted as a plug. Reaching down again, he felt the hook catch a loop. He pulled the wire and the carefully rolled-up and wrapped atlas, which he'd bound with string, appeared from the depths of the tuba. He undid the string and wrapping and flipped through the pages. Once he was sure all the maps were in place he replaced the string. He then stowed the atlas in a large pocket inside his uncle's jacket. He thought it was the last empty one, but wouldn't be surprised if the jacket still kept a few secrets.

* * *

Michael Malik

The front of Hornbeck's map shop was a pleasant mix of brown stone and wood trim. On either side of the door were two display windows featuring different books, maps and globes. The store's name was in big gold letters over the entrance.

Crisp walked inside and looked around. There were at least two levels to the quaint little shop. He spotted stairs going up but none going down. His eyes swept the area again and found what he was looking for. He worked his way past the small cluster of patrons to the checkout desk. A thin young man who must've been in his teens was standing at the counter.

"May I help you, sir?" the boy asked politely.

"I'm here to see Mr. Hornbeck. Is he in?"

"He should be in his office. Who should I say is calling?"

"Detective Constable Crisp."

The young man picked up the phone and spoke briefly to someone. He said "Yes, sir" a few times then hung up and looked at Crisp. "If you would please wait here a moment, Mr. Hornbeck said he would be right down."

Crisp stepped back from the desk and looked around some more as he waited. What he saw was shelves covered with maps of every description. It certainly seemed like he was in the right place. He was about to inspect a fold out map of Cambridge when his eye caught sight of a plump man coming down the stairs. The businesslike attire he wore seemed at odds with his harried demeanor. His protruding eyes seemed to never stop moving and his curly brown hair was disheveled, as were his impressive and quite full side whiskers. The effect was a bit like stuffing a fat squirrel into a nice suit. The man seemed to notice him as well. Once he was off the stairs he made a beeline for him.

"Detective Constable, I'm Josiah Hornbeck."

Crisp shook the hand that Hornbeck offered him. It was limp and sweaty.

"I was told you wanted to speak with me. Is there a problem? The store hasn't had any police issues that I'm aware of."

"Nothing like that, Mr. Hornbeck. I'm not here on official police business. There's a personal matter I could use your help with. Is there somewhere we can speak privately?"

"My office upstairs should do."

Hornbeck led Crisp up the stairs and through the first level of the shop. When they reached the door to the office Hornbeck opened it and went inside without waiting for him. Crisp scanned the room one last time. Nothing appeared out of the ordinary so he opened the office door and went inside.

Hornbeck's office was more like a workshop. There were drafting boards and a computer station. A large and detailed map of Paris and its surrounding area hung on one wall. Some spots were still empty so he assumed it was one of Hornbeck's current projects. A window, which overlooked the street below, let in a thin ray of light. There was a small table with two chairs tucked in the corner. Hornbeck was already sitting in one of the chairs. Crisp sat down across from him.

"Is this adequate?" Hornbeck asked.

"Yes, thank you."

"So, how can I help you?"

"An antique atlas has recently come into my possession. I was hoping to get some information about it."

"An atlas you say? Well, if it's anything worthwhile, I should be able to give at least a rough estimate of it's worth. Did you bring it with you?"

"Yes, I have it right here." Crisp reached for the inside pocket of his coat and pulled the atlas out. After undoing the string, he unrolled the soft, leather-bound book out on the table. He wondered, as he studied Hornbeck's expression, how often he was forced to repeat the same routine. The map expert's bored look suggested he was tired of looking at fancy but false reproductions of old maps for 'friends'.

Hornbeck leaned forward and flipped open to the front page. He barely glanced at the frontispiece before moving on. His examination of the next several pages, however, was done with increasing care. Crisp noticed that when he came upon the first of the two special maps his right eye began to twitch and his cheeks began to flush.

"Interesting, very interesting," he murmured as he leaned even closer.

Crisp saw him discretely rub the corner of the map with his thumb. He flipped through several more pages until he came to the second map with the unique markings. Hornbeck suddenly jumped up from his seat.

"Excuse me—" Hornbeck stammered as he searched his memory in vain. "What was your name again?"

"Detective Constable Crisp."

"Of course—so silly of me to forget. If you don't mind, I'll be back in a moment. I have to go get my magnifying spectacle," Hornbeck said and scurried out of the room.

Crisp was forced to wait for several minutes before Hornbeck finally burst back through the door.

"So sorry," he said as he rushed back to his place at the table. He was waving a round object in his right hand as he walked. "It took me a while to locate this."

The object was a convex piece of glass encircled by a ring of metal. Hornbeck placed the magnifier on the atlas, which was still open on the same spot, and began to inspect various areas. Some he glossed over. Others he stared at intently. Several times the word "remarkable" escaped from under his breath. It was the only word he uttered until he finally finished looking everything over.

"Good news, Detective Constable. Your atlas has features that confirm it to be the work of the Elizabethan period."

"And the atlas itself?"

"It's a treasure. An absolute delight."

"You misunderstand. What I mean to ask is, is there anything special about the maps it contains?"

"Oh my goodness, yes—yes, certainly there is! This means your atlas is quite valuable. In fact, I know of several collectors who will pay a handsome sum for it. I could act as an intermediary for you. I assure you, my percentage is reasonable. The clients I have assisted in the past would be willing to vouch for this."

There was a gleam behind Hornbeck's convulsing eyelids. He was trying his best to contain himself but he

106

lacked the self-control to do so. When Crisp didn't immediately respond, Hornbeck changed course.

"If you would prefer, I could have the atlas prepared for auction. It would be less discrete and riskier, of course. The price it fetches could potentially be much higher, though."

"I think you missed the point I was trying to make. The atlas is not for sale. The only reason I'm here is to get information."

"Information? I just told you, the atlas is genuine. What other information could you need?"

"Is there anything that sets these maps apart from other maps from the same period? It's of considerable interest to me and the elderly relative who gave them to me."

Both of Hornbeck's eyes bulged from behind twitches as he stared back at Crisp. He tugged nervously at his whiskers before answering. "I'm not sure I know what you mean. They're definitely quality maps from the Elizabethan period. There are few atlases currently extant that are of similar workmanship or are as well preserved. As I said, it is quite valuable. If you would allow me to act as your broker—"

Crisp shook his head as he interrupted Hornbeck. "I told you, they're not for sale." He made to get up from his seat. "If there's nothing more you can tell me then perhaps there's another map expert you can recommend?"

"Please, no, wait a moment," Hornbeck jumped from his eat again. "Don't go." He shut his eyes and a pained expression crossed his face. He appeared to be deep in thought about something. After a moment he let out a sigh, opened his eyes, and sunk back into his seat.

"You must excuse me, Detective. I'm a reputable map historian and antique map dealer. I don't care to propagate the myths that sometimes involve my trade. But, as you are so insistent, I will indulge you with a bit of storytelling." He pushed the atlas across the table. The pages were still open at the second distinctive map. "Have you noticed the different texture of this sheet?"

Crisp leaned forward. Now he was getting somewhere. "Yes. It and the other map like it are slightly rough."

"Exactly. It's a special coating of some kind. I can't explain how, but the visual effect it produces is superb. This is an unusual feature for a map from this or any other period. You must've also seen the different symbols around the edges?"

Crisp studied the shapes again. "I wondered about those. Do they mean anything in particular?"

"They're representations of the phases of the moon. The only cartographs I've heard of with such an odd combination of features are called Moonstone maps."

"So there are examples of similar maps?"

"Not quite," answered Hornbeck.

"What do you mean?"

"As I said, it's all mostly legend. The only actual historical reference to Moonstone maps come from some old naval records. Sailors who fought with Sir Francis Drake returned from the Portugal coast reporting of daring night time raids. Drake encouraged them with talk of special maps he commissioned. Because they glowed in the light of the moon he was able to navigate safely close to shore. Despite his contentions, Drake supposedly fumed constantly at the maps' temperamental nature."

"Why was that?"

Hornbeck hesitated slightly before answering. "The records are vague as to why. The important thing is it sheds considerable doubt as to whether the maps ever existed. There are no further comments about them, either before or after, in cartographic history."

"What about the two maps in the atlas?"

"They have the features of Moonstone maps. But they and the rest of the maps all depict parts of England. Drake, the greatest sailor and adventurer of his era, would have no need of them. It's much more likely that its maker heard the same tale I just told you. Seeking to profit from Drake's popularity, he produced some maps that mimicked the Moonstone maps. I grant the result is remarkable. It must have also been a difficult process and therefore hard to make money off of. Otherwise many more would be in existence."

"I suppose so, but—"

"What I told you earlier still applies. They're from the Elizabethan era and very valuable. The fact that two are patterned after a good yarn about Sir Francis Drake may or may not increase their value. That's up to the collectors to fight over."

Hornbeck's nervous energy suddenly manifested itself once again. He rose from his chair with his right eye twitching and paced back over to the window. "Are you sure you do not wish to sell the atlas?"

"Sorry, but yes, I am quite certain."

Hornbeck stared through the misted glass. He took a cloth from his pocket and wiped something from one of the small square panes. "I won't lie to you Detective. I'm extremely disappointed by your answer. And, while I hate to be a poor host, I've neglected my duties long enough. I've told you all I know. I think it is best that you be on your way."

Crisp picked the map up off the table and rolled it back in its string. "Goodbye Mr. Hornbeck and thank you for your assistance." His farewell was met with silence as Hornbeck continued to stare morosely out the window.

10
A Narrow Escape

Crisp couldn't stop thinking about what Hornbeck told him as he walked back to the front of the map shop. Whether the mapmaker knew it or not, his information was potentially very useful. Under different circumstances, it would have been nice to return the favor by explaining why the maps were too important to sell.

He was about to exit the shop's front door when a display case filled with books caught his eye. Hornbeck's name was on the front cover. He moved closer and read the title. *'Compass, Telescope and Sextant – Cartography in the Age of Discovery.'*

He picked one up and headed for the checkout. Having just talked to its author, he wasn't sure how much more it would tell him but making sure Hornbeck hadn't forgotten anything certainly seemed to be worth a few pounds.

After paying for the book, Crisp walked out into the square in front of the shop. He had only taken a few steps when he realized the atlas was still in his left hand and in plain sight. He started to put it back in its secret pocket but he was already too late.

A crowd of shoppers parted across the street, revealing an unwelcome sight. It was Taylor. He wore a heavy leather coat over a black turtle neck and black pants. His left hand was up by his mouth and he appeared to be talking into a small microphone. His eyes, with their familiar icy stare, were locked on Crisp.

Crisp acted like he was putting the atlas in the bag that held Hornbeck's book. Instead, he managed to slip it into its jacket pocket. Taylor reached him just as he finished.

"This is a pleasant surprise. What brings you to this part of town?" Crisp said lightly.

"I told you Detective, I don't like jokes."

"You should learn to like them. I get the feeling the jokes going to be on you quite a bit in the future. Now, toss off before I get angry."

"I will not 'toss off' as you so elegantly suggest. In fact I cannot, under the circumstances."

"What circumstances?"

"You've been careless, Detective. I saw the atlas in your possession."

"So what if you did? I'm not about to give it to a git like you."

"I beg to disagree. In fact, neither of us will leave here until it is in my hands."

"And you said you didn't like jokes."

"I don't. Now, I shall give you one last chance."

"I wouldn't if I were you. I don't take ultimatums very well."

"Enough! The atlas! Give it to me!"

Crisp shook his head and started to leave.

"Don't move!"

The sharp command made Crisp stop short, his curiosity getting the best of him. It was a mistake. As he watched, Taylor reached into his pocket and pulled out what looked like a small lump of clay. With a flick of his wrist, the lump flew the distance between them and hit Crisp on his left foot. It landed with a funny plopping noise and began to immediately deform. As it spread it stuck like tar to the top of his shoe.

Whether intended or not, the projectile's location must have been good enough. Taylor didn't act as if his poor aim was of any consequence. Crisp, in turn, didn't attempt to remove the gray lump. The dangerous looking material now appeared like it would stick to whatever it touched, including his fingers.

Taylor held up his right palm so Crisp could see it. There was a black pad secured to his first finger. A wire ran from it and disappeared into his sleeve.

"A thumbprint trigger. All I need to do is gently press," he moved his first finger toward his thumb as a demonstration, "and the explosive attached to your leg will detonate. And then there will be no more Detective Crisp."

"I almost forgot how much you and your lot like to blow stuff up. Thanks for the reminder."

"You must think that was a clever trick you played." Taylor's lips were compressed in a humorless smile and his voice was laced with disdain. "I'll admit it caused us some confusion and delay. We weren't sure if the book in the package was truly the item sent to you. If it was, then you were of no use to us. If you had the atlas," he pointed at the bag Crisp held, "as it's now clear that you do, you would eventually show up here, or someplace similar. The easiest thing to do was to wait. As predicted, the prey walked right into the trap. Perhaps you aren't so clever after all."

"Still smart enough to fool you and your mates, though, eh?"

"Toss the bag over to me." Taylor said, reverting to a sharp command. "I prefer to have the atlas intact but it won't matter much to me if I turn it into ashes. My objective is achieved either way."

Crisp put his hands slowly above his head. "I have one question first."

Taylor stiffened. "Don't try my patience. You've already stretched it quite thin with your games. It won't take much for me to squeeze the trigger. In fact, I may even derive some pleasure from it."

"That's exactly my problem. After I give you the bag what's to keep you from pushing the trigger anyway?"

"You'll have to trust me," Taylor said with another grim smile.

"I thought that would be your answer."

"Throw me the atlas, now!"

"Okay, okay. Here—"

Crisp heaved the bag directly at Taylor's face, blocking his vision for a split second. The throw also caused his hands to instinctively spread open to make the catch. Crisp moved with lightning speed. Instead of running away, however, he followed the motion of his throw. He and the bag reached Taylor at almost the same instant.

Taylor caught a glimpse of Crisp's movement but it was too late. He put his arms up in a defensive position and let the bag fall to the ground. Crisp didn't bother trying to grab the man's trigger hand. He doubted he could get a good enough hold of it in time. Instead, he just wrapped his arms around Taylor's waist and held on tightly.

"Go on now, push your trigger!" he scowled with as much venom as he could muster. "Push your trigger and join me in celebrating bonfire night early. We'll find out what it's like to be kindling wood together!"

Taylor let out a yell and grabbed Crisp's arms. He tried to push them away but Crisp's grip was like an iron vise. As he struggled, Crisp tightened it even more.

Taylor started to pound Crisp's arms to no effect. "Let go of me!" he screamed. But he didn't press his trigger, which meant, thankfully, that he wasn't as crazy as he looked.

As he fought to hold tight, Crisp worked his shoe off of his foot. Once it loosened enough he kicked it away. It landed ten meters from where he and Taylor were locked together. As best he could, he checked to make sure there were no people around it.

While Crisp made his search, Taylor's struggles became increasingly desperate. He finally managed to dislodge Crisp's left arm with a frenzied blow from his fist. Crisp threw his newly freed arm upwards. His fingers latched onto the cuff of Taylor's leather jacket. He released his right arm and quickly spun his right shoulder inwards. This allowed him to finally get a tight hold of his adversary's right hand.

Taylor's eyes suddenly widened as he realized what Crisp was trying to do. Crisp's right hand was squeezing his trigger finger to his thumb. When they touched the result was instantaneous. The explosive detonated with a tremendous 'WHAM'. White light and heat shot upwards and outwards.

Both men fell over to avoid the effects of the blast. As soon as they hit the ground Crisp rolled away and got back to his feet. The bag with Hornbeck's book was below him. He reached down, grabbed it and took off in the direction of his car. His shoeless left foot padded softly on the road as he ran. He turned the corner onto the road where he was parked. Sneaking a look over his shoulder, he was surprised to see Taylor wasn't following him.

Crisp slowed his pace down to a jog. There was no reason to rush now. Another quick glance again showed no one behind him. Deciding to act less conspicuous, he started to walk.

He was feeling good about his escape. In addition, he learned something from the confrontation. Taylor didn't want or need the atlas for anything. He just wanted to make sure no one else could use it. It meant that his uncle's assumption was correct. The atlas did pose a threat in some way to his plans.

When Crisp finally reached his car, the adrenaline from his recent encounter was gone. His body began to tremble and wave of nausea overtook him. He propped himself on the hood and waited. It took a full minute before the unpleasant combination started to fade. The last thing he wanted to do, however, was linger about. So as soon as felt able, he scrambled into the driver's seat and drove away.

* * *

There was one thing Crisp knew for sure—he couldn't go home. Taylor and his accomplices now knew he had the atlas, which meant any danger that existed in returning there was significantly magnified. He didn't want another confrontation, at least not yet. His number one priority at the moment was keeping the atlas safe. That meant he needed a temporary place to stay.

The aimless route he was driving served to settle him down a bit. It also brought him to Marylebone. This seemed to him like a good place to stop. It always teemed with tourists. Blending into a crowd was often the best camouflage. The area also held some sentimental appeal to him from his time enrolled in the Royal Academy of Music.

Infusions of deep purple and black were starting to creep across the overcast evening sky. It was getting late, he was worn out, and he still had things to do. The sooner he was settled in somewhere the better. He passed a pleasant looking Georgian-style bed and breakfast and decided it looked good enough. A parking spot was available a few blocks down the road. He pulled the car into it. After replacing his lone shoe with a spare pair of trainers from the car's boot he walked briskly to the Inn's

114

front door. Above it was a small sign that read 'Ascot Arms'.

The lobby was cramped but quaint. There were several comfy looking armchairs arranged around a brick fireplace. Cold charred remnants of a long dead fire lay in the hearth. A smiling, gray-haired woman stood behind the front counter. She looked up from a small television as he approached her.

"May I help you?" she asked politely.

"I'd like a room."

"How long a stay will you be needing?"

"One night for now."

As the woman began to rummage through a drawer for a reservation slip an idea came to him. "Do you have anything with a view of the night sky?"

"The top back room has a balcony. Will that do?"

"Yes, just fine, thank you."

The woman completed her paperwork then asked him sign the ledger. Once he finished, she held out a key with a large plastic tag attached to it.

"Just go up the stairs all the way to the top, dear. You're in number eleven at the far end of the hall. The loo is directly across from your room." After noticing he was only carrying the bag from Hornbeck's, she leaned over the counter and peered at the floor. "Do you have any luggage? Gerald can bring it up if you want."

He shook his head. "Needed to get away on a bit of a lark. It was a last minute thing."

"Of course, dear. We get a fair amount of that sort of 'thing'. Just remember to bring her flowers when you go back in the morning." She added a wink to her unsolicited advice.

A chuckle escaped Crisp. The woman obviously thought he needed a room because of a lover's spat. He saw no point in correcting her. Instead, he just took the key and thanked her for her help.

The stairs were to the left of the check in. He climbed the three flights to the top floor. He passed room nine and ten on his left and right. Eleven was in the back left corner. The key slid into the lock and turned with a bit of effort. He pushed the heavy oak door and stepped inside.

A cozy bedroom greeted him. Soft blankets sat in a pile on the bed, which rested against a back wall covered with a print of lavender flowers. Tucked in one corner was a writing desk and chair. A door with a window in its upper half was next to the desk. He saw that it led to a small balcony.

Crisp didn't bother turning on the light. He also ignored the temptation to rest that emanated from the bed. Instead, he closed the hall door behind him and went directly to the balcony.

What he saw disappointed him. It was now completely dark but a thick layer of cloud cover sat like a blanket over the city, completely obscuring the stars and moon. There was no way he'd be able to test the map with such an overcast sky. After a moment he returned back to the room.

Once inside, he laid the bag on the desk and tossed his jacket on the chair. Feeling exhausted, he flopped on the bed. It was as much as he could take. All he wanted was a little moonlight. Instead there was none to be found.

Crisp tried to fight off his drowsiness. He still needed to plan things out, several steps ahead if possible. His narrow escape from Hornbeck's had been too close for comfort and the men who attacked him weren't finished. He was sure of it. That meant he had to stay alert for other obvious danger zones. He also had to have another plan in case his experiment failed. He needed to decide what it would be now and not when it was too late. As he lay on the bed, however, exhaustion overtook him. He fell into a sound sleep.

After three hours of dreamless slumber Crisp awoke with a start. A glance at the bedside alarm clock told him it was close to midnight. More importantly, he realized what roused him. A pale beam of wispy light radiated from the window in the balcony. It was brightest over the top of the bed, exactly where his head rested on the pillow.

He swung to the floor, picked his jacket off the chair and draped it over his arm. With mounting excitement he opened the door and walked out to the balcony. A glance upward confirmed his initial impression. The dense cloud cover was now thin enough that the sky above it was visible. A dim almost full moon and several twinkling stars hung in the sky above him.

Crisp hung his jacket on the balcony railing and eagerly retrieved the atlas from its pocket. After untying the string around it, he flipped through the pages to the first Moonstone map. As the moonlight hit it, a faint glow and an almost imperceptible hissing noise began to emanate from it. For a moment he thought the illuminated portion was trying to form into something. Then, with a faint popping noise, the map switched off. It was like it contained a light bulb that suddenly burnt out.

"No, no, no," he pleaded.

It was no use. The Moonstone map was dark and unchanged from its original appearance. Trying different angles or lifting it higher made no difference. He flipped to the second Moonstone map but the result was the same. It glowed and hissed briefly then flared out without revealing anything worthwhile.

"Bollocks," he muttered as he stowed the maps back in his jacket.

His failed experiment meant one of two things; Hornbeck was right and the maps were nothing more than fancy reproductions or, alternatively, they still held some important secret that eluded him. One persistent fact made him favor the latter explanation. The men who were pursuing him seemed convinced the maps were vitally important. This made it hard to dismiss them as fakes. It also made the next step on his path of discovery fairly straight forward. Find a way to uncover the secret of the maps while avoiding getting blown to bits.

11

A Fickle Flaw

Crisp's breakfast was cold. He had examined it, played with it a bit, but hadn't taken a single bite. The elderly lady who checked him in the night before, whose name he since learned was Helen, wandered through the dining room several times during his meal. On every trip she checked his plate and each time tut-tutted her disapproval. He finally gave up and, after a word of thanks to his server, got up from the table and wandered into the lobby. The hearth was now lit. He chose one of the chairs close to the lightly flickering fire and sat down to gather his thoughts.

Hornbeck's memory, to his dismay, was quite good. Crisp had spent a few minutes perusing his book before coming down to breakfast. The paragraph it contained about Moonstone maps was essentially a replica of the story Hornbeck relayed to him in his shop. Crisp had left his room disappointed, if not terribly surprised, that the text hadn't given him a straw to grasp at.

To make matters worse, he tried contacting Miss Pimsby on his Pitch Stone earlier. She hadn't` responded. After the attack he endured the day before, this worried him very much. She was vulnerable when she was alone. He should have thought of this before splitting them up.

"Cold are ya', young man?" Helen joined him in the lobby. He didn't notice her entering and her question caught him off guard.

"Thank you for asking but no, not really."

"Hmm—I thought I saw you shiver just now. Toss a log on and I'll grab you something to cover up."

The elderly matron scurried out of the room, leaving Crisp to do as he was told. The sparks he made putting another wedge of wood on the fire had barely settled before she returned.

"There you go," she said as she laid a thick wool blanket over his shoulders.

"Thank you, ma'am," he said politely, even though he now felt like he was melting.

118

"My pleasure, young man." It seemed like she was about to leave him again when she paused. "You seem like a nice lad. Don't worry. She'll come around."

Not knowing what else to do, Crisp simply looked back up at her and said, "Thanks". This evidently was the right move. Helen's shuffle exhibited an extra bounce as she exited the lobby.

Crisp returned to staring into the fire and thought about what Helen said. She might have misunderstood what was bothering him but her words still rang true. A bit of luck was bound to turn his way. In fact, there was one small reason he still clung to a sliver of hope. The maps had done something the night before—he didn't know what exactly—but it had been like nothing he'd ever seen before. Maybe Albert had been right. Maybe he just wasn't looking at them with the proper mindset.

He reached down to throw another log on the fire when he felt a tug at his arm. He whirled around expecting to see Helen again, perhaps with a tray of crumpets this time. Instead, a young boy stood next to his sleeve.

"Mister, someone in your jacket keeps talking to you. It sounds like a girl."

Crisp looked down with surprise. The boy was right. He pulled the Pitch Stone from its jacket pocket and noticed its core was glowing a bit brighter than usual.

"Detective Crisp, can you hear me?"

A wave of relief accompanied the sound of Miss Pimsby's voice emanating from the small, innocuous square of rock. Crisp brought the stone up to his mouth and answered. "Yes, I hear you just fine."

"Are you somewhere you can talk?"

"No, afraid not."

"Um—I believe I may have found something—interesting."

Dependable Miss Pimsby, he should have known she would come through. "Meet me in London. We should talk face to face." He gave her the address for the Ascot Arms.

"I can be there in about an hour."

A sudden idea struck Crisp. "Can you take a bit more time and see if the archive has anything relating to Sir Francis Drake?"

119

When Miss Pimsby answered she sounded confused. "Sir Drake was never a member of the Academy. I doubt there'll be anything to find about him."

"Take a bit of time anyway. Cross reference the search with Byrd and Dee. Maybe that'll help turn something up."

"If you think it's important. I've already pulled all the files on those two anyway. Give me an extra hour."

"I'll see you at the Ascot Arms around noon then?"

"Agreed."

"Do me one more favor. Make sure to be careful on your way over."

"I promise I will."

The Pitch Stone's glow dimmed as Crisp replaced it in his pocket. He got up and walked back through the Ascot Arms' lobby. Helen was back in her usual spot. He waved at her but she didn't wave back. She just stared at him with the same look of motherly concern he remembered from breakfast.

* * *

Since there wasn't much else for him to do, he decided to return to his room. He ended up staring silently at the ceiling for most of his two hour wait. Then, certain that Miss Pimsby would be punctual, Crisp left his room a few minutes before noon. He wanted to meet her in the lobby. Treading softly, he worked his way down the stairs. There was one flight left to go when he heard Helen's voice. She seemed to be in a disagreement with someone. He cautiously crept down a few more steps so that he could hear her clearly.

"So you're the one that boy has been pining over. He wouldn't even eat this morning he was so upset over you. I suggest you kiss and make up before he starves to death."

"My dear madam, I assure you, I don't know who or what you are talking about." Miss Pimsby's voice, sputtering with protest, followed Helen's up the landing.

"I know about girls like you. He's a nice polite boy. I have half a mind to—"

Helen never got to finish her sentence. Crisp managed to stop laughing long enough to travel down the final few steps. "That's quite alright, Helen," he interrupted. "I can take it from here." He led Miss Pimsby away by the arm.

"That woman is completely mental." Miss Pimsby looked indignant. "Do you know what she called me? A tart!"

Another laugh escaped Crisp.

"Well I don't see how that's amusing," she said angrily.

"I'll explain everything upstairs. Come on"

When they got to his room, he sat on the bed and Miss Pimsby took the seat next to the desk. Once they were settled, he recounted to her the events of the past day and a half. At first she was horrified by the danger he'd been in. When he reached the part about his arrival at the Inn and Helen's mistaken assumption, however, she joined in laughing with him.

"I can't say that my time has been as exciting as yours," she said when he was done, "but at least I completed the search on Sir Francis Drake as you requested. I even found a scrap of information that may refer to him."

"Does it mention Moonstone maps?"

"No. It's just a short note. I can't even be sure it's Drake that's mentioned. It doesn't actually refer to him by his last name."

"Something must have made you pick it out."

"It's clearly communication from Byrd and he mentions a Francis—I suspect he meant Drake. I thought you'd like to look at it so I made a photocopy and brought it with me."

She reached into her bag and pulled out a small folded piece of paper. After opening it to make sure it was the correct one she handed it over to him. The writing was cramped and hastily scribbled. It took a minute for Crisp to decipher the words."

The experiment was only a partial success. The map did burn brighter with the device but still would only fire if it rested in the spot from whence it came. Francis was disappointed but I see no reason to carry on.

WB

121

"The map he mentioned sounds like it could be the Moonstone map that Hornbeck described. But what device is he talking about. And why didn't the map work properly?" Crisp asked.

"I couldn't find any details about the device but I did find some more information about the maps Byrd was trying to make. It's the interesting thing I mentioned when I spoke to you earlier."

"I'm listening."

"The way I understand it, there was something unusual about the chemical reaction that produced the maps. For some reason it bonded to the surrounding environment. Byrd referred to it as geographic memory. So, like the note says, a map will only respond to moonlight if it's in the same place it was originally created."

"I don't suppose you know where our maps were made?"

Miss Pimsby shook her head. "No. I was hoping the other maps in the atlas would show us where to go."

"I've examined them over and over. There's nothing distinctive about any of them. What's more, there's a map for each region of the country. Based on that, the spot we're looking for could be anywhere."

"There must be a way to narrow it down."

Crisp closed his eyes and began to rub them gently. "Maybe there is. This all started four hundred years ago, after all. Travel was a bit rougher back then. If it was me, I'd pick someplace within a day's carriage ride, which means we're talking about somewhere in or about London. Where is a likely place for Byrd to pick?" He stopped rubbing, opened his eyes, and looked up at Miss Pimsby. "How about the Archives?"

"Sorry," Miss Pimsby said as she shook her head again. "There aren't any access points to the sky there. It's in an underground vault. It seems unlikely they would pick it as a place to view a map under moonlight."

"They must've left some clue as to where the maps work. What's the bit of interesting stuff you said you've found, by the way? Did it have anything to do with the maps?"

"The Academy was heavily involved in the planning of St. James Palace, especially the Chapel Royal. There are several secret hiding places incorporated within the design. I brought a copy of the plans with me. They show where the hiding places are and how to open them."

He saw the connection Miss Pimsby was alluding to at once. "William Byrd was a Gentleman of the Chapel Royal. As a member of the Academy he would have known the hiding places and his position with the Chapel Royal would have given him access to them."

"That was my thought too," Miss Pimsby said as she laid out the plans for him to look at. "There are three different trap doors. One is on the lower level and two are on the upper."

Crisp studied the old plans until he had the relevant parts memorized. "There's a good chance Byrd hid the secret location to activate the maps in one of these spots. It ties together nicely."

"It does."

"Well, what are we waiting for? Chapel Royal awaits us."

When they got back to the lobby Crisp decided it was safer to check out and keep moving. He settled up with Helen, who managed to slip Miss Pimsby the evil eye several times in the process.

Crisp tossed his stuff and Miss Pimsby's bag into the trunk then put the top down. He climbed into the car and, once Miss Pimsby was settled in her seat, shot out of its parking space. He gripped the steering wheel lightly as he weaved through the afternoon traffic.

"But how are we going to get into Chapel Royal?" Miss Pimsby shouted over the noise from the wind. "I don't think we can just walk up to the door, knock and expect to be let in."

"That's exactly what we're going to do." At the next red light, Crisp pulled out his mobile phone and dialed a number. "Hello, Rat, its Benjamin."

"If you don't start using my proper name I'm going to stop answering your calls," replied the voice of Tattingbone, while conveying as much irritation as possible over the phone.

123

"Fine, uh, Rupert. First, your check and your citation of merit from the Queen will be delivered next week."

"Splendid. Father's eyes will pop out of his head."

"Second, is Rose still the organist at the Chapel Royal in St. James Palace?"

"Yes," Rat answered with suspicion. "Why do you ask?"

"I need a private tour."

"When?"

"Ten minutes from now."

"Oh, you do love giving proper notice."

"It's important Rupert."

"I'll call her and have her meet you at the gate," Tattingbone said with resignation. "Someday I'm going to need a favor from you, Benjamin. It's going to be a big one." He hung up with a loud click.

Miss Pimsby had heard only half the conversation. "Who's Rose?" she asked.

"Another old classmate. Both Rat and I dated her at one point. Rat's money ended up being the tie-breaker. She's now Mrs. Rupert Tattingbone."

The car arrived at Pall Mall. After finding a parking spot they walked to the gate at St. James Palace. There was a lone guard with a bright red coat and a large black bearskin hat standing impassively at the door. He ignored them completely.

They waited outside the gate for a few minutes. "I'm going to need some time to look about." Crisp said to Miss Pimsby. "You'll have to distract Rose for me."

"I'll try my best."

When the large wood door finally opened a pretty, red-haired woman stood inside the imposing brick gate. "Benjamin, it's been ages," she said with a beaming smile. She left the palace and gave Crisp an embrace.

"Good to see you too."

"Ahem. Pleased to meet you," Miss Pimsby said. She stuck her hand out at Rose, who gave it a businesslike shake.

"Sorry," Crisp apologized. "Rose this is Miss Pimsby. She's helping me with an investigation."

"Yes, I've been reading about you in the Times," Rose said as she led them through the palace. "You're quite the hero amongst the Royal caretakers, especially here in the Chapel Royal. We're remarkably protective of all our artifacts but the herald trumpets have always held a special place in our hearts. Thank you for getting the missing one back."

"It was our pleasure."

"We're a bit upset, though. We thought it would've been returned by now."

"It can't be returned until it's no longer needed as evidence."

"Well maybe something can be done about that. Now, Rupert said you need to look around Chapel Royal. It sounded important. What seems to be the problem?"

"Probably nothing. I've heard whispers about new plans to steal royal artifacts. The Chapel Royal could be one of the targets. Nothing solid, mind you," he added quickly when he saw a look of concern cross Rose's face. "But since the trumpet thieves are still at large I want to be careful."

Their walk finally brought them to Chapel Royal. It was an elongated rectangular space with oak paneled walls. The lower level was lined with pews. Above them were two full-length balconies, one on each side of the room. The left side balcony held a large pipe organ. The altar was at the point farthest across the room from them. It sat in front of an ornate window with the motto 'All shall be well and all manner of thing shall be well' scrolled across it.

"What a beautiful window," Miss Pimsby said.

"The Golden Jubilee is lovely, isn't it," Rose agreed.

"I would love to learn more about it. Would you mind terribly if we got a closer look?"

"Of course not."

Crisp hung back a bit. "You two go ahead. I need to see if there's anything around that's at risk of being nicked."

Rose seemed reluctant to leave him alone. Miss Pimsby, however, looked directly at her and with a tilt of her head asked, "Shall we?"

Crisp made a show of looking at a tapestry as the women walked away. As soon as he had a chance he ducked into the back left pew. A careful feel along the floorboard identified a depression in the wood. He pressed it and a cleverly hidden shelf popped out of the wall. A quick glance, however, showed that all it held was a ruby encrusted gold cross.

Crisp gently pushed the shelf back into its hiding place and stood up. A look toward the altar showed Miss Pimsby and Rose still chatting away. He headed for the left side upper level. Once upstairs, he counted his paces as he walked on the balcony floor. After six steps he knelt down. Once again relying on his sense of touch, he detected a razor-fine seam. Sweeping his finger along it, he found the point on either end where the line stopped. He put a finger on the exact same spot on each corner. Then, being careful to exert an equal amount of pressure with each finger, he gently pressed down. The segment of floor hinged inwards, revealing a small chamber underneath. He reached into it and pulled out a heavy cloth sack. A good number of gold sovereigns were inside. He reached into the chamber again to make sure he hadn't missed anything but it was empty. He put the bag of gold coins back and closed the secret floorboard.

One more hiding place left. He stood back up again. The women down at the altar were done talking and were looking up at him.

"Do you need any assistance?" Rose shouted.

"Almost done. I'll be down in a minute. Don't bother coming up." He continued along the balcony until he reached the large pipe organ. It took a short search but he found what he was looking for; a panel on the organ's side. A push directly in its center caused it to pop off. He was glad to see the small space held a book. He pulled it out and opened it. His excitement fell as quickly as it had risen. The book appeared to be a young girl's diary. He read a few lines.

> I envisage daily the change in her. Ambition floods her soul like the sun on a summer day. England is my birthright. I fear Elizabeth shall not accept this truth with grace.

Crisp checked inside the front cover. The name Mary Tudor was scrawled across the top of it. "Smart girl," he muttered as he put the diary away and replaced the panel to the hidden compartment.

Disappointed at not finding anything from Byrd in the three hiding places, he went back downstairs. Miss Pimsby looked expectantly at him for a sign of good news. He spoke to Rose but his words were meant for Miss Pimsby.

"Chapel Royal is clear. You can rest assured there's nothing of interest here."

12
The Safe House

"I must admit, that was a bit disappointing" Crisp said once he and Miss Pimsby were back in his car.

"Sorry," she replied, looking guilt ridden. "I guess my information wasn't as useful as I thought."

"Don't apologize. It wasn't your fault the Chapel turned out to be a red herring. It was bound to happen. We are trying to track a four hundred year old trail, after all."

His words seemed to cheer her. "The question now is where we should turn next," he continued. After thinking for a moment he said, "Byrd must've left some mention as to where the maps work. Perhaps we should go to the Archives together and do some more digging."

"I don't think that would help. My search of its records was quite thorough. I even asked my dad to make sure I wasn't missing something. But there's still one more place we can look for clues."

"I'm listening."

"The Academy has a townhouse not far from here. It's used as a common address for the various business dealings the Academy is involved in. Albert encouraged me to use it when we were looking for Doctor Dee. I never needed to stay there but I still have the key he gave me."

"I'm not sure that's the best idea. The thieves know Albert is involved in all this. Chances are it's compromised."

"But it's not listed under his name," she argued. "And he told me he hasn't been there for several months. He also told me that he recently installed some security upgrades. And there's a secret escape passage in the basement. He gave me the instructions on how to open it. They're in my purse."

"A secret passage? Where does it go?"

"I don't know. Albert didn't say. But it should be helpful if there are people watching us. We'll be able to come and go without being seen."

"It sounds like Albert meant it to be a safe house."

Miss Pimsby wasn't finished. "Most importantly, when I asked my father about it he told me the house has a small vault used to store certain records. It may contain information that wasn't in the Archives."

"Another good point," Crisp agreed. "You've convinced me. To the townhouse we go."

Crisp decided to take a circuitous route in the off chance they had been spotted. He turned the car toward the Thames River and then headed south on Abingdon Street. As they drove past the Jewel Tower Miss Pimsby did something odd. She scrunched her eyes shut and stuck her index fingers in her ears. She remained like this for over a minute before slowly opening her right eye. Satisfied by whatever she saw, she opened the other and pulled her fingers down from her ears.

"What was that all about?" he asked.

"Nothing —just a superstition," she replied with a hint of embarrassment.

"Superstition?"

"It's silly, really. I'm sure you don't want to hear about it."

"Actually, I would. You've got me quite curious."

"Promise you won't laugh."

"I promise."

"When I was a little girl my family took walks on Sunday. Whenever we passed this way my father would tell me and my sisters' stories about the old Palace Yard."

"What kind of stories?"

"Oh—mostly about how prisoners were brought there to be executed. Sometimes he would even tell us about the awful things that were done to them before they were hung. It sounds ghastly, I know. I think he believed he was just giving a good history lesson but he scared me and my sisters silly. We started closing our ears and eyes when we came this way. The eight of us would bump into each other and father would get cross but we kept doing it anyway. A bit daft, isn't it."

Determined to keep his promise, Crisp suppressed a chuckle. "No, actually it's quite charming in its own, strange way."

After a few more turns, they arrived at their destination. Crisp pulled into a parking spot across the street from the townhouse. He retrieved their belongings from the trunk and then the two of them walked across the road. Miss Pimsby reached in her purse as they approached the door. The minute she took rummaging around gave him a chance to appraise their lodgings.

The townhouse was a narrow, three-story, Georgian design, much like the Ascot Arms. Its three front steps led to a bright red door. On either side of it sat a pair of large ape statues with flat ugly faces and long hairy arms that reached to the ground. They sat perched on their haunches as if ready to pounce. To Crisp, their appearance was an unpleasant reminder of Taylor's muscle-bound enforcer. As he walked up the steps, a closer look revealed that they were made from a shiny gray metal with a certain magnetic, if slightly tarnished, attraction. They had to have some symbolic meaning for the Academy. He decided to ask Miss Pimsby about them when given a chance.

"There it is," Miss Pimsby exclaimed as she finally pulled the key from the depths of her bag.

A few seconds later they were inside the dark and quiet front foyer. Crisp, having learned his lesson about intruders the hard way, made sure to protect his back and watch for sudden movement as he reached for a light switch. The only thing that greeted them once the light was on, however, was a modest size pile of unopened mail that had accumulated behind the door.

The townhouse seemed comfortable if a bit sparse. A sitting room that was obscured in shadow opened to his left. The bottom of the stairs began next to the sitting room entrance and continued upwards along the left side of the hall. The hall continued straight back toward what Crisp presumed was the kitchen. The door on his right was closed. Miss Pimsby walked over and swung it open, revealing an office, bare except for a wall of bookshelves and a large oak desk like the one in Albert's manor home. The floor was covered with a deep and luxurious looking oriental carpet.

In the interest of time, Crisp decided to divide and conquer. He assigned Miss Pimsby the task of searching the vault. His task was to search the rest of the house and to make sure the tunnel Albert described was in good working order. It would be of little use to them if its hinges were rusted shut or its walls had caved in. He knew from experience that the worst time to discover a problem was after the chance to fix it had passed. So, while Miss Pimsby made a bee-line for the study, he headed to the basement.

A single dim bulb hanging from the ceiling lit his descent down to the cellar. When his feet finally left the stairs and settled onto the tiled floor, he peered toward the back wall. A wine rack lay across it. This was a good sign. The door to the passage was supposed to be hidden behind its collection of bottles.

A closer glance at the shelf indicated Albert's taste in wine was superb. Crisp's first impression was confirmed when he pulled out a bottle of Domaine de la Janasse Chateauneuf-du-Paup and inspected it. He put the bottle back with a shrug. The collection Albert had assembled was impressive but what it hid was far more significant to him at the moment.

The instructions in Albert's note to Miss Pimsby said to find the bottle on the bottom right corner of the rack. He kneeled down and performed a brief search. Once he found it, he grasped it by the neck and, per the next line of instructions, twisted it 180 degrees clock-wise. As the bottle spun into position he heard a clicking noise, like a latch opening. He then took the bottle out of the rack and looked at it. It seemed unremarkable. A closer look, however, revealed that the bottom of the bottle contained a metal ring that he assumed was a magnet.

Continuing the proper sequence, he inserted the bottle into the next space up. He then twisted it 180 degrees counter clock-wise. A second clicking noise was accompanied by the central part of the wine rack popping open. Crisp marveled at the newly-exposed door's craftsmanship. When he first approached the wall there was no sign that it existed.

The wine rack swung open the rest of the way with a faint clinking of bottles; a dark tunnel lay beyond it. Crisp peered into it but saw nothing. He then noticed that his inner jacket pocket, the one that held the Pitch Stone, was

Michael Malik

glowing. He pulled the stone out. An intense light now radiated from it. Some innate property of the tunnel must have activated it.

Supplied with ample illumination, he checked the inner workings of the door. It was a simple knob. The designers must have decided there was no point in concealing how to get out of the tunnel, just getting in.

Satisfied that the first part of the tunnel was open at least, he went back upstairs. While he passed through the reception room, he looked for the security system that Albert supposedly installed. There should have been some wires or a closed circuit camera somewhere. Unfortunately, he didn't see anything of the sort. The only thing remotely interesting in the hall was a pair of enormous barometers, one hanging on either wall.

Crisp walked into the first floor sitting area. Its window was the most accessible from the street. He wanted to make sure it was locked and the blinds closed. It was also the last room that might hold the elusive security system. He doubted its existence now more than ever but it wouldn't hurt to check. If it wasn't in the sitting room he decided he would stop wasting time looking for it.

Crisp glanced curiously at the room's far bookshelf. Set in its center was a bust. He moved forward for a closer look. It was a long faced man with a long pointed nose. A full head of long curly hair draped over his shoulders. A white ruffled collar was knotted loosely below his pointed chin. It was similar in appearance to the bust of Doctor Dee except, instead of being metal, this one was alabaster white.

Crisp peered into the bust's eyes and said, "Hello, is someone in there?" He was met with silence. Suddenly he felt a bit foolish. Not every statue he ran into was going to talk back to him.

A brief examination of the room showed no evidence of any security equipment. He checked the window in the front of the room and found it to be tightly locked. A final glance through it revealed a quiet and empty street. He closed the blinds and exited back into the hall.

Before heading upstairs, he decided to check in on Miss Pimsby. He poked his head into the study but she was

132

nowhere to be seen. He suppressed the urge to panic. "Hello," he shouted. "Are you in here?"

"Back this way," came her muffled reply.

Relieved, he stepped into the room and toward the sound of her voice. He was met by the bookshelf. "How do I get in?"

"Hang on a sec," came her faint reply. He heard footsteps and then a popping noise. He took a step back as the section of bookshelf opened in front of him. Miss Pimsby came through the door with a pile of documents in her hand. He peeked past her shoulder and into the vault. It was impressive; both larger and deeper than he imagined it would be and every shelf filled to the top with stacks of books, files, and other various forms of paper.

"Let me help you with that."

"I'm fine," she answered. "Would you mind closing the door for me though?"

Crisp did as she asked. He was surprised at how heavy it felt.

Miss Pimsby started to sort the documents on the desk. "Did you find the passage?" she asked him.

"Yes and it seems to be in good working order. But I couldn't find the security system that Albert told you he installed. I think he forgot."

"Don't be too hard on Albert. He's a good man."

"I know. And I'm sure he did what he thought he needed to do, for our sake as well as everyone else's. It just seems like he left us completely in the dark. We're like two blind people groping about, hoping to grasp something we can't see. You can't blame me for being a bit frustrated at the moment."

"If it makes you feel better, I can tell you is he thinks the world of you. He talked highly of you every time I met with him."

Crisp felt a twinge of embarrassment. "I wasn't aware I was such a frequent topic of your conversations."

"Oh, yes. Based on what he told me, I'm he sure he left for the meeting because he trusted you to handle this as capably as he would."

"That's a kind thing for you to say. I hope I can live up to my billing."

"It should be simple. Just hold onto your faith in him and what we're doing," she said as she picked up another document and added it to a growing stack on the corner of the desk. "Imagine how bad it will be years or centuries from now, how terrible the consequences will be if we give up."

"That may be true, but we're still stuck with nowhere to go."

"For the moment, but I'm sure you'll come up with something."

Crisp knew she was right. Doubts had to be pushed aside. Too much was at stake and time was running out. With this in mind, he left Miss Pimsby to her work and went to search the rest of the house.

* * *

An hour later he was back in the study. He found Miss Pimsby sitting at the desk, partially hidden by a mound of files and papers.

"Any luck yet?" he asked.

"No. You?"

"Nothing, although it might help if I knew what I was looking for."

She stood up and tried to gather the pile of papers in her arms but it was too much for her to take in one bunch.

"Let me help you with that," Crisp said. He took the lot from her and followed her into the vault. "What do you want me to do with these?"

"Just lay them in the corner with the rest," she said as she began searching the shelves again.

In the back, a fairly large stack of papers was accumulating. He bent down and started heaping the ones he held on top of the others.

"You've been busy."

She looked over at him and then at the disorganized jumble at his feet. "I feel guilty about leaving such a mess but we are in a hurry. If I file everything back where it belongs will slow me down considerably."

134

"I have no qualms about that," he reassured her. He laid the last file on the stack and stood up. "Can I help you find something?"

She shook her head. "The filing system my father created is a bit byzantine. You can take these though."

She handed him a book and several thick folders. He carried them back out to the desk and set them down. She followed him with an equally large collection. He pulled a chair up to the desk and settled into it while she returned to her spot and began sifting through the material stacked in front of her.

Having little else to do, he pulled a file from the stack he carried in and started looking through it. It was a boring collection of invoices as far as he could tell. Even worse, much of it was in Latin. He tossed the file back on the desk and reached for the book. It seemed much more interesting. There was a picture of a strange contraption on its cover.

"What's this book supposed to be?" he asked.

"A catalogue of scientific instruments."

A picture book seemed appropriate for him at his point so he laid it in his lap. "You mentioned your family has been working for the Academy for a long time," he said as he opened the catalogue and began to flip through its pages.

"Over two hundred years. But that's not long at all. I have records in the Archives that go back to Roman times."

"You would think that an organization as old as they are would have something in place to deal with this mess. It doesn't make sense to have a junior detective and an archivist running around trying to pull their bits out of the fire."

"I don't think you quite understand what the Academy is truly all about.

"I suppose I don't," he said as he continued to flip through the catalogue.

"They don't have an army to call on; it's not some sort of secret cult. They're men and women with outstanding scientific minds who are willing to devote much of their lives to bettering man's lot. You heard your uncle the other day. I think he was being far too modest. He didn't even scratch the surface of the inventions and discoveries that came about due to the activities of the Academy."

"But he knew there was something more to it than that, didn't he. Like he said, man's natural instinct is for destruction. That means what we're trying to fix is a bit more complex than a light bulb." He glanced down. The next page of the catalogue showed a globe that seemed to be radiating with energy.

"The Academy members, including Albert, are terribly gentle. Most wouldn't hurt a fly. Your uncle is perhaps an exception in that he tries to stop problems before they happen as opposed to merely reacting after the fact. Nevertheless, even he isn't capable of chasing down mad killers."

"I'd call that a serious oversight on their part."

"Maybe, but in case you haven't guessed, a crisis like this doesn't happen every other day."

"Thank goodness for that."

"I'd say your uncle did what he could, in the little time he was given, to get us moving forward."

"I'll say one thing," Crisp said as he flipped another page of the catalogue and glanced at the ornate instrument depicted on the sheet. It looked like it sifted different sized particles. "When a 'problem' does come up it isn't a minor one. The Academy certainly found a way to make life as difficult as possible for us with this escapade."

"You can't fool me detective," Miss Pimsby said playfully. "You're too much like your uncle. You enjoy a challenge. You just reserve the right to complain about it along the way."

Crisp stared back at her, unsure of what to say. A snappy reply seemed inadequate against the truth. Despite his earlier skepticism, he was now convinced he and Miss Pimsby were entangled in something extraordinary. Instead of discouraging him, each new obstacle they ran into only made him want to figure out the mystery of the maps even more. Besides, how often did someone get a chance to save the world from destruction?

He flipped another page and peered down at it. This time, instead of lazily moving on to the next picture, his eyes were riveted on what he saw. Unlike the rest of the strange devices in the catalogue, this instrument was familiar. He remembered seeing it not long ago.

He showed Miss Pimsby the picture he discovered. It looked like a deformed telescope. "What does the caption for this thing say?"

"Organum Lumen Augmentio," she read. "Loosely translated it means light amplifying instrument."

"That has to be it then," he said, barely containing his excitement. "It all makes perfect sense."

"What makes perfect sense?"

"I saw this recently in the British museum. It was part of the exhibit on Elizabethan artifacts. It was set up against a wall with a bunch of other displaced artifacts but I'd swear it was exactly the same as what's in that picture."

"Are you sure?"

"Yes. And that's not all." He took the atlas from his jacket and flipped it open to the picture on the frontispiece. There was the odd instrument again, in the hands of one of the two men. Its lines were blurry but its features were clearly similar to the instrument in the catalogue. "See, it's here too. And you said it's used to amplify light."

"Which means it should be able to amplify moonlight." Miss Pimsby said as she peered down at the atlas. "It certainly sounds like what we're missing but it's odd. What's an Academy instrument doing in a museum? It should be safely locked away in Albert's lab or in the Archive."

"It was probably supposed to stay with the atlas but for some reason they got separated during the last four hundred years. Why isn't important at the moment. We have to get our hands on it somehow and as soon as possible."

"Umm—won't that be difficult? It's locked away in a museum."

He looked out the window. It was already dark. The museum closed at 5:30. There was no use going over there now. Everyone would have left for the evening.

"Maybe not." He pulled out his mobile phone and started going through his contacts until he got to Fairfield, M. He pushed the number and listened impatiently as several rings sounded. When voice mail picked up, he said,

"Ms. Fairfield, this is Detective Constable Crisp. I need to meet with you at your office as soon as possible. Please return my call when you get this."

"Who's Ms. Fairfield?" Miss Pimsby asked when he hung up.

"Someone I met after the trumpet was stolen. She works at the museum. If anyone can help us, she can."

"But that might not be until morning."

"Most likely. The museum opens at 10. Hopefully she'll call back and get us in before then."

"What do we do until then?"

"Do you have a piece of paper and a pencil?"

Miss Pimsby gave him an odd look but nonetheless searched the drawer in front of her. She found several pieces of blank stationary and a ballpoint pen and handed them to him from across the desk.

Crisp laid the catalogue on the desk and, taking the pen, began to draw a picture of the Augmenter. The three cylinders that made up its body were all the same size and were connected by a series of fancy buckles and locks. When he was through he showed it to Miss Pimsby.

"What do you think?"

"It's a well done likeness. I assume it's to help Ms. Fairfield find what we're looking for."

"Correct." Crisp folded the sheet and stuffed it in his pants pocket. "I figured it was a better option than just ripping the page out."

"I would say so. Perhaps I should put that away before you are tempted again," she said as she reached over and collected the catalogue from in front of him.

"That's an excellent idea. It's late. We might as well tidy up in here, grab a bite to eat from the kitchen and get some rest. I don't know about you but I'm exhausted. And unless I'm wrong, we have an important task ahead of us in the morning."

13
The Security System

"Arise!"

Crisp squeezed his eyes shut and tried to pay no attention to the parade of ghosts that passed by his bed and shouted at him as he slept. He wasn't sure why they were there and didn't care. It was only a dream and he needed to get a bit more rest.

"Thou must arise Benjamin Crisp, quickly now!"

There it was again. More shouting—and it was becoming harder and harder to ignore. Despite his continued and valiant attempt at resistance, the fog obscuring his consciousness started to drift away. Once his head was almost clear, he propped an eye open.

The vision that greeted him was enough to jolt him upright. A glowing ghost floated astride his bed. His prominent nose stuck out sharply from his face, a stream of long wavy hair ran like a waterfall from the top of his head and a silk scarf was knotted lazily around his neck.

"I recognize you. Your bust is in the study," Crisp said as he rubbed his eyes and tried to clear the remaining cobwebs from his brain.

"Aye 'tis my likeness," agreed the ghost. His voice sounded normal, unlike the tinny quality of Doctor Dee's, but its manner was clipped. He was clearly agitated about something. "Robert Boyle is my name."

"But what are you doing here? And why didn't you answer me when I spoke to you earlier?"

Boyle fixed Crisp with a sympathetic look usually reserved for a wayward child. "I was brought here from my usual home at the request of Albert. My duty is to keep watch over this abode. I shan't hesitate in telling thee it has been a dreary job. There has been nothing to do and none to talk to. The boredom has been beyond imaginable—until now. I confess it has caused me to suffer an ill mood. Therefore, despite my dearth of intellectual stimulation, when thou did appear I was much too churlish to engage in small talk. As for thy second question—I am

139

under no obligation to reveal myself unless properly addressed by a member of the Academy of Natural Philosophers. Has thy uncle not explained at least this fact to thee?"

"Actually he did mention it once. Wait a second." Something Boyle said was bothering him. "What exactly did you mean by 'until now'?"

"'Tis what I have been trying to tell thee. There are rapscallions about. I fear they threaten the boundaries of this sanctuary. Thou must arise—arise with haste—and activate the security system."

"What security system? I couldn't find one."

"Thou must learn to not be so limited in thy thinking," Boyle said scathingly. "Speak no more for we waste precious time. Thou must follow me before the ramparts are breached. Come now!"

Crisp scooped his clothes and jacket from his bed stand and scrambled to put them on. Once he was done he watched Boyle sweep through his unopened bedroom door. Crisp paused for a moment to watch the unusual sight then ran over to the door and swung it open with a swift pull. Boyle was already heading for the stairs.

"Hang on a moment," Crisp called out to the drifting ghost. He strode across the hall to Miss Pimsby's door. After a few light knocks it inched open and she peeked out at him through the crack.

"Hello. What are you doing up?"

"Get dressed and follow us downstairs as soon as possible."

"Us?"

"Good evening mademoiselle," said Boyle as he floated up behind Crisp. "I suggest thee do as Benjamin Crisp requests."

"This is Robert Boyle." Crisp said the name like he was introducing an annoying relative. "He says there are people outside trying to get in. We need to leave."

The sleepiness in Miss Pimsby's eyes vanished and for a moment she stood frozen, staring at the unlikely duo. The spell broke with an impatient roll of Boyle's eyes.

"Just give me a moment."

"We do not have a moment," Boyle stressed. "Thou must come now Benjamin Crisp or it will be too late."

"Go," Miss Pimsby said. He hesitated, unwilling to leave her, until she gave him a push. "If there's one thing I learned over the past year it's to take good advice. Listen to Boyle. I'll be down in a jif."

"Hurry up."

Crisp took off in a run after Boyle, who was already sweeping down the stairs. Taking the steps two at a time, he was down on the ground floor in an instant. Boyle was nowhere to be seen but the corner of Crisp's eye caught sight of a soft glow emanating from the sitting room. He rushed toward it and saw Boyle standing before the fireplace. The ghost seemed to be staring into the mirror above it.

"Come hither Benjamin Crisp. Glance at the mirror from this angle and tell me what thou dost see."

Boyle was pointing to a spot on the floor where the pattern of the oriental carpet seemed to coalesce into a bulls-eye. Crisp moved over until he was standing in the center of it and glanced up into the mirror but he didn't see his reflection. Instead, the front stairway was in clear view. Half a dozen men wearing black jumpsuits were crouched on it, just like Boyle said there would be.

The intruders' faces weren't visible but Crisp was still able to pick out three whose height and build indicated they were Taylor and his two cronies. The radio-operator was bent down at the doorknob. It looked like he was trying, without much success, to work the lock. Taylor's body language conveyed a sense of growing impatience over the delay. Two of the other men held something in their hands that he was sure were automatic pistols.

"You're quite right, they are rapscallions. And I can tell you from personal experience they're fond of breaking and entering." He watched as the radio-operator pulled another set of keys from his pocket and bent down at the lock again. "They're trying awful hard to keep quiet. They must think they're going to catch us sleeping."

"They shall not gain access thusly. The lock is not vulnerable to such methods. Nevertheless, their flintlocks suggest they will not be dissuaded so easily."

141

Boyle's statement was quickly proven accurate. The man kneeling at the lock jumped back as if given a sharp command. He was replaced by Taylor, who reached into his pocket and pulled out a small lump of claylike material. He attached the explosive to the door.

"We've got to get out of here." Crisp ran toward the stairs. Miss Pimsby was standing at the top of them. "Get down, now!" he shouted up at her.

Boyle chased Crisp into the reception area. "Too late, too late," he said as he waved his arms frantically. "Thou must activate the security system if thou dost wish to escape."

"What security system? Where is it?"

"Follow me," Boyle said as he moved toward the front door.

"Are you mental? That's going to blow any second." His protest was ignored, leaving Crisp no choice but to follow the surly ghost. They stopped in the center of the entrance hall.

"Now what?"

"There," Boyle answered as he pointed at the barometers.

Crisp was horribly confused. "What do you want me to do? Predict the bloody weather?"

"The valves at each bottom, dost thou see them?"

Crisp looked closer at the barometer to his right. There was a metal knob at the base that was turned to the three o'clock position. The barometer on the left was identical.

"Yes, I see them."

"Open them. Thou must be quick about it."

A faint sizzling noise was suddenly emanating from the lock in the front door. Crisp lunged toward the barometer on his right. He flipped the valve to the left and was amazed to see the mercury begin to drain away.

"Hurry, the other one," Boyle shouted in encouragement from behind him.

Crisp lunged to his left and repeated the same maneuver with the other barometer's valve. This time, instead of watching the mercury empty, he threw himself to the floor. He landed on his side, rolled his back to the door and covered his ears.

The sizzling noise turned to a hiss and then a fast and loud 'BA-BOOM' filled the space above him. The door, followed by a pressure wave, flew over his head. It sailed through Boyle and landed at the foot of the stairs. A scream pierced the air. He searched the spot it came from and saw Miss Pimsby, unharmed, standing at the bottom step with the smoking and splintered door at her feet.

Reassured that no one was hurt by the blast, he turned his attention back to the entranceway. As if out of thin air, a black suited figure emerged from the wall of smoke that now wafted around it. Crisp scrambled to his feet and backed down the hallway, readying himself for an attack. It didn't come. Instead, the person reached up and removed his goggles and triangular mask.

"We meet again Detective Crisp. I do believe, however, your luck has run out this time." With his face now exposed, Taylor's thin, humorless smile was clearly visible. "Ah, good, the girl is with you. That makes things easier. And what's this I see—another pale stooge to interrogate. Too bad we lost the other one. I could've started a collection."

As he moved inside, the men behind him began filing through the door. The ones with the guns pointed them at Crisp's chest. The thick set gorilla-like man was two steps behind his leader and his mask was also off his face. His eyes flashed a menacing look that made it clear revenge was on his mind.

Crisp shielded Miss Pimsby as best he could while he desperately tried to think of a way out of their predicament. Unfortunately, he didn't see one. To make things even worse, turning the valves seemed to have done nothing. It looked like Taylor was right; his luck was gone. He looked over to Boyle for some consolation and saw, incredibly, a broad smile on the ghost's face.

"What are you so happy about," Crisp asked.

Boyle angled his head toward the door. "Watch."

At first Crisp didn't see anything. Then, in what seemed like agonizing slow motion, a pair of shadows grew behind the crowd of intruders. He couldn't identify what was making them until a long, hairy looking, slightly tarnished metal arm swept through the door. It caught the

Michael Malik

man closest to it on the side of the head. He crumpled to the floor and lay there in a motionless heap.

The sound of the man falling made the others look around. They turned just in time to see the rest of the apelike statue leap through the still smoking door frame. Its twin quickly followed.

The men with the guns reversed their aim and began firing simultaneously. The sharp crack-crack-crack of the discharging weapons was followed by a metallic pinging as the bullets ricocheted harmlessly off the apes' metal skin.

Crisp watched in amazement as the statues ran amok. They leapt and spun wildly, striking and knocking down the black suited men. He didn't know how or why but they seemed to be instinctively drawn to the intruders. The thieves made an attempt to fight back but it was a losing cause. Blows that struck the metal-cased dervishes glanced away. The statues responded to each futile attack with surprisingly swift and painful-looking counterblows. The melee quickly turned into a rout. The statues, however, weren't done. Each time someone tried to run away he was knocked back into the center of the fight.

The expression on Taylor's face went from smug self-assurance to borderline panic. Any thoughts of Crisp, Miss Pimsby or Boyle were clearly forgotten. Instead, he watched in obvious disbelief as the ape statues dismantled his team. At the same time, his right hand was urgently trying to unfasten the Velcro that held his jumpsuit pocket closed.

Crisp saw what Taylor was doing and knew exactly what it meant. He brought more bombs and wanted to retrieve another one. If they started flying around, no one would be safe.

"Umm—Detective—" Miss Pimsby was tugging at his sleeve. He tried to ignore her but she tugged it again, only a bit harder, and leaned over to yell into his ear. "Shouldn't we take this opportunity and get out of here?"

Crisp's fists clenched for a moment, the fingers digging deeply into the pulpy flesh of his palms, and his feet felt like lead weights. A minute ago he wanted nothing more than to get away. Now he wanted to stay and watch the thieves get a taste of their own medicine. Despite what his heart told him, however, his head knew that Miss Pimsby

144

was right. It was time to go. He motioned for her to move toward the basement stairs.

"Wait, don't leave me," Boyle shouted desperately at their retreating figures.

Crisp heard the ghost's cry and didn't hesitate. He reversed direction, yelled, "Sorry, almost forgot" at Boyle and, for the second time that night, waded into a danger zone. He was half-way through the foyer when one of the statues catapulted a body across it. The gangly black blob sailed like a rag doll and, luckily, collided with Taylor. The thief was knocked to the floor and more importantly, his hand was wrenched away from his pocket. Crisp took full advantage of his reprieve. He sprinted into the sitting room, grabbed Boyle's bust off the shelf, and then sprinted back through the still chaotic reception room to an anxiously waiting Miss Pimsby.

They managed to get into the back hall without being stopped and were almost at the door to the basement when Miss Pimsby yelled out "Help! Help!" One of the intruders must have seen them and followed them down the hall. He now gripped one of Miss Pimsby's arms and was trying to drag her back toward the fight.

Crisp spun around. "Duck!"

Miss Pimsby obeyed at once. With the bust held tightly in both of his hands, Crisp swung it in a great arc. It connected with a dull thud on the man's temple, knocking him unconscious and freeing Miss Pimsby.

"Good show," Boyle congratulated him. "It has been over three hundred and fifty years since I engaged in fisticuffs. I must admit it is still thrilling."

Crisp was too busy to return Boyle's approbation. Since more men could be heading down the hall at any moment, he quickly led the way into the basement. Once he was in front of the wine rack, he repeated the sequence that opened the hidden door. This time Boyle politely waited for the door to open before passing through it. Crisp ushered Miss Pimsby in next. After one last glance to make sure they were safe he followed her into the tunnel. The door, with a gentle pull, closed silently and seamlessly behind him.

* * *

Despite Boyle's protest that they were perfectly safe, Crisp didn't want to take any chances. Once the secret door was sealed he herded Miss Pimsby ahead of him and rushed down the tunnel. He wanted to make sure they were out of the reach of any more bombs.

"That was brilliant." Crisp huffed as he ran. "What were—those things anyway? I've never—seen anything—like them before—in my life."

"I assume thou speak of the sentinels. They were effective were they not?" Boyle replied as he drifted down the tunnel alongside them.

"Yes, they were—remarkably effective."

"I was terribly—worried we were—next though," said a still gasping and trembling Miss Pimsby.

"Thou were in no danger from them at any point tonight, my dear lady."

"Why not?" Crisp asked as he slowed to a trot and looked over his shoulder. The door was out of sight. He stopped, leaned against the tunnel wall and gave his heartbeat a chance to return to normal.

"Thou were degaussed."

"We were de-whated?"

"There is an ambient magnetic force that biologic entities carry," Boyle explained with uncharacteristic patience. The position of safety they were now in seemed to have softened his demeanor. "'Tis a force that the sentinels are strongly attracted to. Thy charges, however, were dissipated over the past day. The carpets in the office and sitting room were designed to drain the magnetism from thee. Just a few hours are enough for the process to finish. Once done, thou art accepted as proper guests of yon abode. The sentinels would not have harmed thee."

"And the intruders?"

"Their attractive forces were at maximum. The sentinels were drawn to them as moths to a flame. They stood no chance once the beasts were activated."

"What activated them?"

"'Twas thee, Benjamin Crisp." The corners of Boyle's eyes crinkled into his long nose and the corner of his mouth twitched almost imperceptibly upward, "The valves, remember?"

"I don't understand what you two are talking about." Miss Pimsby interrupted. "Can someone please explain so I can catch up?"

"There were two large barometers in the reception hallway. I'm sure you saw them." Crisp explained about the valves at their bases and how he opened them at Boyle's instructions. "What I don't get is where the mercury went."

"Into the sentinels, of course," answered Boyle. "They are crafted from a special alloy of which the most important ingredient is zinc. On its own the alloy is inert. Therefore the sentinels are nothing more than statues when in their dormant state. When infused with the mercury, however, energy is released. With an additional malleability agent that is added to the alloy, the energy allows the sentinels to become animated. Thou witnessed the impressive result of the process tonight."

"But the police must be on their way to the townhouse by now. Won't they get suspicious when they arrive and find statues wandering about?" Miss Pimsby asked.

"When their charge becomes meager the sentinels will return to their original resting places. When the magistrate arrives, they will once more be nothing but statues."

"What about the file room?" Crisp asked Miss Pimsby. "The thieves may search it and find something useful."

"I doubt what thou say'st true," Boyle broke in. "Those jackanapes will flee anon."

"Besides, I sealed it last night before I went to bed. Another bomb might get them into it but even that probably wouldn't work," explained Miss Pimsby. "And it's well hidden. It should be safe."

"Good job," he told her. With the problem of the townhouse settled, he turned to Boyle. "As long as you're in the mood to explain things, will you answer another question?"

"I shall endeavor to do my best."

"Why is your bust white? Is it made from an exotic form of ambrosium?"

Boyle looked slightly embarrassed. "'Tis a remnant

from long ago. The wife of one of my sponsors was not aware I resided within. She felt I clashed with her parlor décor and did not understand why her husband insisted on keeping me. I was treated with the coating to please her whim. 'Twas the compromise he made to keep me."

"I don't see how it matters any," Miss Pimsby said.

"Besides, you saved us tonight," Crisp added. "If you weren't there to show me how to activate the sentinels we would be prisoners right now. Thanks for your help."

"I was but fulfilling my duty Benjamin Crisp. Besides, the events of this evening have gone far in making up for the boredom of the past few months."

"We have a promise to fulfill ourselves, so I'm afraid it's time for us to get going." Crisp held Boyle's bust awkwardly. Despite having almost left it behind a few minutes ago, he now felt an odd reluctance to release it. "What do you want me to do with this?"

"Leave it where thou dost stand. One of the benefits of my position is the ability to pass through barriers others cannot. I shall still be able to keep watch over yon abode from here."

"I hate to think of you all alone and bored, Mr. Boyle," said Miss Pimsby. "We shan't forget you. As soon as we can we'll get you out of here."

Boyle bowed, said, "Take care mademoiselle," and began to retract toward the bust. By the time Crisp placed it on the floor, he was gone.

The bust continued to glow for a moment. When its energy faded away, the tunnel was immersed in darkness. Crisp suddenly felt like a giant snake had swallowed him and he was trapped in its long, cold belly. He shivered at the unpleasant thought, then reached into his pocket and pulled out his Pitch Stone. Following his lead, Miss Pimsby reached into her purse and pulled hers out as well. The presence of the two blazing stones filled the tunnel with light.

"That's better. Let's get going, shall we."

The trek to the other end of the passage was remarkably lengthy. To ease the monotony of the trip, he watched his and Miss Pimsby's shadows bob eerily on the narrow walls and listened to the sound of their footsteps, which created an echo that reverberated in front of and behind them as they walked. Finally, after what seemed like forever, they came to the sealed door at the end of the tunnel. Crisp, with a pang of apprehension, reached forward and tested its knob. The heavy brass handle twisted easily. With a sigh of relief, he cracked the door open and took a cautious peek past it. A narrow vertical tunnel with a metal ladder in its center greeted him. The ladder went straight up and he couldn't see the top.

"I'll go first," Crisp said.

He began to climb, and then continued and continued and continued to climb. His muscles started to ache a bit from the constant exertion.

"Are you going to make it?" he called down to Miss Pimsby when he couldn't see the floor anymore and still couldn't see the top.

"It's a bit tiring but I'll be okay." she answered.

He started to climb again. There was no point in going slowly. Hanging in place was just as exhausting as going up. Thankfully, after another minute he saw what looked like the end of the shaft. He checked Miss Pimsby, saw she was still right behind him, and then hauled himself the last bit of the way up.

Once he reached the top, a square cast iron box surrounded him. An iron handle hung down from its roof.

"We need to be quick. Are you ready?" he asked.

"Yes."

Crisp grunted as he spun then pushed the handle. The side of the iron box facing him began to swing open. It was cantilevered so that as it moved it lifted up above his head. After a minute it was open enough to clamber through. Miss Pimsby followed swiftly behind him.

They found themselves at the intersection of Victoria Street and Vauxhall Bridge Road. There was still a fair amount of activity about but luckily no one was looking their way. The fact that it was still twilight helped as well; the shadows hid their movements just enough to make them barely detectable.

Crisp swung the door closed. It locked itself with a barely audible click. He stood for a moment examining their exit. It was a miniature replica of Big Ben called Little

Ben. He must have passed it hundreds of times before but had never given it a second look. The door was seamless when closed, just like the other end of the tunnel. The door's action was well thought out as well. It prevented a telltale change in the clock's profile while open.

"Let's get going, shall we? It's best we don't stand around too much in the open."

"Where to first?"

"As we no longer have the use of my car I would say there," he answered as he pointed at Victoria Station.

They crossed Vauxhall Bridge Road and walked into the sprawling complex. The station's vaulted glass and metal girder roof hung high above them. They wandered past the many shops and stalls until they found an empty bench to sit on.

"If she doesn't return my message, I'll give Ms. Fairfield another ring when the museum opens."

Miss Pimsby didn't respond. He looked over at her. Her eyes were closed and she was taking slow, shallow breaths. He slid a bit closer to her and gently lowered her head to his shoulder. A faint scent of hibiscus and melon wafted up at him as it nestled in place. It was a nice smell, especially after the dank mustiness of the tunnel.

They were fortunate so far, this much was certain. But luck could change in an instant. She could rest; it was best that she did. He, however, would stay awake and keep watch for the enemies he now knew all too well.

14

The First Map

At 8:30 am Crisp gently shook Miss Pimsby awake.

"Ms. Fairfield called back," he told her as she stretched and yawned. "She's agreed to meet us at the museum at 9 o'clock. We have to get going."

"Can we at least get a bite to eat first?" she asked as she stifled yawn.

They walked to the closest food vendor and bought some muffins. Fortified with something warm in their stomachs they shuffled down to the tube and caught the next train to Holborn station.

Crisp was heartened by the sight that greeted him as he and Miss Pimsby walked toward the front of the museum. Repairs on the damaged wing were proceeding at a decent pace. Scaffolding climbed the damaged wall like a metal skeleton. A pile of pale bricks, looking like lumps of pale flesh, were stacked below it. These were being moved and pressed into place a swarm of efficient-looking construction workers.

When they reached the front door, they were greeted by a security guard. "Detective Crisp?" he asked. Crisp showed him his identification and they were led inside.

The route they took was familiar to Crisp. After all, it had only been a few days since he had last passed through it. Nevertheless, he felt different walking down the brightly lit corridor compared to the last time. It was like someone had pulled the old him out of his body and stuffed another version of him in its place. He sensed the old him was never coming back.

Melanie Fairfield stood up as he and Miss Pimsby crowded into her small office. "Detective Crisp, it's simply wonderful to see you again." She stuck her hand out and he gave it a gentle shake. "And who is this lovely lady."

"Miss Sophia Pimsby."

She stuck her hand out again. "It's a pleasure to meet you. Are you a detective too?"

Miss Pimsby reached for Fairfield's hand and glanced

awkwardly at Crisp instead of answering. "No, not exactly," he replied. "She works for another agency, an independent one, as a kind of investigator. But her help has been invaluable. I couldn't have found the herald trumpet without her."

"Then I am in your debt as well. Please sit down, both of you."

Once they were all settled into chairs she called for tea. "That should take a few minutes," she said when she was done. "We might as well get started. What can I help you with Detective?"

Crisp reached into his pants pocket and pulled out the drawing he made. He put it on the desk and slid it over to her. "I need to have a look at that."

Fairfield studied the drawing for a moment. "I remember this piece. It was in the Elizabethan exhibit, in a display not far from the trumpets. It's a fascinating artifact, one of my favorites. It's also been a bit of a headache ever since we acquired it."

"How so?"

"The Royal Naval Museum claims they should have it."

"Why," asked Miss Pimsby.

"They seem to think it's a nautical instrument that once belonged to Sir Francis Drake."

"And it isn't?" Crisp asked.

"The documents we have clearly indicate it was the property of William Byrd. Have you heard of him?"

"I'm familiar with the name."

"Then you know he was a musician and composer. The odd thing is the caretakers haven't a clue why he would have such a thing or what it was meant to do. Despite what the Royal Naval Museum claims, there isn't any mention of its true purpose in any of the historical records we've reviewed. I suppose that's why I find it so fascinating."

"It sounds like exactly what we're looking for. May we see it?"

"That may a bit of a problem."

"Why is that?"

"Many of the artifacts from the Elizabethan exhibit have been loaned out or put in storage until the building repairs are completed."

Crisp groaned. If the Augmenter was half-way around the world they'd never get it back in time. "Is there some way for you to find out where it went?"

"It should be in the inventory records. Give me a moment."

The tea arrived as Fairfield began to search her computer. He handed a cup to Miss Pimsby and took one for himself. She took a sip from hers but his sat in his lap, untouched, as he watched Fairfield inspect the series of official looking documents that came up on her screen.

"Ah, here it is. You're in luck. It's in the basement storeroom. I can take you to it, if you'd like."

Crisp put his tea back on its serving tray and stood up. "That would be marvelous. Shall we?"

Fairfield led Crisp and Miss Pimsby down a series of corridors and stairways until they reached a large room that was clearly the basement. The lights came on automatically as they descended the last set of steps, revealing a long row of enormous gray statues with lion heads. They passed these and then went by a row of metal shelves covered with smaller stone statues and various sized clay tablets. After this they turned right and went past a collection of oriental vases.

"We're almost there," Fairfield said.

The next turn they made brought to a section of the basement that looked like the one they needed. The artifacts were more modern and clearly of European origin.

"It should be in the fourth section, fifth shelf down."

Miss Pimsby saw it first. "That's it, isn't it?" she said, pointing to her left.

"Yes, you've found it," Fairfield said. She reached down, lifted it from the shelf, and gently handed it to Crisp. "Do be careful."

He turned it in his hands and inspected it closely. It wasn't quite the same as it looked in the picture. All of the pieces were present but the three cylinders were arranged in a different order. There was also one other feature that caught his eye. At one end, a series of numbers was etched crudely into the metal.

51   69   0   34

"Did the museum do this?" he asked Fairfield, showing it to her.

"Heavens no. Those were there when we acquired it."

Crisp thought as much but asked anyway to be thorough. Now came the hard part. He hoped he had built up enough good will with Fairfield to pull it off.

"You've been amazingly helpful, but I'm afraid I have one more favor to ask you."

"It's been my pleasure, Detective. What else can I do for you?"

"I need to borrow this for a little while."

The corner of her mouth drooped a little. "When you say borrow you don't mean—"

"Leave the museum with it. Yes, I'm afraid I do."

For a moment Crisp thought Fairfield was going to pass out and hit the floor. He readied himself in case he needed to catch her on the way down. Luckily, Fairfield regained her composure and managed to steady herself.

"I suppose your request is related to some terribly secret police business that you can't tell me much about," she said in a wavering voice.

"I'm afraid so."

"Can you at least tell me if this has anything to do with the men who stole the trumpet? The ones who got away. Will it help catch them?"

"As a matter of fact, it's the only chance we have of stopping them."

"And if I say no?"

"Then they'll get everything they want."

Fairfield grimaced but didn't answer right away. Crisp understood her hesitation. She was being asked to make a choice between bad and worse. Slowly, however, he saw the necessary courage begin to build in her eyes.

"Alright then, you can have it. But I can't just let you walk out the front door with it. We're going to have to hide it somehow."

"If we took it apart, the pieces should fit in my purse," Miss Pimsby suggested.

Fairfield gazed down at Miss Pimsby's bag. "It's not my

preferred method of transporting priceless artifacts but yes, I suppose it will do."

The three of them spent the next five minutes taking the Augmenter apart and storing it in the bottom of Miss Pimsby's purse. When it was safely tucked away, Fairfield led them back upstairs to the front lobby.

"Good luck," she said, "and, please, bring it back as soon as possible."

"I promise," Crisp said.

After Fairfield left them, Crisp took Miss Pimsby by the hand and led her to a secluded corner of the museum.

"What are you doing? Shouldn't we be leaving?"

"I want to look at something first."

Once he was sure no one was looking, he retrieved the atlas from his coat. Opening it, he flipped to a map that depicted an area east of London.

"What is it you're looking for?" Miss Pimsby asked. "Does this have something to do with the numbers you found at the end of the Augmenter?"

"Yes. There it is." He pointed down at the map. The numbered marking under his finger was identical to the one etched on Byrd's instrument. "I believe we've found our next destination."

"Honestly? Brilliant! Where are we going?"

"Somewhere between Stondon Massey and Ingate-stone."

Miss Pimsby gasped.

"What's the matter," he asked.

"Stondon Massey? That's where William Byrd lived near the end of his life."

"Well, then," Crisp said, "it seems like we're finally back on the right track.

* * *

Crisp figured the safest way to get where they were going was to continue using the train. This way there would always be other people around and, contrary to hiring a car, they couldn't be cut-off or diverted from their route. So he and Miss Pimsby returned to Holborn station and took the tube back to Victoria station. Once there,

Crisp purchased two tickets at the window and they boarded the eastbound train. After finding a comfortable and private place to sit, he passed the time watching the scenery go by and talking with Miss Pimsby about what they might find when they got to Ingatestone. Their eager exchange was interrupted only once, when they made a change at Liverpool station.

As the trip wore on, Crisp realized how nice it was to have Miss Pimsby as a traveling companion. She was irrepressible and it was contagious. Each increasingly unlikely scenario that sprang from her fevered imagination acted like a balm, soothing the sense of urgency he felt since their escape from the townhouse. By the time the train arrived at the Ingatestone station platform, he felt refreshed and ready to take on the next challenge awaiting them.

Crisp stepped onto the platform first, followed closely by Miss Pimsby. He inspected the angular brick structure before him for a minute and then searched the platform for anything unusual. No large men were standing about staring at their shoes so he figured they were safe for the moment.

They hired a cab in front of the station. It took them to High Street. The first order of business they attended to after being dropped off was finding a room to rent for the night. It wasn't easy, but they managed to find an empty one over a baker's shop. Once this was done, they had one more order of business to take care of.

"How are we supposed to get all the way out there?" Miss Pimsby asked as they sat on the bed studying the atlas. "It seems a bit too far to walk."

"That's already been arranged."

"How did you manage that?"

"The baker asked why we were looking for a room. I told him we wanted to get out of London for a bit and explore the surrounding area. It just so happens he owns several bicycles. He was more than happy to rent two of them to us."

Crisp and Miss Pimsby spent the next few hours getting some fitful rest. When he wasn't staring sleeplessly at the ceiling, Crisp was double-checking the map for the best route to their destination.

Close to ten o'clock, they exited the room. Night had settled on the town and High Street was mostly deserted. A quick search around the side of the building revealed the bicycles they were promised. Crisp waved Miss Pimsby toward the closest one with a flourish.

Their trip through the countryside felt strange to him. The night air was cool and still and the bicycles whisked almost noiselessly along the nearly deserted back roads. Shredded wisps of cloud intermittently obscured the moon which made the darkness almost complete. The lack of sensation made his body feel like it was floating through empty space.

Once at their destination, however, reality quickly reestablished itself. The area on the map corresponded to an empty plot of land. It's approximately a dozen acres spread out like a large carpet. The end closest to him was tilled but nothing had been planted in the furrows. At least nothing much appeared to be sprouting from the rich looking soil, although it was hard to tell in the dark. The field sloped gently upwards going away from him. A small copse of trees stuck up like wiry bristles on the far end.

For Crisp it was depressingly ordinary. How could this be a place that would hide an amazing secret? But then he realized the empty patch of sea Sir Drake kept going back to must not have seemed like much either. All that mattered to the map was where it was, not what was there.

Crisp decided the tuft of trees was the most likely place to be hiding a clue. "C'mon, this way," he said, taking Miss Pimsby by the hand so they wouldn't be separated as they made their way across the field. When they reached the trees he became slightly worried. They were quite close knit. He thought it might be difficult to go through them but, to his relief, their branches were supple and he was able to push past them easily. After about thirty yards he bumped into something hard and rough.

"This must be what we're looking for."

Crisp pulled the Pitch Stone from his pocket. If the shed was made by the Academy there was a chance it would light up. When it didn't react he put the Pitch Stone back. He then started to feel around. The roof was covered with slate and some moss. It was remarkably well preserved for its obvious age. Still unable to see much he followed the wall until he reached a corner. He continued to trace the low wall until he came to a door.

After checking to make sure Miss Pimsby was still behind him he ducked down low and went through the door. She entered right after him.

The shed's floor consisted of firmly packed dirt. The walls were plain fieldstone except for a small shelf built into the far right corner. Its most distinguishing feature was an iron frame with two hooks set around a small opening in the roof.

"Would you mind retrieving the item in question?"

While Miss Pimsby pulled the three cylinders out of her purse, Crisp retrieved the drawing he made. As she handed him the pieces, he studied it with the little light that was available. It was good thing he still had it. There appeared to be multiple ways the cylinders could go back together. Without the drawing to guide him, it would have been easy to reconstruct it the wrong way.

"That's seems about right," he said once the instrument was back in one piece. He lifted it and tried to set it on the hooks hanging from the iron frame. It fit perfectly, with one end pointing at the sky and the other at the center of the floor.

Unfortunately, the moon was still shrouded by a large cloud. The interior of the shed was cramped so Crisp and Miss Pimsby clambered back out the door and settled on either side of it to wait for the sky to clear.

Crisp kept his eyes glued upwards. As he watched, a breeze began to whisper through the tiny forest. A moment later, a faint sound caught his well-trained ear. It was hard to distinguish at first from the rustling of the braches. As soon as it began, however, it stopped. He decided it was nothing it and turned his attention back to the cloud covering the moon. It was drifting slowly despite the breeze. Luckily a big patch of clear sky stretched behind it. He figured they needed to wait only a few minutes more before some moonlight broke through.

"This is actually quite a lovely spot," Miss Pimsby whispered.

"Shhh," Crisp whispered back, interrupting her. He didn't mean to be rude but the sound he heard earlier was back again. It was barely audible but getting louder. Whatever was making the noise was moving closer to them.

Miss Pimsby saw it before he did. She pointed toward the road. "Someone's down there," she whispered, sounding a bit shaken.

Crisp squinted through the thicket of branches. A faint glow was making its way across the field. It weaved and bobbed as it approached. The movement of the light suggested a man holding a lantern as he stumbled over rough terrain. The sound he heard was clearly coming from the same direction.

He watched in frozen fascination as the light continued to move unevenly toward them. As it closed in he was able to make out the sound more clearly. It was an unsettling wail of despair. He looked over at Miss Pimsby. She must not have heard it. Her attention was still focused on the light. This was probably for the best. The desperate cry was disturbing and only would have shaken her even more.

He thought of moving somewhere safer but there was no such place on the property. The shed might have thick walls but it also had only one exit. To go in there now would have boxed them into a potential trap. The best thing possible was to stay quiet and still and hope they weren't noticed.

An odd feature about the approaching stranger suddenly became apparent to him. Whoever it was continued to move as though in a hurry, but none of the sounds of a fleeing man reached them. No thudding footfalls or heaving breaths traveled up to their perch. All that persisted was the eerie wail that only he seemed to hear.

As the light moved closer it began to increase in size. The faint amorphous glow also started to take on the outline of a human form. As the figure came upon them it was finally clear who their nocturnal visitor was. He stared in fascination as a wispy imitation of a woman carrying a man's severed head fell to her knees at the edge of the woods. A look of pure fear crossed her face before she turned away from them. Crisp caught enough of it, despite its translucent and hazy form, to see that she was quite pretty. He also managed a glimpse at the severed head she was carrying. It was of a young looking man. There was a definite family resemblance but its facial features carried a look of disbelief as opposed to the terror on the woman's.

The woman's body suddenly convulsed violently. When it did she dropped the head. As soon as it separated from her body the vision disappeared as if it were smoke drifting away from a fire.

Miss Pimsby shuddered slightly and clung to Crisp's arm. "That was scary. I hope she doesn't decide to come back."

In contrast to Miss Pimsby, the apparition left Crisp riveted with fascination. It was like an extremely crude but nonetheless similar version of the ghost produced by Doctor Dee and Boyle. Only this was the natural version—not the harnessed kind that was utilized by the Academy. Somehow he knew its presence in the field was not a coincidence.

Before he could spend much time thinking about it the shred of cloud finally gave way to clear sky. As the moonlight came filtering down he was pulled back to the reason he was sitting in the field at midnight in the first place. He turned to the still shivering Miss Pimsby and said, "Follow me."

They reentered the low stone structure. Crisp was pleased to see a shaft of moonlight filtering down from the window in the roof. A splash of the reflected light spilled out over the dirt floor. He went over to the window and peered through it again. The almost full moon was visible in the top right section of the glass. He adjusted the iron frame accordingly. The lens captured the scattered light and it hit the floor in a concentrated circular beam.

"The original moon roof," Crisp said with a grin.

He opened his jacket, pulled the atlas out of its concealed pocket and flipped to the first Moonstone map. It was the one that included London and areas toward the east of the city. He dropped to his knees and laid it in the center of the bright beam. Time seemed to be temporarily suspended as he watched the map bathe in the thick, almost solid, cone of light.

The map began to glow and crackle, the same as during his other attempts to get it to work, but this time it didn't extinguish itself. His excitement grew even greater as its usual features were washed away and a column of shimmering words took their place.

"Get the pad that you have out of your purse," Crisp said to Miss Pimsby.

She was kneeling next to him and watching the map as if in a trance. His request broke the spell. She pulled the pad and pen out just as the words became clear enough to read:

The pearl of the first map thy hath revealed

Upon a sacred quest now have thee set.

In moonbeam, lit and glowing on yon field

May thy soul with peril ere long be met.

Perchance luck hath obtained for thee these words

Thy heart must prove true friend and nay foul foe

No rogue who shuns fair toil o' morning birds.

Instead, pray thee know all but friend would know.

A place thou still must find amongst the land

Where map insists on length cross'd by leeway

Noted by vassals linked to airy strand,

Without thus it will never have its say.

The moon on map yet fired does align

As seen by friend who turns water to wine.

"Do you have that copied down exactly?"
"Yes."
He pulled the map out of the path of the beam. It immediately fizzled and the words disappeared from view.

161

He flipped the pages of the atlas to the second map. A little more hesitantly he eased it into the moonlight. It began to glow for a moment but just like before it quickly fizzled out.

"That wasn't going to work," Miss Pimsby said as she reviewed the words scribbled on her pad.

"It was worth a try," he said with a shrug.

"That's one map down." Miss Pimsby seemed quite pleased.

Crisp was reminded of his dictum. The way to solve a problem was one step at a time and getting the first map to work was a clear sign that they were on the right path. Miss Pimsby was correct. It was something to be encouraged about. For the moment it would have to be enough.

15
Mind your Manor

A few loose ends needed to be tightened up before Crisp and Miss Pimsby could leave Ingatestone. Where to go next was the most pressing issue. The first Moonstone map was cryptic on this point. When morning came they went over what it revealed, hoping it would help them make the right choice.

"It just doesn't make sense to me," Crisp said after they finished reading the poem carefully for the third time.

"What do you mean?" asked Miss Pimsby. "I think it makes perfect sense."

"I'm not talking about the poem itself."

They sat in the room's small living area. Crisp stood up and began to pace. His ability to concentrate was not being helped by his hunger and the smell of fresh baked goods wafting up from below them.

"Why did they feel the need to make a secret map to hide a secret map? It seems a bit of overkill, wouldn't you say, especially now when we have a deadline hanging over us?"

"Yes, perhaps, but I doubt Byrd and Dee ever thought the compositions would have to be found in a hurry. They might have even been alarmed at the thought of someone rushing to get them. They were obviously much more comfortable with us taking our time and being sure that what we were doing was worth the effort."

Crisp began to rub the back of his head as he walked. "I'm not so sure," he replied stubbornly.

"Let's go over the whole thing again shall we? We'll take it one bit at a time."

"Fine."

He sprawled wearily back into his chair. Despite Miss Pimsby's reasoned explanation he was still feeling disgruntled. His mood, admittedly, was also due to his lack of sleep over the past two nights.

"We agree on most of the broader points."

Michael Malik

He noticed that a businesslike tone now infected Miss Pimsby's voice. She seemed determined to convince him she was right

"This is the first map, the poem says as much. It also indicates that our path to finding the compositions will encompass some risk."

"That's certainly an understatement." A tired grin leaked onto his lips. "I suppose having bombs chucked at us counts as risk. Don't you agree?"

"Hmm—"

Miss Pimsby was still reading and didn't answer him right away. After a moment she looked up. The realization of what Crisp just said seemed to lighten her disposition.

"Yes it certainly would qualify," she answered with a short burst of laughter.

Her reaction to his joke pleased him. Being the Academy's archivist often made her feel the need to act the part. He knew better. She was smart and helpful. She was even more so, however, when she relaxed and trusted herself.

"What's next?"

"There are other hints within the poem that help confirm its purpose." His trick worked. Her eager voice, the one he found so charming, was back.

"You're speaking of the reference to morning birds I assume. That's obviously meant to confirm that Byrd wrote the poem and it's meant to lead us to his compositions."

"Yes, that's one hint. Another one is the mention of airy vassals. Those have to be angels since it's their language the compositions translate. It's all meant to be an indirect way of cluing us in. If we have the proper knowledge then the hints tell us we're on the right track."

"Of course we have the proper knowledge. Who else would be sticking the map under a moonbeam in Essex?"

"You forget, Dee and Byrd had learned others were interested in their attempt to translate angel language. How much had been learned? Who had leaked the information? These questions must have been in their thoughts and I'm sure they hid the compositions with them in mind."

"So?"

164

"So, if the breach was bigger than suspected, if the maps were stolen and the shed discovered then without the extra layer of protection provided by another map, the compositions would be vulnerable."

"It wasn't as easy as you make it sound. We had the inside track and still could easily have missed finding the connection between the Moonstone map and the shed."

"But once we did it didn't take any special ability to stick the map under the moonbeam. We proved that tonight. All we needed was the map, the Augmenter, and a clear night alone in the shed. Even more importantly, there was no special proof of intent involved. We could have the worst intentions for the compositions, like those awful men in the cemetery. The map would reveal itself to us just the same."

"How is a map supposed to figure out if we mean well?"

"It can't. That's my point."

Crisp sat in sullen silence for a moment.

"I concede that the first map isn't a foolproof safe guard. What I don't see is how the second map will be any better."

"Byrd tells us in the poem. He wanted to be absolutely sure the only person who could get to the compositions was a member of the Academy."

"How did he do that?"

"It's brilliant actually," Miss Pimsby answered as she scanned her note pad again. "The poem part is a bit old fashioned but it still works."

"As what?"

"As an instruction manual."

"You're referring to the final line I take it."

"As seen by friend who turns water to wine," Miss Pimsby read out loud. "Yes, that seems to be the essential point."

"But that's mental. We're not miracle workers."

"Sometimes the work the Academy does and the knowledge its members have compiled is hard to believe. But an important thing I've learned over the past year is to never say 'that's impossible'. It's all quite real and what's more it's all based on sound scientific principles."

165

Miss Pimsby's words finally sank into Crisp and he realized he was being a bit of a prat. Negativity wasn't going to solve anything. Unfortunately, despite his decision to stop grumbling, he saw one more problem that he couldn't ignore.

"If you're right, there's one major hurdle we'll need to overcome," he said, trying to sound contrite. "Albert is the only Academy member we know. He also happens to be at his secret meeting." At least he hoped that's where he was. There had been no contact from him or anyone else from the Academy. If Albert had met with his fellow members as planned, word should have come from somebody by now. "Isn't there some way we can get in touch with him?"

"I'm afraid not. Albert told me the meeting is held in total seclusion."

"You must see the problem then. If we need a member to decode the clue in the first map then we're blocked from using it too."

"That's why I think we have to go back to Cambridge and find a way into the laboratory. A text telling us how to do what the map asks should be in there somewhere."

"What about that door in his study. I've examined it pretty closely. Its latch is completely hidden. If it's locked tight it may be impossible to open without instructions."

"I've seen Albert go through that door dozens of times. I'm pretty sure I know how to open it," Miss Pimsby said with confidence.

"How about the archives?" he asked. "Wouldn't they be a logical place to look instead of the manor? We know we can get in there."

"The archives probably hold a document confirming the existence of a way to turn water into wine," Miss Pimsby agreed, "but there are some limitations on what it would reveal. That kind of work has always been kept under close guard in the member's individual laboratories. Plus the archives are in nothing more than a vast storage vault. It doesn't contain facilities for performing experiments. Even if we did find a complete set of instructions we wouldn't be able to do anything with it. I'm convinced the lab in Albert's house is our best bet."

"It's settled then." Crisp said. "We'll go to Cambridge and break into the laboratory."

On the way out, they thanked the baker and bought a few crumpets for breakfast. The baker's assistant drove them to the station, where they purchased their tickets. They ate the crumpets while waiting for their train to arrive.

An empty compartment was available in one of the last cars. A sense of comfort flooded through Crisp as he and Miss Pimsby settled into their seats. It suddenly occurred to him how much time he was spending on the train lately. It almost felt like a second home.

* * *

Several hours later Crisp sat bolt upright. His eyelids were barely cracked and felt like a sandbox. He gently rubbed them open the rest of the way. Miss Pimsby slowly came into focus. She sat on the bench across from him with a magazine folded in her lap.

"What happened? Where are we?" he asked groggily.

"You fell asleep before the train even started moving. As for where we are, I'd say about ten minutes from Cambridge station."

"Why didn't you wake me?"

"You looked like you needed the rest."

"No sign of our attackers?"

"Don't worry," she said as if reading his mind. "If anything dicey started I would have got you up immediately."

Her reply made him feel a bit foolish. If anyone had shown they were good in a pinch she had. He had every reason to trust her. "That's good. It was getting to the point where I expected them behind every bush."

"Maybe we lost them for good when we escaped through the tunnel."

Crisp gave her a skeptical look. "It's worth hoping for but something tells me we haven't seen the last of that crew." He shifted his weight so he could get into his pants pocket and pulled out his mobile phone.

"Who are you calling?" Miss Pimsby asked.

"We'll need a ride to Albert's house when arrive at Cambridge. I'm going to call Sergeant Major Wilkins and ask him to pick us up." He looked down at his phone. "Bollocks. The battery is dead and the charger is in the trunk of my car. Do you have a phone on you?"

"Sorry, no. I spend most of my time in the Archives. There isn't any reception down there so I gave up having one."

"We'll contact him when we get to the station then."

Once they arrived at Cambridge, Crisp immediately went to look for a public telephone. He thought he remembered seeing one of the bright red booths on his last trip down. With Miss Pimsby trailing closely behind him, he quickly found the spot he was searching for. He left the door open as he spoke into the phone receiver since no one was loitering close enough to overhear him.

The Sergeant Major sounded quite pleased and strangely not at all surprised to hear from Crisp again. He just returned from running some tourists to the University. As soon as he refueled the cab he would pop over to the station to pick them up.

Crisp hung up the phone after all the arrangements were complete. Instead of exiting the booth, however, he immediately picked the receiver back off its cradle.

"Who are you calling now?" asked Miss Pimsby.

"I want to chat with a fellow detective in London."

"What for?"

"Our conversation on the train got me wondering about something. He should be able to satisfy my curiosity."

Crisp dialed the number to the direct extension he needed. Three rings sounded before there was a response.

"Detective Sergeant Little"

"Reg, its Benjamin."

"Ben," Little replied heartily, "how's the holiday coming along?"

"I've had an interesting time. But you know me. I can't help wondering what's going on. Have you caught up with the museum thieves yet?"

"I wish," Little said with longing in his voice. "It's been a right mess. I've chased every lead no matter how unlikely. The search has barely left me time to sleep. I thought I might have caught a break a few nights ago. There was an odd bombing of a townhouse in Westminster."

"You don't say."

"By the time Trevor and I got there, though, the place was deserted. Now we're having a hard time even figuring out who owns the place. Like I said, it's been a right mess."

"How about the herald trumpet? It's still safe in the evidence room, I hope."

"It is for now."

"What do you mean?"

"The crowd that manages these things for the Royal family has been clamoring to get it back. We keep telling them if it's returned it could lose its value as evidence. The blokes don't seem to care. They want their stuff back regardless."

"How did you manage to hold them off?"

"Fuller has gotten personally involved. So far he's kept on top of them."

"I don't envy you, Reg. Even with Fuller's help, you've got your hands full."

"Don't I know it."

Crisp saw Wilkins' cab in the distance. "Well thanks for the news and good luck with the investigation. It sounds like it's going to keep you busy for a while yet."

"Wish you were back here helping, mate."

"Sorry. Can you do me one last favor, though?"

"Sure, what is it?"

"If something changes can you give me a ring?"

"I'll try my best," Little answered.

"I'm staying at my uncle's house in Cambridge. You can reach me there for now." Crisp gave him the number.

"Well that answers one question," he said to Miss Pimsby after he hung up the phone.

"What question?" she asked as they walked toward the front of the station.

"The thieves are still at large. I was hoping they'd been caught. It was your mention of the tunnel that made me think of it. Reg checked it out but they got away before he arrived. We'll still have to be on the watch for them."

Crisp finished talking just as their cab pulled up. Wilkins caught sight of them, got out of the auto and shuffled over to where they were standing.

"I'm pleased to see you again sir." He doffed his cap, "and you as well ma'am." He shifted his gaze to their feet. "No bags this trip?"

"I'm afraid not Sergeant Major."

Crisp was well aware of his increasingly rumpled appearance. The distress it would have normally caused him passed long ago. There was something about the events of the past few days that kept him from caring about what he now saw as a minor detail. All the same he was amazed at Miss Pimsby's continued ability to look so tidy.

They left the station with the cab's usual fitful grinding of gears and shuttering start. Wilkins asked a few polite questions as they drove, but none that were too probing. He knew better from his many years driving Albert.

The rest of the trip was eventful only in that they made a short detour to Mrs. Twilliger's house to get Albert's front door key. She was the woman who was keeping house for Albert. Her short plump body moved with remarkable agility as she whirled through her reception room passing out tea and sandwiches. She assured them, as she gracefully poured Wilkins a second cup of tea, that everything was in order at the manor and that Albert's pantry was well stocked with food. Crisp's appetite was amply satisfied before they finally managed to collect the key. And this came only after promising her she could check in on them in a few days.

Albert's home was not far from Mrs.Twilliger's. They pulled up into the circular front drive and Wilkins let them out of the cab. He waited long enough to see that the front door opened.

"Call me when you're ready to leave," he reminded them. He then got back in the cab and drove off.

Crisp and Miss Pimsby entered the front hall. He couldn't help feeling like a hundred years had passed since they were last there. So much had happened. It also felt empty without Albert greeting them from his usual perch at the top of the stairs.

"Let's freshen up a bit. I'll meet you in the study in fifteen minutes."

"I'll be down in a jif," she answered.

Instead of going to his usual room Crisp went upstairs to Albert's. He needed a change of clothes. As the jacket he was wearing attested, they were close to the same build. He took it off and threw it on the bed. A search of the closet revealed some freshly laundered slacks and a jumper that wasn't too old-fashioned. Once he was washed up and changed he returned downstairs. The doors to the study were still closed, which meant Miss Pimsby wasn't down yet. He opened them wide and walked through them. The oak paneled room was beginning to get dark as the sunlight from the windows faded. He strode across the carpeted floor, took a seat behind the desk and began to stare at the bookshelf, hoping as he did that Miss Pimsby was right when she'd said she knew how to open its secret door.

"Oh, you startled me." Miss Pimsby said as she entered the room. She wore some new clothes as well. The colorful blouse and matching skirt looked nice on her. "For a moment I thought you were Albert. I almost went back into the hall to call for you."

"No such luck; it's just me," Crisp answered as he stood up. He turned the lights on from a switch on the desk. "That's better. Now let's get behind that." He pointed at the bookshelf as he walked toward it.

Miss Pimsby joined him. "If my memory is right I need to rub my finger gently down the spine of this book here," she ran her left first finger along it as she spoke, "then press it gently here." She touched the bottom of another book.

Crisp noticed the second book was the *Autobiography of Benjamin Franklin*. As Miss Pimsby's finger pressed against it, the bookshelf popped silently open.

"The mechanism has something to do with a discharge of static electricity I think. At least that's what Albert mentioned to me once. The first book builds it on my finger and the second detects it."

"Well done."

Michael Malik

The door opened into a short but gloomy passage. The light filtering into it from the study allowed them, just barely, to still see as they walked down it.

"Blimey, you can't be serious." Crisp uttered when they reached the passage's far end. He was staring at another door. It was large and impressive and, by the looks of it, tightly locked.

16
Sanctum Laboratorium

Crisp gave the vault-like door a good tug. Predictably, it didn't budge. Miss Pimsby fixed her disapproving librarian look on him.

"It was worth a go. Albert might have left it ajar," he said.

The next thing he and Miss Pimsby did was examine the passage for anything Albert may have left behind. What exactly it might be was hard to say. There was no visible opening in the door for a key. This was not terribly surprising. All of the secret Academy doors they encountered so far contained a hidden latch. They decided to look despite this glaring discrepancy. Their ability to see was so limited, however, that they abandoned the attempt after a few minutes.

Since the top edge of the door's metal frame wasn't reachable without a step or a ladder Crisp began groping around its edges. He concentrated on looking for a depression or groove. When that failed, Miss Pimsby searched along the floor for a secret pedal. Again nothing was found.

Well past midnight, Crisp finally admitted defeat. The skill required to open the door escaped him at the moment. He and Miss Pimsby agreed to get some rest and return when they could inspect things thoroughly and with a fresh perspective.

When morning arrived, Crisp was the first to wake up. He started off the day by pilfering Albert's closet again. This time he chose a Benson & Clegg shirt and pants combination that fit him remarkably well. His jacket was still lying forgotten on Albert's bed. He grabbed it and brought it with him. Once downstairs, he laid it on a chair in the entrance hall.

Instead of waiting for Miss Pimsby, Crisp went into the study and repeated her actions from the night before. The study wall again popped open silently. He swung it as wide as it would go and saw with satisfaction that the tunnel was bright almost all the way to the back.

Once he reached the door the first thing he noticed was two torch holders coming from the wall on either side of it. They were black and set in place above eye level. Their color and position made them easy to miss in the semi-darkness. Crisp grabbed one and attempted to twist and turn it. It was solidly anchored and didn't move. He tried the other one with the same results.

The remainder of the tunnel was no more forthcoming with clues than the night before. The floor and walls were extremely solid looking. He tapped them in several places while listening for a hollow sound. There were no dead spaces that may have given away a paneled nook. There weren't even wires or outlets to indicate a connection to a power source.

"Any luck yet?" Miss Pimsby stood in the entrance of the tunnel, framed by sunlight.

"None whatsoever," Crisp answered with a tinge of disgust. "You're sure this is the only place we're going to get the answer to the map?"

"I'm afraid it is."

"There's no point standing around here then," he said as he moved toward her. "We might as well get back to the study and keep searching. Perhaps we'll find a note from Albert—something cryptic that's written in goat's blood and pinned under the carpet. Then we can bop right inside the lab."

"I hardly think now is the proper time for levity."

Crisp shrugged. "I'm well aware that we're stuck and running out of time. It's just that I refuse to believe that we can't get in. All doors are made to open. We just need the right password. Something tells me 'Open Sesame' won't cut it, though."

"I agree with you, there's something we're missing, but—"

"No buts. There has to be a way in."

"You don't understand. Only full-fledged Natural Philosophers or their apprentices are supposed to be allowed into an Academy laboratory. I thought I was so clever. I thought Albert was so impressed with me he shared something he wasn't supposed to. The truth is, knowing how to open the bookshelf door wasn't important at all."

"It was important," he said as they reentered the front hall. "Besides, we still have time left, so keep your chin up. We'll get in."

"Yes—but—I'm beginning to worry that you were right. We need Albert. We can't go on without him."

"Maybe we'll get lucky. Or maybe Albert will return and save the day."

Not bloody likely. But as quickly as the negative idea popped out it was shoved back into his subconscious. He didn't feel like playing that game at the moment. He promised himself he would stay positive and that was what he was going to do.

"I'll brew some tea and fry some eggs. After we've had a bite we'll go back to the study."

Since she didn't have a better idea Miss Pimsby agreed to his plan. "But let me fix the eggs and tea," she insisted. "You head to the study and see if any ideas come to you."

Crisp watched Miss Pimsby disappear toward the kitchen before going back into the study. He went to the center of the room and peered around. Where to start? After a few minutes of glancing around he flopped down on the couch. He tucked a hand in between the cushions and pulled out a bit of lint. It was the only thing he found. All of the room's other nooks and crevices were not only bare, but sparklingly clean. Even the books that were in such disarray after Dee had been taken seemed to be back in their proper places. He suspected Mrs. Twilliger's hand was responsible for the pristine state he now found everything to be in.

While searching the shelves Crisp found himself becoming engrossed by the quality and rarity of the volumes in Albert's collection. There was a first edition of John Locke's collected works. He picked up another book that turned out to be an 1860 edition of Darwin's *Origin of the Species*. He flipped through its pages but nothing unusual stood out about it. He next spied a seven volume set of the works of Shakespeare edited by Lewis Theobald in

Michael Malik

1733. He was about to lift volume one off the shelf when Miss Pimsby came in with their meal.

"There are several rare books up there," Crisp said to Miss Pimsby as they ate. "If the thieves were a bit more observant when they took Doctor Dee they could have made off with a small fortune."

"For instance?"

He told her what he found during his search. "And I've only been through a fraction of them so far."

Miss Pimsby seemed impressed. "I've never looked things over when I've been here before. Albert always got down to business quickly and gave me quite a bit to do. It sounds like Mr. Oxtail would have loved it here."

"Who?" Crisp asked, once again pleasantly amused by one of her strange tangents.

"Mr. Oxtail, my old grammar instructor. He adored writing and old books. We got along quite well. He even encouraged me to continue my literature studies after I graduated. I wanted to do something more exciting so when the opportunity to become archivist presented itself I jumped at the chance. I thought it would provide more stimulation than teaching English composition."

"I would say you got that one right."

Crisp and Miss Pimsby finished eating and then went back to work. A half hour later they shared a brief burst of excitement when she found something in an original 1776 edition of *An Inquiry into the Nature and Causes of the Wealth of Nations*, but it turned out to be a note from Adam Smith thanking Sir Chauncey Mills for helping him with his theory on free market economies.

"Sir Chauncey was the first Mills to become a member of the Academy." Miss Pimsby remarked offhand as she tucked the note back in its place.

The section of bookshelf that held Albert's theology texts was the last area they checked. Nothing useful showed up. No hidden panels, no notes, not even in the 1455 Johann Gutenberg Bible that he found among the other less famous works, despite his turning the pages one by one.

Crisp put the precious book back where he found it. He then went back to the desk and slumped down in the

176

chair. Miss Pimsby put the book she was examining back on the shelf as well.

"I don't think we're on the right track. We need to take a few steps back," he said to her. "Let's take a look at what the first map said again. Maybe it will inspire us. Do you have your note pad?"

"It's in my handbag up in my room. I'll go get it."

She returned a few minutes later with her purse in hand. She set it on the desk and began to empty some of its contents.

"Here it is," she said finally.

Miss Pimsby tried to hand it to Crisp but he was staring at the small pile she created on the desk. Sitting on top like a cherry was the Pitch Stone. A dull reddish glow radiated from its core once again. He looked from it to the open bookshelf door and back again.

"These gadgets seem to have an affinity for secret passages. They reacted in the one under the townhouse. I wonder if they'll do the same thing here."

He picked up Miss Pimsby's Pitch Stone and carried it into the secret laboratory hall. Its dull glow increased with each step he took. When he finally reached the door it was entirely red and pulsing with what seemed like anticipation. He gave the door another tug but it didn't budge.

"This produced bright white light in the other passage," he said to himself as Miss Pimsby looked on. He searched the door again and his eyes settled on the torch holders. "Of course. How daft can a person be?"

Before Miss Pimsby could answer his rhetorical question he reached up and dropped the stone in one of the torch holders. It immediately burst into bright white light that illuminated every corner of the passage. He tugged on the door once again to no effect.

"Wait here a moment," he told Miss Pimsby. "I'll be right back."

He ran out of the passage and into the front hall. The jacket his uncle gave him was still where he had left it. He grabbed it off the chair and raced back into the tunnel. Once he was in front of the door again he reached into the jacket pocket that held the Pitch Stone. It was throbbing and red just like Miss Pimsby's had been. He placed it in

Michael Malik

the other torch holder. It lit up as well. More importantly, as soon as it settled into place a loud clunking noise emanated from the door. Crisp tugged again. This time the door swung open easily. The portal into Albert's secret laboratory was finally open.

* * *

Crisp stood frozen in front of the door, a mixture of satisfaction and mild shock coursing through him.

"That was brilliant," Miss Pimsby said as she peered through the opening.

"Actually I'd say it was harder than it needed to be," Crisp said sheepishly. "The answer was in our hands all along."

"It was our own fault. Albert told us to keep the things he gave us close at all times."

"It was something else he said that led me to the answer, actually."

He and Miss Pimsby stepped through the lab's entrance as he explained. "When I saw the Pitch Stone I remembered it. He hinted that they're good for keeping secrets. It was like he wanted to tell us how to get in here but couldn't bring himself to do it. The way the stones reacted in the other tunnel then flashed through my mind. For some reason the two thoughts spliced together."

"Thank goodness they did."

"It's all a bit strange, though. It would have been much easier for Albert to leave us instructions. He gave you some for the townhouse."

"The townhouse doesn't have one of these," Miss Pimby said softly. She stood cemented in place as her gaze traveled reverently over the sight before them. "My father worked for the Academy for forty years and never saw this."

Rudimentary looking Pitch Stones set in torch holders lit up upon their entry. The illumination they provided was more than adequate for Crisp to get a good first look of the laboratory. He was willing to admit that it was impressive.

The ceiling was soaring and vaulted. Great arched beams that were intricately carved with inscriptions spanned across it. The words were too high up for him to make out clearly but they seemed to be in Latin. A bookshelf that dwarfed the one in the study took up one entire wall. It went almost all the way up to the ceiling. There were two ladders that ran the length of the shelf. The first was attached to a rail along the floor. A second ladder was on a balcony that split the bookshelf into an upper and lower level. A spiral staircase wound to the upper level at the far end of the room.

"And I thought Albert owned more than enough books already," he said. "That's not going to make it easy to find the formula we're looking for."

"I can take care of that," Miss Pimsby said. "I am an Academy archivist after all. It may take a bit of time but I'll find the formula."

She strode off in the direction of the massive bookshelf with a look of determination anchored on her face.

Realizing it was better to stay out of Miss Pimsby's way, Crisp went back to perusing the room. His attention was drawn to the wall opposite the bookshelf. Its most prominent feature was a large poster that resembled the periodic table of elements only it wasn't quite the same as the one he remembered studying in school. It was arranged with extra elements that were placed intermittently between the standard ones. The ones he didn't recognize were annotated with a Q after their atomic numbers. He searched for ambrosium and found it under the symbol Ab 26Q.

A smaller framed print was hanging next to the periodic table. It displayed a list that was titled The Eight Rules:

1. Be reserved and silent
2. Work in a remote private home
3. Choose your working hours prudently
4. Be patient watchful and tenacious
5. Work on a fixed plan
6. Use only glass or glazed earthenware crucibles
7. Be rich enough to pay for your experiments
8. Have nothing to do with princes and nobles

Crisp thought that the list described Albert almost perfectly.

There was something that appeared to be a large blast furnace built in the far corner. He went to get a better look. A heavy looking cast iron door hung open on its front, revealing its inner cavity. The heavy soot stains he saw lining its thick walls confirmed his initial impression. It looked capable of withstanding enormous amounts of heat.

A large waist high bench in the center of the room was his next stop. It was covered with beakers and test tubes of various shapes and sizes. Copper pipes and Bunsen burners were mixed amongst the glass vials. Some of the beakers were still half full of a congealed substance, which reminded him of the hurry Albert was in the night before he left. There was even a book left lying open on the near end of the bench. He went over to look at it.

Elaborate writing traced across the top of the exposed page. He stared at it for a few seconds before he figured out that it was the instructions for creating a Pitch Stone. Since Miss Pimsby still looked busy, he decided to read them.

Pitch Stones

2 Silicon Fe grain oriented magnetic cores

12 dr. Large Particulate Strontium Aluminate: 63 Q (dopant)

2 lb. Pitch stabilizer

14 un. Germanium coat

8 un. Enamel shell

Place cores in ceramic mold. Orient cores in the center spaced evenly apart. Add SA and use stabilizer to keep particulates well distributed around the core. Add the germanium followed by the enamel coat. Fire at 1250 degrees celcius to create the proper projection. Do not reheat above 1090 degrees Celsius. Split when cooled to 500 degrees Celsius. Rapidly cool in ice bath. Stones will be ready for use when the shell is hardened.

Crisp looked at the periodic table on the wall. 63:Q was listed as avalonium. It was a name he never heard before.

He abandoned the book and went over to investigate the remaining part of the room. It was split into two levels, similar to the book section, except this time the lower level was recessed in a cellar. Each level held numerous sliding cabinets of various sizes. They were all labeled but the names were written in Latin. He pulled one open to see what it held. It was filled with a course brown powder that he didn't recognize. He opened another one. It held three small jars of a claylike paste. He tried a couple more and found several other different substances. Some even held sealed tubes that seemed to contain nothing at all. He assumed these were filled with colorless gases.

There was another bench table set in front of the cabinets. It held a large balance scale and collection of weights and measures. The scale was a remarkable piece of craftsmanship. Its two pans were brass, as big as serving trays and sat horizontally above the table at precisely the same height. The weights were arranged in progressively smaller boxes. Their labels included libra, uncia, drachma, scruplum and grana.

181

Michael Malik

"Eureka!"

Crisp turned his head in the direction of Miss Pimsby's triumphant outburst. His eyes swept the area until he caught sight of her. She was on the upper tier of the bookshelf perched high up on the ladder. It seemed like a dizzyingly precarious place to be from his vantage point.

"I think I found what we need." she shouted down to him. "Stay put and I'll bring it to you. We'll look through it together to make sure."

Miss Pimsby climbed down from the ladder. She was using only one hand to hold on while the other gripped something heavy. She reached the balcony level and once her feet were safely planted she moved quickly over to the stairs.

He was relieved when he saw her in a safe position. His gaze then continued to follow her as she maneuvered agilely down the stairs. As she got closer he could see what she carried more clearly. It was thick leather bound book. He waited for her to reach him with the hope that it held the answer they were looking for.

17

The Formula

Miss Pimsby heaved the book onto the bench next to Crisp, causing the pans of the scale to sway gently from the impact. He looked down at the cover of the massive brown volume. Etched into its leather was the title: *Aquamutatio*. It was the book's only visible outside mark.

"This is the book that will tell us how to turn water into wine?"

"It is the most complete text on the transformation of liquid substances I could find." Miss Pimsby answered. "If the formula isn't in here we're going to have to search through a bunch of smaller, less likely sources. That will take a bit more time. I'm fairly certain this is the right book though. Open it up and let's find out."

Crisp opened the cover and began to flip through the ancient book. He was amazed to see that the pages weren't yellow or brittle. They seemed to be made from a soft cloth-like material. The printing showed no signs of aging either. It was, however, written in the same elaborate calligraphy as the Pitch Stone instructions. Luckily his experience figuring them out made reading the letters easier this time around.

He continued until he reached the index. It listed more than two dozen different types of transformations.

"Another name for alcohol is ethanol. How about this one?" He pointed at the section listed Ethyl Compendio.

Miss Pimsby turned the book so it faced her. "It's between the Dioxide and Ferrous compendiums." She began to quickly flip the pages. She was a third way through the book when she slowed down.

"This should be it," she said as she finally settled on a spot.

Crisp checked the page. Ad Vinum was written in large letters near the top of it.

"To wine," she translated. "This has to be the one mentioned in the map." She took her notepad out from her pocket and then went around the table a grabbed a thick lead pencil. "Why don't you read me the formula while I copy it down? It will be easier for us to work with than trying to repeatedly figure out the writing. It's a trick I use all the time in the Archives. It speeds things up tremendously."

In response to her suggestion, Crisp began to silently read the first line of the formula. It didn't make any sense to him so he decided to skip to the second line. As he read it his confusion only mounted.

"This is a bit cryptic," he said.

"What do you mean?"

"Take the first ingredient." He rubbed the back of his head as he concentrated on what he was reading. "It says we need four ounces of Mary's gold. Well, who the devil is Mary? And how is four ounces of gold going to help make wine?

Miss Pimsby scribbled on her sheet of paper, seemingly oblivious to his consternation. She repeated "four ounces Mary's gold" under her breath as she wrote.

He fixed a questioning look on her she was done.

"Lots of Academy documents are confusing when you first look at them," she said. "Don't worry. It takes practice to figure it out."

"Would you mind telling me what you make of this one then?"

"Mary's gold? Oftentimes the things your uncle asks me to order are natural ingredients; special leaves from Australia or a root from a tree only found in Africa. The first thing I thought of when you read it was Marigold petals. "

"Oh, I see. That certainly makes more sense," he said, feeling foolish. He looked back down at the formula with a new perspective.

"The next additive is four drams of Wives Blush." He didn't have the foggiest idea what Wives Blush was. However, based on what Miss Pimsby said, he figured it must be an herb or bark of some sort.

"Four drams of Wives Blush," Miss Pimsby said again as she wrote it down. "What's next?"

He squinted back down at the page. "The last ingredient is twenty-eight Windsor beans." Finally, something he heard of before.

"Anything else?"

"That's it I think. Hold on," he was using his finger to follow the bottom of the page. "We need Alexander's sacred cane to mix the ingredients, whatever that is."

"How are we supposed to prepare the formula? We need every detail exactly right."

"It says we need to grind the beans. Then we put all the ingredients into six cups of distilled water. The mixture is brought to a simmering boil. The temperature must be maintained at 212 degrees and mixed with Alexander's cane every twenty minutes for twenty-four hours. At the completion of the allotted time period a syrup will have been created, a few drops of which when added to ordinary water will transform the combination to a fragrant and potent wine."

Miss Pimsby reviewed her notes intently for a moment. She finally looked up at him and asked, "That's the lot?"

"Yeah, but—" His protest was quickly interrupted.

"Did you happen to find Albert's apothecary? It's the place where he stores all of his elements and compounds."

The drawers Crisp inspected earlier now made perfect sense. "It's the set of cabinets right behind you," he told her.

She spun around. "Brilliant. Let's get going then. Since it will take a whole day for us to finish, there's no point in wasting any time."

She got up and inspected the closest cluster of cabinets but was quickly stopped in her tracks.

"That's a bit of a bother. Albert has things catalogued by their Latin root names."

"I noticed that."

"There must be a reference book somewhere. Excuse me a moment..." Her voice trailed off as she wandered in the direction of the library again.

Crisp decided to descend the spiral stairs to the lower level and begin examining the cabinets one by one. After searching for a few minutes, however, he began to realize the fruitless nature of what he was doing. Whatever

Michael Malik

rudimentary understanding of Latin he once had was now long forgotten. Looking inside the drawers was also useless. He didn't know what the formula ingredients were supposed to look like.

"Detective, can you hear me?"

He walked back to the foot of the stairs. Miss Pimsby was looking down at him. She appeared pleased about something.

"Yes, what is it?"

"I've found Albert's catalogue for the apothecary in one of the cabinets. It lists everything by their common names alongside their Latin ones. We should have no trouble finding what we need now. The first ingredient will be in a drawer marked *Calendula arvensis*."

"I think I saw it already. Hang on a minute."

He walked back to the spot he just left and glanced down at one of the larger cabinets. *Calendula arvensis* was printed neatly on its label. He bent over, opened it, and slid the drawer it held half-way out. It was filled with what looked like yellow-orange colored petals.

"I found it," he called back to her.

Miss Pimsby reappeared almost instantly at the top of the stairs. "Brilliant. Where shall we put it?"

"I'll bring it up to the work bench."

As Miss Pimsby disappeared from his view again, he removed the drawer, carried it up the stairs and over to the bench. Lying open next to the *Aquamutatio* was an even heavier looking book. He put the drawer of *Calendula arvensis* down and examined the open page. *Saccharomyces cervisiae* was listed at the top.

"Is this the next ingredient we need?" he asked. "Sac-something cerv-something?"

"Yes, that's the second part of the formula," she answered from the corner of the room. "I think it may be over here. Yes, I see it. It's a bit high up though. There's a step stool under the bench. Would you bring it over please?"

He bent over, found the sturdy looking wooden stool Miss Pimsby had referred to and carried it over to her.

"Right there, please," she pointed at the floor in front of her. Once the stool was in place she stepped up and

186

stretched her right arm to a small cabinet. Even with the extra boost it was a reach. She managed to get the cabinet open but as she pulled back on the drawer she lost her balance and began to fall backwards. Crisp threw his hands up, caught her around the waist and then gently eased her back down to solid ground.

"Umm—thanks," she stammered. "The drawer—it's a bit stuck."

"I see that," Crisp said. He released his hands from her waist and hopped onto the stool. His extra height made it easier to reach the reluctant drawer and, with a sharp tug, he managed to break it free. A bag of fine gray-white powder was inside it. He handed the drawer to Miss Pimsby then jumped back down to the floor.

"Let me take that for you," he said.

Crisp carried the *Saccharomyces* drawer to the work bench and placed it next to the *Calendula arvensis*. Between the books and drawers the amount of workspace left on the bench was significantly smaller. He took what seemed to be extra care to make sure everything was safely nestled before checking to see how the rest of Miss Pimsby's search was coming along.

"What's the last ingredient?" he asked her. She didn't look up or answer him. She was gazing down at the book, lazily flipping the pages back and forth.

"Hello, did you hear me?" he said.

She looked up. "Oh, I'm sorry. The last ingredient, is that what you asked?" She began flipping the pages toward the back of the book. "It's called *Vicia faba*," she said. "I haven't seen that one yet have you?"

"No. I'll go back downstairs and see if I can find it. You look up here again. Just be sure to call me if it's on a top shelf."

"Yes, of course. And thanks again."

"For what?"

"For catching me."

He smiled at her. "It was my pleasure. Besides, I'm sure you'd do the same for me."

The search for the final ingredient didn't take long. Crisp located the properly labeled cabinet after only a few minutes. He yelled "found it" in the direction of the stairs then pulled out the drawer. It was half full of large flat light-green seeds.

"That's should be more than enough," he said to himself.

While climbing out of the lower apothecary he noted that Miss Pimsby already cleared a spot on the table and was waiting next to it.

"We should hop to it," he said as he placed the third drawer next to the first two. "We have wine to make and another Moonstone map to reveal."

* * *

Crisp quickly learned that there was much more to making an Academy formula than finding the components.

The first thing he had to figure out was how to use the scale properly. It was easy to place stuff in the center of the large brass pans but not as easy to pick it off cleanly. The yellow-orange petals of the *Calendula arvensis* were not as big a problem since they could be lifted off individually. The problem was more with the powdery *Saccharomyces cervisiae*. It wasn't until he noticed a box of waxy sheets of paper under the bench that he understood what he needed to do.

"If we put one of these on the scale first we can lift the paper away when we're done."

When he put a piece on one of the pans the delicately balanced scale shifted. He realized he would have to account for the weight of the paper before he could proceed so he put another sheet on the other pan to act as a counterbalance.

Once the components were properly measured and the beans ground, Miss Pimsby carried them over to the bench with the beakers and test tubes. Crisp put the drawers back in their proper places. He didn't want to risk accidentally spilling something. If they made a mess of the formula they would need enough of everything to try again.

When he returned to Miss Pimsby she was trying to sort out the myriad collection of glassware. The look of woe on her face told him she was having a hard time picking out which one to use.

"If we start mixing everything in a beaker that's too small we'll have to start all over again." she said as she lined up three likely sized containers. "If we use one that is too big it will be hard to heat it evenly."

Crisp came up with the solution to this problem as well. The one thing they possessed an abundant supply of was distilled water. There was a large tank of it in the back of the lab. He filled each of the beakers Miss Pimsby had chosen with six cups of water. They decided to use the beaker that looked like it would fill over half way when everything else was added.

"How are we going to keep the formula at the proper temperature?" Crisp asked as he set the beaker of water on a metal ring stand over a Bunsen burner. "This torch will probably heat things quite a bit higher than 212 degrees if we're not careful."

His question sent them on another search through the lab. This time Miss Pimsby came up with the answer. She found a submersible thermometer with a probe that could be placed in the beaker. It was attached to a wire that went to a temperature gauge. Because of the wire the gauge could be placed on the bench next to the beaker making it easy to read.

"That should do it," Miss Pimsby said as she dropped the probe in the distilled water.

Crisp turned the Bunsen burner on and centered its flame beneath the beaker. He was about to add the first ingredient when Miss Pimsby stopped him.

"Wait, we forgot something. We still need to find the cane to mix the formula with." This sent them on yet another search. After flipping through the reference book she told him to look for a cabinet labeled *Saccharum officinarum.*

They were experts at searching the cabinets now. It didn't take long for Crisp to find the right one in the back of the upper level. He opened the drawer and pulled out something that looked like a large, sturdy blade of grass.

Miss Pimsby decided to read the instructions one more time. "I'm sure we have everything we need," she declared once she was done.

Crisp took her statement as the cue to finally get started. The water was bubbling gently in the beaker. He checked the thermometer and it was on a perfect 212 degrees. The ingredients were lined up on the bench in the order they were listed in the formula. He added them to the water one by one. After he dropped the *Vicia faba* into the beaker he gave the mixture several good stirs with the cane.

"Now we wait 20 minutes and stir it up again."

They sat together at the bench for a while but staring at the bubbling mixture soon became a tedious chore. He could tell Miss Pimsby was fighting to stay awake, and his energy was fading as well. Crisp decided that if they were going to work through the night the best way was to take turns tending the formula. He sent Miss Pimsby off and told her to get some rest.

An hour later, he began to wonder if sending Miss Pimsby off was the right thing to do. Now that he was all by himself the tedium was magnified. With nothing else to occupy it, memories began to rush into his head. First it was the gaping hole blown into the British Museum's side. Next, the nighttime ritual at Highgate Cemetery came back to him, followed by Albert's dire warning of the consequences it had brought about. Lastly he recalled the smug look on Taylor's face when he thought he had them cornered in the townhouse. They were swift and powerful reminders of why he was sitting in the lab in the first place.

"Bollocks," he said as he gave a forceful turn to the cane.

At four o'clock sharp Miss Pimsby returned to the laboratory. She looked refreshed. "How did everything go?"

"Alright as far as I can tell," he replied. "The temperature stayed steady. I mixed things at the right times."

"Splendid," said Miss Pimsby as she took a seat at the bench. "It's your turn to rest now. I'll see you at six o'clock."

Crisp walked out of the lab and into the hallway. The Pitch Stones were still blazing brightly. He turned away from them and continued on into the study.

The first thing he noticed was the pillow and blanket Miss Pimsby left on the couch for him. He sat down and took off his shoes. Once they were tucked away he lay down and pulled the blanket over him. The couch was soft and still warm from Miss Pimsby having slept there. He gathered up the pillow and put it behind his head.

Despite being quite comfortable he couldn't sleep. The same visions he saw in the lab kept running repeatedly through his head. He needed something to take his mind off of things for a bit. His thoughts turned to the last words his uncle left him with. They were from Lord Byron. Reading a few poems suddenly seemed like the right cure for his overactive brain. He swung off the couch and padded softly over to a bookshelf. After a quick scan, he pulled out an 1868 book of verse by Robert Browning.

Back on the couch, he randomly flipped to different pages of the book. He read a few works that caught his eye. It was enough to do the job. His mind clear, he fell into a light slumber.

This ritual repeated itself through the night. Every two hours Crisp and Miss Pimsby would switch positions. Each time his turn to rest came he was unable to simply fall asleep and the assistance of several more English poets was required.

The arrival of morning meant he and Miss Pimsby were back in the lab together. The formula was taking form and both of them were too excited to miss any of the remaining work. After the seventy-first mixing, the content of the beaker was deep purple.

Noontime finally arrived. Crisp twirled the cane through the beaker and finished with a flourish.

"All done."

"Now we just need some water to test it on." Miss Pimsby said.

She grabbed a clean beaker, filled it from a tap near the blast furnace, and set it in front of him as he took the formula off the flame with a protective glove. The beaker used to prepare the formula was now too large for its condensed contents. He found a more appropriate sized glass flask and poured the syrup into it.

Once the formula had cooled down a bit he lifted the flask and dripped a few thick drops into the water. The drops immediately dispersed evenly through the container and turned the liquid into a rich plum color. Crisp lifted the beaker and took a sip.

"Well?" asked Miss Pimsby anxiously.

"It certainly tastes enough like wine."

"That's encouraging but it's not what I meant and you know it. Do you feel any different? Has the wine revealed anything about the map to you?"

"Unfortunately the answer is no," he said as he put the beaker back on the work bench.

Crisp picked up the flask that held the formula. The thick purple mixture clung to the sides of the glass as he gently shook it side to side. Finishing the formula was an important accomplishment; he was sure of it. But he was missing something, some important link between the Moonstone map and the viscous fluid that he held. With help or more time he was sure he could figure out what the connection was. Since no help was coming there was only one important question left to answer. Could he uncover the mystery before they ran out of time?

18
Eureka

Crisp needed a chance to think so he decided to return to the study. He expected Miss Pimsby would want go with him but, to his surprise, she decided to stay in the lab for a bit longer. Curious, he peeked backwards on his way out the vault door. An amused smile spread across his face as he caught sight of her. She was attempting to clean the congealed substance Albert left behind in several of the beakers. The look of furious determination she exuded seemed to have finally met its match in the brick hard residue.

Once Crisp reached the study he settled into Albert's plush leather desk chair, closed his eyes and began to review everything that had happened over the past several days. He was searching for a mistake; someplace where he'd wandered off the path the clues made. Try as he might, he couldn't identify any obvious missteps on his part. Unfortunately, he was keenly aware that this didn't mean much. How was he supposed to analyze what he might have done wrong if he wasn't even sure how to do it right?

The more he thought about the predicament he was in, the more an irksome feeling built up in the back of his brain. It was a sensation that had waxed and waned ever since he saw what was hidden in the first map. It felt like his subconscious was spinning through a circular file, searching for something. Unfortunately, he wasn't sure what the thing was or whether it was going to pop out anytime soon.

A sudden, brief ringing noise filled the otherwise silent room, breaking his state of concentration. His eyes opened in search of its source, but wherever the noise came from was not in plain sight. When the muffled ring sounded again he got out of his chair and walked toward the center of the study. After a few seconds the ring sounded a third time. From his new position he was able to ascertain that it came from somewhere next to the fireplace.

When he reached the hearth rug the mysterious source of the ringing was revealed. A slightly battered handset from a cordless phone was lying face down behind a small pile of stacked firewood. He reached down and picked it up just as it rang again. He pushed the answer button, lifted the phone to his ear and said, "Hello."

"Blimey Benjamin, I was about to hang up on you. You let the phone ring enough times."

"Reggie," Crisp said once he recognized Detective Sergeant Little's voice. "Sorry about that. The phone was tucked away. I was lucky to find it at all."

"I'm glad you answered at any rate. There's some news about the case. I figured you deserved to know about it."

"Have you finally nabbed the buggers who bombed the museum?" he asked with a flicker of hope.

"Nothing that encouraging, sorry to say."

"What's up then?"

"It's the herald trumpet. Fuller couldn't hold off the miserable sods from the Royal caretaker's office any longer and now they've finally got their way. I've just been assigned to return the bloody thing."

"What! You must be joking."

"That's exactly what I said when I was told."

"Isn't there anything you can do to stop it?"

"Afraid not," Little replied apologetically. "Fuller's been at it tooth and nail with them for a while now but this time they finally pulled the 'Royal property' dodge. After that it was only a matter of when and where."

"But the whole case might be jeopardized."

"Yeah. Fuller told 'em. He even threatened to go over their heads and straight to the Queen."

"And they still want their stuff back?"

"Yup. They promised to provide the trumpet when the culprits are caught, so Fuller was forced to back down. Sorry, mate."

"Is it going back to the museum?"

"Nah. The caretakers feel it'll be safer where it came from—Windsor Castle. I'm supposed to sneak it up by myself. Everyone seems to feel it's a better plan than a big motorcade that would draw a lot of attention. My only consolation is I get one of the armored surveillance vans to transport them."

"And you're bringing them back tonight?"

"Affirmative."

A sense of bitterness filled Crisp. "I suppose what's done is done, then."

"Macbeth. Nice touch, mate, and very appropriate, I'd say." Little's voice broke away from the phone. Crisp heard a few muffled shouts and then, "Sorry mate, but I need to dash off now. I still have a lot of work to do before my trip."

"Sure, I understand. Good luck."

"Thanks mate. Swing by my desk when you get back to work. We'll grab a pint and curse the lot of them."

Crisp said goodbye and hung up the phone. He then began to search for its base, which he found on the bookshelf above the wood pile. Just as he put it back in its cradle he heard a loud clunking noise coming from the tunnel. The shelf buckled slightly and the phone was knocked back to where he found it. He picked it up again and placed it back into its cradle.

"Now I know why Albert doesn't answer his phone," he muttered to himself.

Miss Pimsby emerged from behind the bookshelf door with the Pitch Stones in her hands. "I thought it would be prudent to lock the lab for the time being," she said as she handed him his stone. "What's the matter? You look awful."

He repeated what Little told him.

"What should we do?" she asked.

"We need to get back to London as soon as possible. I need to convince Fuller to hold on to them just a bit longer. If I have to risk telling him everything and getting locked up as a mental case then that's what I'll do."

"What about the second map? We haven't learned where to take it yet."

"We'll have to figure it out during the trip. It's not the ideal answer," he said when he saw the look of concern on her face, "but we don't have much choice. Besides I can't help feeling we already have what we need. We did exactly what the first map told us to. For some reason we're not seeing something that we should. If we talk through it

Michael Malik

some more it may come to us. And hanging around this place longer won't help us solve the puzzle. The chief problem we have now is getting back to London quickly enough."

"I'll call Sergeant Wilkins."

Miss Pimsby's conversation on the phone was brief and not encouraging. From what Crisp could pick out, both of Wilkins' cabs were temporarily unavailable. One was being used and wouldn't be back for several hours. The one he was saving in case they called was suddenly having engine trouble. The part needed to fix it hadn't arrived yet.

"That's inconvenient," Miss Pimsby said with a frown as she hung up the phone. "Hold on. Albert keeps an old car in the carriage house. He hasn't used it in years but perhaps it runs well enough to get us back to London."

When Crisp didn't respond she asked, "Did you hear me?"

"Hmm—yes, sorry, my mind has been stuck on something for most of the morning. It can't quite grab hold of whatever it is. It's like trying to recall a word or a name that's buried away. Honestly, it's a bit annoying."

"Like I said, there's a car in the carriage house. Would you like to come and look at it with me?"

Crisp wanted to see the car she was talking about but he also felt like he might have a breakthrough if only he could concentrate for a little longer. "Can you wait a bit?"

"Of course," she replied. "But don't take too long. I'll gather my things and meet you back here in a few minutes."

* * *

After Miss Pimsby was gone Crisp continued to pace back and forth. He was trying to will his brain to cough out what it held. A few minutes passed without any luck. He finally gave up and flopped down on the couch. As he did, he caught sight of the poetry books he had collected through the night. They were piled on the table in front of him. For some reason, staring at them slowed the spinning circular file in his brain enough that he could almost pick

196

out the card he was looking for, but not quite. Then, suddenly, the file clicked to a stop.

"Eureka!" he shouted as he leapt from the couch.

Miss Pimsby ran into the study from the front hall. "What's happened? Are you okay?"

"Iambic pentameter," Crisp answered.

"Excuse me?" said Miss Pimsby, looking completely confused. "Are you having some sort of delayed reaction to the formula?"

"Never mind that. Do you know if William Shakespeare was a member of the Academy?"

"No, he wasn't, but he was a Special Investigator for a brief time. I saw his confidentiality pledge when I was doing my research at the archives. Why do you ask?"

"Don't you see?" he asked with mounting excitement. When Miss Pimsby's querulous look didn't change he explained, "A William wrote the poem in the first map but it wasn't Byrd like we assumed. It was Shakespeare. It all makes sense now. Byrd was a musician and composer, not a writer. And the William who created the clue for the map used iambic pentameter. I thought I recognized something familiar about the verse from the first map. It just wasn't until this moment that my brain figured out what it was. Oh, I should have seen this so much earlier."

He strode toward Miss Pimsby and stuck out his hand. "May I have your notepad please?"

Miss Pimsby reached into her bag and pulled out the pad. Once she'd handed it to Crisp, he immediately turned to the page where the formula was written then took the pad back to the desk and sat down. He found a pencil in a drawer and beckoned Miss Pimsby to stand next to him.

"This is the original formula that you transcribed from the *Aquamutatio*," he said as pointed to the page.

4 on.	Mary's gold
4 dr.	Wives blush
28	Windsor beans

He took the pencil and made six short underline strokes below her handwriting.

4 on.	Mary's gold
4 dr.	Wives blush
28	Windsor beans

"Do you see it now?" he asked her. When she didn't answer immediately he wrote the underlined words and numbers out on the next page:

Mary Wives Windsor 4,4,28

A wave of sudden understanding swept across Miss Pimsby's face. "Shakespeare's play The Merry Wives of Windsor contains the location where the second map works! That's what the formula was supposed to tell us. You did it Detective, bravo!"

Crisp got up and searched the bookshelf again. He found Theobald's edition of Shakespeare's collected plays. "Act 4, scene 4, line 28 to be exact," he said. He pulled the first of the seven volumes off the shelf. A cursory check of the first few pages told him The Merry Wives of Windsor was one of the several plays it held. He brought it back to the desk and laid it down.

Miss Pimsby took the book from him. She began to rapidly flip through it in the same way as the laboratory texts from the day before.

"I meant to ask you, how do you do that so quickly?"

"It's an acquired skill that's necessary in my job. I usually have to go through quite a bit of information in the Archives to find something for Albert," she explained. "Here we go, on page 290." They both leaned over and began to read:

Mrs Page:
There is an old tale goes that Herne the Hunter,
Sometimes a keeper here in Windsor Forest
Doth all the wintertime, at still midnight,
Walk round about an oak, with great ragg'd horns
And there he blasts the tree, and takes the cattle,
And makes much kine yield blood, and shakes a chain
In a most hideous and dreadful manner.
You have heard of such a spirit, and well you know

The superstitious idleheaded eld
Received and did deliver to our age
This tale of Herne the Hunter for a truth.

"That's got to be it," Miss Pimsby exclaimed. "The second map works in Windsor Park."

"At Herne's Oak tree," Crisp said. "It ties in nicely. The first map includes the area east of London where we found the shed. The second map extends west. I clearly remember seeing Windsor on it."

"We should leave straight away. If we drive fast we should be able to get back up toward London fairly quickly."

"It's close to 4 o'clock now," Crisp said as he glanced at his watch. "We're cutting it close but it just might work. By the time we get to Windsor it should just be turning dark. The moon is supposed to be full tonight. As long as there's no cloud cover it shouldn't have any trouble lighting the second map. Hopefully from there it will be easy to retrieve the compositions."

"I just thought of something else," Miss Pimsby said. "Do you know where to look for Herne's Oak?"

"Not exactly."

"Windsor Park is a big place. How are we supposed to find one tree in it? It might take hours. We don't have that kind of time."

"Excellent point," Crisp said. "Does Albert have a computer?" Miss Pimsby's facial expression was enough to tell him the answer was no. He concentrated for a moment. "I have an idea. Hand me the cordless phone please."

Miss Pimsby retrieved the handset from the shelf and handed it to him. He punched in some numbers.

"Hello operator, connect me with the Crown Estate Office, Windsor branch."

"What are you doing?" Miss Pimsby asked.

"Getting the answer to your question, my dear."

Crisp heard a pleasant male voice over the phone. "Crown Estate office, how may I help you?"

"My name is Morris Finch," Crisp said with a pretentious drawl. "I am the head dramatist for the Cambridge Repertory Theater. We are planning a

199

production of The Merry Wives of Windsor. I thought a picnic with the cast at Herne's Oak tree would help set the tone for a successful show. Can you assist me in my endeavor?"

"The tree you speak of, sir, was chopped down in 1796," the man answered.

Crisp's heart fell into his stomach. "That is a bit of a disappointment. Is there no record of where it originally stood?"

"Yes, of course there is. Edward VII planted a replacement tree on the same spot in 1906."

"You don't say. Well that's splendid—very splendid indeed." Crisp said, his false accent rising a few octaves.

"It's just a bit north of Frogmore House, but that area is not open to the public. A tour of the estate and the grounds can be arranged for your troupe with sufficient notice. That's the best I can do for you."

"I appreciate your assistance my good man. I'll convey what you've told me to my group and see if it will serve as an acceptable substitute."

Crisp hung up the phone and relayed what he learned to an anxious looking Miss Pimsby.

"We should be able to find the spot we need fairly quickly once we get to Windsor Park. We may have to sneak around for the last bit but we'll manage somehow."

Despite his news, a look of unease was still etched on her face. "That was quite clever Detective, but I don't see how we're going to get the trumpet in time."

"We'll have to find some way to head off Little. Once we're in the Park he'll practically be heading straight for us. Hopefully we can catch him before he gets to the Castle."

"Will he agree to give us the trumpet?"

"I don't know. We'll have to figure out a way to convince him if and when the time comes. Right now, we need to work on making our way to Windsor."

"I'll get the key to the house and meet you in the front hall in two minutes." She turned and strode out of the study.

He walked out into the front hall and waited for Miss Pimsby. The sound of her bedroom door closing soon carried down to him. He reached for his jacket, which was still draped on the same chair. After putting it on, he reached into his pants pocket and pulled out his Pitch Stone. Before he could hide it in the jacket, Miss Pimsby appeared.

"Ready to go?" she asked.

He glanced at the Pitch Stone in his right hand. There was something gnawing the back of his brain again.

"Not quite yet. Can I borrow your Pitch Stone?"

"Of course, but what do you need it for?"

"I'll show you in a minute," he answered as he walked back into the study.

Crisp opened the bookshelf door and then used the two Pitch Stones to access the laboratory again. He rushed to the spot where they made the formula, hoping Miss Pimsby hadn't thrown out what he wanted. His heart sank for a moment when he saw the washed and stacked beakers on the edge of the workbench. He then caught sight of the syrup-filled flask sitting on the ledge of an apothecary cabinet. He grabbed it and stuffed a cork in its long neck. Locking the doors behind him again, he returned to the front hall.

"What did you get that for?" Miss Pimsby asked when she saw him holding the formula.

"There has to be a good reason this was chosen as a clue," he answered as he returned her Pitch Stone to her. "Something tells me it will come in handy."

19
The Oak Tree

Crisp wasn't prepared for the sight that greeted him in the carriage house. Based on the way Miss Pimsby described Albert's car earlier, he expected to find a battered old jalopy. Instead a polished and pristine royal-blue 1968 Rolls-Royce coupe sat before him.

He slid the flask of syrup into his jacket and walked over to the car. Its driver-side door swung open for him with a light tug. He got behind the wheel and then watched as Miss Pimsby slid through her door and into the passenger seat. Once she was settled in, he pulled his door shut with a heavy thud. Miss Pimsby's door followed suit with the same satisfying sound. He luxuriated in the car's soft leather seating for a moment then reached for the ignition and pushed the starter. The engine turned over at once. He listened appreciatively to its silky growl while checking the dashboard. The fuel gauge was full.

"Ready?"

"Yes. Let's go."

Crisp slipped the transmission into drive and, as he pulled away from Albert's Manor, took one look behind him. Everything was quiet and dark. The house itself looked odd, as if it was lonely. He shook the feeling off, turned forward and drove the car through the gate.

The route he followed started east. After about fifteen miles he pulled onto A1(M) and headed south. The car was now on the motorway and the trip began to speed by. Since there wasn't much for him to concentrate on anymore he finally noticed something was bothering Miss Pimsby. She had been uncharacteristically quiet since they had left the manor.

"Are you okay?"

"I'm still in a bit of shock," she said.

"About what?"

"The connection between Byrd and Shakespeare. I can't believe I missed it. It was right there. I had the document in my hands and I didn't think twice about it."

"I wouldn't let it worry you too much. There was no way to know he was involved. Dee certainly didn't mention him."

"And I can't stop wondering how he got tangled up in this mess."

"I've been asking the same question about myself for a while now."

Miss Pimsby stuck her tongue out at Crisp's remark. "Okay, okay, you win," he said with a quick laugh. "I'll stay on track."

"Good."

"So, Shakespeare and the maps; there must be a logical explanation for the connection."

"I keep going back to what Dee told us before he left with Albert," she continued. "The plan was to hide the two components of Celestial language separately. Dee completed his task by hiding the herald trumpet in Queen Elizabeth's court. Maybe Byrd wasn't as sure about how to hide his compositions. Maybe he needed help."

"So Shakespeare was recruited? It's possible."

"But why?"

"I'd say you answered that question days ago."

His statement seemed to startle Miss Pimsby. "I did? How?"

"You told me the first map was meant to be an instruction manual. You were right. And since its instructions needed to be clearly understandable, Byrd wanted the services of a writer. It was even more important, however, that the clue was embedded into a work that would endure; something an Academy member would always have ready access to as opposed to something that had ended up on a trash heap long ago. So he chose the best known writer he could find for the job."

"What you're saying is Byrd needed a secret place to hide the compositions. He also needed a way for another Academy member to find them if it became necessary. The plan he came up with involved leaving special instructions hidden in the maps. Then, to insure the hiding place was not only secure but also unlikely to be lost in the shifting fortunes of time, Byrd asked Shakespeare to give him hand. Shakespeare wrote the poem about the formula for the first map. He then wrote a play that included Herne's Oak in it to match the clue in the poem and guide us to the right spot."

"It's only a guess but it does seem to sum things up nicely. If we're right then Byrd was pretty successful. It's been over four hundred years since the compositions were hidden. Nevertheless, we've managed to unearth their hiding place. It wasn't easy. There's no way we would have succeeded without our relationship to the Academy. In the end, though, I would say his plan worked perfectly."

"At least I know one thing for sure," Miss Pimsby said. "Mr. Oxtail would want to be with us now."

"Who's Mr. Oxtail again?" he asked with a laugh.

"He was my literature teacher in school. Don't you remember, I mentioned him yesterday?"

Crisp vaguely recalled the conversation. "I give up. Why would Mr. Oxtail want to be zipping down the A1 motorway in a Rolls-Royce with us?"

"Because he loved Shakespeare but always loathed The Merry Wives of Windsor. It was his least favorite of the Bard's works."

"Why's that?"

"There were several reasons. It's the only one of Shakespeare's plays that takes place in a contemporary Elizabethan England setting, for example."

"What's so wrong about that?"

"It's just so unlike him. Shakespeare wrote romantic plays in exotic locations or historical dramas. Mr. Oxtail never liked the idea of Shakespeare settling for the commonplace."

"I get it. It's out of context with his other works. That doesn't seem like a cardinal sin to me. You'd think Mr. Oxtail could get over it."

"He might have, but there were other things that bothered him about the play even more than the setting."

"Such as?"

"Falstaff is one of Shakespeare's most memorable characters. In the Merry Wives of Windsor he's written as a fool and a cad. Mr. Oxtail hated to see Falstaff diminished in such a way."

"You're building quite a case," he said. "I can see why Mr. Oxtail wanted you to follow in his footsteps."

His compliment pleased Miss Pimsby. He could tell by the way she looked down at her hands for a moment before continuing.

"His lectures were always entertaining. I remember them like they were yesterday."

"I'm still confused about something. If Mr. Oxtail disliked The Merry of Windsor so much why would he want to be here?"

"It's never been clear why Shakespeare drifted so far from his usual routine. We, however, know the truth. The Merry Wives of Windsor was written, perhaps hastily, to serve as a marker for a remarkable secret. It solves a giant mystery about the play that's been a source of great distress to Mr. Oxtail."

"So?"

"Don't you see, silly? He'd have to forgive Shakespeare for something like that!"

* * *

The Rolls-Royce was powerfully eating up the miles to Windsor. In what felt like no time at all, Crisp pulled off the motorway. They traveled along Albert Road, which then took them to Kings Road. The part of the park they needed to enter was now directly on their right.

Crisp looked for a parking spot. He found one along a side road and pulled in. By the time the car engine finally shut off it was dusk. The shadows from the buildings that lined the street were already long and dark.

"We should hurry. It will be much easier to find Herne's Oak if we still have some sunlight," he said.

They exited the car and walked back to Kings Road. Crisp checked the surrounding area with a swing of his head. Another vehicle was moving away from them far down the street. Otherwise all was quiet.

"Follow me."

He walked rapidly through the line of trees that bordered Windsor Park with Miss Pimsby close on his heels. They came out on a narrow but lengthy field with a path running down its center. He skirted toward it. "If we head northeast through that second set of trees we'll be in Frogmore Gardens."

Once they reached the second line of trees they melted into them. A glance told Crisp they'd not been seen. He picked up the pace again. The modest cover supplied by the trees in twilight allowed them to move faster. They stayed in their midst for a few hundred meters to the north. Another field was off to the right. Predictably, there was a large wrought iron fence that traveled the length of it.

"I don't think we're allowed in there," Miss Pimsby whispered once they stopped moving.

"You're absolutely correct," he whispered back. "But we don't have time to request permission from the Crown Estate. I'm hoping that if we're caught our recent efforts on behalf of the Queen's property will keep us out of prison."

"Is that likely?"

"Not very," he said with a shrug.

There were several areas where thick vines grew up the fence. He tested one. It was slippery but the tangled branches held his weight. He climbed nimbly to the top and wedged his right foot against one of the fence's metal ornaments. In order to get even more leverage he wrapped his right arm in the vines. He then used his left arm to hoist Miss Pimsby up. With his assistance, she managed to scramble over the fence. Unfortunately, her grip failed as she climbed down the other side and she dropped two meters to the ground. She landed with a soft thud and a muted, "Ooof".

"Are you hurt?"

Miss Pimsby stood up gingerly. "I might have wrenched my ankle a bit but I can still walk on it."

He worked his body over the fence and carefully lowered himself down. As soon as he was on the ground he bent over and inspected Miss Pimsby's ankle. It was slightly swollen but nothing seemed to be broken.

"I think you'll make it."

"Honestly, it's nothing. Leave it alone and let's get going, shall we."

They set off across another field. He went a bit slowly at first then faster when he saw Miss Pimsby was keeping pace. Another wooded area to the east was their target. As they jogged, a large building with an angular green copper roof came into their view.

"That's the Royal Mausoleum," he said as he tried to get his bearings. "We should only have to go a bit farther that way," he pointed northeast again, "and we'll be there."

The last of the sunlight was fading rapidly now but he noted with relief that a full and bright moon was glowing in the cloudless sky. It would give them some extra light to find their way. More importantly, there were no obstacles to prevent the map from functioning properly.

After a few more minutes of walking, he caught sight of a large oak tree with heavy twisted branches that was growing near the edge of a wood. He also noticed a plaque set near its base, making it even more distinct from the other trees in the area. Crisp was sure it was the oak that they were looking for. He indicated to Miss Pimsby to stay close to him as he headed toward it.

Once they were close enough, the light from the moon reflected off the plaque, illuminating its words:

Herne's Oak
Replanted 1906
King George VI

"This is it."

Crisp unbuttoned his jacket and pulled the atlas from its hiding place. Miss Pimsby reached into her purse as he opened to the page with the second map.

"I hope old George knew the right spot when he planted this."

He knelt down and laid the atlas in a beam that filtered through the oak's branches. The map began to crackle and glow. Instead of writing, however, a faint arrow appeared in the middle of the page. He looked at Miss Pimsby. "Don't bother with the Augmenter. It'll take too much time to put together and I can read the map well enough without it."

"I think it's telling us where to go," Miss Pimsby said in a hushed but excited tone as she closed her purse.

Crisp lifted the map. The faint arrow remained lit. The two of them began to walk in the direction it indicated.

Whenever they started to get off track its glow would start to sputter and disappear.

Their short route led them to a nearby copse of woods. The branches of two enormous oak trees tangled into each other at the edge of the thicket. In the semidarkness the trees looked like two giants engaged in a fierce struggle. The lowest set of crossing branches formed into an archway. A hazy mist swirled in the door-like opening they created. Beyond the mist there appeared to be nothing but thick thorn-covered brush.

"It's a dead end," said Miss Pimsby. She looked over her shoulder. "Did we miss something?"

"The arrow is still pointing forward."

As he looked down at the map the arrow started to pulse in an almost insistent way.

"There must have been a clearing in there at one time," he said as he examined the dense and sharply pointed vines. We're going to have to fight our way in there somehow."

He looked over his shoulder at Miss Pimsby. "Get as close to me as you can, put your arms around my waist and shield your eyes behind my back."

Crisp felt her purse settle against his side as her arms wrapped around him. He put her hands together and formed them into a clasp. "Like that," he said. He then felt her head nestle between his shoulder blades. He waited for a moment to enjoy the warmth of her body against his and then asked, "Ready?"

"Yes."

"Then hold tight."

Holding the map with his right hand, he lifted his left arm so that his jacket sleeve covered his face. Then, bracing himself, he plunged forward. He was momentarily blinded as the shroud-like mist enveloped him, thickened and then began to swirl around his head. To his surprise, however, instead of hitting a barrier he moved forward unhindered.

After a half dozen paces the mist started to dissipate. Crisp examined the map again. As he did, the arrow sputtered a final time and turned dark. He looked up for the moon. Despite the gap in the trees that opened before him, the night sky was no longer visible.

Miss Pimsby gasped loudly behind him. He looked up the path to find the reason for her reaction and was amazed to see a centuries old cottage in the middle of an enclosed field.

The cottage had to be the hiding place they were looking for. Crisp was sure of it. A search of the premises was all he needed to prove he was right. He hoped it was a quick and easy one.

20
Hunter and Hunted

Crisp didn't head straight for the cottage's front door. Instead he spent a few minutes inspecting it from the outside.

The walls of the ancient looking structure were packed mud and stone. Thick piles of golden thatch served as the roof. A chimney was built into one side and, most importantly, smoke was curling up slowly from it. Someone built a fire inside not long ago. This meant it was far from deserted or forgotten.

In the far corner of the front yard he saw a circular well. Sitting beside it was a large bucket of water that looked to have been recently filled. The sides were still wet from having been dipped in the water. A wood hitching post was set above a long trough that was half full of water. Next to the trough there was a small pile of fresh hay.

The front windows were small and square. Each held a pane of glass that was irregular and cloudy. He moved close enough to glance through one, hoping to learn something more about the occupants. All he saw was distorted waves of light that flickered from somewhere within. Several rough-hewn boards were nailed together and hung on iron hinges. They created a crude but sturdy front door.

"Who do you think lives here?" asked Miss Pimsby.

"A gamekeeper is the most likely answer," he said. "Hopefully whoever it is knows where the compositions are. It will make our job easier."

"Just think. The occupants of this cottage have been the guardians of the compositions, unwittingly or not, for generations."

"It's a bit of an odd choice though, wouldn't you say?"

"What do you mean?"

"It's certainly not the most impressive structure we've seen tonight."

"I think it's quaint."

"A bit too quaint..." His words trailed off as he spoke. Something in the bucket drew his attention. The suspicion it aroused was quickly confirmed as he moved toward it for a closer look. A drinking ladle was slung over its lip and rested at the bottom of the pail. He lifted it up and dribbled some of the water back into the bucket. As he did a sudden inspiration struck him. He reached into his pocket and pulled out the flask of wine-making syrup.

"What are you up to?" asked Miss Pimsby.

He waggled the flask in front of him. "Like I said earlier, this particular formula must have been chosen as a clue for a specific reason. This bucket is the only place I've seen so far where it can be used. Maybe it's supposed to smooth the way with the occupants, a sort of gift or peace offering."

Crisp uncorked the vial and tilted it over the bucket. The thick purple syrup inside flowed slowly down the side of the glass. He waited until several drops fell into the water. After they dissolved he leaned down and picked up the ladle. A sip from it told him that the transformation was successful again. He re-corked the vial and replaced it in his pocket.

"That should do it. Now it's time to get what we came here for."

He went over and knocked on the door. Despite the sharp sound his knuckles made against the heavy boards, no one came to answer.

"Nobody seems to be home," Miss Pimsby offered after he knocked a second time. "Should we wait here until someone shows up?"

Crisp grabbed the door's roughly-carved wooden knob and eased it open. He stuck his head inside and shouted, "Hello, anyone home?" He was greeted with more silence. Was it possible Taylor had beaten them to the cottage somehow?

"Hopefully whoever lives here just stepped out a moment. But time's short and we can't be sure they haven't been kidnapped or hurt. We have to go inside and look around ourselves. We'll apologize later if we're caught."

Michael Malik

The door creaked softly as he swung it the rest of the way open and stepped inside. Miss Pimsby followed him in then closed the door gently behind her.

The area they stood in comprised the main portion of the cottage. It was remarkable only in its sparseness. The floor was a rudimentary combination of packed earth and straw. A large table sat in the middle of the room like a heavy wooden turtle. Tucked under its far end was a single chair. The lit remnant of a candle was all that was on the table. An orange flame from its wick provided some of the light he and Miss Pimsby saw from the windows. The rest of the light in the room came from the fireplace, which held a thick layer of embers. Flames flickered and danced from a charred log that sat on top of the glowing pile. A waft of black smoke rose from it and disappeared up the chimney. The inner walls were unfinished and no decorations were hung on them.

As it reached the edges of the room, the light from the candle and fire seemed to be swallowed up. Consequently, the back of the room was barely visible. It appeared to be nothing but a dull gray void. Crisp stepped forward a few paces to get a better look. The gloom eased a bit as he moved and several well-worn buckskins came into view. They were piled on the floor next to a door that was partially open. It was impossible to be sure where it led from their vantage point. Based on what he saw so far he guessed it was a bedroom.

The only sight that intrigued him within the sparse cottage was several lengths of rusty chain that hung from nails by the front door. There was nothing within view that looked even remotely like it might be hiding centuries old documents.

"There's not much in here, is there?" Miss Pimsby remarked.

"No, but it actually makes our job easier. I just hope the compositions weren't used for kindling two hundred years ago," he added with a hand gesture toward the fire. "I'll search along the left side of the room. You search the right."

Despite what he'd told Miss Pimsby, he felt uneasy as he searched the drab surroundings. He couldn't put his

212

finger on exactly what bothered him. Everything just seemed unnatural in a vague way.

It didn't take long before he and Miss Pimsby established for certain what they already knew. The compositions weren't in the front room. They checked the furniture and walls for a hollow spot. Everything was solid. After a few minutes of tapping around they met near the pile of buckskins. A quick lift proved nothing was hidden beneath them. He turned his gaze to the back doorway.

"They better be in there," he said, "or we're done for."

A smaller candle sat on a shelf inside. The light it gave only minimally illuminated the small space. Still, Crisp saw that he was right about the room being a bedroom. It held a straw filled mattress atop a crude bed frame. Crumpled at the foot of the bed was a thick wool blanket.

Miss Pimsby slipped through the door. He was about to follow her when he thought he heard a faint noise come from outside.

"Are you coming," Miss Pimsby asked him.

"You go ahead. I'll watch things out here. Be quick."

He kept one eye on the front door and another on Miss Pimsby. Her figure moved in and out of the shadows as she searched every part of the room.

"There's something in here," she said in an excited whisper. "It's not too heavy. I'll bring it out so we can look it over better."

The sound of something being dragged across the dirt floor came from a back corner of the bedroom. A moment later, Miss Pimsby came back into view. She was pulling a sturdy looking storage trunk behind her. Crisp bent down and gave her a helping hand, pulling the trunk through the uneven doorway.

They inspected the trunk in the light of the fire. It was made from thick oak boards and wrapped with several reinforcing iron bands. More importantly, the initials WB were intricately carved on the top of its closed lid.

"It must have been William Byrd's," Miss Pimsby said as she ran her fingers over the carving.

There was a latch for a lock but it was empty.

"What are you waiting for, open it," he said to her.

The hinges let out a high pitched squeak as Miss Pimsby lifted the top. She gasped softly with a mix of relief and amazement. Crisp took his attention away from the front door for a moment and peered over her shoulder into the trunk. A folio sat in the bottom. A delicate looking wooden tube was nestled on top of it.

Miss Pimsby retrieved the tube and handed it to him. It was a hand-crafted reed instrument, similar looking to a recorder. Several miniature but remarkably detailed deer were carved into each side. He put it aside and returned his attention to Miss Pimsby. She reached into the trunk again and lifted the folio out.

"Careful, that may be fragile after all these years." As soon as he finished speaking he realized his warning was unnecessary. Despite being four hundred years old the book looked remarkably new.

Miss Pimsby opened the folio to the first page. It was a sheet of music. A short but complex series of notes were carefully inked on the rows of lines. She shuffled through a few more pages. It was more of the same, at least four dozen sheets of music in all.

Despite Crisp's initial belief that his uncle was crazy and despite his concern that the task assigned to them was next to impossible, he and Miss Pimsby had found the place where William Byrd's Celestial compositions had been hidden so many years before.

"We did it," Miss Pimsby said, fighting to keep her voice to a whisper. She leapt into his arms and gave him a big hug. "I can hardly believe it. We found them."

"Yes, we have," he said hugging her back. "I admit, this calls for a celebration, but perhaps its best we got out of here first."

* * *

The clear sound of a horse whinnying outside the cottage interrupted their excitement.

"Too late, we have company," Crisp said. "Hurry, put that trunk back and hide the compositions in your bag."

She started to ask him something. "Wait a moment," he said in a barely audible whisper. He was trying to determine how many people had arrived and was listening intently to the noises from outside. When he didn't hear anything more he turned back to her.

"Listen—we have no idea who's out there," he continued in his low voice. "I do know one thing for certain. By hook or by crook, we're leaving with that folio. Now please do as I say."

Miss Pimsby looked nervous but did as she was asked. Crisp waited a moment to make sure the sheets of music were safely in her bag then moved stealthily toward the front of the room. A loud squeak suddenly broke the silence. He looked back and saw the trunk lid half-closed and still in Miss Pimsby's hand. As she looked guiltily back at him he raised his finger to his lips and let out a low "shhhh." Despite the noise, however, there were no shouts of alarm. He heard nothing outside but the soft clip-clop of hooves. He pointed at the bedroom door indicating to Miss Pimsby that she should continue putting the trunk away.

He made his way to one of the windows. The thick glass was unrevealing. All he could see was the shadowy figure of a horse over by the trough. He moved over to the door and stuck his ear to it. There was definitely at least one person moving around. He heard heavy shuffling footsteps and the low deep breathing of recent exertion. The footsteps seemed to be in the area near the horse at first. As Crisp listened they started to travel in the direction of the well. The footsteps stopped after a dozen paces. The next noise he heard was the ladle scraping against the side of the water bucket. This was followed by a low grunt of surprise. The newcomer had discovered the wine he created with the formula. The bucket sloshed as it was lifted off the ground. A moment later, Crisp made out the sound of rapid and greedy slurping. Whoever was outside appreciated his handiwork.

"Who's out there," asked Miss Pimsby in a hushed voice. Crisp was concentrating on the noises from the person outside so he didn't notice her sneak up behind him. He was glad she had. It was easier to protect her if she was close to him.

"I don't know yet but I'm pretty sure it's not the same nasty bunch from before."

Michael Malik

"Perhaps we should go outside and say hello. After all, we're trespassing in someone else's home. Being found inside means we've been caught red handed. If we go outside and immediately apologize we'll look less guilty."

Crisp shook his head. Despite his certainty that Taylor wasn't the one outside he couldn't shake his sense of unease. There were too many odd things about their surroundings.

"I don't think that would be wise."

Miss Pimsby gave him a quizzical look.

"Whoever's out there doesn't know about us yet. I don't want to give up our only advantage to a potentially dangerous stranger."

He looked about the cottage again. Its bareness was even more pronounced at this moment. There was nowhere to hide. All they needed was a few brief moments, just enough time for the stranger to hopefully work his way toward the back of the building. That would allow them to get through the front door undetected or at least with a head start. But there was no chance of concealment in the sparse room.

Crisp heard the sound of an empty bucket being dropped to the ground. The footsteps, which now dragged even more heavily than before, started to move directly toward the cottage. His chance to think of a clever escape plan was gone.

Crisp retreated from the front door. As he did he grabbed Miss Pimsby's arm and drew her back with him. His eyes continued to sweep the room in the feeble hope he could find a way out of their predicament.

They were still backing up when the door burst open. Miss Pimsby let out an involuntary scream and Crisp understood why. A massive man stood in the doorway. He was well over six feet tall and thickly muscled. A patched and frayed hunting cloak was draped over his torso and hung over forest green leggings. Mud splattered deerskin boots covered his feet. Clutched in his right hand was a length of rusty chain. It dragged on the ground four feet behind him. A burn-like scar ran from his left shoulder to just below his right ear. The most remarkable thing about him, however, was his face. His heavy square jaw was

216

covered by a short curly beard but no mustache. His broad nose flared with animal-like anger. His eyes, which seemed to be slightly out of focus, were deep set. Their small pupils glowed in a spectral shade of red from their sunken position. Protruding from either side of his bald forehead were two short spiny growths. They looked exactly like stunted antlers.

"Herne," Crisp whispered in stunned recognition. Somehow, incredibly, Shakespeare's mythical hunter stood menacingly before them.

Herne stared blankly at them for a moment then issued a bellow of rage. He launched himself somewhat unsteadily at the pair and swung his chain down at Crisp. It missed by inches.

Crisp reacted instinctively. He used his grip on Miss Pimsby's elbow to throw her under the table. "The first chance you have, get out of here," he shouted at her. If he could keep Herne at bay long enough she might be able to escape with the compositions. The look on her face, however, told him that she wasn't about to leave without him.

Another swing of Herne's chain crashed into the table next to Crisp. The ricochet caromed into his left shoulder. An agonizing sensation shot down his arm. Despite the burning pain that cascaded into his fingertips, Crisp threw himself at the giant. His momentum propelled him into Herne's left side. The maneuver saved him another painful blow by preventing Herne from reeling his chain in. Crisp, however, felt like he had run full speed into a boulder.

Herne grunted and stumbled backwards. It took a moment before he regained his balance. Crisp used the brief delay to regain some distance between him and the brute. It was a risky move. The reason was Herne's chain. Crisp knew he had no chance against the enraged giant close up. Herne's bulk would easily overpower his much leaner frame. His only chance was to use his superior speed and reflexes. The chain neutralized these advantages by greatly increasing Herne's lethal range. He needed to stay out of its swinging radius until he could find a way to counteract it.

217

Unfortunately, the blow to his side appeared to have further enraged Herne. He recovered his balance and stared at Crisp with eyes that glowed like infernos from hell. It was a fearsome sight that would have cowed a lesser man. Instead, the anger ended up working to Crisp's advantage. Forgetting his chain for a moment, Herne bull rushed him. This decision played directly into Crisp's only advantage. He easily sidestepped Herne, whose momentum caused him to fall near the fireplace.

Herne being momentarily down created an opening. Crisp ran toward the front door. "Get over here!" he yelled to Miss Pimsby. Unfortunately, she was in too much shock to react quickly. In the split second it took for her to register what he yelled, they lost their opportunity.

Herne's eyes were locked squarely on Miss Pimsby. As she started to scramble forward he managed to throw an arm out and grab her by the ankle. She screamed again and tried to kick free but Herne's grip was much too powerful. He began to drag her slowly toward him. Once she was fully captured she would have no chance of escape.

"Bollocks," Crisp swore.

He had a big problem now. It was going to be hard to get Herne to release Miss Pimsby. He would need to get close to the enraged giant to even make an attempt to get her free. That would put both of them within Herne's grasp. And he doubted he could break Herne's hold even if he used all his strength. That meant they would both end up trapped.

He looked around again in desperation and caught sight of the chains hanging by the back doorway. He ran around the far side of the table and pulled one off a hook. The heavy length of chain was unwieldy so that, as he charged forward and swung it, it came down awkwardly on Herne's forearm. A bellow of pain still erupted from the monster and he immediately released his grip on Miss Pimsby's ankle.

"Come and play with someone your own size you big brute," Crisp said as he reeled the chain back in.

Herne dragged himself to his feet and turned to face Crisp. He was stumbling and glassy eyed now. The bucket of wine was beginning to visibly affect him. Crisp, however, wasn't about to let his guard down. Like a punch drunk boxer, Herne was still furious and dangerous. Crisp circled quickly around the far table and toward the front door again. He kept the chain at the ready and his eyes on Herne the whole while.

For a moment it looked like Herne might forgo Crisp's challenge and attack Miss Pimsby again. Crisp decided to force the issue. He drew Herne's attention by swinging his chain. It collided loudly onto the wood table top, eliciting a yelp of fright from Miss Pimsby.

Herne roared with anger and moved toward Crisp. This time he remembered his own chain. He swung it high above his head and whipped it down with tremendous force. All Crisp could do was swing his chain in self-defense. The two chains met in mid-air and let out a shower of sparks.

Miss Pimsby finally gathered herself and was crawling under the table toward the door. "Sorry about that," she called out. "I'm ready now."

"I'm still a bit busy," he called back to her as he dodged another swing of Herne's chain. Miss Pimsby yelped again as it struck just above her then settled limply on the table top.

Before Herne could reel his chain in for another swing, Crisp made a tactical decision. He dropped his chain and grabbed the far end of his foe's. It was the only way to keep from being struck with a single lethal blow.

Herne yanked fiercely on the chain in an attempt to shake it free. Crisp hung on tightly despite the wrenching force that tore at his hands and shoulders. When the chain didn't break loose Herne changed course and began to pull it toward himself. Crisp was slowly being drawn right toward the last place he wanted to be.

Crisp's face grimaced with increasing strain as he fought Herne in a deadly game of tug-of-war. Despite battling with all his might he was inexorably getting pulled closer to Herne's powerful arms and large fists. Just as he was within the radius of Herne's grasp, however, Crisp leapt forward. With both hands still on the chain he swung it directly down on the monster's left kneecap. Herne grunted and bent over in pain. Crisp then used the chain to pull him further down and caught him with a powerful kick that hit just below his right collarbone. The giant was knocked backwards and landed with a thud.

Miss Pimsby saw Herne land on the floor again. This time she shot out from under the table. Crisp turned on his heels and met her at the front of the cottage. He grabbed her by the hand and they swept through the door. Crisp was happy to see her handbag still swinging at her elbow.

"Good girl," he said proudly.

They fled the cottage and ran straight for the opening in the woods. Herne crashed unsteadily out of the door several steps behind them. Instead of chasing them on foot he stumbled toward his horse. He reached the large stallion and attempted to climb into his saddle. Crisp watched over his shoulder as Herne slipped from the stirrup and fell heavily to the ground. Another attempt ended in the same result. He finally pulled himself onto the horse with his third try. Crisp's last sight before he and Miss Pimsby dove back through the misty entranceway was the horse rearing as Herne attempted to spur it forward.

Once he and Miss Pimsby broke through the fog they were again outside the dense thicket. The expanse of Home Park and the moonlight that streamed down from the clear sky were welcome sights. Despite the fact that Herne wasn't behind them any longer their adrenaline kept them in flight for several hundred more yards.

When they finally stopped, Crisp took a moment to catch his breath.

"Blimey, are you alright?" he finally asked.

"I'm fine," she answered despite the fact that she looked anything but at the moment. "But that was absolutely terrify—". She stopped in mid-sentence. Her eyes widened and she pointed mutely over Crisp's shoulder. He turned and saw Herne gallop out of the copse of woods on his horse.

Crisp and Pimsby started running again but they were close to exhaustion. Herne also had the decided advantage of being on horseback. He was catching up to them quickly.

They managed to reach the fence at the edge of Great Park but it was too late. They didn't have time to climb it.

The fence served only to hem them in as Herne got even closer. Despite his trouble staying still on his horse, he had ridden to the point where he was now almost on top of them.

Crisp flinched as Herne lifted his chain above his head. As he went to swing it down, however, he lost his balance and fell out of his saddle. With a great thump he landed beside the stallion. The rider-less horse continued to gallop at full speed. Crisp's last, relief filled sight was Herne being dragged by his stirrups back into Home Park and off into the night.

21
A Little Problem

Crisp slumped against the fence. If it hadn't been there to hold his weight up he would have collapsed all the way to the ground. Miss Pimsby dropped her handbag and gently helped him sit on a soft patch of grass.

As he recovered some energy Crisp reviewed everything that just happened. His first concern was the time. Their initial trek through the misty portal to Herne's cottage now seemed like ages ago. He checked his watch, sure that their deadline had thinned to an impossible margin. Incredibly, it showed that hardly any time had passed since they entered the thicket. He checked to see if was damaged in the fight but it was working fine.

"What time do you have?"

Miss Pimsby checked her watch. "That's odd," she said as she tapped it. "It's running slow."

"No. I have the time as you. It must be accurate," he said with some effort as he tried to stand back up.

"Hang on—are you sure you're ready to go?"

"I'll hold together. How about you?"

"I think I reinjured my ankle on that last sprint," she answered with a half grimace, half smile. "But I'll hold together too."

They clambered over the fence and started to walk back through Great Park.

"I wonder where we just were." Crisp said as they crossed the Long Walk.

"What do you mean?"

"The place that hid Herne's cottage, it wasn't just a nook in Home Park. There was something strange about it. Beyond the fact that it held a giant rampaging lunatic, I mean."

This drew a chuckle from Miss Pimsby. It was infectious and he couldn't help joining her. They shared a few more good laughs as they stumbled along, which for some reason made him feel better. His feet seemed lighter and the aches that only moments ago permeated every part of his battered body began to melt away.

"Look at our watches, for instance," he said once their laughter faded and he finally had a chance to continue his thought. "Time stood still in there. It was like some kind of nightmare looking-glass place."

"I can't agree more. What on earth were Byrd and Shakespeare thinking of when they decided to hide the compositions there? They must have lost control of their senses," Miss Pimsby said as she continued to limp along.

He shook his head. "I've been thinking about that, too. It was a safe hiding place. We just didn't go about soothing the savage beast it held in quite the right way."

"I don't understand."

"We must have done something wrong." Crisp explained. "I can't see Byrd, or Shakespeare for that matter, duking it out with Herne and escaping in one piece. My guess is the wine was meant to neutralize him more effectively than it did. Maybe our formula wasn't strong enough. Or maybe I should have put a few more drops in the bucket.

"There's one thing I know for sure, though. Anyone wandering in there with Herne at full strength wouldn't have stood a chance of making it out with the compositions. It was meant to be a tricky enough job that only a member of the Academy would get it exactly right. We're incredibly lucky to be alive right now."

"Thank goodness you brought the formula with you."

Crisp patted his side reflexively and noticed it was flatter than it should be.

"It's gone," he said as he looked in the pocket. "The formula must have fallen out during the fight. It looks like Herne will get a present in return for the compositions he lost."

They reached King Street but their escape path put them much closer to Windsor castle than where the car was parked. Reversing direction, they walked until they reached the side street with the Rolls-Royce. It was late evening and there was even less activity then when they first arrived. They quickly got inside the car then Crisp pulled onto King Street and headed north toward Windsor castle.

"Unfortunately our work isn't done," he said as he drove. "We still need the herald trumpet. That means we need to stand watch somewhere close to the front of the Castle. With any luck we can find and intercept Reggie before he goes through the gate."

Crisp drove through the next several intersections, hoping to catch sight of the van. After reaching the third one he decided to take a right turn, but stopped when he noticed a pair of headlights approaching from his left. They were larger than a normal car's headlights and, for some reason, moving forward at a relatively slow speed, as if the driver was trying to locate an address. There was something vaguely familiar about the boxy silhouette behind them.

"It's Reggie," he exclaimed.

Crisp jumped from the car, ran into the middle of the road and began waving his arms. The van didn't look like it was going to stop at first but he stood his ground and put his hand up. Fortunately, the tank-like vehicle ground to a halt.

Crisp moved close enough to see through the windshield. A look of utter surprise filled Detective Sergeant Little's face once he recognized who blocked him from moving forward. Little reached over and began to roll down the bullet-proof glass on his door.

Crisp walked from the front of the van to the driver side. He needed to raise his voice to be heard over the sound of the idling engine.

"I must say, you are a welcome sight."

"Ben, is that you? What the devil are you doing here?"

"There's no time to explain, just let me into the van."

"Have you gone mental? You know I can't do that."

"Normally I'd agree with you, but—"

"But what?"

Crisp exhaled slowly, took a few steps closer to Little and looked him directly in his eyes. "Just trust me when I say that it's vitally important that the herald trumpet gets back to London as soon as possible."

A shocked look crossed Little's face. "You can't be serious."

"I'm dead serious."

"I can't do it, mate. The DCI would sack me in an instant."

"Please, just listen—"

"Get out of the way, Ben." Little began to roll the window back up.

"Wait a minute, you don't understand." Crisp called out.

Little stopped rolling the window. "I'm under strict orders to get this thing back where it belongs tonight," he shouted through the half-opening. "Unless you've got signed orders to the contrary I'm completing my delivery."

"Reggie, listen, I haven't been on holiday. I've been working. I can't say much about it—it's been sort of a special assignment. What I can tell you for certain is we have to go back to London immediately.

"I thought so! I knew you'd never go away in the middle of an investigation."

"So open the door and let's get going."

"You know procedure as well as I do, Ben. Even though I believe you, without proper orders there's no way I can disobey Fuller."

Little's reaction put Crisp in a major bind. He needed the trumpet but didn't have the orders that would get Little to cooperate. Reggie was a good bloke. He didn't want to get him in trouble or, even worse, have to resort to force.

He began to go through his jacket in an attempt to stall for time. "Fine, if you insist," he said and tried to look like he was searching for paper work. As he desperately rummaged around his right hand brushed across the pocket holding the shaker of Sleep Sand. Praying silently that it was the solution to his dilemma, he worked the hidden flap open with his fingers.

"I'm only supposed to use this in an extreme emergency but I suppose this counts as one."

He acted like he was shuffling through a set of papers as he took the lid off the jar. Once it was ready, he stepped even closer to the half-open window, but not too close. He wanted to conceal what he was holding. He also wanted

225

Little to stick his arm out as far as he could reach. The trick worked. Little stretched his hand out to grab what Crisp was supposed to be passing over. Crisp tilted the shaker and spilled a few grains of the Sleep Sand into his open palm. Instantaneously, Little's eyes winked shut and his body hunched over. Crisp leapt to the open window to check him. He was in a deep sleep.

"Thank heavens," he muttered as he carefully replaced the cap on the Sleep Sand and stowed it away again.

"Is your ankle okay? Can you come over and help me?" Crisp called out to Miss Pimsby.

"Don't be silly, I'm fine," she answered.

As she limped toward him, he climbed up the side of the van, unlocked the driver's door through the partially open window and swung it open. Little's body slumped out. Despite his slender frame, Little was surprisingly heavy. It took extra effort for Crisp to heave him back into the passenger seat. Once he was sure Little was comfortably positioned, he climbed into the back of the van. A long case rested in the middle of its floor. He flipped it open and saw with great relief that it held one shining brass herald trumpet. It was packed in a fitted plastic mold with a red velvet liner. He closed the case and passed it out to Miss Pimsby.

"Take this to the car and get back in your seat. I'll be there in a minute."

"We're not taking the van?" she asked. "Won't it be safer?"

"Possibly, but it's also slower and much more conspicuous. We need to get back to Highgate Cemetery as quickly as possible."

Before exiting the front cab Crisp checked Little one last time. He was still breathing deeply and slowly. His chin rested on his chest and a smile was on his face.

"Sweet dreams mate," he said quietly.

He turned off the engine, locked the driver's door, and jumped out of the van. The driver's door clicked loudly as he closed it.

"That should keep you safe enough," he muttered. Despite not having much of a choice, Crisp still felt a bit guilty about the way he tricked his colleague. In order to make amends, he was doubly determined to make sure it was all worthwhile.

* * *

Speed was now the utmost priority in Crisp's mind. The case with the herald trumpet was safely wedged in the trunk. Miss Pimsby carried the compositions in her handbag. The only remaining obstacle in front of them was getting to Highgate Cemetery before time ran out. He was in his element, though, and the Rolls-Royce responded once again with gusto as he pressed on the accelerator. By his calculations, if they didn't meet any major delays, they would get to their destination with less than an hour to spare. Not exactly a huge margin but still enough to get the job done.

"When we get to Highgate we'll need to hurry," he said. "We should try to figure out which composition we need before we get there. It'll save time."

Miss Pimsby flipped a dash light on, opened her purse and pulled out the folio. "I don't read music," she said apologetically. "I don't know what any of this means."

"Just look at the titles. Dee told us the name of the composition that we're supposed to counteract. It was the *Repeto Domus*. The name of the one we need will hopefully have some relation to it, like the anti-*Repeto Domus*."

"Hold on, there's a sheet in the back with some regular writing on it. Maybe it's instructions of some sort."

She pulled the last page from the book and began to read it to him:

Salutations,

If thou hath absconded with hither

Music thou must truly be friend and

Philosopher. Herne shall be sorely

vexed. The reed hath acted

as means for him to value and

227

Michael Malik

guard the pages we hath left behind. His spectral presence hath but few amusements to pass time in the nether land. As fellow Friend we bid thee act with care. The works thou now possess have worthe beyond measure. If thou doth possess the horne, blow always with solemn judgment.

William B
William S

"Sporting of them to leave a nice note—a bit late on the uptick, though, wouldn't you say?"

"Better late than never, I suppose," Miss Pimsby said with a shrug.

"Well, at least it helps confirm a few of our suspicions."

"Yes. And it also explains why they felt safe leaving the compositions in Herne's possession."

"Anything else?"

Miss Pimsby flipped the poem over. The back of the page was blank. "That's all there is."

"Keep looking for the sheet we need then."

She continued to shuffle through the papers. To Crisp it looked like she was having a bit of trouble in the dim light, especially since she was taking extra care not to miss anything. After inspecting half the folio, however, she pulled out one of the sheets and gave it a second going over.

"I think I found something." She was squinting at the page, which was a few inches from her nose. "This one's called the *Repeto Terra*. Do you figure it's the one we're looking for?"

"We have no way of being absolutely sure but it sounds about right," he answered. "Maybe you should finish checking the rest. That way you can make sure there isn't another one that sounds close."

Miss Pimsby did as she was asked. When she was done examining the last sheet she closed the folio.

"None of the others sound right to me."

"What did you do with the *Repeto Terra*?"

"I made it the first page so we can find it quickly."

They were almost to their exit, which meant they were only ten miles away now. Their next destination was North Hill Avenue which headed directly into Highgate.

Before long the Rolls was traveling up Swains lane. The street seemed even more claustrophobic to him this time around. Despite this being his second visit to it in a short period of time, nothing seemed familiar or comfortable to him. Perhaps having been nearly killed the last time around was the reason his spine tingled.

He tried to shake the feeling off. It shouldn't be anything like that this time. It was going to be a lark. Just go in, play the *Repeto Terra* on the herald trumpet, call the angels back, restore the balance of good and evil in the world so that centuries of death and destruction is averted, and go home. Once it was over he would give the lot back to Albert. Hopefully he would decide to melt the trumpet and burn the compositions so that no one would have to go through the same trouble again.

The west cemetery gate they previously entered came into view. Crisp pulled the car over to the side of the road. He turned the engine and headlights off but kept the electrical system on. Both doors opened noiselessly as he and Miss Pimsby exited the car together. Crisp made it to the trunk first. He saw why. Miss Pimsby's gait was clearly worse.

"I think my ankle stiffened during the ride," she said when she saw his expression.

Crisp opened the trunk, pulled the case out, and retrieved the trumpet. A barely noticeable scratch and an almost imperceptible dent marred its otherwise perfect metal surface.

"Do you have the *Repeto Terra*?"

"Yes, right here." Miss Pimsby opened her purse. She retrieved the folio and took out the first page. "That's it," she said and handed it to him.

Michael Malik

Crisp took the page from her and held it up close to the trunk light. *Repeto Terra* was written across the top of the sheet in elaborate calligraphy. His eyes shifted lower and he scanned the notes composed four centuries earlier by William Byrd.

"Genius," he said with a trace of awe. "It's complex but doable." He was rubbing the back of his head as he studied the lines. "All of a sudden I wish I kept up my tuba playing."

Once he absorbed the information on the page he folded it and stuffed it in his jacket. Now came the hardest part. He managed to avoid it ever since they left Windsor but now he didn't have a choice.

"Miss Pimsby, I—"

"You have to go on without me," she interrupted him. "I know. My ankle will slow us up and we don't have much time left. I'll lock things up here and try to catch up with you as fast as I can."

Crisp was extremely relieved. He thought she would fight him over staying behind. Instead she made it easy.

"We'd never be standing here without all the work you've done. It doesn't seem right for you to miss the payoff."

"You can tell me all about it when we meet up again. Now go before it's too late."

He started to leave but then suddenly stopped and stood squarely before her.

"Before I do, it's my turn."

"To do what?"

"Say thank you."

"Whatever for?"

"I have a bit of a confession to make. That day, the one when you waited on my stairs, I meant to send you packing. Like I told you, I was convinced I couldn't help Albert; that there was more important business I needed to attend to."

"But you did help, that's all that matters."

"You don't understand—"

He hesitated for a few heartbeats. It was just enough time for him to find the words and courage he needed.

230

"I've spent a good part of my life running away from things—problems I didn't want to face. Each time I've ended up regretting my decisions, mostly because they always hurt the people closest to me. Yet, for some reason I always kept making the same mistakes. If it weren't for you I would have gone and done it all over again. So, like I said, thanks."

He bent over and kissed her softly on the lips.

Miss Pimsby looked at him oddly for a moment. He felt like she was looking right through his outer shell, the part he put up to protect himself, and seeing the heart of him. He suddenly felt a bit warmer in the chilly night air.

"I think you're being a bit hard on yourself," she said as she reached up and lightly caressed the fading bruise on his cheek. "But in any case, you're welcome. Now get going."

Crisp stood glued in his spot for a moment wondering if there was more he should say. When nothing came out, she gave him a soft shove to the chest and said, "Go. We can talk more later." He picked up the trumpet and trotted toward the cemetery. He took one last look back at Miss Pimsby. Her eyes looked damp as she waved him forward and then limped back to the front of the car.

He reached the gate and plunged into the darkness. Once his eyes adjusted, he found the same path he and Miss Pimsby followed last time. He jogged along it, looking carefully for the opening in the brush that would take him to the clearing. The cemetery was a big place and he could waste a lot of time if he got lost.

Keeping his gaze trained on the side of the trail helped guide him. He soon found the broken branches that marked their old detour. He pushed through them again, careful to keep the trumpet tight in his grip. After a struggle he broke into the clearing on the other side. He immediately zeroed in on a large pedestal that was in the distance. It had once held a lovely angel statue. Now, only the lower half of the angel's body stood there. The clearing he needed was just to the other side of it. He rushed forward, the excitement of being so close to his goal overwhelming him. After only a couple of strides, however, the base of his spine was tingling again and he felt the sudden urge to turn and retreat. Before he could act on his instinct, a fast rushing sound filled the air followed by a tremendous roar. The ground erupted in front of him in an enormous shower of dirt and rocks. It was as if a new mountain was growing suddenly and violently from the earth. He was thrown backwards like a rag doll and landed hard in an awkward tumble of limbs. The darkness of the evening started to take second place to the gloom that filtered through his brain. One last thought crossed his mind before he lost consciousness. His luck had finally run out.

22
The Improper Spirit

The first sensation that returned to Crisp was pain. A wave of intense and unremitting agony washed over him. As his awareness slowly increased, he isolated the wracking feeling as coming from somewhere below his waist. He moaned softly and made a feeble attempt to move. This brought a new sensation. He was suddenly dragged from the ground and propped into a sitting position. The movement brought forth another blaze of fire, which helped him identify the pain as coming from his lower legs. They were, at the least, badly broken.

Once the worst of it started to fade, he began to take a mental inventory. In addition to his legs, there was a throbbing sensation that pulsed from around his left ear. Something wet and sticky, which he assumed was blood, was running down his neck on the same side. His ears, especially on the left, were functioning as if cotton was stuffed in them. Noises that sounded like distant murmuring started to filter through the fog, but they were muted and garbled.

As he took several deep heaving breaths he could feel that his back was resting against something hard and cold. There was also a stitch in his right side that worsened with each gasp of air he inhaled. At least it was a familiar sensation. It was the same pain he'd felt in the SAS when he cracked a rib after a jump.

His evaluation was interrupted by a chillingly distinct voice. Somehow it managed to penetrate the thick shield that seemed to envelop his head. "Hello, Detective Crisp. Welcome back to the land of the living—although I suspect just barely so."

Crisp lifted his right eyelid, which felt like it was made of lead, and looked in the direction the voice came from. It was just as bad as he suspected. Coming slowly into focus, dressed in his black bug suit and with his mirthless sneer back in place, was Taylor.

"You are quite a fortunate man. I instructed my team to ignite the explosives when you were directly above them. The sentry who first saw you coming was slightly premature with his trigger. A few more steps and we wouldn't be having this conversation. I'd be picking pieces of you off the ground."

Crisp tried to think of a clever retort but the pain once again overwhelmed him. All he managed to respond with was a wince as he gritted his teeth.

Taylor savored the sight of Crisp in agony for a moment and then said, "Ahh, how liberating—the thorn has finally been removed from my side. I must say, it's about time. I am quite tired of your jokes. Please, try to relax. None of your police friends are going to come charging to your rescue here, and I doubt these statues will come alive to fight on your behalf.

"You are, I assure you, alone—foolishly alone. Oh, I almost forgot your female friend—the secretary. But of course we've already accounted for her."

Worry filled Crisp and he began to look frantically around. All he could see was that he'd been dragged to the clearing and that the hard, cold object he was leaning against was a tombstone. Taylor's body blocked his attempt to get a view of much else. Luckily, the smug villain was satisfied with his taunts and started to walk toward the center of the small open area. This allowed Crisp to continue his search. He swept his head until he caught sight of another figure sitting on the ground. He opened his other eyelid and tried to focus. When the blurriness began to diminish, he saw with relief that the other prisoner was indeed Miss Pimsby. She was gagged and lashed to a tombstone. Most importantly, however, she was alive and didn't seem to be injured in any way.

She noticed his gaze and stared back with what looked like a combination of fear and concern. Crisp knew it was for him. He was probably a frightful sight.

Having located Miss Pimsby, Crisp began to survey the rest of his surroundings. He immediately noticed the reason he felt the cold tombstone so well. He was no longer wearing his jacket. It was lying on a crypt on the opposite side of the clearing. The thieves had somehow discovered its secret pockets, emptied all the elemental tools, and piled them on top of it. He looked for the atlas, expecting it to be with the rest of his kit, but didn't see it.

The more he looked around, the bleaker the picture became. There were faint traces of movement all around the clearing. He figured at least a half-dozen men were dispersed just beyond the circle of angel statues that formed its border. Their black suits and his blurry sight made recognizing further details difficult. Even so, it looked like they were deployed efficiently enough that every possible avenue of escape was covered.

The case that had held the herald trumpet sat in the center of the clearing. It must have been taken from Albert's car when Miss Pimsby was captured. The trumpet sat flared-end down on top of it.

There was one sight that he was having a deuce of a time figuring out. Stacked in the center of the clearing, less than ten meters from the trumpet, were about twenty small wooden barrels. Some open box crates sat on top of the pile. Three smaller square bundles rested around the base of the strange pyramid. Whatever the structure was, it was distinctly separate from the rest of the cemetery. Which meant Taylor and his accomplices must have brought it with them.

Crisp admitted there was little to be optimistic about. The trap used to catch him was well thought out. Nevertheless, he refused to give up. There was still a slight chance he could at least get Miss Pimsby to safety, but he needed to wait for the right moment

"He's awake," Taylor called out from his position in the center of the clearing.

At first Crisp thought the man had gone soft. He was talking to a rock set on a crypt. Then Crisp noticed something unusual about the clump of material. It wasn't stone. It was metal and about the same size and shape as a human head. As he stared intently at it, trying to figure out what it was, the clump began to glow. The added light assisted his vision just enough that he recognized the thing that Taylor was addressing. His shock and surprise could not have been more complete. It was an ambrosium bust. Despite his growing confusion, he was absolutely sure of it.

235

The pulsing light that emanated from the bust grew in intensity. A glowing ball of light materialized then rose from its center. It freed itself from the bust except for a thin cord-like wisp that maintained a tenuous connection. The orb then moved slowly outwards. It drifted directly toward Crisp with what seemed like purposeful curiosity. As it did, the amorphous luminescent ball started to take a human form. The ghost that was revealed wore pantaloons and a short velvet coat with full lace collars. His long, narrow face was blunted by a full beard. A tall broad brimmed hat sat on top of his head. Thick shoulder-length hair tumbled out from beneath it on either side.

The ghost's glowing figure illuminated an area several feet around him. The light allowed Crisp to catch a glimpse of a rumpled and portly figure standing next to Taylor. Despite the black camouflage, his squirrel-like features were unmistakable. The addition of his erstwhile map expert, Josiah Hornbeck, to the company of thieves was another unpleasant surprise that only added to his increasing desperation.

The ghost was now fully formed and staring intently at him.

"As Mister Taylor hath expressed to thee already, Detective Crisp, welcome back to the land of the living." The voice that accompanied the ghost was deep and raspy. "I cannot return the favor of course. As thou can see I am but a lowly spirit, much the same as that black hearted John Dee. Thou art the fool who so nobly rescued him nigh a fortnight ago. Despite thy lack of wisdom thou hath managed to give us much trouble—and so unnecessarily. Thou hath been placed on a false path. For his pride Albert did insure thy destruction."

The shock Crisp felt at the sight of this new ghost had one beneficial effect. It dulled the pain he felt. Instead of dwelling on his misery his mind was filled with questions. The main one was where this ghost, who was obviously familiar with Dee and his uncle, came from. He thought only the Academy of Natural Philosophers knew how to create ambrosium busts. Was this also a ghost of the Academy? Had he been struggling against a colleague of theirs this whole time? It was a logical conclusion, but at the same time it seemed so wrong. This ghost spoke of Dee and Albert with such obvious contempt and outright hatred. He looked and acted nothing like a scientist.

"Who are you?" he finally blurted out. "Why are you here with these madmen?"

"All in good time, Detective, all in good time."

The ghost floated away from him and toward the center of the clearing. Taylor seemed to be ready and waiting. He held up a piece of paper for the ghost to inspect. Crisp, whose mind and senses cleared considerably in the prior few minutes, immediately recognized it as the *Repeto Terra*. The ghost seemed to be entranced as he stared at the composition for a full minute. He then nodded curtly. Taylor pulled a heavy metal lighter from his pocket and, with a flick of his thumb, a tall orange flame shot from it. He touched it to the corner of the sheet of music. Crisp watched in horror as it was engulfed in fire. Taylor dropped it to the ground where it turned to ash almost instantly. A gust of wind picked up the charred pieces and, just like that, the *Repeto Terra* was gone.

* * *

The ghost floated back to Crisp. A barely suppressed smile curled the corners of his mouth. He was obviously pleased with his triumph.

"Thy still hath perhaps a few dozen minutes before the deadline passes. It is of no matter now. With the *Repeto Terra* destroyed thy last hope is gone." The smile twitched with satisfaction. "We may now talk as long as you wish. First, let me introduce myself. My name is Guido Fawkes. Most know me by the first name Guy. Thou art surely familiar with me already. A holiday is celebrated in my honor in this country, as I knew it someday would be. Perhaps now the world will follow suit."

Crisp hardly believed what he was seeing and hearing. The person responsible for the bombings, the thefts, and playing the Celestial music wasn't a person at all. It was Guy Fawkes! His ghost was somehow preserved in an ambrosium bust.

237

He began a rapid search of his memory. It wasn't hard. Every English school boy and girl knew the tale. Guy Fawkes—1605— November 5th—that's the day he tried to blow up parliament in the infamous Gunpowder Plot. He was caught in the nick of time. Afterwards he was taken to the Tower of London, where his torture was supposed to have been merciless. Once he confessed he was hung in the Old Palace Yard. He was supposed to have been drawn and quartered too, but somehow broke free from his captors and jumped to his death, sparing him from the most gruesome part of his execution.

"What—what—are you doing here? How did you—find us?"

Fawkes' response to his question was a laugh. It was not from amusement. Harshness and cruelty instead resonated from the short outburst.

"It was only a matter of time. I knew that if thou desired to reverse that which we wrought thou must return here. Thou were but a mouse to my cat."

Crisp shuddered slightly. Even as the pain from his injuries made him weaker, however, his curiosity continued to grow stronger.

"How did you become a ghost? The Academy—they didn't make you." These last words faded into a faint cough.

The cruel laugh escaped Fawkes again.

"Thou art so full of questions Detective. Tis quite remarkable for a man in thy position. Is not the pain exquisite? Trust me, I know something about pain. The torture that I suffered in the Tower was unrelenting." Despite their ghostly glow, Fawkes eyes now appeared distant and hollow.

"You haven't—answered my question."

He saw that Taylor and Hornbeck were staring in rapt fascination at their exchange. Even the men outside the clearing turned into frozen shadows.

"Twas a remarkable thing in many ways, a curse in others, and so long ago. William Byrd and I were kindred spirits, both still loyal to Rome in a country that was mad with anti-papist furor. At one of our meetings he hinted that he was working on something that would lessen our torment. He was coy, and never would speak directly of what he planned. I took to prying whenever we were together and found his early attempts at Celestial language amongst his papers."

"You were the one Dee told us about—he found a leak—their secret wasn't safe."

"I confess readily to my intrigue. I was patient at first, eager to learn how Byrd meant to use the discovery. With each debate I drew him into, my disappointment grew. Byrd, like most of the sheep he kept company with, desired peace and harmony above all else. He didn't see the power that dwelt in his hands.

"I made one foolish mistake at this point. My more ardent associates needed encouragement. I whispered to them what Byrd whispered to me. I, however, spoke of the Celestial language as a way for us to gain an advantage. My associates' tongues lacked discretion. Thus did Dee, who is a charlatan and beggar, learn that their secret was forfeit."

"He caught you at your own game."

"'Tis true Dee suspected me, but he never knew for certain where the breach came. I had one more chance. Byrd and I met. After some cajoling he confessed there was something he was trying to hide. I was sure he meant the compositions. Before he took his leave I succeeded in pilfering a single sheet from his valise. 'Twas tricky and I was nearly caught. But my effort gained me the *Repeto Domus*."

"You must have been disappointed."

"Very perceptive of thee, Detective. I could not make the language work, despite having the finest musicians play the notes. I decided to put the sheet aside and pursue other methods to fight the heretics. When Dee learned of my plan to bomb Parliament the foul blackheart leapt at his opportunity. It was that spawn of darkness who alerted the guards and caused my capture and subsequent torture.

"One of Mr. Taylor's ancestors was an original associate of mine. After narrowly escaping arrest, he sought retribution against Dee. While waiting for his chance, he observed Dee doting over three lumps of a strange metal. He stole all three that night and tried to barter them for my freedom. The guards he approached refused his advances. The metal may have been strange and worth much to Dee, but contained no worth to them. The next day he watched forlorn as I was brought to the gallows. He stood directly beneath me as the rope did its work. Later he found, to his amazement, that one of the lumps carried my likeness. To his greater amazement, I flowed forth from the bust in my present form. So the belated answer to thy question is 'twas a most fortunate accident."

"You blame Dee—that's why you sent the angels away?" Crisp asked with barely a whisper. His back was sliding down the tombstone but he didn't dare right himself. "This has all been for revenge?"

Anger flashed across Fawkes' face. "Revenge! Dost thou think my intellect so vulgar that revenge wouldst be my goal?"

He turned to Taylor. "The minds of the men engaged in the imprisonment of the soul do not readily change. It is just as we have discussed, my friend. It is just as it will ever be unless we are victorious."

"You've lost me," Crisp said weakly.

He glanced over to Miss Pimsby. She was struggling to escape so that she could help him. Her efforts were now almost frantic. He wanted to send some sort of signal to her, to reassure her, but it would likely be in vain. He doubted Taylor and Fawkes would let them walk away scot-free once they got what they wanted. They probably weren't going to kill them. If they planned to, it would have happened already. Even so, Crisp was fully aware that there were ways to punish someone without killing them.

Fawkes turned back, eager to explain. Crisp could tell the ghost held onto centuries of anger and resentment. He was using his moment of triumph release some of the pent-up pressure these emotions had caused.

"What Dee suspected but Byrd was too noble to grasp was that I had, and still have, a specific purpose. Quite amazingly, even after four centuries, he still has not figured it out."

"Figured what out?"

"I, my dear Detective, am an anarchist, dedicated to the restoration of man to his natural state. In order to accomplish this, the corruptors of man must be eliminated. After my capture and torture I understood the truth. Achieving my goal meant abolishing every form of government and religion from the world.

"Through the centuries I have worked with a loose band of confederates to bring about these aims. We have managed some successes. But it was always the same. Destroy something or kill someone and chaos reigned for a brief period. The world seemed to right itself no matter the tragedy we invoked.

"Then I remembered Byrd and the composition I stole. I realized that as long as mankind could call upon his basic virtues we would never reach our goal. But now, by chasing off the angels, we have finally dealt a fatal blow to the troublesome power they wield."

"What power are you talking about?" Crisp blurted out, interrupting Fawkes.

Fawkes' malicious grin spread even wider. "Dost thou mean to say thy precious Academy did not tell thee? What trust thou must have in thy masters to risk so much with no understanding. Blind fool."

When Crisp didn't answer Fawkes floated even closer to him. The ghost stared down with eyes that were as cold as stone and a grimace of contempt seeped beneath his mustache.

"Byrd thought the angels were here to guide mankind, to help see him through the most troubling times and endure. I, however, saw the truth. The forces Byrd spoke of create only subservience—to Queens and Kings and Popes and Captains. They are invisible chains that need to be broken."

"You have it all backwards."

"I am certain thou wilt refuse to heed my words but they are nonetheless true. Men are nothing but dogs led by a leash. The tethers that harness them exist naturally and are all around us. Some are so slight that they break, like a cobweb, with the least effort. Others create bonds that are much more durable—and influential. The ability to trust, to believe, to feel a sense of loyalty; that, my poor, misinformed young fool, is the purpose of angels here on

Earth, to imbue the masses with this kind of faith." He sputtered out the last word like it burned his tongue.

"Without them, men shall turn on each other like the animals they truly are, but this time they shall not stop until the wheat is separated from the chaff—once and for all."

"You can't. It's madness."

"Ah, thou art so wrong. 'Twill be a hard road, I admit. Many may perish. In the end, man will benefit beyond any measure thy corrupted mind can conceive. We will give him back the freedom to live in a natural state."

"Someone will stop you."

Crisp's threat was unimpressive even to him.

"Thou were our last obstacle. Thou hath been conquered." The bitterness faded from Fawkes expression and was replaced once again by a grim smile. "Now if thou will excuse me, I must still decide thy fate."

23
A Ghost of a Chance

Fawkes turned his back and started to float away.

"Wait. Water—I need water."

Fawkes stopped and looked back at Crisp. There was no pity in his expression.

"I cannot help thee. As thou can clearly see, I have needed neither food nor drink for centuries. I have none to give," he answered with a smirk.

"My flask has some. Please—give me some water."

Fawkes' expression went from smug to annoyed. He swung around to Hornbeck, who jumped back, startled.

"Mapmaker, check his flask."

Hornbeck looked terrified as he rushed over to the crypt where Crisp's jacket rested. He rummaged for a moment then picked out the flask from the pile of objects.

"Here it is," he said, lifting it for Fawkes to see.

"Don't just stand there; make sure it is what he says it is." Fawkes ordered.

"How?" Hornbeck asked with a blank look on his face.

"Taste it, dunderhead."

Hornbeck twitched nervously. He was obviously worried Crisp was attempting some sort of trick. After twisting off its cap, he sniffed at the flask's small opening. The lack of odor seemed to satisfy him and he took a small swig. A smile broke across his face.

"It's just water."

Fawkes' annoyed expression intensified. He seemed to be caught in an internal dilemma. After a moment of thought he said, "I am not the same beast that my captors were. Therefore, I shall be generous and afford thee a small comfort amongst thy suffering." His decision made, he swept away without another look.

As Hornbeck moved toward him, Crisp noticed something that lifted his hopes. There were fewer human-shaped shadows outside the clearing than earlier. Fawkes' henchmen seemed to be disappearing. He watched as a large dark figure off to his left silently vanished. His options when it came to fighting back were suddenly and mysteriously expanding. Fawkes and Taylor were in a deep conversation and hadn't noticed anything out of the ordinary. Once Hornbeck finished giving him his flask, though, he would have nothing to do. He might notice what was happening. There were several more men still standing guard. If he could distract Hornbeck long enough the entire outside ring of guards might be gone before an alarm was raised. His chance for an even fight would be considerably improved.

"Here." Hornbeck knelt down and was pushing the flask into Crisp's limp hand. He held it like it would burn him if he gripped too tightly. "Take it. Drink quickly before he changes his mind. I doubt you will receive any more charity after this."

"What's your part in this?" Crisp asked as he lifted the flask to his lips, took in a generous mouthful of the Aquae Vitae and swallowed it down.

Hornbeck looked over his shoulder. Once he was sure they were not being scrutinized he started to answer.

"My part? It's simple. You owned something I wanted. Now it's mine."

Crisp looked down and saw the atlas tucked in Hornbeck's belt. Now he knew why it wasn't with the other stuff from his jacket.

"So that day, in your shop—"

"Was the most incredible day of my life! I spent years studying what I thought was a legend. And then all of a sudden there you were, sitting in front of me, with an actual Moonstone map in your possession. But then you refused to sell it to me. That was a mistake. If you did as I asked none of this would be happening."

Crisp took another swallow from the flask and noticed that his hearing in his left ear now seemed better. The stitch in his side also was receding. He decided to test his right leg by carefully stretching it out. It was less painful but still felt weak and stiff. His left leg was the same. The Aquae Vitae was working but its effects were still incomplete. Hopefully, in another minute he would be healed enough to move. It was all the time he had left.

"That doesn't explain how you got here."

"I saw what happened that day through my window. I saw Taylor attack you. I watched you get away. I figured I found an ally so, after the explosion, I hid him in my shop until it was safe for him to leave. We made an agreement that day. If I helped him, the atlas would be mine when you were caught."

The cartographer's face started to twitch with what Crisp assumed was giddiness. "It should bring me untold fame and fortune. I suppose I have you to thank for that, Detective."

"So you're an anarchist with a profit motive. It must get confusing for you."

Hornbeck looked aggrieved. "I'm no anarchist. I'm an opportunist." He tossed his head back to the center of the clearing. "Taylor's the true believer. His family has been following Fawkes' orders for four hundred years. Even so, he's more practical than he would like everyone to think. He's been promised the herald trumpet when this is over. It should bring a handsome sum in a secret auction. I guess even an anarchist likes the rewards that come from a successful effort."

He snorted with irony at his own comment. The laugh was cut short when he suddenly realized how much he just revealed. His eyes settled on Crisp with a suspicious glare.

Hornbeck retrieved the flask from Crisp's hand and stood up. "This will be another nice little souvenir for me." He gazed down at Crisp like he was a traveler about to go on a long trip. "You shouldn't have gotten involved with this bit of business. Fawkes is not a man who has much kindness left in him."

"He's not a man at all, now is he?" Crisp retorted irritably.

"No he's not," Hornbeck conceded. "But the anarchists who follow him are and there are more of them than you would care to guess. Believe me when I tell you, they do just as he says. Fawkes may be nothing but smoke but the power he wields is fire. And you, my unlucky young man, are about to get burned."

Crisp was tired of the twitchy little thief. As subtly as possible, he looked around the cemetery. He hoped all the guards were gone so that he could be rid of Hornbeck.

There was one shadowy figure still left. Hornbeck spared Crisp the trouble of trying to distract him anymore, however. With the flask in his hand, he started to move back to Taylor and Fawkes.

Crisp's body tensed in anticipation. There could only be a few more minutes left before the deadline passed. His time was almost up, and he knew he had only one chance to get things right.

* * *

A loud shout suddenly penetrated the still night air. "Oi, who are you! What have you done to my brother?"

Fawkes, Taylor and Hornbeck all turned to inspect the spot the shout came from. Crisp decided it was as good a distraction as he was going to get. He leapt from the ground and ran toward the herald trumpet in the center of the clearing.

Taylor caught sight of him first. An astonished expression filled his face. "Impossible! Impossible!" he screamed. Lifting his wrist, he began to yell into what looked like a small transmitter. "Engage, all of you, engage. Leave your posts immediately and engage the enemy in the central staging area." He looked up expectantly. When nothing happened his expression went from astonished to furious. He lifted his wrist again and yelled "Engage now. Where are you? Where are you!?"

Crisp ignored Taylor and continued to make a bee-line toward the trumpet. A feeling of relief shot through him like an electrical shock. Minutes earlier there was no way he could have reached the trumpet and freed Miss Pimsby before being subdued. With Taylor's men out of the picture he had a chance to finish the job and still save her.

"Someone get him," screamed Fawkes, his raspy voice now shrill.

Hornbeck was closest. He hesitated for a moment, clearly less than eager to fight.

"Mapmaker," Fawkes yelled, "Help not and I will bury thee where thou doth stand."

The threat hit home. Hornbeck shuffled a few steps to his left and placed himself directly between the trumpet

246

and Crisp. Once in position, he went into a defensive crouch. He was less than a daunting sight.

Crisp didn't bother to slow down. At another time, he probably would have enjoyed stopping and teaching the portly mapmaker a lesson. At the moment, however, his mind was cemented into a set plan. When he reached Hornbeck, he simply ran through him. The collision sent Hornbeck flying backwards. He was thrown to the ground and rolled over several times before coming to rest flat on his back.

Crisp's body was knocked sideways. Slightly off balance, he halted for a moment. The sight of two bodies crashing through the outer ring of the clearing held him up further. Through the corner of his eye he identified the radio-operator who helped attack him in his flat and who played the *Repeto Domus* a week earlier. He was dressed in the same black camouflage as his compatriots but his facial features made him easy enough to recognize. He appeared to be fighting with a man he never saw before. All he could discern from his brief glance was that the man was lanky. He appeared to be at least three of four inches above six feet and quite thin. A somewhat large but well-shaped nose dominated his facial features and a shock of slicked back blond hair covered his head. He was wearing a jacket that was newer but similar to the one Albert gave to Crisp. And he was desperately grappling for something with Taylor's radio man.

The appearance of the two men caused Crisp to delay for a split second. It was enough time to allow Fawkes to gain back a measure of control.

"Mr. Taylor, it is left to thee to deal with the Detective," his raspy voice commanded. "Thou knoweth what to do. I shall help Basil with his unexpected nuisance."

Without hesitation, Taylor rushed toward Crisp. Fawkes swept toward the other pair of combatants, who were still wrestling furiously.

Crisp met Taylor a few yards from the center of the clearing. He stretched out his arm to grab Dee's trumpet, which was still standing upside down on its case. Taylor was able to knock him sideways at the last moment.

Michael Malik

"It ends as it began, Detective." Taylor taunted as he dug his heels in between Crisp and the trumpet.

"All out of little bombs to toss around, eh?"

"It doesn't matter much. I have no need for them. My tactical situation is superior. The *Repeto Terra* has been destroyed. At this point I am merely protecting what I have rightfully earned."

"Stolen, you mean," Crisp said coolly.

"You have so little to gain. By my calculations, which I assure you are accurate, you have only minutes left to get past me. After that the trumpet will be worthless to you. Are you willing to risk so much simply to satisfy the whims of your Royal masters?"

The crunching sound of breaking glass caught Crisp's attention. He decided to risk a quick glance to see what caused it. The object the men had been fighting over lay shattered on a tombstone. A thick cloud of gas now emanated from the spot where it hit and was beginning to dissipate into the atmosphere. The new man reacted instantly. He knelt to the ground and threw his coat over his head. Basil was not so lucky. Caught in the center of the gas cloud, he fell to the ground like a sack of potatoes. His eyes were open and he seemed awake but he was apparently unable to move. When the edge of the cloud reached Miss Pimsby her head slumped over as if her neck lost all of its strength. Then, in the blink of an eye, the vapor seemed to evaporate into the night air. The newcomer leapt up almost as quickly as he had crouched down and shrugged his coat back into place.

Hornbeck was now back on his feet. Any sense of attachment he may have felt to his fellow thieves seemed to have disappeared utterly in the chaos that surrounded him. He turned and attempted to flee. Despite being surprisingly fleet of foot, the path he took was not wide enough. The stranger managed to intercept him at the edge of the clearing. With one hard tug he ripped the atlas from Hornbeck's waist belt.

Crisp thought for a moment that Hornbeck was going to fight to get the atlas back. The mapmaker stood his ground and stared greedily at the hands of the thin stranger. But fear must have overtaken him once more. With a low

248

whimper, he turned and raced out of the clearing. The darkness swallowed him in an instant.

Taylor was now outnumbered. Crisp pounced at him but the anarchist was still a strong and capable opponent. He managed to intercept and easily deflect Crisp's attempt to get past him. Crisp was reminded that his injuries were not truly healed and, despite the Aquae Vitae, he was already beginning to wear down.

"Do not let him near the trumpet," Fawkes yelled at Taylor.

His apparition was now floating in tight circles around the center of the clearing. In a fit of rage, he stopped and pointed at the stranger, who stowed the atlas in his jacket and began closing in to help Crisp.

"Hold thyself, foul interloper."

Fawkes swept down at the man and passed straight through his body. The stranger, however, ignored his momentary meld with the ghost and continued toward Taylor. He attempted to grapple with the anarchist but was quickly thrown to the ground.

Taylor couldn't fight two people at once, though. The seconds he spent defending himself gave Crisp an opening. He brushed past Taylor and grabbed Dee's trumpet. Once it was securely in his grasp, he carried it to the edge of the clearing. He stopped next to the crypt where his jacket was laid out. Praying silently that his memory was accurate, he lifted the trumpet to his lips and began to play the *Repeto Terra*. A beautiful and haunting melody escaped from the end of the instrument. It reminded him of the *Repeto Domus* but with more languid and flowing notes and a sharper finish.

As the last note sounded, the sky above the cemetery began to change. Thick clouds rolled in, seemingly from nowhere, obscuring the previously bright moon. Violent gusts of wind began to swirl in circles. Suddenly, a giant rent formed in the middle of the blanket covering the sky. A shaft of light pierced the opening like a sword and stabbed down toward the earth. The path it took carried its point directly into the center of the clearing. When it hit the ground, the column of light burned with a white hot intensity. It then shattered into countless small glittering

Michael Malik

particles of light. The particles seemed suspended for a few moments, as if waiting for permission to move. Then, instantaneously, they scattered in a dazzling firework-like display. Some shot directly upwards. Others flared up before fizzing to nothingness. Still others shrunk then disappeared as if sucked into a vacuum. The blinding visual cacophony kept everyone glued to their spots and temporarily washed out Fawkes ghostly glow. After reaching a crescendo, the flashing and whizzing dissipated, allowing the night to settle back into semi-darkness. Fawkes and the moon were once again all that remained to illuminate the clearing.

The night vision Crisp lost in the display took a few moments to reestablish. Once the spots cleared he reassessed the scene around him. Miss Pimsby was still secured to the headstone and listless. The timely and life-saving stranger was already moving toward her. He kneeled at her side and gently lifted her head up with one hand. Reaching into his jacket, he pulled out a small glass phial. It cracked in half easily with pressure from his thumb. He wafted it beneath Miss Pimsby's nose. After a few passes her muscle tone started to return. The stranger removed his hand from her chin and she held her head up on her own. He whispered something to her that Crisp couldn't hear. She nodded her answer. The stranger then moved behind the headstone and started trying to untie her.

Taylor covered his face with his right arm when the sword of light had exploded. He now brought it down and started his own reconnaissance. After watching Crisp and the stranger warily for a moment he looked for Fawkes. The ghost was sputtering with disbelief and anger.

"No, no, no, it cannot be. It cannot be." he kept repeating. "All my plans, all the years waiting have come to naught. It cannot be."

"It's over Fawkes." Crisp said. "You might as well pack it in."

Taylor shook his head defiantly. "Not quite yet, Detective."

He reached back into one of the open box crates on the pile of explosives and pulled out a stick of TNT. A long fuse stuck out from one end of the deadly cylinder. He then

250

retrieved the heavy lighter he used to burn the *Repeto Terra* from his pocket. It ignited with a quick flick of his thumb. The tall flame it produced easily lit the end of the fuse.

"Tell your new friend to back away from the girl or she will catch this in her lap."

Crisp didn't have to repeat Taylor's threat. The stranger stopped trying to untie Miss Pimsby and moved back into the open, several paces away from the headstone holding her. His posture was relaxed as he waited for Taylor's next move.

"Your friend is smart. He doesn't wish to be a hero. Now Detective, you'll return the trumpet to me. Your friend will wake Basil just as he did the girl. Perhaps playing the *Repeto Domus* again will reverse your meddling. It's worth a try, I think."

Crisp hesitated.

"Do it now!" Taylor screamed while lifting his arm in a throwing motion.

Fawkes noticed Taylor's actions and zoomed toward him. "Yes Mr. Taylor, blow them up, bring the inferno if thou must." He was practically babbling with excitement. The failure of his plan seemed to have unhinged him.

A furtive glance toward Miss Pimsby was the only signal Crisp dared try to convey. He was sure the stranger saw him, though. His glance was returned with a deliberate eye shift. The man then moved toward Basil slowly, trying to prevent returning an ally to Taylor any sooner than necessary.

"Hurry, Detective. My fuse is literally getting short," Taylor called insistently.

"You win," Crisp answered. "Just don't hurt anyone and you'll get what you want."

He moved toward Taylor with deliberate caution, not wanting to do anything that might spook the anarchist into tossing the TNT. When he was close enough he held the trumpet out for Taylor to take.

As soon as Taylor's hand gripped the instrument Crisp yanked on it hard. Taylor was pulled off balance and he stumbled forward. Crisp raised his injured right leg and kicked upwards. His foot caught Taylor on the hip, causing an unpleasant sensation to shoot from his shin to his knee.

Michael Malik

It wasn't normal pain. It felt like a frostbitten extremity; numb but in an uncomfortable way.

The kick's effect on Taylor was more important than the feeling it created in Crisp's leg. The anarchist went flying backwards and landed against the pile of gunpowder barrels. Several tumbled on top of him, knocking him down. As he fell, the lit stick of TNT flew from his hand and landed somewhere in the center of the explosive pyramid. Two of the barrels he knocked over rolled toward the crypt holding Fawkes' bust, finally coming to a halt at the base of the cement structure.

Crisp reacted instantly. Not knowing how much time he had, he turned and ran back toward his coat. He grabbed the Magic Flute and looked over at Miss Pimsby. The stranger was no longer guarding Basil. He was kneeling next to her and desperately trying to untie her bonds.

"Get down."

He passed Fawkes as he ran toward his friends. The ghost was paralyzed with disbelief. His own store of gunpowder was about to obliterate the bust that sustained him for four centuries.

Crisp's strength drained increasingly with each step. When there were only a few yards left to go, he dove. He landed at Miss Pimsby's feet, on his side with the injured rib. A sharp stabbing sensation ripped through his side. He quickly stifled a grunt of pain then, after taking a second to get his breath back, raised the tube to his mouth and blew as hard as he could. Three different streams of gases shot from the elemental tool. They began to swirl and mix above his head just as the explosive pile erupted. He braced for the deadly impact from the blast. A wave of pressure and heat roared toward him and the friends he wanted to protect. Just as it began to squeeze and sear his lungs the gases from the Magic Flute coalesced into a crystallized shield. The main part of the explosion hit the barrier and was deflected safely away.

Crisp watched the shield vibrate and glow as it absorbed the blast's energy. The fury from the explosion quickly dissipated behind it. The last thing he remembered before losing consciousness was the shield disintegrating and disappearing, as if it never existed.

24
Miss Pimsby's Fib

The beeping sound that filtered into Crisp's slowly reviving brain was oddly familiar. It was rhythmic, like a clock, and unrelenting. He knew he wasn't quite awake yet. The beeping, however, seemed like a summons to change that fact, even though his body didn't feel ready to interrupt the rest it was getting.

At first he tried to shut the persistent noise out. When that didn't work, he decided the easiest thing to do was to wait for it to stop. Only the beeping noise wouldn't cooperate. After several minutes the regularly timed annoyance was as persistent as ever. He finally realized it wasn't going to be silenced without some effort on his part.

Calling upon an extra dose of willpower, he cracked his eyelids open. His effort was met with a painfully blinding glare. He immediately squinted to reduce the discomfort, which was only minimally effective. Luckily, the stabbing pain that accompanied the waves of light started to relent. Despite the protests of his still fog-filled brain, he finally managed to open his eyes wide enough to examine his surroundings.

It took him a few seconds to find the source of the beeping. It was an ECG monitor hanging on the wall next to him. He tried to sit up so he could turn it off but his legs wouldn't swing around normally. There was a good reason why. There were side-rails on his bed and its crisp white linens were tucked tightly under the mattress. The thick casts on his lower legs didn't make things any easier, either. Neither did the intravenous tube that ran into his right arm. It was attached to a bag of fluid which hung from a metal pole next to the bed. The clear liquid it held was slowly dripping down the tubing and into a vein.

"Bloody hospitals", he muttered to himself.

Unable to quell the beeping, he examined the small square space he found himself in. Its white walls were bare but clean. Partially closed curtains covered most of the Plexiglas door across from his bed. He attempted to peer

Michael Malik

between them. At that moment the door slid open, the curtains were pulled back, and a matronly woman in a nurse's uniform walked in.

"Good to see you're finally awake," the nurse said to him from the foot of his bed. Her face was plain and round and her teeth were crooked but that didn't stop her from giving him a wide and charming smile. "Are you comfortable? May I get you anything, dear?"

He shook his head.

"I need to check a few things in here. Then, if you feel up to it, there are some people who have been waiting to talk to you. Doctor Bragg has held them off until now. He said they could only come in once you were fully alert. He was worried they might not understand."

"What do you mean?"

"You've been unconscious since you got here. That hasn't stopped you from mumbling some unusual things. I can't say that any of it made much sense to me. It was mostly a bunch of nonsense about ghosts and angels. Doctor Bragg said it was delirium brought on by your ordeal. He didn't want anyone to see you until you were healed and fully awake."

"I'll have to thank Dr. Bragg when I see him. So, how long have I been an unconscious mumbling half-wit?"

The nurse laughed. "Just a day. Now let me adjust that I.V. rate and hang your antibiotic. Then I'll let your visitors in."

She moved over to the clear bag and hung another packet next to it. She then adjusted something on the line going into his arm.

"There, all done." She gave him another smile then walked over to an intercom next to the Plexiglas door. "You may send Detective Crisp's first visitor in now."

The sound of footsteps echoed from the hospital corridor. They got louder until at last Detective Chief Inspector Fuller entered the room.

The appearance of his superior from New Scotland Yard caused Crisp to feel a twinge of discomfort that was unrelated to his recovering wounds. His continued involvement with the Museum Case while he pretended to be on holiday was now impossible to deny. And he interfered with the duty of Detective Sergeant Little without proper orders, which, of course, prevented the trumpet from being safely delivered to the Royal caretakers. What was worse, he was sure it was destroyed in the explosion. All the good he did was now just as completely undone. It was for a worthy cause but Fuller didn't know that. More than likely he was at the hospital to sack him.

As he moved to Crisp's bedside, Fuller's face looked grave. This seemed to confirm the worst.

"Detective Chief Inspector, I can't say I'm surprised to see you here."

He wasn't sure how he could explain what happened in a way Fuller would accept. At another time he might've been able to invent a plausible story. Unfortunately, his injuries were interfering with his ability to concentrate. He was drawing a complete blank. If a suitable excuse didn't come to him, he would have to give him the truth, whether he believed him or not.

As his brain continued to search for what to say, the slender form of Miss Pimsby slid silently into the room. Crisp caught a glimpse of her behind Fuller. The guilty look on his face must have been plain for her to see. She attracted his attention with a slight wave then shook her head and lifted her finger to her pursed lips.

He wasn't sure what was going on but he took the hint. He stopped trying to think of an explanation for everything that happened. Instead he focused on trying to change his guilty expression to one of blank innocence.

The nurse also saw Miss Pimsby enter. "I'm sorry miss, but no more than one visitor at a time. Doctor's orders."

She wasn't the type to make an exception to the rules and quickly moved to usher Miss Pimsby out of the room. Miss Pimsby stood her ground and gave the nurse a wilting glare.

"You can be next to visit, I promise," the nurse said in response, but with a conciliatory tone that was absent a moment earlier.

"If I must," Miss Pimsby said, while leaving the clear impression that she was holding the nurse to her word. She exited the room with a final glance at Crisp that left him even more certain he should stay mum for the moment.

Crisp wasn't sure but it seemed that the corner of Detective Chief Inspector Fuller's mouth twitched with barely suppressed amusement during the exchange between the two women. The older man watched Miss Pimsby leave then turned and addressed Crisp.

"You've given us an awful bit of bother to deal with, I must admit, Detective Constable. The pile of paperwork on my desk is impressive. The calls from the Royal caretakers alone have been exhausting. It has, of course, all been worth it to have the men who practically destroyed the British Museum either dead or behind bars. Once again, you've performed a great service for your country."

"I'm afraid I don't remember much of what happened, other than the explosion. I hope there wasn't too much damage done."

"The crater from the blast is actually quite impressive. It will take some time before the cemetery is restored. It's a miracle that you didn't end up like the two men whose bodies we found in the rubble.

"None of the blame rests on your head, of course. That delightful young lady friend of yours has explained everything. You can file an official report once you've sufficiently recovered from your wounds."

"Thank you, sir."

Fuller turned to the nurse, who was still fiddling with one of the machines hanging next to the bed. "I need a moment alone with the Detective Constable, if you don't mind."

There was something about Fuller's tone that made it clear he was not to be questioned. Unlike her exchange with Miss Pimsby, the nurse gave in without a word of protest.

Once she was gone, Crisp decided to take the initiative. "I know the name of at least one person who escaped, sir. It's Josiah Hornbeck."

"So, old Josiah is wrapped up in this too."

"You know him?"

"Not personally. Remember that smuggling operation you were investigating before all of this happened? The few items that we were able to track were related to his area of expertise. There was never any real proof he was involved, mind you. That's why I put you on the case. I was hoping you would find some. And now you have."

"Does that mean you know where he made off to?" Crisp asked.

"No, but now that we have proof that he's bent, I'm confident we'll catch up with him eventually."

"When it happens I hope you'll let me pay him a visit. He took something that belongs to me. I'd like it back, if possible."

"I think that can be arranged."

Fuller fidgeted silently for a moment before continuing. "Frankly, Benjamin, you've performed an incredible bit of police work. I'm still have no idea how you managed it. All I can say is well done."

"Thank you, sir."

Crisp appreciated the compliment. He knew it wasn't in Fuller's nature to dole out praise lightly. He couldn't help but wonder, however, what Fuller would say if he knew of the special tools and help he received during it all.

"I wanted to check that you were getting better with my own eyes," he said. "Now that I see you are, I must be going." Fuller moved toward the front of the hospital room. "Several more preservation groups have scheduled meetings to lodge their complaints. Despite your injuries, I do believe I would trade places with you for the next several hours." A twitch of a smile formed in the corner of his mouth.

"Get well soon Detective Constable. We need you back at Scotland Yard." With the sliver of a smile still in place, he slid past the Plexiglas door.

* * *

Several minutes after Fuller left, Miss Pimsby entered the room. She took a chair from the corner and set it next to Crisp's bed. The nurse was off taking care of another patient so they were alone.

"Thank goodness you woke up when I was around."

"It was all part of my master plan. I wrote it down after 'get blown to bits twice in one night', so you shouldn't have

Michael Malik

worried. How are you? Is the stuff that paralyzed you out of your system?"

"I'm perfectly fine," she replied, brushing away his question. "The nurse said the Detective Chief Inspector was to see you first. I had to get in here and pass a message somehow. Even then, I wasn't sure you would follow what I was getting at."

"You've given a lot of good advice over the past several days. It seemed natural to take it even when I've just regained consciousness and have no idea what it may entail."

The worry Miss Pimsby exhibited when she entered the room began to fade in the face of Crisp's relaxed demeanor.

"It looks like you're recovering fairly quickly," she said with relief.

"My head is throbbing a bit and these casts itch. Otherwise, so far so good. Don't try to change the subject. I want to know what you told Fuller. Whatever it was seemed to pass muster with him. How'd you do it?"

"I was given a chance to practice charming a policeman not long ago. I learned my lesson well."

"Very clever, but what did you tell him?"

"I told him that we were on holiday together in Windsor when, by pure chance, we saw the van get attacked. The thieves incapacitated Detective Sergeant Little and took back the trumpet. We followed them back to Highgate Cemetery. In the fight that followed there was another explosion. We were lucky that a large crypt shielded us and that you, in particular, were just injured instead of killed."

"Impressive," he complimented her. "I'm inclined to believe your version over what really happened."

"It's not so hard. The trick I learned from you is to make something up that the person is likely to believe in the first place."

"What happens when Little or the anarchists that were captured get questioned? They aren't going to corroborate your version of events."

"I don't think that will be a problem. Detective Sergeant Little doesn't remember anything that happened. I guess it's one of the side effects of the Sleep Sand. As for the others, they seem to be sworn to a code of silence, similar

258

to the one you signed for Albert. Detective Chief Inspector Fuller told me that not one of them have uttered so much as a how do you do. They're committed to their cause. It's a bit scary, actually."

A knock at the door interrupted their conversation. It was the nurse again.

"Excuse me Detective Constable, but there's someone else here who'd like to see you. He says he's from the offices of the Royal estate and is quite eager to speak with you. I know it's against the one visitor rule but would it be alright?"

"I have a few more questions for my friend. I was hoping she could update me on my uncle's whereabouts. He left on a trip not long ago. I'm eager to see if he's back and, if so, how it went."

"That can wait." Miss Pimsby said airily. "You should meet with the Queen's representative. I imagine he's here to discuss something important." Despite her casual response she suddenly looked slightly uncomfortable.

"I suppose you're right. He probably wants to give us a bill for the damages. You might as well let him come in and get it over with."

The nurse left. A minute later she was back with a tall, gray haired, regal-looking gentleman. He wore a blue pinstriped suit and an umbrella hung over his right wrist. Thick black-rimmed glasses bridged his nose and his chin was deeply dimpled. A polite smile seemed permanently frozen on his face.

"Very pleased to meet you, Detective Constable. My name is Grant Bartholomew. I hope I'm not disturbing you."

"I seem to have a bit of time on my hands at the moment, Mr. Bartholomew. How can I help you?"

"The Crown has sent me to express its appreciation for your herculean efforts to protect and maintain its valuable property. It would like to extend a debt of gratitude and ask if you and your associate would attend a ceremony to be given in your honor."

"But the trumpet was blown to bits in the end," Crisp protested. "I didn't expect you to be chuffed about it."

Michael Malik

"Yes, well—despite the loss of the aforementioned herald trumpet, the Crown realizes the overriding importance of maintaining the proper law and order. Apprehending the men who were causing wanton chaos and destruction in the fair city of London is of greater value to the Royal family than any artifacts it may possess. Will you accept the offer?"

"Don't worry, Mr. Bartholomew. Detective Constable Crisp and I will be happy to attend," Miss Pimsby answered.

"Where exactly will this ceremony take place?" asked a still doubtful Crisp.

"Once you are sufficiently recovered the plan is to arrange a formal recognition of your efforts at Frogmore House, in Windsor Park. It is, I must say, a singular honor for you both."

At the mention of Frogmore House Crisp and Miss Pimsby exchanged looks. Then, simultaneously, they burst into laughter as Mr. Bartholomew watched on in a state of utter bewilderment.

25
The Newest Member

Over the succeeding days Crisp grew increasingly bored and restless. Lying in a hospital bed at the mercy of others was a foreign experience for him. To make things worse, whenever he asked about events in the outside world Miss Pimsby deflected his questions with meaningless small talk. She seemed determined to keep him focused on his recovery. The only activity that helped pass the time was his physical therapy. The exercise involved was painful and taxing but it was also just what he needed. With each session his strength increased. It also reminded him that he would not be in the hospital forever.

After three weeks of the same routine the casts were finally removed. His legs felt slightly stiff and were still uncomfortable but at least he could walk without help. Dr. Bragg was amazed at the how fast he got better and declared him ready to be discharged.

"The doctor says you still might need some assistance from time to time," Miss Pimsby informed Crisp once the doctor's decision to let him leave was made. "That's why you're going to spend the next couple of weeks in Cambridge. Don't argue," she said before he could protest. "Your uncle insists."

"So he's back then?" Crisp asked. "I was beginning to wonder. You wouldn't say much about him."

"Albert's car is in the hospital garage," she continued unabated. "I was instructed to drive you up to the manor once you were released. There's no reason to linger here. I'll even help you pack."

Considering how eager he was to leave, the decision to go with Miss Pimsby was an easy one. It took only a few minutes to collect his things and put them in a carry bag. Miss Pimsby then left to get the car ready. He said his goodbyes and thank yous to the nurses and staff. The obligatory wheel-chair ride to the front of the hospital then took him down to the waiting Rolls coupe.

261

Miss Pimsby held the door open for him as he shuffled the few steps from the curb to car. She tossed his bag in the boot then got behind the wheel. A few moments later the car was accelerating down the road.

The hospital disappearing in the rearview mirror was a welcome sight. When it was completely gone Crisp tried to get comfortable in his seat. After a few minutes of fidgeting he realized it wasn't going to happen. He then watched Miss Pimsby for a few minutes. She didn't return his gaze. Her attention remained focused on the road ahead.

After a few more minutes of silence he couldn't take it anymore. He'd understood Miss Pimsby's reluctance to talk in the hospital. There was a chance they could've been overheard. But they were alone in the car now. There was no longer a reason to stay silent.

"Sophia," he said softly, "you said that Albert was back. How is he doing? And how did the meeting go? Did he convince the other Academy members about the growing threat he detected? Have you told him what we learned about Fawkes and the Anarchists?"

Her expression was hard to read. To Crisp it seemed to carry a trace of sympathy. She obviously understood how he was feeling.

"I know how eager you are to find out what's going on, Benjamin," she replied. "But I think the answers to your questions are things you should learn from Albert."

The rest of the trip went by uneventfully. They chatted some more. The news on the radio helped pass the time a bit as well. Crisp then slept for a while. When he woke the scenery had the familiar look of the Cambridgeshire countryside. Miss Pimsby greeted him and told him they were only fifteen minute away from the manor.

Crisp stared out of the car window for the last few miles. As he watched each lush green field come and go he decided Miss Pimsby was right. It was only proper for his uncle to answer his questions. Making him understand why they'd been abandoned for so long was going to be tough enough. It was better to wait a bit and get the whole story all at once.

They reached the gate not much after noontime. The house was as impressive as ever as it soaked in the midday sun. Miss Pimsby pulled up to the front door.

"I'm going to put the car back in the carriage house. You go straight to the study. Your uncle will be waiting for you there."

Crisp left the car and walked up to the front door. It was unlocked and swung open silently. The entrance hall was unchanged. All the portraits and vases were in the same exact places. Nevertheless, the room felt different to him somehow. Perhaps it was the warm feeling given by the sun streaming in from behind him? Or was it how still and peaceful the air seemed? The combination, for some unknown reason, filled him momentarily with a sense of hope mixed with anticipation. He just as quickly rejected the sensation. It was out of sync with his present state of mind.

Despite the light that filled the front hall, the study was steeped in shadow. The contrast made it difficult for Crisp to see through the open doors. He walked through them and looked around. The blinds were down, which explained the darkness. He did, however, pick out the silhouette of a man sitting on the couch.

"Albert?" he asked as he moved further into the room.

"Sorry, no." The answer came in English with a noticeable Eastern European accent.

Crisp moved forward. After a few paces he recognized the tall man who helped him and Miss Pimsby in Highgate Cemetery. He stood up as Crisp approached. His thin face was handsome with inquisitive eyes. The expression it carried was gregarious and open. His frame was gangly but still athletic. He appeared to be the type of person who would be difficult to dislike.

"I'm sorry, we haven't been properly introduced. I'm Benjamin Crisp, Albert's great-nephew. Do you happen to know where my uncle is?"

The man's expression lost a fraction of its humor.

"Yes of course," he answered solemnly. His arm lifted and pointed at the bookshelf. "He is right there."

Crisp turned and looked at the spot where the man pointed. It was the area of the bookshelf that was once reserved for Doctor Dee. In its place was a new bust with a bald head and a folded chin. Crisp recognized the face instantly. It was his great-uncle Albert.

* * *

All of the negative thoughts Crisp carried flooded out of him. None of the anger he expected to surface materialized. The only emotion he felt as he stood before the bust was sorrow.

"Albert, why didn't you say something?"

As if answering a summons, the bust began to crackle and glow. A moment later the ghost of Albert had emerged from it.

"My dear Benjamin, you must forgive me," he said with obvious remorse. "I have burdened you in ways I never intended. I hope you will accept my apology and at the same time my appreciation. You have faced many grave challenges recently. Despite this you succeeded in reversing the damage that was done. Splendid work!"

"What happened to you?" Crisp asked as he struggled to adjust to the strange sight of his uncle as a ghost.

"I've been ill for quite some time. It comes with the territory at my age, I'm afraid. I didn't want to tell you at first because I was sure you would assume my illness caused me to fall into a delusion. You suggested as much when you first visited me, remember? Then I was worried my illness would burden you unduly. I was sure that figuring out the maps and finding the compositions would take great effort on your part. Your mind had to be free from worry."

"But you didn't look that sick when I last visited," Crisp protested.

Despite his words he couldn't help noticing how different the ghost of Albert was from the often befuddled man that had left for the Academy meeting. He was back to his old professorial form.

"I'm afraid I must plead guilty once again. I imbibed Aquae Vitae during your visits. I've been using it intermittently as the need arose for many months. It didn't reverse my failing health but I did get a temporary lift from it. It was enough to allow me to feel like my old self again for short periods. With its assistance I managed to go out and do a bit of investigating. Something quite calamitous was being plotted. I was sure of it. This led me to another problem."

"What problem?"

"The Academy hasn't been without a member from the British Isles since before the Industrial revolution," Miss Pimsby answered from the study door. "But Albert was the only member left in this part of the world."

"Welcome back, Miss Pimsby, and you are absolutely correct," Albert said as she walked into the room and settled on the couch. "Normally this would not be a problem. The Academy has many other members from different countries. Eventually they would select a successor. But the threat was more immediate. Someone needed to be here to combat it now, not in months or years from now. I needed to find a person who could adapt to unusual circumstances quickly and still function normally. Then Dee suggested we send the atlas to you. You are, on the outside, a gentle person with a good sense of humor, Benjamin. Those traits, however, are welded to a confident and capable interior. As my nephew, I also felt that I could trust you more than anyone else. You were the perfect choice and my best hope. I agreed to send you the atlas and waited for your response. What I failed to anticipate was the attack on my home and then, more importantly, on you. It was an error that I deeply regret."

"So what happened at the meeting then?" Crisp asked. "We thought you forgot about us."

"I must apologize once again. When you left to find the angel compositions I didn't have much time. I only managed to make three elemental tools. The Aquae Vitae I gave you actually came from the last of the stock I made for myself. But I miscalculated the strength I had left.

"When I arrived at the meeting I fell into a coma. It lasted for several days before I finally died. In my state I was unable to do anything to assist you and Miss Pimsby or convince the other members of the threat we uncovered. Fortunately the other members voted that I should be preserved as a ghost. It's a great honor that I'm still not sure I deserve. But it did allow me to finally meet with the other members.

"I'll admit, they were skeptical at first. There hasn't been much conflict to resolve as of late. It was hard for them to accept that a new threat was arising when so many of the old ones seemed quelled. They are scientists and intellectuals, however, and kept an open mind. Copernicus was perhaps my most vocal supporter. He thought help should be sent immediately. The question then became, who should go? A bunch of mostly elderly scientists and intellectuals are not helpful against men armed with explosives. Fortune smiled on us again. There was one person at the meeting who might be able to do what was required." Albert paused to search the room with his shining eyes. They found the thin stranger. "Ah good, I see you two have met properly."

"Not exactly," Crisp said, still unaware who the man was.

"Tsk tsk, that won't do. Benjamin I would like to introduce you to Franc Pawlik. He's an Academy apprentice from Poland. Apprentices don't usually attend meetings such as the one I went to. Luckily for us he had a new invention to exhibit. Also luckily for us, when Copernicus asked him, he was willing to be of assistance. He invented the Curare Mist that was used to subdue Fawkes' men in the cemetery. Without him all might have been lost. I would say his actions have proven his worth beyond any measure."

Crisp turned to Pawlik. "It's nice to finally know who you are. Thanks for saving us."

"It was my honor," Pawlik replied in his Eastern European accent. "When I arrived here I saw that you had come and gone. Sir Price-Mills gave me his Pitch Stones so I was able to access the lab. The work you had done indicated you were close to retrieving the compositions so I went to Highgate Cemetery, hoping to catch you there. I found the anarchists had set a trap but was unable to warn you in time. Once you were captured I saw only one way to help. Fortunately the Curare Mist worked well."

"After your demonstration at the meeting I was sure it would work splendidly," Albert said.

The shock Crisp initially felt at seeing his uncle's bust had finally worn away. He now noticed the ache in his legs from standing in one position for too long. Miss Pimsby and Pawlik were on the couch so he made his way to the desk. As he settled into its chair a thought suddenly struck him.

"Where's John Dee? Since you're in his spot does that mean he's been relegated to the carriage house?"

Albert chuckled. "No, nothing like that. He was elected to the Hall of Elders at the meeting. After four hundred years of field work it was overdue. Speaking of Dee, once Miss Pimsby delivered her report we were able to piece together much more of what transpired back in his time. William Byrd heard an old story of a murdered girl and her beheaded brother when he went to stay with a patron in Ingatestone. The reports of her ghost being seen meant one thing to him; a possible source of ambrosium. His investigation led to an amazing discovery. There was more of the element in the field than he had ever seen in one place before. Dee was sent to help mine it. They built the small shed to hide their activities. The time they spent in it together gave them a chance to talk. It was this close association that led to a discussion about Celestial language. Byrd quickly figured out that the missing part of the language was music."

"It was brilliant," interjected Pawlik.

"Yes it was, but still inconvenient," Albert said.

"Inconvenient? What does that mean?"

"It means it caused the big mess that we just barely got out of," Crisp said.

"What you say is true. Unfortunately it's not quite all there is to it," continued Albert. "As I mentioned earlier, the ambrosium deposit was very large. The amount Dee and Byrd recovered caused them great excitement. There was enough to produce three busts plus a little extra. No member delegation had ever presented that much ambrosium to the Academy at one time. Suddenly, the language they discussed plus the ambrosium they found became a way to ensure that they would be enshrined as ghosts together. They felt two such enormous discoveries would make it a fait accompli. That same sense of exhilaration also temporarily blinded them. They no longer saw the dangers that accompanied their undertaking. You're all too familiar with the near disastrous consequences of what happened next."

"So that's where the lump of ambrosium came from, the one that created the ghost of Fawkes I mean," Crisp said.

"Yes, it and two other complete ones were stolen, as Fawkes stated. All that was left was a less than satisfactory amount to create a bust. Because Dee held the knowledge of where the trumpet was hidden it was decided to preserve him with it anyway. It explains why he's never been quite right. The use of insufficient ambrosium left his energy field weak and some of his memories never stored properly. It took some direct questions to jog his memory but Dee was finally able to confirm the version of events I've given you."

"You said three lumps were stolen. What happened to the other two?" Miss Pimsby asked.

"They could be anywhere. Even worse they could be anyone. The news of their existence was quite distressing to the Academy. The members voted unanimously to make their retrieval a high priority and to devote significant resources to the task. That reminds me about another important thing happened at the meeting. It's something you need to know about in particular, Benjamin."

"What is it? Please don't tell me there's more bad news. If there is I want Franc to brew some Aquae Vitae right away."

"Nothing so severe," Albert answered with a chuckle. "Because of recent events the Academy decided to forego the usual initiation period and elected you as a full-fledged member."

Crisp felt a stunned feeling creeping over him. "There must be some mistake. I'm not a scientist. I don't belong in the Academy."

"I think recent events quite clearly contradict your assertion. Fawkes was devoted to a flawed and discredited ideology. That didn't make him any less intelligent—or dangerous. He would have figured out what the ambrosium was and how it worked. We must assume he made contingency plans in case his plot failed. You are exactly the man we need for the challenges that lay ahead of us."

"You won't exactly be alone," Miss Pimsby said. "I'll still be here to help you."

"I must admit, that is a first-rate incentive." Crisp said.

"Besides, if I remember correctly, we never finished the talk we were having."

"You mean the one outside Highgate Cemetery?"

"Yes, that's the one."

"You do bring up another excellent point." He gazed at her and she smiled back. They were simple but important gestures because of what they implied.

"And while Franc must go back to Poland and continue his work with Copernicus, he promises to return if you need him," Albert interjected.

"Tak," Pawlik said. "I would be honored to help."

"It seems like an appropriate time to let you know another important bit of information," Albert continued. "As my last remaining relative you've inherited my estate. Of course this includes the manor house here in Cambridge and the laboratory it holds. That should make things a bit simpler for you."

"I'm flattered," Crisp said. "I do have a few more questions to ask before I can accept your generosity, however."

"By all means," replied Albert with a kind and patient smile.

"What exactly did we stumble into when we found the compositions? Herne wasn't some scientific manifestation of a specially prepared element. And he definitely wasn't a ghost. He was solid and downright terrifying."

"An excellent question," answered Albert. "Unfortunately I don't have a clear answer for you. Phenomena like Herne have been an area of study for the Academy for centuries. There seem to be pockets throughout the world where unexplained inter-dimensional planes of existence occur. Members who've studied them refer to them as Nether Worlds.

"The Academy has discovered and gained access to several such areas. Byrd secretly discovered the pocket that contained Herne. He used his knowledge and the assistance of Shakespeare in order to provide a safe place to hide the compositions. How such planes come to be and what sustains them is, I must admit, still a mystery."

"You should also know that Franc and I put the compositions back in the cottage," said Miss Pimsby. "None of us could think of a better place to keep them safe. Herne has been enjoying the wine formula you lost. He was sleeping like a baby when we saw him. We tip toed in and out as safely as going into a nursery."

The idea of such an easy stroll past Herne was more than Crisp cared to envision. "What about the Augmenter?" he asked, changing the subject. "Did you return it as well?"

"I delivered it back to Miss Fairfield personally."

Everything seemed to be tying together nicely. Nevertheless, there one final question he needed to ask.

"Please don't take this the wrong way. I'm proud of what we accomplished. Stopping Fawkes and the Anarchists kept a lot of people from getting hurt, I'm sure of it. And the Academy has shown itself to have amazing resources. I've seen numerous things I wouldn't have believed before now. But, even after everything that we've been through and despite your logical explanations for everything that's happened, there's still something that bothers me."

"What is it?"

"We found the compositions and played the trumpet just like you said to," Crisp explained. "I saw a bunch of bright flashing lights. But I still don't know if the angels came back, or left in the first place or even exist at all for that matter."

"I understand," said Albert, "and your question is not surprising. It is a universal and enduring part of the human experience. Perhaps this explanation will help. Many great accomplishments have come from believing in something. This includes believing in things beyond the world we currently exist in. How dull and dreary our lives would be if this was not so. Imagine that the only things we could conceive of were the ones right before our eyes. Mankind would still be living in caves, trapped by the barren rock walls of the here and now. Great inventions like the radio or light bulb would never have come to be. Art could not blossom. Justice would be limited to brute force. Our quest has been and should always be to elevate our minds. We must use them to consider not only realities but also possibilities.

"It's true you never clearly saw any angels leave or return. But accepting that they likely did, or even might have, is enough to build a future upon. I admit this may not be the direct answer you wanted. It is, however, the essence of what drives us to better ourselves and the world we live in."

Crisp took in his uncle's explanation. It wasn't a direct answer, like Albert admitted. Nevertheless, it was a logical and convincing argument. He glanced across the study. Miss Pimsby was looking at him with the eager expression that he remembered from their first meeting. But it wasn't exactly the same as before. It was now mixed with genuine affection, which made him like it even more.

"Then it sounds like I'd be crazy to not accept."

Miss Pimsby beamed at him. Pawlik clapped his hands together enthusiastically. Albert's expression was pure pride.

"We'll just have to change the old expression."

"What expression?" the others asked together.

Crisp flashed a mischievous smile. "Instead of give up the ghost it should be the ghost will not give up." The smile continued to grow as he settled back in his chair. For the first time in a long time he knew he was where he was meant to be.